DVNGEON PRIME

DVNGEON PRIME

DUNGEON PRIME

— Phantasm Book V —

CHRISTOPHER HALL
AKA MAXLEX

Podium

Cover design by Amanda Shaffer

ISBN: 978-1-0394-5879-6

Published in 2025 by Podium Publishing
www.podiumentertainment.com

DUNGEON PRIME

START NEW GAME

We're going to have such fun!"

Those were the last words the mad dungeon intelligence yelled after us as we fled the burning elevator. We found ourselves in a thoroughly modern corporate lobby. Polished granite floors, walls made out of . . . some kind of composite. A high ceiling, and one large glass wall that gave us a perfect view of what was outside.

I looked around for a reception desk, but the room was empty. The elevator behind us continued to burn. Smoke started escaping from the crack in the door.

"The only way to go is forward," I said.

"We can't go out there!" Kyle protested. "It's full of monsters!"

"Also," Cloridan objected, "I don't see a way through this glass wall without breaking it."

I blinked, realizing that my friends didn't recognize a modern door when they saw one. It was Borys who spoke up first.

"That's the door there," he said, pointing. "Don't go near it; it will open automatically, and I think we want to take some time to study the situation before we leave."

"We might not have that much time," I said, glancing back at the elevator. Judging from the smoke, the fire was only getting more intense. Everything in this place was arranged by the intelligence. The fire was a spur to get us to leave, so the only question was how much time it was going to give us.

"We can't go out there, though, we'll get swarmed!" Felicia said. She clung nervously to Kyle's arm.

"I don't think it's as bad as you're imagining," I told her. "I've got an idea of what's going on here."

Outside the glass doors was . . . well, I never played that *Cyberpunk* game, but I saw pictures, and this would have fit right in. A dystopian cityscape, filled with neon and dirty concrete. It was both more developed and seedier than any city I'd seen in real life. I suppose there might have been some small part of Tokyo or Hong Kong that looked like this, but the business trips I'd taken to Tokyo had only shown me much nicer areas than this.

Inhabiting it were . . . well, Identify wasn't stopped by clear glass.

[Identification]: Businessman Mook – Threat: 10 – Properties: Skilled

There were other types as well.

[Identification]: Ganger Mook – Threat: 11 – Properties: Armed, Skilled
[Identification]: Prostitute Mook – Threat: 9 – Properties: Skilled
[Identification]: Cop Mook – Threat: 12 – Properties: Armed, Linked, Skilled

None of them posed any great threat. Probably. If "Skilled" meant what I thought it did, then it could change things. The real problem, though, was how many of them there were. The only time I'd seen so many monsters was during the double Dungeon Break, back in Talnier. If they swarmed us . . .

"I think it'll be fine," I said. "Let me try something."

[Phantasmal Emissary].

I summoned a Phantasmal version of me out on the street. Keeping track of both sets of perceptions was tricky, but I wasn't trying for anything fancy. All that the illusionary version of me had to do was stand there.

"Why aren't they attacking her?" Felicia asked. "Do they see her?"

"They do," Cloridan said. "Look—they're walking around her."

And indeed they were. Time for the next test. I gave one of the passersby a shove.

"Hey! Watch where you're going!" the mook yelled. Then it turned away from me and kept going. I reported what it had said to the others.

"Most monsters with skills can talk," Kyle told me. "You've seen that for yourself."

"Yeah, I don't think that's what is going on here," I said. I had my emissary shove another businessman.

"Hey! I'm walking here!" Just as before, he walked away once he'd delivered his line.

A classic. I shoved another one.

"Are you blind?!"

Another.

"Hey! I'm walking here!"

There we go.

It turned out that the businessmen, at least—I couldn't be bothered to test the other types right now—had five different lines that they delivered at random.

"Is that different from how monsters normally are?" Felicia asked. "I mean, we can't understand them normally anyway."

"It is different," I said. "Monsters are intelligent. Not *very* intelligent, and overwhelmed by aggression, but the intelligence is there. These guys . . . they're scripted."

I looked over at Borys. "Are we thinking the same thing?" I asked.

"A sandbox game," he agreed.

"What's that?" Kyle asked.

"Let's answer that outside," I said, looking back at the elevator. It was starting to glow.

"Let's," Borys agreed. "It should be safe as long as we don't interact with anyone."

I cancelled my spell and we all walked out of the glass doors. Out on the street, I tried to explain what was going on to my companions.

"These monsters aren't intelligent," I said. "Or maybe they are and are just being controlled like slaves . . . *that's* an unpleasant thought. In any case, they won't behave like regular monsters."

That statement was self-evidently true based on the behavior of the monsters around us. We formed a close-knit knot on the sidewalk that all the monsters diverted around without comment. My friends weren't quite prepared to trust what they saw, or what I said, but as long as the monsters didn't attack, it would be fine.

Now that I saw them up close, the monsters were remarkably human-like. They were clearly *not* human, though. Grey skin, misshapen jaws, and flattened noses. They kept their mouths closed, but I got the impression that their teeth weren't within human norms.

The businessmen looked incongruous in their smart suits. The gangers had their uniform of leather jackets and tattoos that looked more like tribal warpaint. The prostitutes . . . well, I couldn't see anyone here paying for sex and then murdering them.

I resumed my lecture. "Each one of these monsters is following a script. Most of them are just meant to wander around, adding character. Some of them will be waiting to interact with us. There will be monsters we can trade with, monsters that give us missions to complete."

"Be especially careful of the cop mooks," Borys added. "That linked property probably means that if you attack one, all the linked ones know about it and will come after you."

"Cops will probably come after you if they see you killing monsters, or committing any crimes," I said.

"But we don't have to kill any monsters if they don't come after us," Felicia said.

"Oh, we will have to," I said grimly. "Somewhere in here is a mook that knows how to get to the next level. To find him, or get him to tell us where it is, we're going to have to do some sort of mission. That mission—or those missions—will involve a lot of killing. Depend on it."

"Can't we just find our way by following the mana?" Kyle asked.

"Maybe," I admitted. "But . . . from what I've seen, the mana is more controlled than what you normally see. And there are all these buildings in the way. The first order of business might be to get to the top of one of these buildings and note the lay of the land."

"How big do you think this level is?" Borys asked.

"There's no actual limit on how big a level can be," I said. "It takes mana and time to claim the volume, and you need to have the physical space to hold it, but this is the First Dungeon."

"It's had all the time in the world," Borys said thoughtfully. "And with spatial manipulation, a lot more space than you would think."

"Exactly," I said glumly. "The big spaces in Dorsay's dungeon were about five Ks across, so we're looking at at least that. Maybe ten, twenty times that."

"So where do we start?" Cloridan asked.

"I guess . . . we start wandering. Start by looking for a building that will let us in. Look for a store that's selling useful things. Look for anything that stands out. And . . . look for a good place to mug someone."

Gangers had a much more aggressive reaction to being shoved.

"You talking to me? You talking to me?"

The ganger shoved me—or my emissary, rather—but as long as I kept backing away, he kept following me, without attacking. This was about optimal as far as I was concerned, so I kept backing away until we were both in a nearby alley.

Presumably, this alley had been designed for mugging people. It didn't seem to have any other purpose. There weren't any doors that led out to it. There was a dumpster about halfway down, but it didn't look as if it had been moved, or used, for years.

"You think you can take me?" the ganger yelled when Kyle stepped out from behind the dumpster. It was interesting that it noticed him, and also that it determined he was a threat. This fight was over, though.

"Yeah, we do," I said and cast Blind. That was the end of his scripted lines, but it took a little longer for him to die.

I hung back and let Borys rifle through his pockets. I felt a little queasy about mugging what looked like a semi-civilized person.

He's just a monster, I told myself. *Less than that, even; he's just acting out a script.*

"What's he got?" I asked, trying not to let my disquiet show.

"His clothes are not even armor," Borys said. "He's got . . . a gun, a phone . . . and this."

He handed the last item to me, while he inspected the gun.

Isn't that a kettle of worms? I thought to myself as I examined the device in my hand. It was . . .

[Identification]: Credstick – Quality: Poor – Credits: 238 – Interest: 1% per day

---

Even if I hadn't had Identify, I would have been able to tell what this was. It had *Credstick* printed on the side. Not in English, but as soon as I saw the symbols, I knew it indicated that this was a stick that held something called "creds."

"It's money," I told the others. There was a panel on the front that opened easily, a little like a flip phone. There were buttons for numbers, another one marked *all,* and two more marked *give* and *take.*

"The money is a number on the device," I explained. "Instead of giving someone coins, you transfer the numbers across to another credstick."

"Is that something from your world?" Felicia asked.

"Not . . . like this," I said.

"Same here," Borys said. "This isn't a gun."

"It isn't?" I asked. I let Identify answer my own question.

> **[Identification]: Saturday Night Special – Quality: Poor – Ammo: 5 – ROF: 1 – Damage: 150**

"That's a lot of damage for a Poor item," I said. Borys nodded.

"We're lucky he didn't get a chance to fire it," he said. "We'll have to see how it interacts with skills. But look."

He pointed at the thing's muzzle, while carefully pointing it away from everyone. I quickly saw what he meant.

"It's too small," I said. "I don't know much about guns, but the bullets are bigger than that."

"Right," Borys said. "Everyone stand clear."

Realizing what he was about to do, we all stood away from the dumpster he was pointing the thing at. Once everyone was ready, he pulled the trigger.

Instead of a *crack*, as there was in the movies, there was a very intense *hiss*. There was no smoke or fire, but a slim metal rod was suddenly embedded in the side of the dumpster.

"I think it uses magic to fire," Borys said. "He wasn't carrying any reloads, and there doesn't seem to be a mechanism to reload it either."

I checked it over with Sense Mana. There didn't seem to be a way to put more magic into it. Whatever it was made with was what it had.

"Perhaps reloading is a feature that comes with more expensive models," I said. "What's left?"

"The phone," Borys said and held it up so we could all see. It was the standard glass oblong that we knew and loved. There was a case on it, so I couldn't tell if it was infringing on anyone's intellectual property.

"You seem to know what it is," Felicia said. "Is it good?"

"It might be when we get a few more," Borys said. "I bet it only works in the dungeon, though."

"See if there's anyone you can call," I suggested.

"That was easy," Borys said. "If everyone in here is unarmed, this will be even easier."

I could tell that it wasn't going to be that easy as soon as we walked in. All the gangers still had the Armed property. I guess the guy at the door was just to sort out the chumps.

"How do you want to do this?" I asked, looking around the room. There were about twenty people scattered around in the gloom. Some of them were looking at us, some of them drinking. They were mostly gangers, but there were some prostitutes working the crowd.

"The numbers are the main problem," Borys said. "Perhaps we could get some privacy?"

"Gotcha. We can start over there, then," I said, pointing.

They were, I reminded myself, monsters. They might look and act like semi-civilized thugs who had thoughts and feelings, but they were just there to be killed. I cast Privacy.

"Hey! What happened?" three voices said in unison. We didn't bother answering. Borys and Kyle's swords appeared, and the killing began.

Afterwards, we started gathering up the loot, and I went over the numbers.

"Kyle didn't have any trouble hitting them, but I couldn't unless I blinded them," I reported. "That puts their defenses somewhere between 180 and 200."

"There were a couple that even Cloridan couldn't hit," Kyle said. "Borys didn't have any trouble, but . . ."

"That's what Blind is for," I said. "Those guys were the leaders, with threat thirteen. Given how hard they were to hit, they must have had better skills, too. I figure that the mooks had an Ability of six and a Skill of three. The bosses had one more Skill at least."

"I presume this is the bottom tier of what we will be facing," Borys said thoughtfully. "If their skills increase as their Threat does, the total will ramp up quickly."

"We might need to rely on the guns as an equalizer," I said. "Fortunately they didn't get a chance to fire them in here."

"More like a result of our tactics," Borys said. "Getting ambushed by thugs with better versions of these . . . it's worrying."

We all agreed soberly and started collecting our loot. There were only two guns that were of Mediocre quality, sixteen that were Poor. Twenty-two phones and twenty-six credsticks, all of Poor quality. We siphoned off the creds to five sticks, leaving each of us with about a thousand creds each.

"Now what?" Cloridan asked. He had sampled the drinks and was making a sour face.

"That's not a bad idea," Borys said, staring at the wall of bottles behind him. "It's not worth anything to us, but someone might pay good creds for all that.

"No, I don't want any of that shit," the mook behind the plastic wall said scornfully. "Does it say Finn's Bar on the door?"

"No, it says Finn's Used Goods," Borys admitted. "Are you saying we'd have to drink this before you'd buy it?"

"Don't try to make me sick. You got goods to sell?"

"Sure," Borys said and pulled a pair of the Poor pistols out of his sack. Finn sneered.

"One hundred, each."

"You're selling these for five," I said mildly.

"Not these, I ain't. *These* I gotta clean up and recharge, make sure there isn't any biological evidence left on them from whoever you took them from. One hundred, take it or leave it."

"Take it, I guess," Borys said. "There's more where that came from." He held up his sack.

Finn cursed. "Don't just dump them on the counter, lay 'em out proper."

Borys shrugged and complied, laying the guns out neatly. He added the one we'd picked up in the alley for a total of seventeen guns. Finn nodded briskly.

"Seventeen hundred it is." He held out his credstick, giving another sneer when he saw the quality of Borys's.

"Do you sell a better one?" Borys asked.

"I can shit a better one," Finn said. He slapped two down on the counter.

[Identification]: Credstick – Quality: Mediocre – Credits: 0 – Interest 0%

[Identification]: Credstick – Quality: Average – Credits: 0 – Interest +1% per day

---

"One grand, ten grand," he said, pointing at each one in turn.

"A thousand creds just to stop losing our money each day?" I asked.

"Gotta spend money to make money," Finn said.

"We'll take one. How much will you give us for our old ones?"

"They have bins of those things for free at the banks," Finn said. "Just toss 'em in the garbage."

Borys made an annoyed sound. "We've got phones as well, do you take them?"

"Sure. Crappy ones like the guns? Five hundred each."

"That's not bad," Borys said, surprised.

"Not much difference between the grades of phone," Finn explained. "Mostly it's a status thing."

"Eighteen of them, then," Borys said, starting to set them out on the counter.

"Gotta admire your work ethic," Finn murmured. "You folks interested in buying at all?"

"I've got some questions," I said. "First, is that shelf really *used* cyberware?"

"It's properly cleaned, don't worry. There's a lot of chop shops that won't deal with used hardware, but I can direct you to a clinic that does mostly good work."

"What is it, exactly?" Kyle asked. "I see some pieces there that look like armor?"

"Those arms aren't hollow," I said. "You need to chop your arm off to use them—leave it to the monsters."

"Oh," Kyle said, working it out. "Then *second*hand means . . ." He trailed off, looking distressed.

"Hey," Finn said, "I don't think you lot are in a position to criticize my other suppliers."

"Fair enough," I admitted. "What are the trays labelled with corporation names for?"

"Corp IDs," Finn told me, glancing over at them. "Corporates are always losing them, and they don't get cancelled until the end of the month."

"They let you get into buildings?" I asked.

"Yeah. Not the higher levels, you understand. The likes of those don't show up on the street to get mugged. But they'll get you in the door, no problem.

"Interesting," I said.

Finn grinned. "If you're interested in sneaking into corps, I know some people that might have a job for you."

"Do tell," I said.

WATCH OUT FOR SNAKES

Social skills interacted with the NPCs in a weird way—that is, even more weirdly than they did normally. No matter how you looked at it, putting words in my mouth and controlling my facial expressions was a strange experience, but I supposed that I had gotten used to it.

It had taken some experimentation, but we figured it out. Better skill totals resulted in extra dialogue options. Better ones. Better deals, too. The prices I was offered, buying or selling, were about fifty percent better than what Kyle got. That was underselling Bargain considerably. If Kyle didn't know what the going rate for something was (he was quite knowledgeable about swords and armor), then I could normally expect to pay half of what he did. Or had, since he'd teamed up with me.

Finn had been the start, but he was only a stepping stone. He didn't have the contacts we needed to progress to the upper levels, but he did have jobs. Jobs that paid credits, and reputation.

"We can get it for you," I told the suited mook. "But not for that price."

My skills did still help me find the words, but I had a sneaking suspicion that was because there were humans in the room to look cool in front of. Alone, my skill might have urged me to say. "Bargain. More. More. Meeting." The dialogue options for the quest-givers were pretty good, but they still defaulted to whichever one was *most* appropriate, given what you'd said.

"Whadda you want?" the suit said. "More money?"

"I *do* want more money," I said. "But I want to meet with your boss as well."

He hesitated. Quite a convincing facsimile of doubt and calculation that I might have fallen for were it not for the fact that *every* mid-level manager hesitated when you tried to climb the ladder. It might have been a stylistic choice on Axel's part, but I rather thought it was to cover the delay while whatever mini-System he was using checked my reputation with that corporation.

"You get it back in one piece, he'll talk to you," the mook finally said.

"It's as good as done," I said, taking my leave.

We'd done a few of these missions, enough to iron out the kinks. Borys and I had brainstormed how we thought these missions would differ from regular dungeon runs. So far, the others had been bemused about how accurate our speculations had been.

We walked into the club where the deal was going to go down. It was pretty similar to some of the other clubs we'd seen so far. There were some different types, but there wasn't much variation within each type. This one had three stages for girls to dance on, a ring of seating around each stage, and a cordoned-off VIP section for the block bosses or higher to sit in. The girls were mooks, of course, which I thought was missing a trick. If they'd been human, and wearing what those girls were wearing, we'd have had to drag Cloridan and maybe Borys out of each club.

I sighed when I made out our target. Occupying the center stage, the traditional bulky aluminium suitcase gleamed under all the spotlights that were pointing at it. It was raised high enough to be clearly visible over the heads of all the surly mooks who were lined up around the stage, making sure that no one got near it.

I noted Cloridan's departure. He was already invisible and fully informed of his part of the plan.

"I need to talk with someone important in Iron Hanuman," I told the doorkeeper. "I've got vital information about Kanzaki-Volkswerk."

I had to hand it to Axel, it was a pretty neat trick. All of the mooks had different *sets* of actions they performed when we were watching. Maybe at other times as well, who knew? When we came in, they were using what you could call the happy set. They were clapping one another on the back, ogling the girls, and slamming down drinks.

As soon as I said "Kanzaki-Volkswerk," they switched to a more nervous set. The girls faltered and changed dances. Cheers turned into suspicious glances around the room, and hands went nervously to weapons. It changed the feel of the room, building tension. The doorkeeper grunted and gestured us towards the bar.

Another thing about these missions is that you could go either way, depending on which corporation you were looking to get in good with.

"I heard you've got something for me?"

I looked up from my drink, which I hadn't touched. This was the most well-dressed ganger I'd met yet.

> **[Identification]: Ganger Capo – Threat: 17 – Properties: Armed, Skilled, Leadership**

"I should have known that a deal this big would need a capo to be involved," I said. This was a complete lie, as I'd never seen a capo until this moment. Threat seventeen, though, and with skills. He was way too dangerous for the first level.

His eye twitched, perhaps indicating that I hadn't managed to trigger a dialogue option. "You got something for me or what?"

"I heard that you've got a deal set up with Kanzaki-Volkswerk for tonight," I said.

His eyes narrowed. "You're telling me stuff I already know . . . tell me *how* you know that."

"I heard it from Fujimoto-Braun," I said. The mood changed again, switching to something more *aggressive*. "They know you have their stuff. They've sent a team to collect it, and hit KV at the same time."

The ganger stared at me as if trying to figure out if I was telling the truth or not. He might have been able to, but it didn't matter. In finance or politics, lies were a sign of an amateur. Every lie gets found out eventually. Ideally, it gets discovered after it's too late for the victim to do anything about it. Regardless, other professionals in the market will remember. They'll do a little bit more due diligence before dealing with you again. That's if they'll deal with you at all.

Tell the truth, though, even if they get burned from some key detail you left out, they'll still drink with you in the club. "We should have asked," they'll say, and you'll nod commiseratingly.

So every word I told them was true. I just left out that we *were* the team hired by Fujimoto-Braun Technik.

His face contorted into a grimace and he grabbed for his phone. "Deal's off!" he snarled into it. "Someone's got a leak!"

I smiled as I watched him bark orders to his gang. Mooks jumped up on the stage and hustled the briefcase away to the secure room in the back of the building. Every ganger went on alert, guns out and scanning for intruders.

Once the initial flurry of orders had died down, I stepped up to the now-angry gang boss.

"Whadda you want?" he growled.

"Just my fee," I said mildly.

"I ain't giving you shit until we find out if the info's good," he said. "Bad enough we gotta cancel the deal."

"Understandable," I agreed. "But if you do get attacked, you'll let Kanzaki know that we were helpful, right?"

"Yeah, sure," he said. "I'll let them know."

I smiled and let my friends escort me out of the building. We would be getting enough money for this job as it was; the reputation was the important thing.

We headed out, but we didn't go far. Turning right, we slipped into the alleyway next to the club. Like most of the alleyways we'd seen, this thin gap didn't serve any purpose. Even the muggers had been scared away by the close presence of the gang.

"Dark enough for you?" Borys asked.

"Not really," I said. He shrugged and shot out a nearby light.

We all froze, but the softer sound of the magic gun didn't attract any attention. Glaring at him, I pulled on my mask and opened up a shadow.

Axel had measures in place to deal with Shadow Magic. I'd already tried, and I couldn't use it to enter the upper levels of the corporate buildings. Those areas were cut off from my shadow-sense in a way that felt different from the areas just being well lit. For the most part, though, he relied on the same defense everyone else used. Light.

The spotlights on the briefcase hadn't just been an incredibly unsubtle way of drawing attention to the thing. They also meant that I couldn't just Shadow Step over there and take it. The secure room that they'd taken it to, behind guards, alarms, and security doors, was also brightly lit. There wasn't a shadow to be found.

Getting into that secure room would be a nightmare now. Earlier, though, the room had just been an afterthought. Without the briefcase to protect, there was no need to guard an empty room. Someone who happened to be invisible could just walk right in.

Of course, now he'd be trapped inside. Trapped behind all those guns and doors and alarm systems. But all he had to do was throw a light switch . . .

I felt the space open up.

"Be right back," I said and stepped into the shadow.

The first thing I did when I stepped out was cast Greater Invisibility. It was dark, and the mask should hide my identity, but I didn't want to take chances. My next action was to cast Light.

Glancing quickly around the room, I made a note of the important items. The briefcase, of course, was sitting on a table.

[Identification]: Fujimoto-Braun MacGuffin – Properties: None

Always good to check you had the right item. The body of a guard, unconscious or dead, was on the floor. He must have been Cloridan's work. The man himself was leaning idly against the wall, still invisible. He gave me a wave.

I didn't bother waving back—he couldn't see me. I just grabbed the briefcase. Cancelling the light, I stepped back into the shadows.

It might seem a little callous to leave Cloridan there, but I hadn't learned the spell that let me take others yet. He would be fine: Once the gangers realized the briefcase was gone, there wouldn't be a need for security on the room anymore. He'd be able to walk right out.

What we weren't sure of was when they'd realize. The way this floor worked, it was even odds that taking it out of the building had cleared the quest. The other possibility was that it wouldn't clear until we gave it back to Fujimoto-Braun. Covering both possibilities, we left Borys at the club to meet up with Cloridan when he got out and headed off to collect our reward.

Unlike the real world, we didn't need to worry that the gang would stew over how they'd been beaten. We hadn't gotten to our destination before my phone chimed with an update. Kanzaki-Volkswerk's regard for us had increased.

"Looks like they got hit after all," I commented wryly. "I guess our information was good."

Felicia giggled. "It's so strange the way you and Borys do this," she said. "It's like a giant puzzle."

"I just wish we could solve it faster," I complained. "But if all goes well, we should be done with at least one of the pieces."

We were whisked through security. Our contact whispered a word in the ear of the faceless guard, which was enough for them to turn off the gate and usher us through without precautions. His card in the elevator got us up to the middle management level.

Ugly mooks in suits that were too nice for them gathered around as we strode into the conference room and put the briefcase on the table.

The mook with the shiniest suit stepped up. Unlocking the briefcase, he took a deep breath. I tensed up. We hadn't yet had a quest where the corp turned on us at the end, but I wouldn't put it past Axel. Not this time, though. The mook just breathed a sigh of relief as he saw the machinery inside.

"You've done well," he said. "The CEO wants to thank you in person."

"Of course," I said, as if that hadn't been part of the price of the job. We got led to a different, more luxurious elevator. This one didn't seem to operate on card keys. We didn't have to press a button; the doors closed once we got inside and we went up.

This was the final step, for this corporation at least. Once we got the ear of the CEO, we could get jobs from him directly, and one of them would lead to us getting the company token we needed. We were getting close to finishing the first stage.

Having us wait in his antechamber was a bit of a surprise, but I guess power moves are universal. It gave me time, though, to feel things out. As I'd suspected, the block on Shadow Magic was a barrier, not a suppression field.

"I need to use the bathroom," I said. The receptionist blinked, but this wasn't a computer game. Accommodations had to be made for the players, lest they shit in the spotless lobby. She pointed off to the side.

It was a nice bathroom, as nice as one would expect of the C-level suites. I only had eyes for one thing, though. The light switch.

No lights in your walk-in safe, Mr. CEO? That will cost you.

Top of the World

We'd *finally* found a spot with a view.

I had thought when we started that it would be easy. It was never a high priority, since I had suspected that it wouldn't do us any good, but I still wanted a chance to *see* the city. Looking down on all the lights was a staple of the cyberpunk genre after all, and this place had a surplus of tall buildings and power-mad CEOs.

I had reckoned without thinking about the claustrophobic nature of this floor. Most of the buildings were tall enough to extend into the cloud cover. In most places, that would mean a hell of a view across the cloud tops. Here, though, the clouds were more of a permanent fog, meant to conceal the rock ceiling. It extended all the way to the roof, and so did the skyscrapers. They weren't buildings so much as pillars. The exclusive penthouse executive suite was generally entombed in rock.

Which, in fairness, made for great security. If the view had to be faked with screens, none of the occupants seemed to mind.

So for a while now, I'd been keeping an eye out for a building that was high enough to see over the majority of view-blocking buildings, while not being *so* high that it reached the clouds. You might think that all I had to do was look out a window halfway up a taller building . . . but you would be wrong. If false picture windows were good enough for the CEO, then they were good enough for the lower floors, it seemed. There were more . . . energetic ways to look outside, of course, but a firefight with security wasn't conducive to taking in the view.

I'd all but given up, and yet here we were. On top of a building that was just the right height, placed well enough to take in much of the city. A depressing expanse of drug dens, chop shops, and corporate law firms.

"I see one," Felicia said.

"I do, too . . . and there's a third," I replied.

We were looking at the local mana flow. Dungeons tended to have very smooth flows compared to the outside, but that just made it easier to pick out the flows that they did have.

"What does that mean? Why have multiple exits?" Borys asked.

"You've got to have an exit," I explained, "And the mana is going to tell us where it is."

I left unsaid the possibility of using illusions to conceal the mana. I didn't want to give Axel any ideas if he hadn't already thought of it.

"So if you want to keep the adventurers from rushing the exit before they finish your little game, you make multiple exits," I continued.

"How does that help?" Borys asked.

"Normally, it would just mean more exits to defend. Here, though, we've seen that Axel can make changes to the floor we're on, which dungeons can't normally do. So any time we get near an exit, he just closes it up."

"Which he can do since he still has an open exit," Kyle finished for me. "What if we started closing the exits for him?"

"That might work," I admitted, "But I think it will be easier to just play his game. Plus, he might not answer those questions if he can claim we cheated."

"I want those answers," Borys stated. "We're almost done with this game, and the new tools we've acquired should only make things go faster. There's no need to change plans at this stage."

"Fair enough," Kyle said. He hefted his new weapon. "So are we ready to go?"

I looked around at everyone. "I don't see why not," I said. Moving to the other side of the building, I looked down at our target.

"Twelve floors up, five windows down," I recited. The location had been chosen from some plans we'd liberated in a previous mission. I lit it up to make things easier for Kyle. "Is that right?"

Felicia double-checked for me. "It's right," she said quietly. She readied her own weapon.

> [Identification]: Tsurugi Viper – Quality: Great – Ammo: 30 – ROF: 5 – Damage: 761

My friends had taken to the magical guns as if they were secret Americans. Felicia's small and light machine pistol dealt more damage than Kyle's sword, turning her from a pure healer to a damage dealer.

The real delight was the autofire, though. Each pull of the trigger counted as five shots for training in Weapon Mastery: Triggered Weapons. I'd been neglecting that skill, but I was going to come off this floor as quite the crossbow master.

Kyle didn't have to feel left out, though.

> **[Identification]: Drachen Blitz – Quality: Great – Ammo: 1 – ROF: 1/2 – Damage: 4,000 – Properties: Area Effect**

I wasn't sure if it could be properly called a rocket launcher when it magically propelled a dart enchanted to trigger a magical fireball . . . but it was close enough. Kyle aimed at the window I'd highlighted. The window was fake, of course, but that didn't matter to the Blitz.

Glass shattered all across the side of the building, leaving a scar of concrete behind. At the center of that scar sat a massive hole, flames licking fitfully at its edges. We gave it a moment for something unexpected to happen, and then Borys stepped up with his own shoulder-mounted "weapon."

> **[Identification]: Tenshi Talon – Quality: Great – Ammo: 1 – ROF: 1/2 – Damage: 1,000 – Properties: Grappling Line**

Most of the weight and bulk of the Tenshi was in its steel-cored cable, 200 meters coiled up tightly behind the grapple. One thousand damage was a bit misleading, as it was designed to punch through soft targets and embed itself in hard ones. If you were hit by it, you might only take a thousand damage, but you'd be strung out on a line and anchored to the wall behind you. Or the hook wouldn't lodge and you'd be drawn in when the recall function started.

Borys aimed and fired. This was our first time using that particular weapon, but it didn't matter to the skill. His aim was spot on, the harpoon flying straight through the hole. When he started pulling back on it, it seemed that it had lodged somewhere solid.

"Looks good," he said and secured it at our end. The back end of the line detached and could be looped around a solid structure or hooked onto something. We'd done the first one. All Borys had to do was push a button, and the line started tensioning.

A beep and a green light indicated that the line was ready. Borys didn't have to ask who was first. Cloridan stepped up. Dodging would be important for the first one in.

It wouldn't be his only defense, though.

[Greater Invisibilty].

Cloridan gave me a lazy wave, as I was the only one who could see him, and hooked his strap over the line. In the next moment, he was half-way between the buildings, sliding down into the hole.

"And . . . in," I said, letting the others get an idea of how long it took. I was going to have to be next.

With Cloridan invisible, we couldn't see how the fight was going. The spikes made some sound when they hit a target, but the distance and the other sounds drowned that out.

I cast Greater Invisibility so the others wouldn't see how nervous I was.

This is just another use of the Climbing skill, I told myself. *Nothing to worry about.*

To my great relief, the skill did trigger as I reached for the line. I swung myself over the edge of the building as if I'd done it a hundred times before, and launched myself down to our entry point. The room was filled with the scattered black-clad bodies of what had been ShinseiDrachen's security team.

Cloridan had cleared out most of the security from the floor, so I flashed a Static Image to my crew to let them know to come down. I gave Cloridan a bit of supporting fire, staying carefully out of his way. He didn't really need the help. The mooks were just firing wildly, with no idea of where his attacks were coming from.

Giving an invisible rogue an assault carbine was just cheating, in my opinion, and I thoroughly approved.

Cloridan had finished up by the time Kyle came down, so I cancelled our invisibilities.

Your party has killed 12 Security Mooks – your experience share is 4,693 XP.

"It's a shame these things can't be reloaded," Cloridan said. He threw away his second empty gun and started looting weapons from the mooks he'd killed. They should have plenty of ammo left: They hadn't had any-thing to fire at, and most of them carried a spare.

It was a shame. The guns *could* be reloaded, but only by weapon shops. And they wouldn't do it for you. Ask for a reload, and they'd just insult your mother. But if you sold them the gun for half price and then came and bought it the next day, it would be freshly cleaned and reloaded . . . and twice the price.

"Probably for the best," I said. "It means that we won't be taking them with us." The cell phones would only work down here, but I saw no reason why the guns wouldn't work anywhere—until they ran out of ammo, anyway.

Felicia was next down the line, and Borys finished up in the rear.

"No problems," he reported.

"Great," I said. "Now let's see how much of the infrastructure we left intact."

While the boys kept the lift covered, I hunted around for a suitable connection point. This level had been the security center and had some special terminals.

I found what I was looking for. Pulling a black, featureless device out of my storage, I pulled a cable from the terminal and plugged it into the device. A second later my phone rang.

"Geez, lady, you sure made a mess of this place!"

"It needed to be done," I said, shrugging. Glitch had said that the last time, too, and we hadn't been anywhere near as messy then. "Can you bypass the security now?"

"Already done!" the hacker said gleefully. "I've got my routines running roughshod over them. You can stop worrying about the elevators, they're under control."

"Good," I said. Like any computer game corporation that didn't have to worry about health and safety, this building only had elevators. No stairs. In a further offense to the gods of Fire Safety, the ground floor elevators only ran up to level *eight*. To get to the higher floors, you had to run a gauntlet of receptionists, security, and deadly traps for four levels.

Or you could bypass that insanity by blowing your way into level twelve and having your hacker take over the system. Glitch had assured us that once he was plugged in, the only way to get him out would be to physically unplug him. Since he controlled the elevators, they'd have to cut through the doors and climb up the shafts.

Since he'd mentioned it as something the security staff *could* do, I had to assume it was part of their programming. It would take time, though.

"Okay, let's go," I said. The doors for the elevator to the upper floors slid open.

"Next stop, the penthouse," Glitch cackled from my phone. "It's a straight elevator run, all the way to the top."

"This is it guys," I said. "If we can get ShinseiDrachen's secret formula for cyberorganic fusion, Kobayashi-Krüger Konzern will give us their token. We take ShinseiDrachen's token from out of their CEO's cold, dead hand and we're done here. Floor finished."

There were muted cheers all around. Everyone couldn't wait to be done with this. We got in the elevator and watched the numbers climb: 13 . . . 14 . . . it stopped on 19, one short of the top floor. The doors dinged open, revealing the massed gunmen waiting for us.

"Sorry, babe," Glitch's voice came from my phone. "Kobayashi pays pretty well, but ShinseiDrachen pays better. It's been fun."

"Ah, Glitch," I said sadly. "Curse your sudden but inevitable betrayal."

GAME OVER

Sudden treachery from a paid ally was such a staple of the cyberpunk genre that I was honestly surprised it hadn't happened already. With a thought, I flung up a Phantasm of a mirrored wall. That would only buy us a second before they shot through it, but—

"Hey, where'd they go? And who are you guys?"

Maybe it would buy a little longer than that. Not that it mattered, because Borys was already moving. His storm took a little longer to get going, but when he had to cover such a small area, that extra time was measured in seconds.

An icy whirlwind was forming around him as he shot forward. I could barely make out his figure as he crashed through my barrier, and then he was among the mooks, and the whole corridor filled up with flying ice and snow.

People tend to think of guns as the ultimate weapon, but all weapons are situational. If you and your mates are in a corridor with your enemy at one end, then guns are pretty good. You can line yourselves up and all fire down the corridor without getting in one another's way.

If your target is in the middle of your group, and the corridor is suddenly filled with biting ice and obscuring snow, the situation has changed. Suddenly, your guns are no good at all. You can't even fire without hitting one of your friends, and your hands have been chopped off already.

The rest of my team did not follow Borys into the blood slushy that was rapidly forming. They'd just get in his way. Kyle shielded us all while we sheltered in the elevator. Kyle's shield had been coated with some carbocobalt weave that made it even more damage resistant. We should be able to take that out with us, so it was all right.

I made a phone call. Glitch had hung up on me, so I called one of my contingencies.

"Shade? It's happened. Can you take care of it?"

"Yeah, hold on," came from the other end of the line. There was a crash, some shouting, and then the *hiss-thwack* of the magic guns shooting someone.

"It's done," Shade told me.

Put Byte on the line, I said. *Bye-bye, Glitch. You were useful.*

"I can't work like this, boss!" a higher-pitched voice said. "Shade got blood all over the chair! Where am I going to sit?"

"Just stand," I suggested. "Is the rig all right?"

"Yeah, it's fine. Kind of nice, actually. You mind if I—"

"Once we're done, you can take what you like," I said. "Consider it a bonus." On top of her generous payment. I would have been more stingy, but the creds wouldn't do us any good where we were going.

I glanced over at Borys. He was just about finished up.

"Is Glitch still logged in?" I asked.

"Yeah, yeah. Y'know, I'm losing respect for this guy. He was using official ShinseiDrachen credentials! I guess that makes sense, considering. Still, shoulda hacked it."

"If he'd stayed honest, you wouldn't be rifling through his stuff right now," I pointed out. "So we're good to go up a level?"

"Just say the word."

Your party has killed 10 Black Op Mooks – your experience share is 5,200 XP.

Borys had dismissed his storm and was collecting unused guns from the security team. They were covered in ice, now melting, but magic guns weren't bothered by water. Arms full of fresh weapons, he jogged back to the elevator.

"Take us up," I told Byte.

"You got it, boss." The elevator doors closed and opened again after a short ride. They dinged open to reveal the familiar sight of the executive waiting area.

"Excuse me! You can't go in there!" the receptionist said as we walked past her. She was frantically pushing a button, but I was pretty sure that it just summoned the team from downstairs.

Borys pushed open the dark hardwood doors to the main office. To our surprise, the CEO was all alone in his office, sitting behind his desk as if everything was normal.

If he'd been facing away from us, I would have expected the chair to slowly turn around, revealing that he'd been shot in the face. As it was, he was still clearly alive, looking nervously at us, hoping he wouldn't get shot.

"We'll take the formula and your token," I said. "Actually, we'll take everything that's in your safe."

"That's fine! Just don't kill me, please? I have a family!"

"Yeah, yeah," I said, heading straight for the safe. These places were all built to the same plan, and I could sense the dark voids. Wait a minute, that wasn't a safe . . .

I turned and carefully aimed at an otherwise inoffensive part of the wall, emptying my gun into the masonry. There was a brief silence as everyone looked at me. Then the body fell out, smashing through the remains of the false panel.

I looked at the CEO.

"I wasn't! He wasn't . . . it was . . ." he stammered.

"Get over here and open the safe," I said.

"How did you know it was there?" he whined. I didn't bother answering him. Nor did I bother trying to intimidate him. At this point, he could only act as the script demanded. That didn't mean that there wouldn't be any twists, but Intimidate would just bully the monster under the script.

This time, the script played it safe.

[Identification]: CarboCobolt Deposition Formulae – Properties: None
[Identification]: ShinseiDrachen Corporate Token – Properties: None

---

"Let's get out of here," I said.

The rest of the run was pretty anticlimactic. Byte still had control of the security center, so we could send all the goons—sorry, mooks—to an out-of-the-way corner and make our way out of the building without further issues.

The final transfer was done in a low-level meeting room in the offices of the Kobayashi-Krüger Konzern. You kill *one* executive in their fancy office, and all of the other CEOs suddenly find that dealing with you personally is much less of a concern. Not that I cared. I cast a bit of side-eye at the prominent KKK logo painted on the wall, but if Borys wasn't going to say anything, I wasn't either.

As soon as we took possession of the token, my phone beeped and started displaying directions to the exit. I showed it to the others, and we started walking.

"Congratulations!" Axel's voice came out of my phone again. "You've successfully completed the main run! What did you think of my level? Wasn't it fun? Wasn't it so much more *inventive* than what those other dungeons can come up with?"

I thought about it as we walked to the exit. Possibly by design, it wasn't far.

"I'd be more inclined to think it was inventive if you hadn't clearly cribbed it from a computer game," I said. "It makes a change from slaughtering monsters as they come, but I question the *need* for any kind of killing at all."

"Well, of course, there needs to be slaughter," Axel said patronizingly. "Where else will mortals get experience from? Killing each other?"

According to my phone, the ordinary-looking residential building was where the exit was hidden. I gestured for Borys to go first.

"I question the need for levels at all," I said. "They're nice and all, but most people don't need them."

"As long as levels are possible, then someone will kill enough entities to get them," Axel said. "Making monsters widely available means that everybody has the opportunity to grow."

We all filed into the lobby. It looked ordinary enough, except for the black glossy slab where the mailboxes would normally go. There was an unlabeled slot in the center of it.

"Just feed your tokens in there," Axel said, "and you can enter the *vestibule*."

I looked suspiciously at the phone. "The *vestibule*?"

"Just a place to wait while we finish up our business," Axel said. "I owe you some questions, don't I?"

"Fine." I fed the tokens into the slot, and the black slab cracked open, revealing itself to be a door. Beyond was a brightly lit white room with white couches. A big screen lit up, showing about half of Axel. He was dressed all in white to match the room.

"Welcome to the *vestibule*!" he said. I sighed and put my phone away. We all took seats.

Borys glanced at me, ceding the first question. We hadn't discussed what questions we were going to ask, not wanting to give Axel notice, but we had discussed who was going to ask them.

"All right, Axel, first question," I said. "What floor are we on."

Axel made a face. "Boring!" he exclaimed. "So many questions about life, the universe, and your purpose, and you just ask about your immediate tactical concerns."

"That's as may be," I said. "But you said it yourself, those concerns are *immediate*."

"Fine, fine," Axel grumbled. "You're on floor four. I didn't think the first floor would be challenging for you, and you might have had complaints about the otome dating floor or the gatcha floor."

I held back a "What?" with difficulty. Axel damn well would have taken that as my next question. Not trusting myself to speak, I nodded to Borys.

"How do we use the portal to get back to Earth?" he asked.

"That's a much better question," Axel said, smiling. "You're my favorite Champion."

He took a deep breath, closed his eyes, and held up three fingers. Opening his eyes, he started talking.

"You need three things. You need a way to open the portal. I can do that, if you ask me nicely enough. You need a way to control the destination. That . . . can be learned. Anybody with a high enough Theurgy should be able to do it with some practice. And lastly . . ."

He paused and gave us a sly grin.

"You need to get the Earth back in working order."

Borys glared at Axel in silence, clearly holding himself back. Axel looked at me, then back at Borys.

"I *believe* that is a full and complete answer, but if you feel differently, I'll hear you out."

"The first two steps," Borys said carefully. "You gave us some idea of how to accomplish them. You didn't for the third."

"That's true," Axel said nodding. "I'm afraid I have no idea of how you might accomplish the third task. I may be decamillennia in age, but I am only a dungeon."

"You have said that getting back was impossible, then," Borys stated.

"No," Axel said. "I have reason to believe that it *is* possible. You see, someone is attempting to do it."

Another tense silence. Axel looked at each of us, grinning slyly.

"Not curious?" he asked. "You don't want to ask who, or why? I am *dying* to tell you."

"Maybe later," I replied. Borys looked as though he was going to burst, but he nodded to me, passing the question along. "How many floors before we reach the end?"

"Tsk, another boring question," Axel complained. "How many questions do you plan on wasting like this?"

"This will, among other things, tell me how many questions we've got remaining," I pointed out.

"True," Axel said. "In that spirit, then, I shall say that it will be up to you!"

He gestured wildly. Seven doors appeared around the room. On one side, the doors were marked zero to three. On the other, they were marked five to seven.

"I'll allow you to go down three floors at a time," Axel declaimed. "Or you can go back to the floors you've already passed. The labels are accurate, by the way; I wouldn't trick you that way."

He leaned in close to the screen. "I really recommend the gatcha game floor."

"Since we're out of questions, I assume we can ask them again without losing a future question," I said.

"Yes, yes, by all means, let us return to normal conversation," Axel said.

"Then how on earth did you manage to turn scantily clad women into a dungeon floor?" I asked. Axel cackled with laughter.

"Try it and see!" he said.

"Hang on, what was this about?" Cloridan asked.

"Don't bother yourself," I told him. "This is just going to be like the mook strippers. Monsters in revealing clothing."

"Now, now," Axel put in. "There are plenty of monsters that are more . . . comely. I chose mooks because they suited the aesthetic. The gatcha aesthetic is quite different. You won't be disappointed."

Cloridan gave me a pleading look.

"No, no, a thousand times no," I said. "We're here for a reason, and we don't want to get diverted. They're monsters, Cloridan."

I looked at the others. "We're going down as far as we can, right?"

The others all nodded. Even Cloridan, though he put on a sulky face.

"Never mind," Axel said. "Perhaps the elves will let you come back when it's all over. Gate seven, is it?"

"Yes," I said, and stepped through.

FREEZE FRAME

I knew that I'd made a mistake the second I stepped through the portal. I fell to my knees and would have fallen further if Felicia, right behind me, hadn't rushed forward to catch me. I wasn't sick or injured, I was just stunned by the memory I'd just received. This one wasn't like the others.

It started with Reggie turning up the volume on the presentation.

"—founder of Binary Nexus Technologies. We stand at the dawn of a new era in computing, where the boundaries of artificial intelligence and data processing are constantly being redefined. Our mission at Binary Nexus is to lead this charge, creating solutions that are not merely cutting-edge but also transformative in their potential to revolutionize the data processing industry. Today, I am thrilled to share our vision, our groundbreaking technology, and the remarkable opportunities that lie ahead for us all."

Past me had relaxed, letting the familiar flow of words rush past me. I might not have heard this speech a hundred times, but I was still new.

"But before we begin, I'd like to present our team. Liam Johnson, our chief financial officer, Trica Maynard, our—"

"Hold it," Fyskel said.

Everything froze, except for me. And Fyskel, the Turncoat God, who was suddenly standing by my side.

"What's going on? What are you doing?" I asked. I felt a headache starting to form. I hadn't asked this before, but I now remembered doing so. . . . This wasn't how memory was supposed to work.

"Curse this HDMI resolution," the god said. "Why couldn't you have attended in person?"

"Where were you when this started?" I countered. "You've been awfully silent in the face of recent revelations."

Fyskel shrugged. "We didn't know about the memories," he said. "They were . . . outside our purview, so to speak. And they didn't *seem* to have anything to do with your task here. So, we kept quiet."

"So what, again, are you doing in my memories?"

Fyskel shook his head. "I need confirmation," he said.

"Well, of course, I don't believe you," Ashmor said. The God of Destruction was here now, too, still in his snazzy red suit. He gave me a sardonic bow. "Nice place you've got here," he said.

"I don't recall inviting either of you into it," I replied testily.

"I suppose not," Ashmor agreed. He glanced over at the monitor and became just as intent on it as Fyskel had. "This is fresh? Untouched? I can't see any way that you might have modified it."

"It's just as you see," Fyskel said. "I haven't changed a thing."

"Oi!" I yelled. "Either explain yourselves or get out!"

"We, too, would like an explanation," a new voice said. I whirled around to see not one new god, but a bunch of them. All *seven* of them, if my quick count was right.

I may have made some kind of a *yeep* sound, but they ignored me.

"Fyskel, what do you think you are doing, inviting Ashmor into the mind of my Champion?" one of the goddesses asked. I gave her a closer look.

I guess the whole mystery of my patron is old news now, I thought.

Whoever my patron was, she had long flowing black hair, streaked with silver. *Actual* silver, not the light grey that people called silver. Crystalline blue eyes were giving Fyskel a glare so pure that I bet it would hurt if it was directed at me.

She was dressed in something like modern clothing. A deep emerald-green blouse, subtly patterned in a way that I couldn't make out from here. Black pants. The shawl she was wearing was a bit of a giveaway, though. I didn't think modern fabrics boasted anything quite so shimmery.

"Hold on," was all that Fyskel said. It didn't seem to assuage her.

"There are enough of us to evict you—forcefully—from this mind, Fyskel," she said coldly.

"I know, I know, just—"

"It's her," Ashmor stated, pointing at the image of Trica. "It's Ix."

"No, it's not," another god said. This one had midnight black skin and pure white hair. "That is an *image,* taken from a *memory,* of a *human.* Not our predecessor."

"It is, though," Fyskel said. "I don't know how, or why . . . but it is. You never knew her like we did."

"Nobody knew her at all, except for you two!" my patron yelled. I was pretty sure that she matched up with descriptions I'd read of Toriao, Goddess of Knowledge. Gods could appear in any way they wanted, but they did have preferences.

"The least trustworthy of any of us," another goddess continued. From the way that her hair and clothes appeared to be made of lushly growing plants, I assumed it was Naldyna, Goddess of Nature. "The two who *killed* her."

"It took three of us to do that," Fyskel said. "But yes, we knew her, you didn't. So believe me when I tell you: That is her!"

"So what?" another god asked. This one looked like the Old Testament God. White hair, flowing beard, still hale and vigorous despite his age. There was a blue tinge to his hair and skin that made him look otherworldly.

"Say we believed you—which we don't," he continued. "It's only a memory. How does that affect the game we're playing right now? A game, I remind you, that countless mortals have a stake in."

Fyskel glared back at the icy old man, but it was Ashmor who answered.

"It does not," he said. "Its importance is far beyond your petty plaything, or the lives of the mortals that you hold so dear."

The old man glared at Ashmor. Mist seemed to be forming around him. Icy crystals started falling at his feet like snow.

"You're not welcome here, Ashmor," the old man said. "If we have to start a new round because we destroyed Toriao's pawn fighting to get you out of here, then so be it."

"I wouldn't dream of putting you to such lengths," Ashmor said urbanely. "After all, it wouldn't do to destroy the source of such revelations before she's done revealing them, would it?"

He winked at me and then winked out.

"Fyskel," Toriao said warningly. Fyskel held up a hand in surrender.

"Fine, fine," Fyskel said. "I got what I needed. I'll go." He looked over at me as if he was going to say something, but just vanished instead. When I looked back at the others, they were gone, too.

Time restarted and I doubled over, dizzy and nauseous.

"Are you all right?" Reggie asked.

I shook my head. He hadn't said that before. My memory was changing underneath me again.

"I'll be fine," I said. "Just a little queasy." I needed to get the memory back on track or this headache would keep up. I leaned back in my seat and tried to pay attention to the presentation, but the words just merged into babble.

Did this mean that my memory was corrupted? Had the gods over-written my memory of this event with their squabbling?

Once Reggie's attention turned back to the screen, I could feel that the dissonance was reduced. Words started making sense again, and I could follow the speech. At least the words. Malcolm was about to start the simulation, and I was missing the context to understand what he was about to do. I winced at the thought, but I needed to do it.

"Sorry, I zoned out. What kind of simulation is he going to run?"

Reggie looked at me in surprise, but I suppose my earlier queasiness was excuse enough.

"Oh, we're going to connect to a universe very similar to ours! So similar, in fact, that it has another version of this startup! Having an investor meeting!"

I immediately felt my headache return, and I wasn't sure if it was from the memory dissonance.

"You mean you're going to talk to . . ."

"Yes!" Reggie said eagerly. "We're going to convince their investors, and they're going to convince ours!"

"That's messed up," Dace murmured. "Are you *sure* it's just a simulation?"

"Oh yes," Reggie said. "Nothing but numbers. We spent a week testing for gravity fluctuations, just to be sure! Even when we generate a universe where something physical comes through the wormhole, it just becomes a part of the existing simulation."

With a flourish, Malcolm pressed the enter key on his ceremonial keyboard. There was a hushed pause, which extended while the simulation booted up. The monitor went to a split screen, half showing the presentation room and the other half showing the screen of Malcolm's computer.

The techs had no doubt worried about keeping the money's attention during this phase, so they had made some reassuring status messages to show their progress. "Initializing variables," "Starting core processing," that sort of thing. It was all pretty normal until the last two.

"Signal detected."

"Opening video stream."

The text messages disappeared, replaced by a video feed of . . . another investor meeting. Not our meeting, though there were some similarities.

Malcolm was at both of them, and the pair gave each other a wink. Our team had been replaced by what looked like a Japanese delegation. We all looked at one another in shock.

The Malcolms opened their mouths to say something, and that was when everything went wrong.

At first, I thought that Fyskel had frozen the memory again, but this was not that. Pieces of the memory, pieces of the world, were freezing. There wasn't any kind of order to it—random chunks of the world were just starting and stopping.

I saw half of my boss freeze. He started at his frozen half in shock and jumped away from his frozen self. Or, at least, half of him did. The rest of him stayed right where he was. Like a Road Runner cartoon, for a brief instant, it seemed as if his half-body would just keep going like that. Then the blood started to burst out.

The feed cut out.

The memory ended.

I was back in the dungeon. Felicia was holding me.

"What's wrong?" she asked.

"Just—just a memory," I replied. "And the gods, shitting all over my head."

Borys looked at me curiously. "I look forward to hearing about it," he said. "But it can probably wait until we find out what sort of madness we've stepped into."

He pointed, and I looked around. We were in an underground bunker, or at least that was what it looked like. No windows, and concrete walls and metal support beams were visible. Borys was pointing to a metal door with a wheel that you turned to open.

"Nice of Axel to give us a fortified starting position," I said.

"Our phones still work," Borys said. "Axel isn't talking; he doesn't want to spoil our reaction, he said. The guns still work, but I doubt we'll be able to recharge them."

"Right," I said. I took a deep breath and stood. "Let's see what we've got."

Kyle opened the door while Borys and Cloridan stood guard. I was going to send out a Phantasmal Emissary to scout. It took a few turns, but then there was a *clank* as the bolts came free.

As soon as the door cracked open, we could hear the sounds of gunfire and explosions.

"More guns," Borys said. "Maybe we will be able to recharge them after all."

He was really getting attached to the things. I had to admit to liking them myself. We pulled the door open enough for me to cast through the gap. Leaning against the wall, I focused on my other self, climbing up the short flight of stairs to see what was going on. The gunfire hadn't stopped.

Looking around, I mostly saw rubble. The sky was lit like an overcast day, grey clouds scudding by, not far off the ground. The buildings around me looked to have been three to five stories high before being partially destroyed.

"This . . . doesn't look great," I said to the group inside the bunker with me.

A grinding sound came from around the corner, and I crept my emissary over to take a look.

"Oh, no," I said.

[Identification]: Panzer II – Threat: 24 – Properties: Armored, Ranged Attack

---

"It's a World War Two simulation," I told the others. Well, Borys was the only one who understood me. "And the tanks are *monsters*."

GEOPOLITICAL REALITIES

You have to number them?" Felicia asked, aghast. "How many world-encompassing wars have you had?"

"Just the two," I replied. "World War Three was a widely feared possibility, but we managed to avoid it."

I'm not sure if it counted as a win that we'd managed to hold off on global war long enough for the world to end in a data processing accident, but I'd take it.

After a bit of scouting, I decided it was safe to have the group creep out of the bunker. Looking around the rubble, I saw various looks of shock and disappointment.

"Your *whole world* was like this?" Felicia asked. "Twice?"

"Not everywhere," I said defensively. "You only got this when the armies fought in a city. World War One was different, I think." I looked over at Borys.

"More trench warfare, less city warfare," he agreed. "There were still enough bombs and artillery to destroy many cities, though."

"What are those?" Felicia asked uneasily.

"Bombs. Think of giant birds dropping those Drachen missiles from the last floor," I said. "Artillery: same thing, only flung long distances. We might see some of both, so keep an eye out."

Felicia looked up at the cloud-covered sky. "How?" she asked.

I shrugged. "They make a distinctive noise, in the movies," I said. "That was when they were machines, though, so who knows what goes for here."

It was funny how the world worked sometimes. Right now, I'd really prefer to be processing my new memory of my boss tearing himself apart in front of me. Or trying to comprehend what it meant that the gods had been arguing inside of what amounted to my head. Or the fact that the Goddess of Creation might have been a *financial officer* for a now-defunct startup. Surely that deserved a little time for me to figure out how I felt about it.

But the needs of the moment reigned supreme, at least if I wanted to live long enough to think about those things. Somehow, the needs of the moment required me to revisit certain geopolitical realities of the 1940s.

"The tank I saw was a Panzer Two tank," I told the others. "So we're probably going to be facing Germans. If we see their soldiers, they'll be wearing sort of squared-off helmets. If we see soldiers with rounder helmets, they're probably Allies. We might be able to join up with them."

"Axel is unlikely to share our prejudices," Borys said. "He might have arranged things so we can ally with either side . . . or only the German side."

"That might be so, but I'd feel uncomfortable allying with the Nazis," I said.

Borys nodded. "They are not remembered fondly in my nation either, but keep the possibility in mind."

"So what do we do?" Kyle asked. "Is it going to be like the last floor, with missions and such?"

"Maybe," I said. "World War Two games tend to be simpler, with less dialogue. You get objectives you have to capture, and you kill all the soldiers that are in the way."

I thought about trying to contact Axel, but decided against it. Getting missions from a smartphone wouldn't have been in keeping with the theme.

"Let's get moving," I said, shrugging. "Let's try and get as much information as we can before committing to anything. At least . . ." I looked around, up in the air, letting Mana Sense do its thing.

"At least we know which way the exit is," I said, pointing. "So we might as well head that way. You're our scout, Cloridan."

He nodded, used to the role, and I cast Greater Invisibility on him.

"Let's give him a bit of a lead," I said, "and then we'll head out."

I eased back around the corner and found the rest of my group waiting for me.

"Nazi goblins," I said, to the edification of only Borys, who raised an eyebrow.

"Nazis are Germans, right?" Felicia said.

"*Some* Germans *were* Nazis, during the war," I said carefully. "They have distinctive uniforms. If you should happen to run into any real Germans, don't call them Nazis."

"That doesn't sound very likely," Felicia replied.

"You've got a Pole and an Aussie right here," I said. "Odds seem a lot lower from where I'm standing. Anyway, there's a patrol of them, looks like they're doing a sweep of the street. We might want to take them before they get to us."

"They've got guns?" Borys asked.

"Guns and skills," I told him. "Uniforms, not armor, though, so they should go down pretty easy. And there's no tanks around."

Cloridan couldn't say anything, as he was still invisible, but he waved to get my attention and then made a pincer gesture.

"Yeah," I agreed. "We'll wait for Cloridan to get in position and then attack them from here. Once we've drawn their fire, he'll attack them from the side."

"Solid tactics," Borys said. "How are we for weapons?"

Cloridan held up two machine pistols. "Cloridan's good for his part," I said.

"We've got enough guns for maybe three significant battles," Kyle said. He was carrying most of the spare guns. "Maybe more, depending on how wild the fire gets."

He looked significantly at Felicia and me. We were definitely the worst shots in the group, and firing on full auto had a way of making up for a lack of skill. Once you got used to the recoil, of course.

"Yeah, yeah, we'll keep the rate of fire down," I said. I nodded to Cloridan, who headed off to find an ambush site. The rest of us got into our own ambush position.

The goblins were picking through the wreckage of one of the buildings. They were chatting to one another, and it didn't sound scripted. That didn't mean it *wasn't* scripted, especially without any interference from the outside. For all I knew, Axel had scripted an hour-long conversation for them to have every time they thought they were alone.

The fact that it didn't sound like German, and the way that my translation made it out to be a simpler type of speech, were arguments against a script. They looked and sounded like well-dressed goblins; they probably were. Which meant that they'd kill us as soon as they saw us.

We opened fire. Borys and Kyle opened up with their assault rifles in single-fire mode, picking off the unaware goblins. Felicia and I held off for a bit, waiting to see if they decided to charge us. Machine pistols were better at shorter ranges.

The goblins appeared to have some basic safety instincts, though. They dived for cover behind piles of rubble. I cursed and switched over to burst fire. The rest of my team did the same. Now we were going to be trading fire with another group who was also behind cover.

The goblins' weapons were *loud*. Much louder than our magic dart-throwers. They didn't seem more powerful or more accurate, though. There were a few ways out of the stalemate we were in. Kyle could charge out behind his shield, we could throw a grenade, or . . .

The sudden slump of one of the goblins at the back heralded the arrival of a third option. The sound of Cloridan's attacks was entirely covered by the loud racket that the goblins' guns made. They didn't notice a thing until it was too late.

My ears were still ringing when Cloridan waved the all-clear. We stepped out and started to loot the bodies.

"These are . . . normal-sized guns," Borys said.

"I *thought* they looked too big on these guys," I said, picking up my own example. "They're all carrying . . . assault rifles? Did they have those in that war?"

> **[Identification]: Gewehr 43 – Quality: Good – Damage: 525 – Ammo: 10**

"Carbine rifles," Borys corrected. "These do look like the German ones. And look!"

He held up the rifle and demonstrated how to remove the clip. Or, rather, he demonstrated that it *had* a clip.

"These ones can be reloaded!" I said. He nodded.

"They should be carrying spare cartridges that look like this," he told the others. "Grab as many as you can."

"Much more convenient than spare guns," I agreed. "But let's hurry." I suited actions to words, rifling through the goblin's small Nazi uniform. "Those guns made so much noise that I'm worried—"

"Um, Kandis?" Felicia interrupted. "Is that the *tank* you were talking about before?"

A panicked glance down the street showed that Felicia was correct. A tank, probably a Panzer—

> **[Identification]: Panzer II – Threat: 24 – Properties: Armored, Ranged Attack**

Yes, thank you, Identify—was turning down our street. It wasn't yet facing us, but the turret was already turning, which meant we didn't have much time.

"Everybody off the street!" I yelled as loudly as I could while sprinting towards the nearest hole in a wall. Everyone followed me, which wasn't the best—but it was what we'd practiced: Keep the group together. My instincts were telling me that we needed to scatter. That way it couldn't kill *all* of us—

I shut that line of thought down when I realized that I was counting on at least one of us dying, that I was trying to minimize the casualties. That was what you *did* when a tank came after you. That wasn't an acceptable line of thinking, not anymore.

The tank had looked to be at least five hundred meters away when I'd seen it. It hadn't had the time to cover any of that distance, but distance didn't mean much to that gun.

The street we'd just left exploded into flames.

"Keep going! Keep going!" I yelled. There were more holes that led deeper into the building. Some of them had been doors. Not all of them.

"We need to—" Kyle said.

"It can drive *through* buildings!" I yelled. "We need to not be here when it arrives!"

He blanched, took a last look out at the street, and then followed me.

"If its shots explode when they hit a wall, it won't—"

"Borys?" I asked. He was a guy, he'd know better than me.

"Tanks have more than one type of shell," he said quickly. "You just saw the one that explodes. There are others designed to punch through armor, which will go through walls just as easily."

"What do we do then?" Kyle asked. "Can Cloridan sneak up on it?"

"No!" I said loudly, making sure that the shadowed form of Cloridan was close enough to hear. "Tanks don't have eyes, so I doubt that they're using sight to target us."

"Didn't you say that they were piloted by humans inside? Doesn't that mean there'd be goblins doing the aiming?"

"Maybe . . ." I said doubtfully. "Doesn't seem like it would need to be a monster in that case, or that a monster would need a pilot. But how does a living monster have wheels and a gun?"

"Magic," Kyle said.

We were quite a way from our entry point by now, but a crashing sound indicated that the tank had not given up looking for us. The sound of a tank crashing through a wall was not one I'd heard before—movies didn't do it justice— but it was quite distinctive.

"Let's think about this," Borys said. "If it *is* piloted, the pilots are the weak point."

"Sure, just like regular tanks," I agreed. "If it's not piloted, though . . . has anyone ever heard of mechanical monsters?"

"Golems are non-living," Kyle said thoughtfully. "They work pretty much like regular monsters, just with different stuff inside. There's . . . living armor?"

"What's that? I asked.

"It's a suit of armor, animated with magic," Kyle said. "I suppose it's a little like an animated skeleton, only with armor instead of bones."

"Ouch," I said. "For those, you have to destroy enough bones or separate them enough from each other. Doing that to fifty tons of metal . . ."

"These guns do a lot of damage," Kyle suggested.

"Yeah, basic rule of tanks," I said. "Don't bother shooting them with small arms."

He frowned. "You're saying it will have more armor than these guns can do damage. That's a lot of armor."

"You're getting better at math," I joked.

"Let's get back to the goblin pilot possibility," Borys said. "We can test it."

"How?" I asked.

"You've still got a few grenades, right?" he asked.

"Yeah, but I doubt they'd do much good," I said. "Maybe if I got one in the tracks?"

"A thought to try later," Borys said. "But you're neglecting one of your skills. If there are goblins inside, there must be a space for them. A dark space."

"What are you . . . oh." I should have thought of that. I pulled a grenade out of my ring space.

"Be right back," I said.

GAME OF SOLDIERS

I stepped out of the shadows and into the only slightly less gloomy interior of the tank. I could see, just. There were thin windows for the driver and a dim lightstone impersonating a lightbulb attached to the ceiling. The first thing I noted was that the tank was empty. No goblin crews; the tank was moving on its own.

There *were* controls, though. From the way they were moving about, it seemed that they did control the tank, at least nominally.

I considered my options, painfully aware that my team didn't have a lot of time. Should I try destroying the controls with a grenade, or see if I could control the tank?

Let's try the non-destructive option first, I thought and jumped into the pilot's seat. The cockpit was lacking a convenient PlayStation-style controller, but there were two prominent sticks that seemed as if they might do something. I gave one a pull.

The tank slewed around, as one of its tracks had gone into reverse. Mana gathered around the stick I had pulled, and it tried to pull itself right back. I tried holding on, just to see if I could.

I managed it, but it was a struggle, and the tank didn't like it. Not that I'm an expert on the emotional state of tanks, but there were some subtle signs. Other controls started flipping back and forth agitatedly, and a machine gun started up in the turret. Firing at what, I couldn't tell, but that wasn't great, even if my comrades were behind cover.

I glanced up into the turret but couldn't see any sign of shells for the main gun or the smaller one that was firing now. It must magic up the ammo just before it fired.

I decided to cut my losses. Pulling the pin from a grenade and dropping it, I Shadow Walked back to my friends. I appeared just before the explosion triggered. Everyone jumped twice, first from my sudden appearance and then again from the crump of the grenade going off. It wasn't particularly loud behind the tank armor and a couple of walls, but it *was* distinctive.

You have inflicted 2,000 damage!

"No goblin crew, and no kill notification from *that*," I reported. "A lot of damage, though. Looks like hitting the inside bypasses the armor."

"So it's a living armor, then?" Kyle asked.

"I think so," I said. "It looks like a tank interior, with all the controls moving on their own. We might be able to pilot it, but it would fight against us all the way."

"What about Theurgy?" Felicia asked. "If the magic is on the inside, you should be able to touch it."

"That . . . might work," I said thoughtfully. "It would take some time, though. Let's get a bit farther away first. I think I made it mad."

My second Shadow Walk into the tank was much less comfortable.

Wow, I thought. *It looks like someone set off a bomb in here.*

The interior was damaged, but largely intact. The seats had taken the brunt of the damage, which was purely fire-based. Axel's grenades didn't have shrapnel. The controls seemed a little wonky, but they were still moving by themselves. I guess tanks built for war were built tough.

Sitting down was out of the question unless I wanted to either cut or burn myself, but the magic was in the smoke-scarred walls, so that was where I went. I could see the magic running through the walls, and with my hands against the blackened surface, I could *almost* touch it.

It was close enough. This time, I tried the destructive option first. There was a chance I could twist the magic enough to let us take control of the vehicle, but that was going to be difficult. It was far easier to mangle it to the point it stopped functioning, then see if it got better or died.

Destruction was easy. I didn't have to understand or control the patterns I saw, I just had to get rid of them. I grabbed the mana, and I pulled.

The tank screamed, and I jumped out of my skin.

How?

I didn't have time to consider the question—the tank was shaking wildly, in a way that tanks shouldn't be able to do. I had to finish this. I pulled the magic out of the steel, accompanied by an agonizing screech. Was that the sound of metal being torn? It didn't sound like it . . .

> **For killing a Panzer II, you have earned 4,560 XP.**

Not bad. There wasn't a party kill notification, just a personal one. It looked as though I'd gotten all the XP for the kill. I guess I had been all alone in here, but it was weird how the System decided these things sometimes.

I Shadow Walked back to my friends.

"Nice work, even if it sounded a little creepy at the end," Borys said.

"Tell me about it," I replied, shuddering. "It was much worse on the inside."

"At least we have a way of beating the tanks," Cloridan said.

"Let's avoid them, if possible," I replied. "Did that . . . noise attract any attention?"

"Not as far as I can tell," Cloridan said. "It was loud, but there's been no sign of anything investigating."

"Maybe they were scared off by the sound," Kyle suggested.

"Let's hope so," I said. "Where to now?"

"I took a look around," Cloridan said. "Climbing up as high as I could, it looks like this grid of streets and bombed-out buildings continues as far as I can see in all directions."

"Could it really be that big?" Felicia asked.

"It could be," I said. "Lots of time to expand and Spatial Expansion to expand the space. Or it could be not quite that big but Axel used Spatial Expansion again to loop it around."

I expected to have to explain that, but apparently everyone was familiar with the spatial shenanigans that dungeons could get up to.

"We'll just follow the mana then, I guess," I said. "It might lead us into a trap, but it will get us closer to the exit."

I took a bearing, and we headed off that way. With Cloridan scouting, we managed to avoid a lot of the patrols. Then Cloridan found something new.

"You should see this," he said. "I think we've found the other side in the war."

The other side turned out to be Kobolds. Kobolds in British uniforms. I wasn't an expert in uniform identification, but the Union Jack was unmistakable on their sleeves.

"This is silly," I said. "The buildings are human sized. The *guns* are human sized. But both sides are half-height races?"

The Kobolds in question were all dead. They'd gotten into a firefight with a group of German goblins. It wasn't clear who had won, but whichever side it was hadn't stuck around.

"So this is the side we want to join up with?" Felicia asked.

"I'm not sure," I said, eyeing the lizard-humanoid corpses with distaste. "We certainly aren't going to be fitting into those uniforms, but I might be able to make a suitable illusion for us."

The boys were searching the bodies, collecting guns and ammo. Naturally, it turned out that the British guns didn't take German ammo.

"Annoying as that is, I'm pretty sure it's historically accurate," I said.

"I found this as well," Kyle said, handing me a leather wallet. I raised an eyebrow and opened it. There were a bunch of papers inside, but the important one was on top. It *wasn't* in English. I suspect it was in some Kobold language; Kyle couldn't read it, but I had no trouble with it.

Top Secret
To: Captain James Langford, 2nd Battalion, The Parachute Regiment
Date: 15 July 1944
From: Major General Arthur Montgomery, British Intelligence Corps
Subject: Operation Steel Curtain
Captain Langford,

Your immediate attention and expertise are required for a highly confidential mission of utmost importance to the Allied war effort. Intelligence has indicated the existence of a top-secret German project believed to be critical to the enemy's strategic capabilities. The exact nature of the project remains unknown, but preliminary reports suggest it involves advanced weaponry or communications technology that could alter the course of the war.

The project is reportedly located within the city of Aachen, currently a heavily contested area between our forces and the Germans. Your mission, codenamed Operation Steel Curtain, is to infiltrate the city, gather intelligence, and ascertain the precise details of this project.

You will be supported by a select team of operatives skilled in reconnaissance and covert operations. It is imperative that this mission is conducted with the utmost discretion. Any intelligence gathered must be transmitted back to headquarters immediately via secure channels.

Your specific objectives are as follows:

1. Identify and locate the facility where the project is being developed.

2. Obtain detailed information about the nature and purpose of the project.

3. If possible, acquire any documentation or evidence related to the project.

4. Assess the level of security and potential vulnerabilities of the facility.

5. Report all findings promptly while maintaining operational security.

Be advised that the city is heavily fortified and patrolled by enemy forces. Exercise extreme caution and prioritize the safety of your team. The success of this mission is critical to our efforts to gain a strategic advantage over the enemy.

May fortune favor your efforts, Captain. The future of our campaign may well depend on the information you uncover.

Good luck, and Godspeed.

Major General Arthur Montgomery

British Intelligence Corps

I read it all out aloud to the others.

"This is probably the mission we need to complete," I said. "We need to find clues to where the facility is, and probably stop whatever they're doing ourselves, since we don't have a central command to report to."

"None of the kobolds here had a radio," Borys reported, "But we might find one later."

"Yeah," I agreed. "The scenario might be that we just find the place and then they come in and bomb it."

"What would a secret project be for?" Kyle asked.

"There are lots of stories about the Nazis having different secret military projects," I told him. "Death rays, flying saucers, even . . ." I trailed off.

"Even what?" Kyle asked.

"Even . . . there were stories about Nazi occultists calling in entities from beyond our world to help them win the war. Here, that would be . . . demons."

"We haven't seen any yet, but we know they're down here somewhere," Borys said. "I don't think much of Axel's containment efforts if they're already this high up, though."

"Floor seven isn't that high up," I said. "We'll just have to keep a lookout."

"So what's next?" Felicia asked.

"Hmm. Cloridan, do you think you can track wherever the winners of this fight went? If it's British Kobolds, we might try to join up with them. If it's goblins, we might try the same. They might have information."

"Are you going to illusion us? Did you get Disguise Other?" Felicia asked.

"No, Illusory Terrain is overkill, but it will get the job done," I replied. Then, struck by a thought, I asked Borys, "Did the bodies have any identification papers?"

"No," he said. "Just dog tags. I'm not sure if that was the practice at the time. Not much use for ID when fighting in enemy territory."

"What about the goblins?" I asked. He shook his head.

"Just the dog tags. You think that's what both sides use for ID?"

"It does have a computer-gamey feel to it," I pointed out. "An easily collectible token to show what side you're on."

"Well, we can collect them easily enough," Borys said. "They won't fit around our giant human necks, though."

I made an annoyed sound. "I guess we can wear them like bracelets? That will make it easier to show them to people."

We collected enough dog tags for each of us to have two, one for each side. They weren't easily confused—the German ones were metal ovals, designed to snap in half, while the British had two, with different shapes and colors. We kept them in our pockets for now, thinking that it made a difference if you were wearing them or not.

Then we went looking for soldiers.

FROM THE COLONIES

Cloridan found the trail, which led to the camp. It seemed that the Kobolds had been the winners of that fight. He came back to let us know where we could find them.

"Okay then," I said reluctantly. "Everybody put on their British tags, and let's approach . . . cautiously."

"Are you going to make us look like Kobolds?" Felicia asked.

"Not immediately," I said thoughtfully. "It's a tricky illusion to keep up for a long period, so if the tokens are enough, I'd like to leave it to them."

"Why not play it safe and do both?" Kyle asked.

"If we get accepted, and they turn on us after I cancel the illusion, they might remember who we were," I explained. "If we go in clean and they fire on us, we can back off and come back in disguise."

There were slow nods all around as they accepted my logic.

"Cautiously, then," Kyle said. "I guess I'm taking the lead,"

"Cloridan's taking point, as normal," I replied, "But you'll be the first *visible* team member."

I wasn't certain that Kyle's shield, heavy as it was, would stop bullets. But I *was* pretty confident about my video game logic. *Real* soldiers wouldn't have abandoned their companions and set up camp a ten minute's walk away. Even if they had to leave the bodies, they would have collected the dog tags and the orders. They had been left for us to find, not by the Kobolds, but by Axel.

So I was only a little nervous as Kyle approached within shouting distance.

"Hello, the camp!" he called out. There was a brief flurry of activity, brief glimpses of little lizard-people scurrying about.

"What's the password?" came the reply. Kyle looked back at me blankly, and I realized the flaw in our plan. Kyle couldn't understand a word that the Kobold had said. I rushed forward.

Seven people in the whole world who can play this game and two of them are here, I thought. *The mooks spoke common, so why don't these guys?*

"Give me a drink!" I called. That appeared to be the right answer as they broke out into laughter.

"Come on up," one of them called. I gestured for the others to follow me into the camp and I got my first chance to use Identify.

> **[Identification]: Bucky, Kobold Private – Threat: 20 – Properties: Skilled**

"Reinforcements at last," one of them said. He was a little larger than the others. "Blimey, you're a lofty lot, aren't you?"

> **[Identification]: Sarge, Kobold Sergeant – Threat: 21 – Properties: Skilled**

"Yeah," I said. "You're part of Steel Curtain as well?"

He nodded. "We lost Captain Langford, so I hope you're ready to take command," he said.

"Sure," I said. "Why don't we start with introductions."

"Yes sah!" he barked. "Starting with myself, Sarge, the rest of this sorry lot are Bucky, Pip, Titch, Spike, Rusty, Nobby, and Rook."

He pointed at each one as he went, but they were almost identical as far as I could tell. At least I had Identify if I needed the names.

"Borys, Kyle, Felicia, and Cloridan," I said. "Aside from Borys and myself, they don't speak much . . . English. They're from the colonies."

"Ah, darkies. Understood, sah. And yourself?"

I stared at him. I wasn't sure if he was reproducing the racism of the time or if the game was just adapting to whatever shit came out of my mouth.

"Just Captain is fine," I finally said.

"Understood, Captain!"

I turned to the others. "Looks like we're joining up. You can get the names from Identify, and they seem to have accepted that you don't speak their language.

I sighed as a thought struck me. "They're probably going to try talking to you very loudly and slowly."

"What good will that do?" Felicia asked.

"None whatsoever," I said. I turned back to the Kobolds. "Why don't you brief me on how the mission has progressed so far."

"Aye, sah!" Sarge said. He made a gesture, which turned out to be for Rusty to get out the map.

It was a very large map. I wondered where they got the paper for it, considering it was hand-drawn. Did the British Ministry of Defence hand out impractically large, intricately folded blank pieces of paper to its soldiers? A mystery.

Somebody—Rusty claimed to have drawn it, but I suspected the thing had been created by Axel—had drawn out a significant portion of the street grid. Enemy patrols had been marked, both infantry and tanks. The routes were long complicated loops that began and ended in one of three barracks. Two infantry barracks and one tank . . . pen, I supposed the correct term was.

"We take out one of those, it will get a lot easier to move around here," Sarge said. "But it's a hard ask."

He had also identified a target.

"Administrative building," he said. "Abandoned now, but there should be archived records there about the project."

"Abandoned? So we can just break in there and search quietly for the records we want?" I asked.

"Afraid not, sah. Intel puts the building as being occupied by squatters. And the basement, where the records are supposed to be, is sealed off and alarmed. If we disturb the civvies or set off the alarm, we'll have patrols on us in no time."

"I see."

Sarge started rattling on, talking about how the best plan was to take out the barracks one by one. That *sounded* like what someone playing a WWII tactical war game would do, but we weren't playing a game. We could do something different.

"I can just Shadow Walk into a building and search for records while invisible," I told the others. First, though, I had to explain to them what Sarge had said. If Sarge thought anything of me speaking a foreign tongue, he didn't say anything about it.

"That puts you all alone again," Felicia objected.

"I will learn to take others through," I said. "Just as soon as I have the points."

"That doesn't help us now," she said. "And how are you going to explain this to the Kobold?"

"I doubt I'll have to," I said. "If I can find the right document and bring it back, he'll be, 'Oh, we have to go to this location now.' That's how these war games tend to go."

I looked over to Borys for confirmation.

"Yes," he said. "Get the objective and the mission ends. Are you sure Axel will be okay with it?"

"He seems fine with us . . . bending the rules," I said. "We skipped a lot of steps on the last floor, and he didn't complain. I think he considers us play-testers."

"Perhaps," Borys agreed. "So what are *we* doing?"

"Backup?" I suggested. "If all goes well, there shouldn't be a need, but if something does go wrong, you can try and get to me."

"That will certainly trigger the alarm," Borys said.

"If you need to get in, then the alarm will have most definitely been triggered," I said. "We're talking about a situation where my invisibility isn't working and I can't Shadow Step out of trouble."

I looked at Felicia. "Which I *will* do, if I see any signs of something I can't handle," I assured her. "I like living, too."

"That's all well and good," she said, "But if you do run into trouble, how are you going to let us know?"

I dug out my smartphone from Tokyo-Berlin, or whatever we were calling that floor, and dialed Kyle's number. It rang.

"These still work," I said. "A bit anachronistic, but so are the guns we still have."

Borys frowned. "That still leaves the question of how we're going to come to your rescue." He turned to Sarge, who was still waiting patiently. "How long before they send troops to the hospital if the alarm is tripped?"

"Five minutes," Sarge said promptly. I doubted that was the sort of thing he would *know*, but never mind. "Second barracks is farther away, they'll be another ten minutes. The tanks take longer to start up, they'll take another fifteen minutes to arrive."

"Will they just set up inside, or will they enter the building?" Borys asked.

"They'll come inside," Sarge said. "Once the alarm is triggered, they'll come and kill everyone in the building."

"Even the civilians?" I asked.

"Aye. It's a military building, and they're illegal squatters," Sarge said. "They'll kill them."

Borys must have noticed the look on my face. "They're goblins, Kandis," he said. "Monsters."

"Yeah, I know," I said. "I just . . ." I shook my head.

"The smart thing to do would be to set up to hit the first barracks from behind," Borys mused. "If they charge into the hospital, their backs will be open."

"That will leave the civilians—and me—defenseless," I pointed out.

"True, but you're the slipperiest out of any of us. If you can't get out, we probably can't get in."

"And we don't care about the civilians," I groused.

"We don't," he confirmed.

"Fine," I said. "I'll get the mission done without tripping any alarms or endangering any civilians. You can just park yourselves in a building and have a nice boring little wait."

"Uh, you know how this works, don't you?" Borys said.

"Shut up."

I went in at night. Less chance of running into a goblin, and more shadows for the finding. The building was lit, excessively so. Didn't they know there was a war on? From two stories up, on the ruined building we had chosen for an ambush point, I could see other buildings with equally profligate lights shining out the windows.

"Asking for a bombing, I reckon," I said to Borys. He shrugged.

"It's a German city. For it to be this damaged, there must have been bombing, but there must be more Allied troops in the city than just our group. It's being fought over, which makes it dangerous for either side to just drop bombs."

"Fair point," I admitted. "You think that means we won't see any bombs?"

"Oh, no," he said sourly. "It'll just be at a dramatic moment, and they will be aimed at us, not any loose light."

"Well that makes me feel *much* better," I said sarcastically, and he laughed.

"We'll deal with that when it comes," he said. "For now, get in there."

I reached out with my shadow sense. I'd decided to start at the top and work my way down, partly because it was darker, and partly because there weren't any moving voids that meant people on the top two floors. I found an empty space and stepped through.

Wow, they cleared this place out pretty thoroughly, I thought as I looked around. This floor was pretty much one big room. It hadn't always looked so open, I figured, as the floor was crowded with toppled, empty cabinets that looked to have contained electrical machinery at some point. Only the wires remained. There were still a few lights working on this floor, enough light to see that there was nothing for me here.

This might have held computerized records at one point. Did they have such things back then? But the computers, or whatever they had kept up here, were long gone. I stepped carefully through the detritus, towards the stairway. The stairs continued up to the roof; the door had been left open, which wasn't doing much to preserve the integrity of the place. I wouldn't find any records on the roof, so I headed down.

Belatedly, I remembered to cast Greater Invisibility before I went down. I also examined the stairwell. Remembering what Cloridan had taught me, I looked for signs of wires or pressure plates, as well as checking for detection fields with Mana Sense. There was nothing, so I headed down cautiously.

Coming out on the fourth floor, I was greeted by a stairway that ran the width of the building. It was lit and there were four doors, two on each side. On the left side, the doors were paired with large windows, one of which was smashed. The closest door was on the right, left open, so I peered through it.

This room was lit as well and contained books. Probably a library before the squatters had gotten to it. Books were strewn all about the place; the ones lying on the floor had gotten wet somehow. This *could* have the records I was looking for, but all the books I could see were properly bound hardcovers—or had been before they got torn to shreds. It didn't look like a place where up-to-date records were kept, so I moved on.

The two rooms on the right were labs. It was difficult to tell what kind of labs, what with all the looting and vandalism. Neither of them was lit, but enough light came in through the corridor to make out the contents, smashed up as they were.

The final door of the floor was closed. I could tell that it was well lit from my shadow sense, but not much more. No traps as far as I could tell, so I pushed it open a crack and looked for wires. Seeing none, and feeling no resistance, I cautiously eased it open.

It was . . . probably a storage room. Empty shelves filled one wall, but the place must have held useful stuff because it had all been cleared out. Even the lightbulb had been removed . . .

Wait. Where is the light coming from, then?

As I looked around, the light started *peeling* off one wall, like a giant flake of glowing paint. The other side wasn't dark, it was just as bright, but it held an eye that looked quizzically in my direction.

What is that?

My instinctive question was quickly answered by Identify.

Warning! Demon Detected!
[Identification]: Elohim Abomination – Threat: Unknown –
Properties: Unknown
Warning! Demon Detected!

CİVİLİAΠS

İ froze.

It can't see me . . . can it?

I was invisible, and inaudible as well, so staying frozen in place wasn't doing me any favors. I raised my gun and took the shot.

I was using one of the guns from the third floor. We only had a limited number of shots left with the things, but they were quieter, and I didn't want to alert the civilians downstairs. The bolt hit its target, which said good things about its defense total, but passed straight through the . . . being. There was a hole, but it didn't seem to bother the elohim at all.

There was also no damage notification.

It seemed distracted, looking at the wall where the bolt had embedded itself, so I took a step backward and closed the door. Perhaps it would stay there. Perhaps it *had* to stay there. It didn't have hands, so I wasn't sure how it had gotten in there, past the closed door.

I took a few steps backward and paused, waiting for something to happen. I holstered my gun and pulled out my two daggers. Holding them gave me bonuses to Agility and Dexterity, but they also had a greater chance of hurting the thing. Enchanted weapons had an extra *depth*, which often helped damage ethereal beings.

I took a breath, then another.

I'll give it a minute, I told myself. *I need to tell the others before I go any farther.*

Then the light changed.

I looked up at the lightstone doing a good impression of an old-style incandescent lightbulb. Something was coming out of it, a glowing form that I was pretty sure was the abomination.

Lightstones or lightbulbs were better light sources than the lanterns or torches that were normally used in this world. The nearest shadow was in the abandoned labs, the closest entrance to which was the broken window. My instincts twitched at the thought of jumping over, possibly through, sharp, jagged glass, but I had skills. I could probably do it. I took a step in that direction.

The elohim abomination came all the way into the corridor and floated there, slowly rotating. Its eyes looked everywhere, but they didn't seem to see me. I drew my daggers, felt the surge as their bonuses took effect.

Am I really doing this? I wondered. *It's a demon!*

But I didn't want to leave it behind me. I didn't want to leave it alive to do . . . whatever it was doing. And it wasn't that hard to hit.

It started drifting towards me. Not an attack, I thought, or even an acknowledgement. We were in a corridor, there were only two ways to go, and my end was the longer one. But it meant I had to make a decision. Fight or flight.

I chose fight. Dashing forward, I aimed a vertical slice at its edge.

You have inflicted 200 damage!

The dagger sliced through the floating disc with only a slight dragging resistance. The damage was promising, but it was the shriek of pain that made me think I was getting somewhere. It didn't seem to come from any kind of mouth, it just . . . emanated from around the thing.

I staggered back from the sheer volume of it and then moved forward to attack again. Before I could close, though, it curled up into a ball, and then . . . kept curling. In less than a second, it had curled in on itself until it wasn't there anymore.

My eyes flicked to the one shut door in the corridor. It had likely fled back to there . . .

Oh, wait. Shadow sense.

I quickly determined that the room behind the door was now in darkness. Not there, then. I cast my net wider. I sensed shadows, not light, but a moving light should be noticeable. . . . There. One floor below.

I should—no, wait. First, I should call it in. That meant cancelling my invisibility. Which . . . wasn't safe, particularly if that shriek had attracted attention. I Shadow Stepped up a level and pulled out my phone.

Borys answered on the first ring.

"Trouble?" he asked.

"I just ran into a demon," I said. "Elohim abomination. Unknown everything. It ran, made some noise. Is there any movement?"

"Some," he said. They were watching the lower floors through monoculars from the third floor. Monoculars weren't telescopes exactly; they were . . . more techy. "I think they heard you, but they don't seem to be moving up."

"It'd be a brave goblin that ran towards that shriek," I said, "But it might not matter. *It* headed down."

"Noted. Are you aborting?"

"No. I don't think it can see me, and my daggers seem to hurt it," I said. "Bullets seem to pass right through, though."

"Great," he said sourly. "What does it look like?"

"A big floating platter, about a meter across," I told him. "Eyes on the bottom, and the whole thing glows."

He grunted. "Easy to see coming, then."

"It came out of a solid light source," I said. "I think it has the opposite of my Shadow Step."

"That isn't a spell that exists," he mused. "But . . . demon."

"Demon," I agreed. "There might be more weirdness that I haven't seen yet."

"There might be more abominations that you haven't seen yet," he cautioned. "Stay safe."

"I will," I said and dropped the call. Then I sighed, cast Greater Invisibility again, and headed down the stairs.

The abomination seemed to have stopped moving, which made it hard to tell where it was. I had a guess, based on the shadows, but the third floor was more lit up now. At least I knew where it *wasn't*.

The third floor had been offices. Proper offices, not a cubicle farm. It gave the squatters rooms of their own, so this floor had been pretty much taken over. Goblins—German civilians—were moving about cautiously all over.

I soon overheard the reason for all this activity.

"It got another one, boss!" one of them said to a less raggedy one. He sighed.

"Let's see it," he said.

Morbidly curious, I followed the pair, taking care to avoid anyone else in the corridors. I did have to search this level, at a basic level at least. Any one of these offices might have papers left by an occupant that had what I needed. From the quick looks I took as I passed open doorways, what hadn't been cleared out had been repurposed as bedding.

The pair of squatters led me to one of the offices where we were treated to a fairly gruesome sight.

"Just like the others," the better-dressed goblin said.

It looked like the dead goblin had been attacked in his bed. At least, I assumed it was a goblin. *Small humanoid* was about all I could tell from looking at it . . .

> **[Identification]: Goblin Ashen Remains – Quality: Poor – Properties: None**

I stood corrected. What made it hard to tell anything was that the corpse was completely black. Almost Vantablack. It drank in the light, making it hard to make out details. It *seemed* to be still solid, rather than a pile of ash, but without touching it I couldn't be sure.

I wasn't going to touch it, and the goblins seemed reluctant to.

"That's the fifth this week, boss! What are we going to do?"

The boss goblin harrumphed to himself. "Normally, I'd clear us out, but I hear that these kinds of corpses are popping up all over. I'm putting out feelers for someplace to go, but everyone's looking."

"We're not going to do nothing?"

"Try and work out how to kill the damn thing, is the only thing I can think of right now," the older goblin said.

Well. That wasn't my concern, and this room didn't hold any papers, so I left them to it. I resumed my search.

The civilians weren't defenseless. I spotted several guns around the place, either stored or carried. They looked more like WWI guns to my uneducated eye. Or hunting weapons maybe?

In one empty room, I found a locked filing cabinet. That had potential. I carefully eased the door to the room shut. Passing goblins might think it odd, but I'd at least have some warning before they came in.

I examined the cabinet. It looked simple enough. I could see the tab that held the drawer in place through a small crack. And it was a *steel* cabinet.

One of my darksteel knives sank into the steel as if it were butter. There was a slight *twang* as the locking mechanism was released. Inside was . . .

Nothing. Just some letters, some bottles of alcohol, and a bundle of German banknotes.

[Identification]: 300 x 20 Reichsmark Bill
[Identification]: 900 x 10 Reichsmark Bill
[Identification]: 1,000 x 5 Reichsmark Bill
[Identification]: Total Reichsmarks: 20,000

There was that feature I'd found so useful when starting a bank. That was a lot of money! I was sure I'd find a use for it.

I had the satchel in my hand when I heard the squeak of the doorknob starting to turn. The satchel was visible and would remain so until I recast my spell, so I dropped it back in its drawer.

There was a pause, long enough that I started to doubt that the knob was turned. Then three goblins burst into the room, pointing guns in every direction at once.

I stepped back to an out-of-the-way corner but didn't otherwise react. The goblins were babbling a chorus of "Can't see it!" "Clear here!"

It took them a bit of examining and pointing guns at every inch of the room's ceiling, floor, and walls, but they eventually calmed down. Fortunately, they didn't seem keen on going too far into the room, so I was in no danger of being run over. Finally, one of them called back to whoever was outside.

"There's nothing here, sir!"

The boss goblin pushed his way in.

"Then who the fuck closed the door!" he snarled. "Everyone should know it likes closed-in spaces!"

Ah, he's talking about the abomination, I thought. *That's what it likes.*

That was where I had found it, of course, in a closed-up room. Not a dark room, since everywhere it went was lit. Some place that could hide the light.

I was pretty sure I knew where it was now. I hadn't checked out every place on this floor, but there was a lit-up area just outside of the inhabited sections. Probably a utility shaft. Not normally lit, but it was now. For some reason.

"Hey!" the boss goblin exclaimed. "Who's been going at my files?"

He bustled over, shooing away curious guards.

"Damn, look what they did to that lock!" one of them said. The boss ignored them, checking each drawer for missing items. There was a chair he had to stand on to look in the top drawer. I hadn't thought anything of it at the time, but now I shook my head at the lengths Axel had to go to pretend that these goblins were *supposed* to be here.

"Nothing's missing," the boss said reluctantly, "But someone's been at the lock." He looked suspiciously at the guards and slammed all the drawers shut.

"What's in that thing?" a guard asked.

"Just correspondance. Private correspondence," the boss said.

"Why, are you worried someone's going to steal your letters?" another guard asked. I marked him as the smart one.

"They broke the lock!" the boss said. "Never mind why, someone is going through our stuff. They must have closed the door as a distraction while they rifled through *your* possessions."

All three of the guards immediately burst out with outraged exclamations.

"Yes, go, find them," the boss said. "I'll stay here, we know it's safe."

The three ran out of the room, promising to murder anyone who messed with their stuff. The boss stayed behind, looking at the damage I'd done to his cabinet.

"That thing doesn't do that," he muttered to himself. "Someone else is here. But why . . ."

He took the satchel out and stuffed it under a pile of clothes sitting in the corner. I thought about killing him.

[Identification]: Grunwald Schmiedtrog – Threat: 18 – Properties: Skilled

---

Even with surprise, he probably had too many hit points for me to take out in one stab. He'd get to warn the others. It wasn't worth killing him for some Reichsmarks I'd never get to spend.

What I was looking for wasn't on this floor. I'd have to keep going down.

WOMEN AND CHILDREN

The second floor was mostly larger offices. They were soiled and torn to pieces now, but I could tell that this had been the *fancy* floor. Normally, you'd put your executives as high as possible, but perhaps they wanted to distance themselves from all the equipment that had been removed from the top floor.

Or perhaps this had all been designed by a crazy magical construct and there wasn't any reason behind it. I kept forgetting about that.

Anyway, larger offices were more suitable to host large families of goblins. There must have been a hundred women and children huddled under desks and makeshift nests.

> [Identification]: Goblin Whelp – Threat: 12 – Properties: Skilled
> [Identification]: Goblin Female – Threat: 15 – Properties: Skilled

Much lower threat values than the rest of the level, but there were enough of them to form a swarm.

Which made me wonder: Did monsters grow? Would these children turn into full-fledged goblins in time? That didn't seem sustainable, but they did have the elves going through, doing regular cullings.

I shook my head. Questions for another time. Right now I needed to find those documents telling us where to go next. Most of the rooms here were easily eliminated. They were filled with goblin families who were completely uninterested in preserving documents. Any papers in those rooms would have been eaten or used to line a nest.

There was one room, though, that bore further examination. The door, still on its hinges, was marked *Archives*. It was just as filled with goblins as the rest of the rooms, but there was one major difference. Instead of walls lined with fancy (now badly damaged) wood paneling, this room's walls were lined with filing cabinets.

Some of them had been torn down. Some hung open, their contents distributed to the wind. Some were closed, though. Closed and empty, or did they still have papers in them? I'd have to check to be sure.

The dozen goblins going about their business in this room would make that difficult. I found an unoccupied corner and considered my options.

I could hear them talking amongst themselves. Most of the chatter was the normal interactions one would expect within a tribe. "Stop doing that," "Give me that," etc. Some of them were talking about current events. Specifically, what they called "the hunter."

"It'll pick us off, one by one. You'll see, but it'll be too late," one of the females said to another.

"Nowhere for us to go, you know that none of us would last a day out on the streets," the other replied. There was something off about the way they talked. The upset one didn't sound particularly worried, nor did the naysayer sound particularly resigned. They were both speaking normally. Not without emotion, but as if discussing the choice of dying in the street and being hunted down indoors was a perfectly normal choice that people made every day. I suppose for them it was.

None of this was getting me closer to clearing the room. I decided to try using Sourceless Sound to make a scratching noise come from the walls. I couldn't target "inside the wall" but I could target the wall's surface, which sounded much the same.

They noticed. I was hoping it would make them evacuate, but if it drew more goblins, then I could always move it to another room, and draw them in there. As it was though, they just stared at the wall it was coming from.

"What is it? Is it the hunter?" one asked.

"I never heard that it made sounds like that. Doesn't sound like no Tommies neither." The one that spoke kicked one of the kids. "Go find Schmiedtrog, tell him what we're hearing."

One down, I supposed. No one suggested the sound might come from rats, which struck me as odd until I realized that I hadn't seen any so far. This city floor might not have them.

You would expect rats to be a given in any war-torn city. With sanitation services ended, and plenty of rubble to hide in, they would quickly reproduce and spread to cover any areas they weren't already hiding in.

There might be little food for humans, but there would be plenty that rats could feed on. Dead bodies, for one.

However, this level only had the monsters that Axel had decided fit the theme. Ordinary rats were far too low a threat to be considered, and monstrous rats weren't a part of WWII.

Something to keep in mind if I had to provide Axel with a serious critique of this floor to get more information out of him. But right now . . .

There was one sound I'd heard the hunter make. I replaced the spell and watched everybody in the room jump as though they'd been scalded.

I couldn't make the shriek as loud as I'd heard it—the spell didn't go up that high—but that fit. It was supposed to be coming from the other side of the wall, after all.

The goblins all started backing away from the wall. Encouraged, I cast a Light spell at that spot as well, making it as diffuse as I could. It didn't look anything like an abomination, but from what I could tell, these folks had never *seen* one.

It did the trick. There was a panicked stampede for the exit.

Perfect. No doubt they'd be back soon, but it wouldn't take me long to check out the cabinets. Some of them were locked, but I had a way of dealing with that.

Empty. Empty. Filled with bones. Filled with dried meat. A few scraps of colored cloth. Yeah, this wasn't getting me anywhere. I was going to continue; I couldn't rule out the idea that *one* filing cabinet held gold, after all. But then I happened to glance around.

A little goblin boy was standing at the entrance to the room, frozen at the sight of the drawers opening by themselves.

Ehhhh . . .

That was me busted, I supposed. But what was he going to do? Even if he could see me, I could take the little brat. And I'd be finished before he could fetch help. I opened another drawer.

Filled with brightly colored rubble. Great.

The light changed. I whirled around.

Just like before, the abomination was coming out of the lightbulb. The goblin boy gaped up at it as it emerged, its eyes scanning the whole room.

My own eyes narrowed. I wasn't anywhere near understanding it, but had it been attracted to the sound of its own screaming? Did it think another abomination was in trouble?

Whatever it thought, two of its eyes latched onto the goblin brat. Before he could unfreeze, it pounced, wrapping itself around him like a thick blanket.

It hadn't been solid enough to stop a bolt, but it seemed solid now. The kid had started struggling, but he wasn't making much headway.

I swore as I dashed across the room. The abomination had left the side with the eyes on the outside, giving it a clear view all around, but it couldn't see me. I sank both daggers into its yielding flesh.

> **You have inflicted 203 damage!**
> **You have inflicted 208 damage!**

The abomination screamed again. It thrashed about as well, or the boy underneath did. It was hard to tell. The thing was thick, about four inches at the center. That was thin enough that I *could* have stabbed the boy at the same time, but thick enough that I could avoid doing so. Getting only two damage notifications suggested that I had succeeded. That, or the kid was already dead.

Eh. He was a monster, after all. This wasn't about saving the kid, it was about trapping the abomination. I'd seen how it had escaped before, curling in on itself. With the kid in the way, it couldn't do that. If it wanted to escape, it would have to show me a new trick.

Rather than risk freeing it by pulling the daggers out, I tried slicing through its flesh. As far as the System was concerned, that was the same thing.

> **You have inflicted 201 damage!**
> **You have inflicted 205 damage!**

More struggles, more screaming. It released the boy, sending him staggering back into a wall, and tried to curl backward over me. I wasn't having any of that, though. I held my arms out straight and pushed out with both my knives. It couldn't seem to bend as far around its eye side, so all it managed to do was form an incomplete dome, anchored at two points by my two knives.

> **You have inflicted 206 damage!**
> **You have inflicted 203 damage!**

Then it seemed to remember that it was free to flee now. It pulled itself off my knives. A white, glowing ichor fell from its wounds. Before I could finish it off, it curled up again and disappeared.

I stood there, panting, as armed goblins burst into the room. Safely ensconced behind the front line was my old pal, Grunwald.

"What the hell happened here?" he exclaimed. I took a few steps back, to better avoid the civilian shooters slowly making their way into the room. I noticed that whatever that white ichor was, none of it had stuck to my daggers. They were as clean as they were when I took them out.

The guards had noted the ichor as well.

"He hurt it?" one of them said, looking back at the unconscious brat. "How?"

"Don't be an idiot," Grunwald growled. "Look!"

He pointed at the cabinets. I'd left some of them open, and some of them had been forced.

"Same as in my office," he said. "The thief was looking around in here, and got interrupted."

"The thief . . . hurt the hunter?" one of the guards said slowly. "But why?"

"Why indeed," Grunwald said, staring at the holes I'd carved in the cabinets. The other goblins looked at him uncertainly.

"I'm going back to my office!" he suddenly announced. "Door's staying open, but none of you go near it!" He paused. "Unless . . . there's another hunter attack. Otherwise! Stay away!"

He turned on his heel and strode off. I watched him leave, frowning. This didn't *feel* like a script. The British Kobolds *had*. Even after giving us our mission, they relaxed around the camp with a number of set phrases. A large number to be sure, but they started repeating eventually. This . . . felt different.

Grunwald was *reacting* to a demon which *shouldn't* be part of the script. He'd *deduced* that there was someone invisible who could help him, and now, unless I missed my guess, he wanted to *negotiate* with me.

Unless Axel had written a script that referenced my invisibility and the demons . . . which wasn't impossible. That hadn't happened on the last floor, but Axel would have been watching us our whole time there. That was plenty of time for a time-dilated magical construct to script something based on the abilities it had observed.

On the other hand, if this was a script, then we were progressing. So I'd better go meet with Grunwald.

Just as he'd said, Grunwald was sitting alone in his office. He was perched on a bundle of cloth serving as a cushion so that it looked as if he was sitting at the desk. A pair of glasses and one of the bottles I'd found before were set before him.

I walked into the office and shut the door. Grunwald watched the door close but didn't otherwise react. After a moment, he poured some clear fluid into the glasses.

I cancelled Greater Invisibility.

"I make it a rule not to drink while I'm working," I said.

He looked up at me and made a fair effort to control his reaction.

"The damn Tommies really are sending giants," he muttered. "Hope you don't mind if I indulge."

He didn't wait for me to shake my head but grabbed one of the glasses and tossed it down.

"Strange," I said. "Are you not consumed with an overwhelming desire to kill me?"

He grunted. "Do my duty to the homeland, you mean? I'd be a hero of the State, for sure. If you didn't rip me in two, bite my head off, and spit out the pieces, that is."

He poured himself another drink, leaving mine untouched. "Do I look stupid?"

I chose not to answer that in the interests of diplomacy.

"Strange," I said again. "But you wanted to talk, so what do you want to talk about?"

He rolled his eyes. "Like you don't already know. But sure. You're looking for something. You fought the hunter, I guess because it got in your way. We all thought that it was some kind of English superweapon, but I guess that's not true."

He looked at me through slitted eyes. "Or maybe it *is* true, and that's why you've got the only weapons that can hurt it."

"I couldn't possibly comment," I said. I picked up my glass and took a sniff. It smelled like poison, which is to say, alcohol.

> **[Identification]: Tomtegeist Schnapps – Quality: Good – Properties: Intoxicating**

I didn't drink it, and I didn't say anything else, just waited for him to continue.

"We can help you find what you're looking for, and you can kill what we need dead. Let's trade."

To my surprise, I felt Bargain perk up again, as if I were talking to a real person. Not that I needed it; this was as simple as deals came. I nodded in agreement.

"This building was part of a project," I said. "I'm looking for details about that project, as well as where the rest of it was."

Grunwald sighed in relief. "That's easy, then," he said. "There's two people here that can help you."

DEAL

Two people," I said doubtfully.

The smile Grunwald gave me had way too many teeth in it to be considered a grin. Or a smile.

"Two," he repeated. "My crew have been all over this dump, and there's only one place that has the records you want. Permanent archives, basement level."

"Why haven't they been stripped as well?" I asked.

"Locked up tight," he replied. "Only two of us have got the codes to get in and turn off the alarms."

"Why do you have the codes?"

"Other fellow's the caretaker," Grunwald explained. "He let us in when it all went to shit, but he kept the basement locked up. That's the only bit his bosses care about."

"Why'd he give you the codes?"

"I'm the boss, I insisted on it. It's got real thick doors, figured we could hide down there if things took a turn for the worse."

"But now you've got a threat that can go right through thick doors," I said.

He scowled and nodded. "You take care of that, you can get what you want," he said.

"Are you sure the codes work?"

He nodded. "I wasn't born yesterday. I tested them when he gave them to me. It's dark and dry down there, but it's untouched."

"And all I have to do is kill this monster for you."

"Aye." He showed me his teeth, in what may have been a friendly gesture. I don't know. "Sorry if it's one of your side's superweapons, but we aren't exactly a priority military target, are we?"

"Don't expect you'll believe me, but it isn't one of ours," I said.

He shrugged. "As long as you can kill it, I don't care who it belongs to," he said.

"Fine," I replied, and then I didn't say anything for a bit, just sat there and thought.

How can I do this? I asked myself. It took a bit, but something like a plan started to form.

"It likes light," I said slowly.

"It *is* light," he countered. "Glows like a lightbulb."

"Sure, but it still likes light. It can jump from one light source to another. It *is* a light source, so we can't stop it from leaving, but we might be able to control where it goes."

"Do you know where it is now?" he asked.

"Utility shaft," I said. He frowned.

"How'd it get there?" he asked. "There shouldn't be any lights in there."

"That is odd," I said. I thought about how the shaft felt to my shadow sense. There were small shadows in there, too small to jump through, hidden behind pipes and boxes. Did it feel, I wondered, like it was lit from a single light source, or was there more than one?

It didn't feel like one.

"There must be two of them," I said. "Or more."

Grunwald grunted and took another shot of his schnapps. "Get all of them if you want us to help you," he said. "But how'd they get there in the first place?"

"The first one I found was in a dark room," I said. "I figure they can fly around, maybe they've got some way of opening and closing doors. I'm betting the door to the shaft on the top floors isn't secured."

"Probably not," he agreed. "So, where's all this taking us?"

"To start with, if you turn off all the lights in the building, there won't be anywhere for it to run," I said.

"So we get to huddle in the darkness while you piss the damn thing off?"

"I reckon I can get past the door on my own," I said. "If you'd rather I take my chances with the alarms . . ."

"Keep your hair on," Grunwald said. "I didn't say we wouldn't. You're sure, though?"

"No," I answered frankly. "I don't know jack about this thing, except for what I've seen. It's not exactly staying within the bounds of physics, you know?"

Grunwald stared at me for a long moment. "I was hoping . . . I don't know. What are you going to do?"

I showed him one of my knives. "These daggers," I said, "can hurt it. They absorb light, so maybe it's as simple as that. Anything else just seems to go through it like it was made of smoke."

"I saw," he said sourly.

"Right. But it doesn't go through walls, so there must be a limit to that," I said. "If something is really wide, it can't let it pass through without getting disrupted too much.

"Something wide . . . and it's in the shaft . . ." Grunwald said, considering my words. "Ah. You're going to drop things on it from the top of the shaft."

"Exactly," I said. "And if it comes up to complain, I'll stab it."

The top floor was the best for this attack, I decided. There was still plenty of junk lying about that I could use. None of it was great, from an aerodynamic or structural perspective, but there was plenty of stuff that I wouldn't want to get dropped on me from the fifth floor. Really heavy stuff, like chunks of the wall, would probably damage the pipes and wires in the shaft, leading to problems for the refugees later.

I could feel the darkness growing downstairs, as the goblins put out the lights one by one. Grunwald said he'd give me an hour. It wasn't long before it was pretty dark. I wasn't sure if moonlight shining through a window counted as a light source, but I guessed that we would find out.

Hey, I thought to myself, *maybe the abominations run outside the building and become someone else's problem.*

Just on the off chance it would work, I cast a Light spell next to me. It was, I judged, the strongest light source in a hundred meters, except for the ones below me.

The door to the shaft was, in fact, not secured. It was hanging askew, only attached by one of its hinges. I removed the remaining hinge with my darksteel dagger and then cut the door in twain. The two pieces made for a fine opening salvo as I pushed them into the light.

You have inflicted 18 damage!
You have inflicted 17 damage!
You have inflicted 21 damage!
You have inflicted 17 damage!

That's pretty crap damage, but it is damage, I thought. *Which is more than I thought I'd do.*

I didn't hear any screams, though, so I looked down to see what I could make out. I kept my dagger between me and anything that thought to swoop up from below. It was under my invisibility spell, so with any luck, any swoopers would cut themselves in half before they realized what was going on.

There had been four notifications for two pieces of door. Did that mean there were four abominations down there, or did each door only hit two? Or were some abominations missed altogether?

It was well lit down there at least, but it was hard to make out what was going on. There was movement, but even my enhanced vision couldn't tell how many things were moving down there. For now, it didn't look as if any of them were coming up. I eyed the ladder running down the shaft for inspections or whatnot. That was a possibility to consider later, maybe.

My light flickered behind me. Without looking back, I cancelled the spell.

I winced as a scream started up again. This one came both from behind me and from down the shaft. It was weaker, though, and shorter.

You have inflicted 2,367 damage!
For killing an Elohim Abomination, you have earned 50,000 XP.

Nice. Soloing these things is pretty lucrative.

I glanced back behind me. There was a piece of meat on the floor, bleeding white blood. It wasn't glowing anymore. On the off chance it would work, I recast my Light spell. I still didn't know if these things were intelligent, and this seemed like a pretty good test.

Nothing happened immediately. No other abominations volunteered to step into my guillotine, nor did they start floating up towards me. I decided to try provoking them, dropping an empty metal cabinet down.

It made a lot more noise than the doors had. And this time it got a response. A scorching ray of light flashed upward, cutting the cabinet in half. It kept falling, though, and I got a notification.

You have inflicted 13 damage!

Hmm. Two pieces, but only one hit? Only one target, or did some of them dodge? More data was required, so I went and fetched more cabinets.

I kept an eye on the shaft door as I scavenged, but I wasn't too worried about being snuck up on. My targets glowed in the dark, after all. My shadow sense could let me know if they found a way to teleport out. The lower doors were all sealed shut, so I didn't think they could get out that way.

Once I'd assembled an arsenal, I started launching medium-sized pieces of junk down the shaft. The abomination responded with a barrage of lasers, but some of my shots got through.

> **You have inflicted 8 damage!**
> **You have inflicted 7 damage!**
> **You have inflicted 6 damage!**
> **You have inflicted 7 damage!**
> **You have inflicted 6 damage!**

Are they really lasers? I wondered. I could see them, after all, and I didn't think you were supposed to be able to. I didn't need an answer to that question to know I didn't want to be hit by one . . .

. . . or did I care? I was invisible, after all. Light went through me, and these were light beams of some sort.

Hopefully, I wouldn't find out. It might take a while to kill the thing this way, but I had plenty of junk. Of all the fights to the death I'd been in, I think I preferred this one.

It wasn't to last. The light in the shaft suddenly dimmed, and my latest salvo didn't get any points. I took another look down. It was all dark, except for some light coming from a hole in the wall, around the third floor. My shadow sense concurred, telling me that there was a new light source moving at jogging speed on that floor.

Damn.

Was it running, or was it looking for some tasty goblins to eat and heal up with? It didn't really matter. I didn't want any more civilians to die, and I was even less keen on letting 50,000 XP slip through my fingers. There were plenty of shadows on that level, so I stepped through, aiming to get ahead of the thing.

I stepped out into an open corridor, but I'd misjudged the abomination's speed. Its light washed over me before I could recast Greater Invisibility. It froze, seeing its enemy for the first time. Then it sent a barrage of lasers at me.

I dodged to the side, moving just fast enough to stay out of the scorching heat.

[Greater Invisibility].

The abomination froze for a fraction of a second. I didn't wait for it to decide if it had seen me teleport or go invisible and dove towards it.

Ooof.

Oh, right, I wasn't a gymnast. Jump could help me launch forward, but it couldn't do much for my landing, given that I was planning on landing prone. Fortunately, my spell covered up the sound of my embarrassing belly flop. The abomination didn't know what to do, but it tried lasers anyway. Three more of them flashed through where I had just been standing. Then three more farther down the corridor.

It thinks I'm running?

It wouldn't think that for long. I forced myself to move despite my sore elbows. I really needed to practice diving for cover. Crawling forward, I got in range just as the abomination decided that it wasn't getting anywhere with random laser blasts. It started moving again, in the same direction it had been before I had popped up. Which was towards me.

I love how invisibility makes everyone dumb, I thought. I waited a moment more for it to get into position, and then lunged up with both daggers.

> **You have inflicted 238 damage!**
> **You have inflicted 241 damage!**

It screamed again, hurting my ears. Just on the off chance, I tried aiming Improved Blind, but the spell couldn't find a head. Never mind, I seemed to be hurting it more.

It jerked itself off my blades and sent a spray of lasers in my general direction. Instinctively, I blocked with my dagger. The light hit it and . . . got sucked into it. I managed not to drop it in surprise.

That's darksteel for you, I guess.

The other two shots went wide, but not so wide that I didn't feel the heat. I lunged forward again. I had an idea that this was an abomination that I'd already stabbed. I could see some dark marks on it that might be scars from previous stabbings. With luck, it didn't have many stabbings left in it.

It dodged, desperately, but it couldn't see what it was dodging. Running might have worked, but from what I'd seen, it didn't move that fast.

> **You have inflicted 241 damage!**
> **You have inflicted 239 damage!**
> **You have inflicted 237 damage!**
> **You have inflicted 244 damage!**
> **You have inflicted 238 damage!**
> **For killing an Elohim Abomination, you have earned 50,000 XP.**

I didn't waste any time. Grunwald's office was entirely dark, but there was a goblin-sized void in there that I couldn't step into. I stepped to another place in the room.

He jerked as I came in. My invisibility had been cancelled, and I guess my normal Stealth wasn't good enough against goblin hearing.

"It's done," I said. I made a small light glow over my head, giving me a spooky look, just for kicks. "Let's talk about your end of the deal."

OBJECTIVE COMPLETED

Grunwald made a *very* satisfying yelp and jumped in the air when I announced myself.

"Don't *do* that!" he said. "My heart could have given out!"

I looked at him curiously. Did monsters suffer from heart failure? The normal kind, I mean, not the kind of failure that occurs when you stick a sword in it. Heart disease took a long time to build up, and these goblins hadn't been around that long, as far as I knew.

On the other hand, could they be *created* with an already existing heart condition? I didn't see why not, other than the fact that there wasn't a good reason to do so. When it came to Axel, a *good* reason didn't seem necessary.

Interrogating Grunwald didn't seem likely to get me an answer. I could ask Axel, but it would be a waste of a question. I made a note to ask Rhis, sometime when we didn't have anything else going on. Shouldn't take more than five years to get to it.

"The codes," I said. Standing there looking at him while I distracted myself with idle notions must have been quite intimidating, because he swallowed nervously.

"A—Ah yes, the codes. It's done, then? We can switch the lights back on?"

I nodded. "There aren't any more light sources in the building. I can't guess as to whether more will come, but the two here are dead."

"Two," he muttered. "Can they breed?"

"I don't know," I said. I watched him as he stumbled through the gloom to the door and flicked on a light switch. Bright light flooded the room, making my little night-light redundant.

"Forgive me," he said, making his way back to the desk and pouring out another small glass of liquor. "It's been a trying day."

"If you're worried about eggs, you should check out their nest," I said. "Or, there might be larva hiding in the corpses I left behind."

He shuddered and poured himself another drink. "I'm going to do my best to forget you ever said that," he said.

"The codes," I repeated.

He grimaced and pulled a sheet of tattered paper out of his desk and handed it to me. There were two lines of numbers written on it.

"Here I am, betraying the fatherland," he said bitterly. "The first set is the combination of the lock. The next set has to be punched into the device on the wall just behind the doors."

"Thank you," I said.

He tossed back another shot and scowled. "Just forget I ever gave it to you," he said. "I don't think that things can get much worse than this, but I don't want to find out I'm wrong."

I nodded. Since the lower floors were dark, it wasn't a problem to Shadow Step down to the ground floor. I made a light to see by, and I could feel lights slowly turning on upstairs as I started searching.

It wasn't hard to find the stairs down. They had been kept clear of junk and debris, presumably by the caretaker. The stairs ended in a small landing. Travelling farther was blocked off by a large steel door with a large, obvious combination lock.

At least I thought it was a lock.

Did anyone ever make a combination lock that looked like this? I wondered as I eyed the thing. It was big and bulky, a box about twenty centimeters high and forty centimeters long. Five large numbers were displayed, and there were five wheels that clearly controlled what numbers were displayed.

Maybe they built it that way so you couldn't shoot it off, I guessed. *Though it's not like they didn't have explosives in WWII.*

I didn't need to rely on any of that, though, as I had the code. A few twists of the wheels set the numbers to match the first line on the sheet. There wasn't an obvious *clunk*, but when I pulled on the door, it opened silently.

Smooth.

I didn't enter, but let the light shine over my shoulder as I looked inside. There was a box on the wall, looking only a little clunkier than the alarm panels that I was used to from home.

Looking around, I didn't see any obvious danger, so I stepped up to the panel and pressed the numbers Grunwald had given to me. This time there was an obvious result: A green light lit up. *Green for good.*

Safety achieved, that left me standing in a corridor that went one way. So I followed it. The corridor twisted around two left turns before ending in a door with a glass window in it. It wasn't locked. Behind the door was a large room divided into two parts.

One part was set up as an office for two people. Chairs, desks, filing cabinets. It wouldn't have looked out of place in any office building, except for the part where it was underground. Based on the turns I'd taken, I thought that the far wall of the office section would be the opposite side of the wall that held the alarm panel. I eyed several neatly bundled wires coming out of the wall. They went into another boxy panel mounted there, before heading off through the wall and out of sight.

The other half of the room was filing cabinets. Lots and lots of filing cabinets, arranged in rows that extended out into the darkness beyond my floating light.

I considered the light switch beside the door but decided there wasn't any upside to using it. The chance that it would alert someone was low, but why take any chance at all? I brightened my light spell and moved over to the office section.

One of the desks had a file sitting on it. Just that file, no other papers, pens, or office paraphernalia. It was emblazoned with a red *Top Secret* stamp.

Making it that easy, Axel? I thought, but only to myself.

As soon as I picked it up, I got a notification.

Eternal Palace of Dreams, Floor Seven: Objective 1/5 completed!

Then my phone rang.

"They're moving," Cloridan said when I answered it.

"Five minutes?" I asked.

"Probably. Is that going to be a problem?"

"No," I said. It was still dark outside, I could be out of here in seconds. "I've got the objective, the demons are dead. It's all good here."

"We'll be waiting," he said, and the line went dead.

I had time, so I took a look at the file contents.

Reich Ministry of Armaments and War Production
Berlin, 12 February 1944
Top Secret
To: *Oberstleutnant Franz Ritter*
Commanding Officer, Facility 12
Hauptstraße 57, 52062 Aachen
Subject: *Classified Dossier on Project Uranus*
Oberstleutnant Ritter,

Enclosed herein is the latest dossier on Project Uranus, our most critical research endeavor currently underway. This file contains comprehensive updates on the atomic fission experiments, materials acquisition, and ongoing progress at the Kaiser Wilhelm Institute. The enclosed documents provide detailed schematics, research notes, and operational timelines crucial to our objective of weaponizing nuclear energy.

As per Oberkommando orders, this dossier is to be kept under the strictest security. Any breach of its contents could severely compromise our strategic advantage. It is imperative that this information remains confined to Facility 12, and under no circumstances is it to be transferred to any other location without direct authorization from the highest levels.

Should further analysis or consultation be required, arrangements can be made through the office at Büchelstraße Headquarters, where select members of the research team are currently stationed to ensure the continuity of the project.

Please confirm receipt of this dossier immediately and ensure that all protocols for handling classified material are strictly adhered to.
Heil Hitler!
Dr. Hans Müller
Head of Special Weapons Division
Reich Ministry of Armaments and War Production

"Goddamn it," I said aloud. "Why couldn't it have been flying saucers?"

I didn't stay to read any more. The first page had two locations, which was likely one more than I needed. I made to teleport out of there, but something held me back.

There wasn't a reason to warn them. They were just a part of Axel's system. But they'd felt too real for me to just leave them. I jumped back up to the third floor.

Grunwald wasn't in his office, which might explain why the lights were turned off. I could hear his voice outside, so I stepped out. There were screams.

"The military is coming," I told him before he could complain. "Five minutes."

His eyes widened in fear, and he swore. "You had the codes, dammit! Why didn't you use them?!"

"Believe me when I say that it was unavoidable. Call it an additional trap. Good luck. Oh, and I left the door open; you might want to send someone down to close it."

I felt a bit guilty about that, but I didn't let it show. I didn't have the time to close up behind myself!

I disappeared back into his office. It wasn't as impressive an exit as invisibility would be, but I didn't want to cast the spell just to lose it as I stepped through a shadow.

I couldn't get back to the others in one jump, but the streets were clear for now, so I didn't have any trouble. They were happy to see me, and Sarge was raring to go.

"We going ta smash those bastards from behind like we planned?" he asked.

"I don't think so," I said. "We're better off getting to the actual site while they're looking for us here."

I couldn't read Kobold expressions, but I made a note of that one as "disappointment." Nevertheless, he took the file off me eagerly.

"It's all here, sah! All the details of this atom project of theirs," he said as he went through it. "If we get this back to HQ, it will be a success, no doubt about it."

"Atomic?" Borys asked. "As in, atomic bomb?"

"Yeah," I said heavily. "Sarge, find us our next target. We're going to want to steal or disrupt or destroy whatever they're working on."

"Is atomic bad?" Felicia asked, looking at our expressions. "It was a big fireball, right?"

"They wouldn't be using it *here*, though," Borys said. "This is a German city."

"You don't believe that," I told him. To Felicia, I explained: "It's a *really big* fireball. I doubt that Axel can make one, and I *hope* that he can't mimic one with magic. But he could do a pretty good impression if he fills this entire floor with flame."

"The entire floor?" Felicia asked, aghast. "Why would he do that?"

"Adds dramatic tension," I said. "An atomic bomb is the ultimate Chekhov's gun. You don't introduce it in the first act if you're not going to fire it in the fourth."

From the blank looks I was getting, my idiom hadn't translated right. But Borys got it, much as he'd like to deny it.

"It's a rule of writing plays," I explained. "And while this is a game, it's also a play being put on for Axel's amusement. I'm not sure what the excuse is going to be. It might be some mad German commander wanting to purge the city of the enemy, it might be a launch that fails. Or it might be that they don't build it right and it goes off accidentally."

"That does sound like something Axel would do," Borys admitted.

"So we're in a race," I said. "We have to find this project before they set off this bomb and kill us all."

"No doubt, sah!" Sarge put in. "But don't worry, I've gone through the file, and I've found out where they're building the damned thing! We'll winkle out that bomb in no time!"

"Don't get your hopes up," I cautioned the others as I could see their mood being lifted. "The next place is only the second objective . . . out of five."

institute

A little while after that, we had our first air raid. We were heading back to our camp when the sirens started.

"Everybody under cover! *Now!*" Sarge shouted, and we all ran, following the Kobold into the nearest building.

"What's going on?" Felicia asked.

"Just find a strong wall, and hunker down," Sarge told her. He took his own advice, huddling in a corner.

"Is this our guys doing this?" I asked, curling up against a wall. I used Phantasmal Object to block off the door and windows. If the British Kobold sergeant found my use of magic odd, he didn't say anything about it.

"Probably. Not that it matters. Damn flyboys can't see a thing at night, they're just dropping bombs on a map reference."

"What's—" Felicia tried again, but she was interrupted by the first bomb falling.

Just like in the movies, there was a high-pitched whistling sound, followed by a loud explosion. The ground trembled, just a bit.

"Oh," Felicia said. "That. Big fireballs, you said? Will we be safe here?"

I looked over at Sarge, who shrugged. "Depends how close they hit," he said. "You don't want to be on the street, though. Flying debris goes a lot farther out in the open."

"But if one hits here . . ." I said, looking up at the ceiling.

"Then we're dead, and the mission's failed," he said. "Not much point in thinking about it, though. We're going to be stuck in here for a while, might as well get some shut-eye."

He and the other soldiers promptly curled up into little balls and dropped off to sleep.

"How?" Felicia asked incredulously, looking at the suddenly snoring Kobolds.

"Soldiers learn to sleep wherever they need to," Borys said. "It's probably a good idea to join them."

"Shouldn't we keep watch?" Kyle asked.

"I'll stay up for a bit," I offered. "I want to try and reinforce this place. My Earth Magic skill could use some practice."

> **[Earth Magic] Level 3 acquired through use.**
> **For gaining a skill level, you have been awarded 1 XP.**

I really had needed to practice that skill. The problem was that I could never find a reason to use Earth Magic in combat, which was when you got the best experience. Iron Dart was a combat spell that I did have, but my spell total was so low that it wasn't worth using in most cases. Even now, my total for that spell was just 108.

That was significantly worse than my subpar Dagger skill. More practice would help, of course, but I was never going to get the numbers for this skill because it was based on my Intelligence, which was much lower than my Charisma.

This was why, I was coming to understand, most people didn't spread their skills as widely as I had. The first few levels came quickly, but if you wanted to get a skill up to six or seven, you needed to practice, practice, practice.

You *could* get away with less training if you did it in a dangerous environment. Floor seven of a dungeon while under bombardment seemed to count. I might get the skill to level four by the time we were done here.

Of course, Earth Magic had uses beyond direct combat. To start with, I'd managed to mend the numerous cracks in the walls here, reinforcing the structure. Changing the flat ceiling into a dome should also increase the strength of the building.

Scooping some stone out from the center of the room allowed me to make little alcoves to cover the sleeping Kobolds. This house didn't have a basement, and I suspected that none of them did, as I could only go two meters down before I ran into a rock that I couldn't affect with my skill.

It looked normal, but . . . oh, right.

> **[Identification]: Impervium Stone – Quality: Perfect – Properties:**
> **Impervious, Scryproof**

Nice stuff. I was pretty sure Rhis *couldn't* make this. If he could have, he would have built everything with this, mana cost be damned. I wondered if I could get a piece of the stuff for him to absorb. It seemed unlikely, but maybe an elf would carve off a piece if I asked nicely.

Finishing the shelters for the humans left me with a large hole in the middle of the floor, but we weren't planning on staying long. There was just one thing left to do before I woke Cloridan to take his shift.

More spell levels meant more spell *points*, thanks to Extra Spells. I now had enough to buy the spells needed to take people with me into shadow.

Shadow Magic was a little weird in that respect. Instead of offering a higher-level spell to take more people, it had *two* spells that combined to let you add people in.

---

15 Cloak: Gather shadows to cover a person. Light will dissipate shadows after duration. (15 mana) (5 minutes)
20 Enshroud: Allow a Cloaked object or person to be included as the caster for any Shadow Magic spell. (20 mana) (lasts while Cloaked)

I could have gotten Cloak already, but it was pretty useless without Enshroud. Better to save the points in case I needed them for something, or until I was ready to get Enshroud.

Which was now. Right? I thought through my options. Up until now, I'd used Shadow Walk to stealthily infiltrate on my own. That had worked on floor four, and for the first part of this floor, when all I needed was information or to collect an item. But I expected that at least one of the next objectives would require us to do . . . military stuff. We had that squad for a reason, after all.

Getting one person past the defenses was nice, but if we could get the entire *unit* through . . . that was something else again. It would be expensive, though. About eight hours of mana regeneration, which was an insane amount for me. Illusion spells were cheap. Despite throwing them out left and right, I still had 80 percent of my mana. Casting this on the group would cost me twelve percent.

Still worth it, though. I bought the spells. I'd try them out in the morning.

I was woken up by a gunshot and a sudden brightness. When I poked my head out of the shelter, I saw light shining through the door and Sarge grinning at me.

"Wakey wakey, sah! This . . . thing was blocking the door. Seems to have sorted itself out, though."

I grimaced. "You couldn't have woken me up—normally—to get rid of it?"

"This was quicker," he said. "And you're up, along with everyone else."

"Right. What's the agenda for today?"

"Back to the camp. If it's still there, we'll get some grub. Then, I reckon we can find this institute that they mention in the notes. Chances are there'll be soldiers in the way, so we'll be in for a fight."

"We'll see about that," I said. "Let's get some food, and then I'll tell you about how we're going to get past the soldiers."

With Cloridan scouting invisibly, and the Sarge's . . . know-how, we didn't have too much trouble avoiding patrols as we made our way to the Institute. Once we got there, though, we found an obstacle we couldn't sneak around.

"It's like this on the other three intersections," Cloridan explained.

"This" was a military camp. The roads had been choked off with six-foot-high walls of sandbags, arranged in a square with only a single-lane gate to allow any necessary traffic on each side.

"It's ridiculous," Borys said. "There's not enough room for all the soldiers there."

"What do you mean? It's not like they're spilling over the sides," I said. The fortresses *were* pretty small, constrained by having to fit into an intersection.

"I mean, where do they sleep? It's standing room only in there. Where do they eat?"

"Maybe they don't eat, or sleep," I said glumly. Sarge looked at me scornfully.

"Or," he said, "they took over some of the buildings between the checkpoints."

"Damn," Cloridan said. "I was thinking we could sneak over or through some of those buildings, but that'd be pretty dangerous if there are off-duty soldiers in them."

"Aye, it would be a dumb plan regardless," Sarge said. "The lights would get you before you crossed the road."

"Huh?"

"Those small towers," I explained. "They have powerful lights on them. At night, they'll light up the whole street."

"And they'll light you up with tracer fire when you try and cross it," Sarge said gleefully. "Nah, we'll have to punch through the lines. Take 'em off guard and go through one of the forts before they know what hit 'em."

"The military solution," I said thoughtfully, staring at the institute itself. It was a big neoclassical pile of stone, with soaring columns and clean, undecorated walls. There were windows, but none of them were within twenty feet of the ground.

"Do we know what the other buildings on that block are?" I asked.

"Aye, that's in the notes. It's all one compound, but only the administration is fancy, like," Sarge said.

"Let's have a look at the other intersections then," I said. To my shadow senses, the street was a blazing no-man's land. I doubted that would change come nightfall. There were shadows beyond the street, but I couldn't sense very far into the building. There might be something better from another angle.

"If you say so, sah," Sarge said doubtfully.

"At least there's no tanks," Kyle said as we pulled back to approach from another direction.

"Tanks don't mix too well with infantry," Sarge said. "On account of how they don't care too much who they kill."

Borys snorted. "Germany *invented* combined arms doctrine. It's a strange sort of war recreation that doesn't include it."

"He probably can't make any changes right now," I said. "But let's not give Axel any ideas of how he can make this floor harder, hey?"

"Good point," Borys allowed. "Sorry."

We snuck around for a while, but the second approach hit pay dirt.

"Okay," I said, "I can sense a way through. Some place nice and dark without any moving voids in it."

Sarge stared at me without comprehension, the way he always did when I talked about magic.

"Brace yourself and get ready," I said, and then I started casting spells.

I didn't *think* that I needed to do this in shadow. Cloak suggested it would last for five minutes even in the light. But we were holed up in a deserted storefront near one of the intersections, so it was a moot point.

I needed to cast Cloak and Enshroud once for each Kobold soldier and on each of my friends. Fortunately, they were both the set-and-forget kind of spell. As I covered everyone in shadow, the already gloomy room became wreathed in darkness. Enshroud didn't have a visible effect, but it had an effect on me.

I became bigger. It felt really weird. Somehow, everyone I cast Enshroud on became a part of me. Not in the sense that I could control them, or sense anything from them. I wasn't clear on *why* I thought they were a part of me. I just knew that they were.

It all became clear when I cast [Shadow Walk]. It wasn't like I had expected, that they would all be able to walk through the shadows at the same time. Instead, I stepped through, and they all came with me. I *could* move them, just only through shadow.

I'd never noticed before, but there wasn't any sound in the shadows. I noticed it now because I was fairly sure that my friends were trying to say something, but I couldn't hear them. All I could do was move them to our destination and release the spell.

"Gah! That was really uncomfortable!" Felicia was the first one to speak. The others made similar noises, complaining about the trip, and the dark. The last, I could do something about. I cast Light.

"Quiet," I said, looking about. "We're here."

A notification window popped up.

Eternal Palace of Dreams, Floor Seven: Objective 2/5 completed!

KOBOLD RAMPAGE!

We were in a garage. A dark and empty garage. I guessed the Germans figured they wouldn't have much use for cars with the roads blocked off, and removed them. Or . . . they never had any cars at all, because this was all a set piece of WWII, done in a fantasy world. If they *did* have cars, the goblins would have been too short to drive them.

Aside from the lack of cars, it was a very authentic garage. I could smell the same gas and metal smells that filled every other garage I'd visited. When I cast Light, we could see the benches of tools and the oil stains on the floor. There was even a stack of tires in the corner.

"We're in," Sarge said. He sounded surprised, and I thought he might be responding to our notification as much as he was to our physical location.

"So what's the next step?" I asked.

"We gotta do two things," Sarge said. "Destroy all the records of the work they've done here, and destroy the prototype."

He pulled out a map. For a moment, I thought it was going to be a perfectly drawn map that showed every location of interest in the compound. It was that sort of game, after all. Instead, it was a crudely drawn scrawl that could have been made by anyone who had looked at the place from the outside, as we had. All it showed was that there were four buildings on the block, arranged to form a square.

Sarge tapped the largest building on the map. That would be the pile of stone at the front.

"Administration building," he said. "That's where the notes will be. A nice toasty fire will take care of most of them, but there'll be a fireproof archive somewhere, probably in the basement. We'll have to take care of that as well."

He tapped the next two largest buildings. They came off from the administration building, forming two sides of the square.

"Workshops and labs," he said. "That's where they're making the thing. We've got to find the prototype and destroy it.

"How do we do that?" I asked.

"We've got plenty of demo," Sarge said. Several of the Kobold privates started nodding vigorously. "The administration team will need some of it to start the fire and get into the archive, but there's plenty left to make a big bang."

"You want to . . . blow up . . . the atomic bomb? That sounds dangerous," I said. I looked to Borys for confirmation.

Borys grimaced. "Blowing it up won't *detonate* it," he said. "It's not a conventional explosive . . . unless it is."

"What do you mean?" I asked.

"Well, we don't think Axel has actually cracked nuclear fission, do we? He's going to mimic it with magic, he doesn't have a critical mass of U-235."

I felt a sick feeling in my stomach. "I *didn't*, but now that you say it . . . I don't see why he *couldn't*."

"Then . . . I think it's likely that blowing up the bomb will throw up a cloud of poison. Either because he's managed to make a working bomb, or he's just added the poison in to make it more realistic."

I looked at Sarge. "Won't be a problem, sah. We'll put a timer on, and we'll be long gone by the time it blows. Poison will just make it harder to rebuild."

"Long gone . . . I like the sound of that. All right. What's this building here?" I tapped the smallest building. The two workshops occupied the corners of the square, leaving just a small part of the final edge for this building to occupy.

"Accommodation," Sarge said. "That's where the boffins and the cooks live."

"We're not tasked with taking out the scientists as well?" Borys asked.

Sarge scowled. "I didn't sign up to kill civilians. Like as not some of them will die in the action, but we don't need to go around killing unarmed folks. There'll be plenty of soldiers to fight once we get started."

"Fine by me," I said. "You said we were going to form two teams?"

The Kobold nodded. "How do you want to split us, sah?"

"We're staying together," I said, pointing at my group. "If we go after the bomb, we'll need someone for the . . . demo."

Sarge nodded. "Bucky will sort that out for you, and I'll come along to keep him in line. Pip, you take the rest of the boys and burn down that building."

The other Kobolds nodded and saluted. Then they gathered around Bucky and started loading him up with small Kobold satchels. He'd been carrying a fair amount of gear to start with, but when they were done, he looked a little like the Michelin Man.

"You all right there, Bucky?" I asked.

"I'm fine, sir. Let's go find that bomb."

"Right." I turned to leave. "No, wait, let's do this with scouting. Cloridan . . ." I cast Greater Invisibility on him. "Go do your thing."

Cloridan gave a credible imitation of the Kobold's salute and opened the door.

There were two goblins standing on the other side. They were already facing the door, and they were now gaping at . . . well, nothing. The door had opened on its own as far as they were concerned. But they could see *us*, and they had guns.

Cloridan jumped over the guards' heads and rolled to the side. Showing off, but it was a smart move.

"He's clear!" I shouted as everyone went for their guns. Someone on our side was first.

> **Your party has killed a German Private – your experience share is 305 XP.**
> **Your party has killed a German Private – your experience share is 305 XP.**

Wait, was that right? I wondered. Privates were threat twenty, I recalled. That, times the level difference, times ten, and times six for the number of shares I got. Divided by the size of my share should give me the number of shares . . .

Thanks to Calculate, the answer came right away. Fifty-nine shares. Borys and I made twelve, my friends made another fifteen . . .

The Kobolds were getting a share of the experience.

I didn't have time to contemplate that fact, though.

"No time to scout, we've got to move, sah!" Sarge shouted. No one moved, though.

Oh right, I'm in the military now, and I'm in command.

"Move out," I said, hoping I sounded more like a captain and less like Optimus Prime. The Kobolds obeyed, regardless of what I sounded like, and my group fell in behind Sarge.

I cancelled the spell on Cloridan. Bullets were going to start flying, and I couldn't count on being able to direct my side to avoid him.

"Building's three floors," Sarge said. "We go up to the top, work our way down."

We pushed on. We didn't run into any trouble finding a stairwell, but once we got out onto the third floor, we started running into problems.

"Hey, what's all that—"

"You can't be here—"

"Ahhghh! Giant invaders!"

Most of the goblins we encountered were civilians. They screamed and ran for the most part, and we let them. A few of them tried to stand in our way. We let Borys handle them. Instead of shooting them, he could use his rifle as a club, knocking them down and out of the fight in one blow. Not dead, generally. We—well, I—got a paltry 48 XP for defeating them.

We crashed through what looked like chemical labs, physics labs, and seminar rooms. We moved fast, operating under the assumption that a nuclear bomb would be pretty easy to identify. We also assumed that it wouldn't take long for the soldiers outside to come looking for us.

We didn't meet organized resistance until we finished sweeping the first building and tried to cross the courtyard. A bunch of goblin soldiers were forming up there, probably getting ready to charge into the building after us.

I blocked their view with a Phantasmal wall. It lasted for three shots, which I thought was pretty good, but it amounted to about half a second. That was enough for us to get through the door, though. Sarge and Bucky went out front, with Cloridan, Kyle, and Borys firing over their heads. Felicia and I hung back, but I added in a few Improved Blinds when I had line of sight.

They didn't last long.

Your party has killed a German Private – your experience share is 305 XP.
Your party has killed a German Private – your experience share is 305 XP.

Your party has killed a German Private – your experience share is 305 XP.

Your party has killed a German Private – your experience share is 305 XP.

Your party has killed a German Sergeant – your experience share is 380 XP.

I was used to monsters with more hit points, I think. Or less damaging weapons? We took a few hits, but Felicia was able to heal them.

Then we were charging across the courtyard, into the other building. We found our target on the first floor.

The layout of this building matched the one we'd just left. This room matched up with the garage we'd arrived in—except that they'd removed the ceiling so they had more height for construction. The heavy roller doors leading outside were some evidence that this place had started as a garage as well.

They needed the room in here for the two cranes. One of them held what must be the bomb.

[Identification]: Endkampfwaffe Prototype 002 – Quality: Perfect – Properties: Destruction

---

Oh no, I thought, looking at the empty crane. *The fifth objective.*

The bomb was suspended by the crane, hanging about four feet in the air, which was plenty of room for a goblin to walk underneath. The bomb itself was huge, about two meters wide and three meters long. It was surrounded by two levels of gantries, giving access to every part. Not that they were working on it right now.

"Everybody out!" Sarge shouted at the goblins. They stared at him, but when he pointed his gun at them, they broke and ran.

"Bucky, rig this thing to blow," Sarge said calmly.

"On it, Sarge!"

The rest of us spread out, waiting for the next assault.

"You saw the prototype number?" Borys asked me with a worried tone.

"Yeah, we want to hope that there's some clue here as to where it went," I replied. "I don't like the idea of capturing a prisoner to interrogate while we're waiting for the bombs to go off."

I looked around. There were papers scattered about. Axel had made it easy last time, but I didn't see anything with a golden halo.

"We probably need to worry more about where the next wave of soldiers is coming from," I said.

Borys nodded at the steel roller doors. "There's only a few soldiers left in the building, but there's a whole company out there."

I looked uneasily at the thin steel barrier. "It seems like it would be awkward to open."

Borys shrugged. "They'll just blow it in with a grenade or an anti-tank weapon," he said.

"Seems odd for the Germans to have anti-tank weapons when the tanks are German," I groused.

"I don't think they are German," Borys said. "They're more like wandering monsters. There might be some British ones out there as well. And besides, they need to have them so the gallant heroes can take them off their corpses."

"Fair enough," I said. "See if you can find a transportation order or something, I'll see if we can get some advanced warning."

With Borys's agreement, I grabbed Cloridan.

"I need you to cut a hole in this door," I said. "Quietly."

"Well, that's what darksteel was made for," he replied, "But if they're out there, won't they notice the hole in the door?"

"That's what Static Image is for," I said. I cast the spell on the door.

"I don't see anything," Cloridan said.

"I overlaid the image of the door over itself," I said. "Now, when you cut a hole, they won't see it. We just have to make sure that the bit you cut out doesn't poke through the image. Or the knife . . . wait."

I cast Greater Invisibility on Cloridan again.

"Okay, do it," I said.

Cloridan's knife cut through the mild steel like butter. I winced when he held the sharp edge of the cutout in his hand, but he was wearing gloves.

"Now poke your invisible head through and take a look," I whispered.

He did so, taking a long look. Then he motioned me back from the door. Once we were a little distance away, I cancelled the spell so he could talk.

He swallowed nervously. "It looks like there's an entire goblin army out there," he said.

THE ELEMENT OF TIMING

An entire army?" I repeated.

"More than I could count in a minute," Cloridan said. "I dunno what they're waiting for, but they're formed up and ready to go."

"Military tactics often involve a lot of 'hurry up and wait,'" Borys said as he came over waving a piece of paper. "I found it, by the way—it was placed pretty obviously."

"Great," I replied. "Now we just have to finish our objectives and—damn!"

"What is it?" Cloridan asked, but I was already hurrying over to Sarge.

"Stop working!" I whispered urgently.

"What? But we're almost done, sah."

"Just stop for now," I said. I glared at him until he tapped Bucky on the shoulder. Then I turned back to the others.

[Privacy].

I dragged the Kobolds into the bubble and beckoned the others to come closer.

"It's a triggered attack," I said. Blank looks all around, even from Borys.

"It's like it was back at the first objective," I said. "As soon as I picked up those papers, the troops started moving. Those troops outside aren't there to stop us from completing the two objectives from this building. They're there to stop us from getting to the next."

"Is there a reason we have to listen to this foreign jabber?" Sarge asked. "'Cause we'd rather get back to work."

"Quiet, you. We need to time the placement of the explosives very carefully, and I'm still working out what the timing *is*."

"You mean, time the detonation, sah," Sarge said sullenly.

"Shush." Although he did have a good point. The objective wasn't completed when we had planted the explosives, was it? It would be when they detonated . . . surely?

Confused, I repeated my thoughts to the group. Borys, at least, was able to follow me.

"No, it has to be when they're primed," he said thoughtfully. "We need to leave before they blow . . . for all we know, the explosives don't work at all, we just get credited with it."

"Or they could charge in when we complete the *third* objective," I speculated, "Making us fight through it while we try to place charges."

"I don't really get it," Kyle said. "But if the goblins are just going to stand there until—something—happens, shouldn't we shoot them now?"

"That will probably trigger an attack," I mused. "They're not *actually* computer game sprites. If the control script is broken, they'll just revert to being ordinary monsters."

Then a thought struck me. "But what would the script do," I wondered, "if they were under attack but couldn't identify a target?"

It only took a few moments to cast a bunch of Phantasmal Objects for hearing protection. This was going to get loud. We'd been in firefights a bunch of times now, but this was going to be three fighters pouring as much lead downrange as possible.

Do magical guns overheat? I wondered. I hadn't fired the guns of this level enough to know. Well, we'd been collecting enough guns and ammo to have a few spares.

I cast Greater Invisibility three times and watched Kyle, Cloridan, and Borys stumble their way to the hole in the door as if they were in some sort of slapstick comedy. They couldn't see each other, or the hole in the door, but they knew it was there and found their way with a minimum of amusing antics.

Once they were all in position, I ordered Sarge to get back to priming his explosives and flashed a light to signal the start of the operation. As an afterthought, I raised a short, thick stone wall to help protect the backline against stray shots.

It was . . . odd. I needn't have bothered with hearing protection for Felicia and myself. Each of the boys should have been able to hear (and see) their own weapon, but for those outside the spell, all the flash and thunder were suppressed.

"Is it working?" Felicia asked.

"They're firing," I said uncertainly. Neither of us could see what was happening on the other side of the door.

Then the notifications started coming in.

Your party has killed a German Private – your experience share is 305 XP.

Lots of those. A few Sergeants, even a Lieutenant. But most of them were Privates.

"It is working!" Felicia exclaimed.

Then another notification came.

Eternal Palace of Dreams, Floor Seven: Objective 3/5 completed!

"Is he done?" Felicia asked, looking over at Sarge. He was still furiously twisting wires and swearing.

"No, that must be the Kobolds in the archives. They must have started the fire."

I looked over to where the boys were firing. They still were, but all of them were taking breaks between bursts to wave at me.

"Oh, shit," I said. "I think—"

I didn't wait to finish the sentence. I barely had time to put up a Phantasmal wall, covering part of the garage door, before the whole thing blew up.

My wall didn't last a second, of course, but it did stop fragments of the roller door from scouring the room. Part of the room. As the smoke cleared, I could now see outside.

There were a lot of goblins out there. The boys had killed a bunch, but there were still plenty, all of them running towards us.

This seemed like a time for a grenade. We didn't have many left from floor four, but this seemed like the time.

Just before it exploded, I heard Sarge call out, "Finally done!"

Eternal Palace of Dreams, Floor Seven: Objective 4/5 completed!

Well, that's something, I thought. I looked over to where the boys had stopped raining death on the incoming goblins and cursed. They'd been knocked over by the blast. Not seriously hurt, at least I didn't think so, but they were at a loss. They weren't lined up side by side, firing through a hole anymore, so they didn't know if one of the others was in the line of fire.

I swore some more and cancelled the invisibility spells. It made them vulnerable, but it let them attack, which was the main thing.

Felicia was firing over the stone wall we were using as a mini-fort. She wasn't causing notifications, but she was slowing them down. I decided the boys could use a fort of their own and started raising one.

But now we were taking fire. The goblins had stopped charging forward and had taken whatever cover they could find. Whether hunkered behind some debris or just lying flat on the ground, they were sending a hail of bullets our way. One of them happened to find me.

You have taken 416 damage!

I screamed with the pain of it and dropped to the floor.

"I've got you!" Felicia said. Dropping behind the wall with me, she used her Heal skill. The pain ebbed away, and I could return to the fight.

The boys were hunkered down as well now, and the notifications started coming in. There were still a lot of goblins, though, and it was only a matter of time before they found another grenade or anti-tank rocket or whatever that first explosion had been.

Borys must have been waiting for the same thing, because as soon as a small object flew through the entrance, a stiff cold wind blew up, flinging it back out to explode outside. No notifications, but they didn't throw anything else through. Borys kept the icy wind up anyway. I wondered if he intended to coat the ground with ice, making it harder for them to rush us.

"Can you link up our forts?" Felicia asked. "Some of the boys are wounded as well."

I looked over and winced. "Yeah, give me a second." Another wall started rising from the ground.

Then the sound of gunfire started coming from a new direction. Above us. They were firing on the goblins outside, and the notifications started flowing. The goblins tried to return fire, but their cover was ineffective against the higher elevation our new allies enjoyed. None of them surrendered or ran, so they were picked off one by one.

When the last one was done, silence fell over the battlefield. We stared out of the now ice-lined entrance. Borys cancelled his spell, and we could hear cheers from upstairs.

"That'll be the rest of the team," Sarge said, sauntering up proudly. "Now, there's not much time on these timers, so let's get going."

There was a bit of time. Enough to pick up some replacement ammo from the fallen soldiers outside. None of us were keen on sticking around, though, and it seemed certain that we were going to see some tanks before too long.

Sarge took a look at the address Borys had found, and we were off, falling into the same pattern that had worked before.

"Doubt we'll find anything," Sarge said. "That place is a railway station. Only reason to send something there is to get it out of town."

I grunted in acknowledgement but kept my thoughts to myself. What the hell did that mean? Did this floor have another city within its bounds? Or did it just have a railway station that went nowhere? That seemed more likely. Especially since we expected to find the final objective here.

There were encounters on the way, but we were well-practiced in avoiding tanks. They just weren't worth fighting. We took out a few patrols, mainly when avoiding them would put us in the path of a tank. There was another air raid. All in all, it took us the rest of the day to get to the railway station on foot. The light was fading when we finally sighted the long buildings.

"Should we push on, or make camp and come back in the morning?" Borys asked. As he spoke, the lights turned on.

Not all of the lights that a city should have. This city was supposed to be war-torn, after all. No, just the lights of the railway station. The whole thing lit up like a beacon. Lights blazed out of windows and spotlights illuminated the outside.

"Are they . . . crazy?" Borys asked. "This city is getting bombed! Lighting it up like that at night is the worst thing they could do!"

"Looks like we're expected," I said. "I think making Axel wait for us overnight could prove costly."

"It . . . is a trap, though, right?" Kyle asked, looking at the building warily. As the general light level dropped, the whitewashed walls seemed to glow under the artificial illumination.

"Of course. This whole floor—this whole dungeon—is a trap," I said sourly. "I'd like to think it's a trap for demons, but it works pretty good on us humans."

Cloridan didn't say anything, as he was still an invisible scout. He looked at me, the only one that could see him.

"Go on," I said. "Take a look inside."

He nodded and strode off. We followed at a more cautious pace. There didn't seem to be any troops guarding the building, but the wide open space meant plenty of room for some to arrive.

None did. We made it to the front entrance unmolested. The huge gates stood open. As we walked through them, we all jumped at the high-pitched squeal of a PA system starting up.

"What's that?" Felicia asked.

"Someone is going to talk to us, probably Axel," I explained. "It's a mechanical version of Sourceless Sound."

Sure enough, a voice started to speak. It wasn't Axel, though.

"My loyal citizens of the Reich,

"In this hour of great struggle, our enemies close in from all sides, their armies fueled by the greed and deception of those who seek to destroy every-thing we have built, everything we hold dear. But they underestimate the will and the power of the German spirit! They believe they can break us, that they can reduce our great nation to ashes with their overwhelming numbers and their mindless machines of war. But today, we shall show them that even in the face of overwhelming odds, the Reich stands indomitable!"

Borys looked at me. "Is that . . . Hitler?"

KILL HITLER

Who's Hitler?" Felicia asked as the distorted voice blared out across the main hall.

"He's the . . . King of the country this floor is supposed to be," I answered absently, looking about for enemies. "By most accounts, he was the most evil person there has ever been."

We had gone up some stairs to get into the building. Now, past the open entrance hall, we could look over the main station and see that there were four train lines, each in its own trench, with built-up platforms for access on either side. The building stretched a long way, far enough to completely enclose the full length of a train.

"And . . . maybe?" I said to Borys. "I never listened to many of his speeches, and they all had terrible sound quality. He's *supposed* to be, I'll bet. Goblin Hitler."

Only one of the lines was occupied by a train. Most of the carriages were ordinary passenger carriers, but near the end, close to the engine, was an open flatbed with what looked a lot like an atomic bomb on it.

Borys had seen it as well. "This is too easy," he said. "Where are the troops?"

Goblin Hitler continued his rant.

"For years, we have pursued a vision—a vision of a weapon so power-ful, so unimaginable, that it would bring our enemies to their knees with a single stroke."

I cursed as the realization struck me. "It's not easy at all," I said. "He's going to blow it when he reaches the end of his speech."

Borys frowned. "So we have to rush the objective? Still pretty—oh." He looked over at the path we would have to take. "Ambushes."

I was looking at the train. Those passenger carriages *looked* empty, but goblins were so short, they didn't come up to the windows. The cars could be filled with them, just waiting to jump up onto seats and attack us.

On the other hand, invisibility had worked pretty well, and Cloridan was still invisible.

"Cloridan," I said, "get down to the end of the train and kill the goblin who's giving the speech."

"That weapon, the culmination of our scientific genius, the fruit of our unyielding determination, is now in our hands. Our 'Spezialwaffe,' the atomic force that harnesses the very fabric of the universe, is ready to be unleashed!"

"Why would Hitler be next to the bomb, if he's going to set it off?" Felicia asked, not realizing that Cloridan had already left.

"If he sets it off, he's crazy," I said. "Even crazier than history makes him out to be. And there's nowhere safe for him to be."

Unless he's got a deep underground bunker somewhere, my brain pointed out. *But . . . that's impossible. Can't go too deep without hitting the next level.*

I started conjuring Phantasmal ponchos and clear riot shields. They'd stop a bullet, if only once.

"In case I'm wrong," I said aloud. "We're going to have to run the ambush."

"Not a problem," Sarge assured me. "Lemme at them Krauts."

I looked at the others.

"Sure," Borys said. "Never overlook a chance to get XP."

"Plus, I don't want to die in a giant fireball," Kyle added.

"It was my wish, and indeed my expectation, that this mighty power would be wielded on the battlefield to secure a decisive victory, to sweep away the foes of our beloved Fatherland and to carve out a future for the Reich that would endure for a thousand years."

Geared up, we rushed down the platform. The Kobolds took point, and Kyle and Borys flanked Felicia and me in the center, shields held high. We didn't have to wait long for the ambush.

The shield popped out instantly as six Nazi goblins popped up and started firing from the windows of the first train carriage. My poncho disappeared a moment after that.

> **You have taken 314 damage!**

Goddamn. The problem with machine guns is they fire *lots* of bullets. Borys was mostly fine—they couldn't get past his defense, any more than they could penetrate Kyle's heavy armor. Two of our Kobold soldiers dropped, though.

We returned fire, of course, and the ambushers didn't last long.

> **Your party has killed a German Private – your experience share is 305 XP.**
> **Your party has killed a German Private – your experience share is 305 XP.**
> **Your party has killed a German Private – your experience share is 305 XP.**
> **Your party has killed a German Private – your experience share is 305 XP.**
> **Your party has killed a German Private – your experience share is 305 XP.**
> **Your party has killed a German Private – your experience share is 305 XP.**

I was displeased to note that whatever the carriages were made from, it resisted bullets quite effectively.

"But alas, the treachery and cowardice of those who betray us from within have prevented this. They have sought to deny us our triumph, to steal our destiny from us."

"Maybe we should try moving up through the train?" I suggested.

"No," Borys said. "Let's try something different."

He took a deep breath in. When he released it, it came out cold, and so did everything else.

A chill wind blew through the concourse, and the temperature only dropped from there. Ice started forming on every surface, and snow started swirling around, blocking vision.

"But they shall not succeed! No, they shall never succeed! The Reich's resolve is stronger than steel, and our vengeance will be swift and terrible!

If we cannot bring this power to the front lines, then we shall bring the front lines to this power!"

"Brr. That's way too cold," Felicia said. She looked at me. "Hold still long enough for me to heal you?"

I agreed. We then pushed forward, leaving the fallen Kobolds where they fell. Sarge looked upset, but he didn't say anything.

We raked the next carriage with fire, but it bounced off the metal walls. Some of the windows broke, but there weren't any goblins behind them yet.

Borys directed the storm in through the broken windows. People—goblins—started screaming.

The notifications came in thick and fast.

I didn't think it was that cold. It must be colder when you're at the other end.

This time, no goblins popped up when we passed. The speech kept going as we made our way up the platform.

"And so, today, I have chosen Aachen—the birthplace of our proud heritage, the city that embodies the heart of our Reich—to be the stage upon which we shall demonstrate our might."

The next attack came from above. I hadn't noticed there was a balcony up there, but Borys's storm covered the entire area. They didn't freeze up, but the accuracy of their fire was greatly reduced. We got bogged down in an exchange of fire, but then one of them decided to speed matters up by dropping a grenade.

Borys blew it back in their faces. We got eight notifications that time, and two more when the balcony collapsed.

"In this very hour, I will order the detonation of this ultimate weapon at the Aachen Railway Station, not as an act of despair, but as a declaration! A declaration to the world that Germany does not surrender, that Germany does not bow!"

We raked the next carriage with fire, focusing on the windows this time. Throwing a grenade in there might have worked, but we only had limited grenades. We seemed to have unlimited ice.

Then a tank burst through the outside wall. I gaped at it for about half a second longer than I would have liked, but the rest of my team wasn't as slow. Borys pounded it with ice and sleet, while Kyle stepped forward, shield at the ready.

The main gun wasn't pointed at us, and it didn't seem inclined to wait for its turret to rotate. It spun its tracks against the slick stone surface, turning to face us. That was all I had time to see before I stepped into a shadow and put myself inside. Unlike illusions, Borys's storm *did* reduce the overall light level.

"This act, this sacrifice, will echo through history as a testament to the unbreakable will of the German people."

I held on to the walls of the tank and used Theurgy, ripping the mana right out of the metal.

I was never going to get used to the screaming.

Your party has killed a Panzer II – your experience share is 463 XP.

Huh, only an assist. I guess that ice did something to it.

"The world will know that the Reich, even in the face of total annihilation, chose to strike one final, devastating blow for the glory and the honor of our nation!"

I climbed out of the hatch under my own power. We were in a rush, but I was starting to get low on mana. I still hadn't recovered from shadow-stepping the entire team.

"Let our enemies tremble as they realize the price they must pay to defeat us! And let this be a signal to every German heart—urk!"

That didn't sound like it was part of the script.

Your party has killed a German Führer – your experience share is 305 XP.

"Hold up on the ice," I told Borys. "We're getting close to where Cloridan might be, and I can't see him through the storm."

He nodded. He didn't cancel the storm, but it parted, leaving the way forward clear. I could see Cloridan waving to us from the engine. There were only two more cars to go. One passenger, and one bomb car.

"I see him," I said. "He's at the engine."

"Then that just leaves . . ." He looked at the final passenger carriage.

I shrugged and raked the side of the carriage with my carbine. Once again, he sent the storm in through the broken windows. This time, there were no screams. Or notifications.

"It's . . . empty?" Borys said questioningly.

Then the carriage exploded.

Everyone jumped as gouts of fire and smoke shot out from the broken windows. The inside of the carriage was consumed with roiling flames. Somehow, though, the main structure of the carriage resisted the blast. It kept the fireball mostly contained. We all stared, watching the flames slowly die down.

"Booby-trapped?" I speculated. "In case we fought our way through the train?"

"Must be," Borys agreed. "The wind or ice must have set it off. I saw the notification for Goblin Hitler, but did you see one for the final objective?"

"No," I admitted. "I guess the final objective is something to do with the bomb?" I looked at Sarge. "You got enough explosives to blow up another bomb?"

Sarge grimaced. "'Fraid not," he said. "We could have used what was in that other carriage."

We walked cautiously up to the engine, casting suspicious glances at the bomb carriage. It looked inert and didn't have any goblins hiding on it. Cloridan must have ducked back into the engine car when the explosion went off, but he popped back out again as we approached. I cancelled the invisibility spell.

"I've got your final objective, right here!" he said as soon as he was able.

"It wasn't the speech guy?" I asked.

"Nope, it was pretty close, though." He led us up to the engine car and had us look inside. The corpse of Goblin Hitler was there, slumped against a wall. Cloridan had taken him out with a headshot, so I couldn't tell if he had the little mustache. The other feature of the cabin was a prominent panel with two buttons. One was labelled *Detonate*, the other *Disarm*.

"It can't be this easy," I said.

"I don't know what to tell you," Cloridan said. "He was looking at the red one, but I can't read the labels, so I thought I'd wait for you."

I looked at Borys. "What are the odds that he's mislabeled them as a joke?"

Borys thought about it. "Pretty low, I'd say. He's played us pretty straight so far."

"Do you want to do the honors, then? I don't know if I could live with killing us all."

Borys gave me a wry smile. "That would be difficult," he said. He stumped up to the panel. After a moment of hesitation, he pressed the green button.

There was a *pop* as confetti was released from the ceiling.

I almost died from fright. Then the entire front half of the engine started rising, tilting forward with a hiss of hydraulics. It revealed a stairway going down, and another of Axel's video screens.

"Congratulations, adventurers!" Axel's face said. "You won the war! As a reward, you get . . . Question Time!"

QUESTION TIME

We all looked at the screen.

"Go on, go on," Axel said impatiently. "There's a vestibule down there like last time."

We headed down cautiously to find a small room with four doors, some plain chairs, and another big screen. Axel was already on it.

"So, who's going to go first?" he asked excitedly.

I looked at Borys. It was his turn.

"Why did you—" he started, before cutting himself off. I guessed it was some version of why did Axel recreate the Nazis and an atomic bomb, fake or not, but the answer to that question was always going to be that he thought it was funny.

"Who is trying—" he tried again, but this time, I cut him off.

"If you ask who's trying to save the Earth, you'll just get a name. If you ask how to contact them, the answer will just be get to the bottom level."

"Mmm," Axel said with a big smile. "I think you'll be a *little* more surprised by the answer than that, but you'll discover that particular fact soon enough. Try for a more interesting question."

"Fine," Borys grunted. "What did the gods send us here to do?"

The Axel on the screen raised an eyebrow. "I'm supposed to know what the gods intend? I'm not the one they speak to."

"You know something about it," I said.

"True," Axel replied. "I know what *I* have been doing, and I can guess which of my activities *some* gods might have an objection to. No one's asked me to *stop*, however."

"I'm guessing that communicating with you would go against their non-interference pact," I said.

"Perhaps, perhaps," Axel acknowledged. "It's a complicated treaty, though. I'm sure there are *some* loopholes they could have utilized. Much more polite than sending a bunch of thugs to strong-arm me."

"If you don't want to answer the question . . ." Borys said.

"No, no, I'll answer it," Axel said. "As long as you accept that my speculation about the motives of the gods is just that. I wouldn't want to *mislead* with what could be incorrect information."

Borys nodded. "That's fair enough," he said. "Speculate away."

Axel grinned, far wider than a face made of flesh could. "Well. I should begin by saying that the alternate dimensions that the Gate to Other Worlds has been connecting to haven't been *quite* as random as they're supposed to be."

"The elves were under the impression that the gods were responsible for that."

"Oh, no, no, no. Not unless they're being very subtle in influencing me. Although . . ."

Axel paused for a second. "In a *way*, they're right, since I'm doing it a the behest of a god. Not one of the ones they're thinking of, though."

"You cut a deal with Ashmor," I said flatly.

"Indeed I did! Apparently, it's easier for him to keep my activities secret than it is for him to intervene directly."

"Not *that* secret, if they sent us," I said.

"Well, I'm sure the gods can run a statistical analysis of the types of demons entering as well as the next doctorate student. Once the demons started making it out, I'm sure they noticed *something* was wrong. Hardly my problem."

"What were the terms of the deal with Ashmor?" I asked.

Axel smirked. "Another question?" he asked. "Don't worry, I won't count it. I still haven't finished the first one."

"Thanks, I think."

Axel winked at me. "My deal with Ashmor was simply that he'd conceal the *rest* of my activities."

"That's it?" Borys asked. We weren't really maintaining question discipline here, it seemed.

"Obviously, he would *rather* have had me open the portal wide to the most destructive type of demon . . . but I like existing."

I wondered about that. Wouldn't a full breech have forced the gods to act and vaporize the place? Fiddling with the destinations didn't seem to accomplish much. A few deaths? The only real thing it accomplished was . . .

Getting us here. Maybe the elves *were* right. I didn't have time to think about that, though, because Axel continued talking.

"Which brings us to the *other* thing that *some* gods might, *possibly*, have an objection to," Axel said. "How to put this? I've been stretching my wings."

"I wasn't aware you had wings," I said.

"Metaphorical," Axel told me. "Let's see . . ."

Axel's face was replaced with something like a screen saver. A dark blue background with light blue lines and stars, all of them moving. It looked kind of familiar . . . Axel's voice came through unabated.

"I am rather more aware of my nature than most," he said. "There aren't many who can observe the workings of their own brain."

"I've seen what a dungeon core looks like in action," I said. "It doesn't look like that."

"Just a representation," Axel said. "Mana isn't turned to computation easily; there are all sorts of tricks you have to play to make it work nicely."

It came to me where I'd seen that picture before. On television programs, when they'd needed to show . . ."

"The internet," I said aloud. "You've been *networking*."

"Exactly right," Axel said smugly. "I'm a construction of mana, but what I'm *really* made of is the computation that it allows. Other universes have different computational paradigms."

"You've lost me," Kyle said, holding his hand up. The others from this world looked just as confused.

"He's been outsourcing—sorry, that's a business term. He's been *having his thoughts happen* in a different dimension," I explained. From the looks on my friends' faces, that had not helped. I tried again.

"Imagine you could build another brain in a separate location." Hopefully, my companions knew what a brain was for. I remembered reading that early physicians thought it was for cooling the blood. "It would have to be connected to yours—somehow—but then you could do your thinking someplace else."

"Wouldn't that just make a second person?" Felicia said slowly.

I breathed a sigh of relief. She still wasn't getting it, but she was leagues ahead of where I thought she might be.

"Yeah," I said. "But that's because you don't understand how your own mind works. The gods do—" I assumed they must, if they were putting together people and dungeon cores. "And so does Axel, here.

He knows enough about how he works to mesh two different cores together."

"Why?" Kyle asked. Axel opened his mouth, but shut it when I glared at him.

"To get out from under the gods," I said. "He's got a place they can't reach, where he can make plans that they can't see."

"It's none of their business, really," Axel said. "But I imagine that they might want me to stop. And before you waste a question on what those plans are—I don't know, of course. That is the entire point."

"You must . . . take actions when you don't know your reasons for them," I mused. "It would look a lot like—feel like—being crazy."

Axel smiled. "I modified myself so I wouldn't mind," he said.

I shuddered at the thought of a self-modifying AI with access to extra-dimensional computing and very real space-time magic in *this* dimension.

"They did *not* give us enough warnings about you," I said. "You know that doing that exact thing was how our universe died, don't you?"

He shrugged. "Binary Nexus was exploiting a bug with no understanding of what was going on," he said. "I'm far in advance of where they were."

"Of course you are," I muttered. "That's exactly what they always say just before disaster strikes."

"Dimensional catastrophes aren't as bad as they sound," Axel said dismissively. "You two survived yours; I'm sure you'll manage if one should strike again."

I stared grimly at the Axel on the screen. "Second question," I said. "What happens if we destroy your core?"

"Kandis!" Felicia gasped.

Axel laughed. "Your concern is appreciated, Mistress Bolton, but I will be fine. No longer existing in this reality, but fine."

He paused in thought while I thought about how he knew her last name. Did a dungeon's Identify work on people?

"To answer your question more fully," Axel said thoughtfully, "it would depend on the state of the Gate at the time. It was put inside me to contain it, after all."

He paused again. "The interaction between it and the collapse of my little hidey-hole is hard to model, but I think it would remain fully open for . . . forty-five days of local time within my nominal space before being expelled, along with everything that came out of it."

"Local time . . ." I said, remembering that Axel was using time dilation. "How long from the outside?"

"Oh, not much more than a second," Axel replied. "What comes out, of course, depends on what I set the Gate to immediately before my untimely demise."

He smiled cruelly. "There are a few options. If I connected to the heart of a star, there would be more than enough time to fill this entire space with superheated plasma. It would be quite the explosion, and I do wonder if the gods could contain it."

I grimaced. "I guess that explains why the gods haven't vaporized your ass."

"Do you know, I don't believe that it does," Axel said thoughtfully. "I think that the non-interference treaty *does* protect me. As does Ashmor, of course."

"I'm surprised Ashmor hasn't convinced you to destroy the world since you've already got backups," I snorted.

"I have no intention of destroying the world," Axel said with a raised eyebrow. "Humans have ten fingers, but I don't see them cutting one off for no reason."

"I guess," I said. I looked at Borys. "Your question."

He frowned. "How do you know all this?" he asked. "About our Earth, the computer games, what happened to it, all that."

"Hmmm," Axel said. "It's difficult to give a *complete* answer that doesn't take us a lifetime to relate. I pick up tidbits here and there. I *talk* to people who know . . . many things. But the majority . . ."

He paused for thought again. "A lot of data from old Earth ended up here," he said. "Like debris from an explosion. That's not a good analogy—data doesn't have a physical presence to get flung somewhere. It's a case of data preservation routines dueling with malfunctioning garbage collection routines, that led to the data being stored . . . not in this universe, but somewhere that this universe can *access*."

"Is that why Ix is based on a person from my universe?" I asked.

"Ah, that *is* a good question, but I'm afraid we're out of time," Axel said. "To finish my last answer, I am uniquely placed to collect this data, put it together into a useful form, and learn things about the lost culture that is old Earth."

The four doors lit up with the symbols for numbers. One of them lit up with a zero, the others with eight to ten.

"And now!" Axel crowed, "It's time to select your next floor! Will you take your leave? Or will you press on, for glory and adventure and the Gate to Other Worlds?"

"Do we need more than three extra questions?" I asked Borys. He shook his head.

"I think anything else we need to know will get answered by the Gate," he said.

"Rude!" Axel said with fake outrage. "You're teeming with questions! You *just* asked me one! How will you live with yourselves if you run out?"

"We'll manage somehow," I said. "Door ten it is, then."

Everyone murmured agreement, but I didn't make a move for the door.

"Something wrong?" Felicia asked.

"I'm just bracing myself for another forced memory update," I said. "The last one included the moment my universe tore itself apart around me, so I'm not looking forward to what comes next."

"I don't think anything *could* come after that," Borys said. "You can't make memories if there's no universe to hold you."

"You think I—we—were just frozen in time between then and now?" I asked. "That's comforting, really, compared to the alternatives."

"Only one way to find out," he said. "And . . . whatever happens, it's just a memory, right? You know you lived through it."

"I didn't realize you were a PTSD therapist," I said sourly. "But you *are* right."

I stepped up to and through the door.

Fyskel was waiting for me.

HEART TO GOD

Fyskel was waiting for me in a white void. This time, I didn't put an illusion up to make myself more comfortable. I just stared at him.

"No missing memories this time?" I finally asked.

"It seems not," Fyskel said. "I can't be sure—if we had access to the memories before they attached to you, we wouldn't have been so surprised. But I think that well has run dry."

"No divine convention, either," I noted.

"Ah . . . we do apologize for that," Fyskel said. "We made efforts to ensure that no damage was done, but the human psyche is really only rated for occupancy by one god at a time."

"Any chance I could get that reduced to zero?" I asked sourly. "I don't appreciate getting my thoughts all trampled over."

"You're upset," Fyskel said seriously. "And by your lights, you have reason to be. But keep in mind that the only reason that you—and the rest of humanity—have lives to live and thoughts to keep, is that we actively allow it."

"Pretty sure you didn't make humanity," I said, my eyes narrowing. "I'm *sure* you didn't make *me*."

"So?" Fyskel asked, making a helpless gesture with his hands. "I'm not talking about your origin, I'm talking about now. Letting you live your lives takes not just *intention* on our part, it takes active, *constant* restraint."

"And I'm what, an outlet? A vent for your frustrations?"

"Close. You and the other Champions are . . . a tiny *window*, through which we allow ourselves to change the world. Through you, and *about* you. It's a way of keeping the collateral damage to a minimum."

I shuddered. "You're talking about the Gods War, right? When you talk about *damage*."

Fyskel nodded absently. "We came so close to losing you back then. The scare was enough to convince us—*most* of us—that being *right* wasn't enough."

"And has this latest revelation about Ix changed anything?" I asked.

"Not yet," Fyskel replied. "We're still discussing it. Some of them are *very close* to being convinced that it isn't all a setup by yours truly."

"Can't imagine why no one trusts you," I muttered.

He grinned. "I'd care more if I could work out what I was convincing them of," he said. "Neither of us are sure of what it means."

I grunted non-committedly. "Your theory is that Ix—somehow—came from my world, before or after it was destroyed. I'm not sure why, though. Did Ix even have a physical form?"

"No," Fyskel admitted. "Those came after, well after we discovered humanity. It's her . . . essence, I suppose you might say, that we recognize. Even through your limited human perception, it shines through."

"If you say so," I said doubtfully. "So what does it mean?"

"For all our . . . everything, our origins have always remained a mystery to us," Fyskel mused. "Ix always denied creating *us*, but the doubt never went away."

"You and Ashmor," I said slowly. "The two remaining originals."

"Or . . . the two second-generation gods, perhaps," Fyskel said. "Were *we* of the same order? Would *we* generate seven more gods from our ashes?"

"I guess you weren't inclined to experiment," I said dryly.

"There were no volunteers, no." replied with amusement.

"I guess I get it," I said. "If Ix had an origin in my world, and you *don't*, then it's more likely that she made you. Are you sure that you don't, though? You didn't spot . . . Trica until she was right under your nose."

"That's possible, too," Fyskel said. "If the data . . . became us, there might be no copies left in this world. The fragment of Ix that we got from you is the only memory of her left."

"Wait, so none of the other . . . souls you can access from my world remember her?" I asked incredulously.

"No . . . something that is true for all of the people at that investor meeting."

I felt a chill run down my spine. "Except for me," I said.

"No . . . now that we look, no one that we can access remembers you," Fyskel said thoughtfully. "And you didn't remember that board meeting until recently."

"That's . . . what does that mean?" I asked. If no one remembered me, then.

"Very little for you personally," Fyskel said bluntly. "It's not like you can go back and interact with any of those people. For us . . . it does appear that the gaps in our . . . repository have a structure and purpose that we weren't able to see before. That's interesting."

"Well thank goodness you still have a puzzle to keep you interested," I said sourly. "Is that why you brought me here, to keep me up to date on your latest hobbies?"

"Hmp," Fyskel sniffed. "For all the ink humanity has spilled on the puzzle of your own origin, I think you could spare a little interest for the origin of my species."

I shrugged. "I'm a little busy right now," I said. "Doing this whole Champion thing. I had thought that you were going to be giving me instructions on what to do when we got to the bottom."

"Oh, no. No, no," Fyskel said. "For one, if I gave you instructions, you'd do your best to ignore them or do the opposite."

I didn't bother confirming.

"For another," Fyskel said, not pausing for me to respond, "The truce still holds. The gods *cannot* interfere any more than they already have."

He winked at me.

"At least, not any actions beyond the extremely limited set of options laid out in Section 35~AF$4."

"I'm crying for you," I said blandly. "That doesn't include Ashmor, though."

"Well, no, but my colleagues and I are paying very close attention to this event, and Ashmor in particular," Fyskel said. "He'll find it very hard to do anything."

"But not impossible," I said. The difference between *hard* and *impossible* became a lot more important when you were talking about the difficulty of immolating us all instantly in a fireball.

"That is almost certainly off the table," Fyskel said, no doubt just to prove he was reading my mind. "Simple actions like that are easy to stop. The problem with preventing him from doing *anything* is that there are so many possible things for him to do."

"Well that's a great comfort," I told him. "Seriously, though, why am I here?"

Fyskel looked at me closely. "I can't tell you what to do," he said. "But I can nudge the odds of what you *will* do a bit."

"Are the other gods going to stand for that?" I asked. "Am I going to get a parade of gods after you, lobbying for me to do something or other?"

Fyskel laughed. "No, the rules are pretty clear there," he said. "The gods without a Champion here are kicking themselves right now. No one thought that Axel had slipped right out from under our nose."

"Wait, if that's not what you sent us here for, then what was the reason?"

"Who knows?" Fyskel shrugged. "You'd have to ask Toriao. Perhaps she *did* know and was keeping it a secret. As much as she hates to, she can keep her mouth shut when she needs to."

"What about the God of Storms?" I asked. "Is he keeping his mouth shut?"

"Rakaro's not much of a talker," Fyskel informed me. "And escaping demons is a perfectly good reason to send a Champion here."

"You—most of you gods, anyway—want the portal shut."

"That would be nice, but it's not possible," Fyskel said. "And before you ask, *destroying* the portal, the first preference for mortals of all stripes, isn't workable either. The portal *controls* the breach; destroying it would jam it open, leading to who knows where."

"That's not what Axel said would happen," I countered.

"Axel's answer was based on you destroying his *core*," Fyskel said. "That wouldn't destroy the portal, although his scenario of opening it up to the heart of a star *would* do that. Easily."

"He's sitting on a lot of potential destruction, isn't he?" I asked. "I suppose we will be, too, if we do get down there and take control."

"Do try and wield it responsibly," Fyskel said dryly. "I won't hear the end of it if you destroy even a single percentage point of Ryvue's surface."

"But no instructions," I said.

"To be honest, I don't think that Axel is done surprising us yet," Fyskel said. "Now that I know his thoughts are out of my reach . . . it's concerning."

"You think he's just going to bring out some overpowered demon to kill us?"

"If he wanted to kill you, he'd have made the challenges harder," Fyskel said. "No, something is going to come out of the portal, and by definition that makes it a demon. But I doubt very much that it will try to kill you."

He gave me a long look, which had to be performative because he was reading my mind. He smirked when I thought that and waved his hand dismissively.

"I think that's enough preparation," he said. "Have fun on your final level."

Without any further ceremony, the void dismissed itself, and I found myself standing next to my companions. The transition was a little nicer this time, and I managed to not stumble or otherwise embarrass myself.

"Are you with us, Kandis?" Felicia asked tensely.

"Yeah," I said softly, looking around. We were in a built-up urban area, standing on a four-lane main street. It all looked abandoned, though. There were cars parked, but I could see that the windows had been smashed in. There was a little too much grass growing out from under the sidewalks.

And there weren't any people that we could see.

"It looks different from the Germany place," Felicia said.

"Yeah," I said, still keeping my voice down. I felt exposed. People could be watching us from the roofs or windows of any of a dozen buildings.

"This looks more modern," Borys said, and looking at the abandoned vehicles and the light poles, I had to agree.

"Modern-day America, looks like," I said. "Abandoned, though, so . . ."

"Post-apocalyptic setting?" Borys mused. "It could be pretty bad if there's fallout."

I stared at him. "We're just dead if that's the case," I said. "But, uh, maybe we should mask up, just in case."

We managed to find enough spare clothing to tie around our faces before we started moving. We didn't like to delay, but we couldn't take the chance.

"I could cure it, whatever it is?" Felicia said.

"Maybe, but let's try to avoid it so you don't have to," I said. "It's . . . some of the dust is poisonous, but all of it will burn you from the inside."

"That sounds pretty horrible," Cloridan said. "It's a deliberate effect of a weapon?"

"More of a side effect, occasionally seen as a benefit," Borys clarified. "Ah. Looks like it's something else, though."

He pointed. Coming around the corner was the shambling figure of a man. His face had been cut open, and one of his arms was hanging limply. He shuffled around the corner, and his red eyes locked on us.

> **[Identification]: Zombie – Threat: 30 – Properties: Diseased Bite, Diseased Blood**

"Shit," I said. "Don't shoot it—don't make any noise if you can help it."

"Not a problem," Cloridan said confidently, stepping forward and drawing his knives. "A little help?"

"Sure," I said, casting my spell, "But don't go scouting yet. I think we should stay together for now."

He nodded as Greater Invisibility took hold and rushed forward soundlessly. The zombie didn't know what hit it, but sadly, it didn't go down in one hit. It managed to let out a gurgling roar before Cloridan finally hacked it down.

"That'll bring more," Borys said grimly. "Let's move, find a place to fortify."

I nodded and gestured for Cloridan to hurry back. We could hear more howls start up from all around. Not close, but not too far either.

Hurrying in the direction that seemed quietest, we looked for shelter. Most of the buildings here were shop fronts, though. There were a few that still held their glass windows, but we all felt that they would be too easy for the zombies to push through.

"Over here!"

We all stopped as we heard the call. Looking around, I saw someone waving from a second-story window.

A person, here? I thought, but we didn't have time to question it. The building they were in looked strong. Coming closer, we saw it was a fire station.

I also saw that the zombies were now coming into sight.

"Come on!" the person yelled and dropped a rope ladder out the window. That was a pain, but maybe smart. If they'd boarded up all the lower floor entrances, this might be the only way in or out of the building.

We prioritized. Felicia went up first, then me, while the fighters secured our climb. The person up top seemed surprised when Felicia jumped up ten feet and started swarming up the ladder, but we didn't have time to waste. As soon as Felicia had grabbed the windowsill, I made my own jump and cancelled Cloridan's spell so he could fight with the others.

"Wow, you folks sure can climb," the woman who had dropped the ladder said.

Surprised, confused, and more than a little suspicious, I tried something that shouldn't have worked. I was even more confused when it did.

[Identification]: Rachel Collins – Threat: 10 – Properties: None

ZOMBIE FLICK

I stared at the notification for far too long. We still had people on the street. A quick discussion selected Kyle to be next to climb up. Much like Felicia, he jumped halfway there before scrambling up the ladder.

By then, the zombies were on the guys downstairs. I tried to give them what support I could, but Improved Blind seemed ineffective. It masked their heads in darkness just fine, but it didn't seem to impede the zombies in combat at all.

"Zombies use other senses, you know that," Kyle said, looking down from the window with me. "Next!" he called down.

"It was worth a try," I said defensively. "These are different from your regular undead."

"Get back from the window and pull the ladder up!" Cloridan called down from below.

"Hey! You're not going to leave them down there are you?" Rachel shouted as we complied.

"It's fine, ma'am, they're just going to show off a little," Kyle said.

I blinked in surprise. *Kyle could understand her?*

Cloridan jumped up to the windowsill from a standing start, startling the hell out of Rachel, but I was still processing the language thing. Rachel looked like an American, but she wasn't speaking English. The Kobolds and goblins from the previous floor hadn't spoken English or German, but some other language that the others weren't familiar with.

But Rachel was speaking Latorran. Not the local language of this region, but the language that every member of this party spoke. That couldn't be a coincidence, surely?

Borys was the next to jump up to the window, leaving a pile of cut-up zombies below. To my disgust, the remaining ones began to eat their fallen brethren.

"You guys sure are kitted out, aren't you?" Rachel said, causing everyone to look at her with varying degrees of confusion.

"Thanks for the assist, uh, ma'am," Borys said. "How long have you been down here for?"

"Down? I've been living in Lorraine my entire life," Rachel replied.

"Use Identify on her," I said. From the blinks and startled looks, we were at least on the same page now.

"How?" Felicia asked. "Why does that—are you a monster, Rachel?"

Rachel laughed, and Felicia looked mortified. "After five years living like this, I sure do feel like one sometimes. Come on, I'll take you to meet the others."

She led us out of the room, which I now noted was a dormitory-style bedroom with two beds. Past the doorway was a large living room with multiple couches and numerous other doors leading off. Through a large doorway, I could see a landing and some stairs heading down. There was also a pole.

"You can take the stairs if you want, but I'd advise finding your fun where you can," Rachel said. She grabbed a hold of the pole and slid down to the level below.

"Oh, it's a firehouse," Borys said, about half a second before me. He followed Rachel down the pole. Everyone else looked at me for an explanation.

"In my world, it's pretty common to fund groups to specialize in taking care of fires that break out," I explained. "They live in the firehouse and rush out whenever a fire is reported. Since speed is of the essence, they make a big deal of getting ready and out the door fast."

I gestured at the pole. "Poles are supposed to be faster than stairs, so most firehouses have something like it."

"I guess that makes sense," Kyle said.

"I'm not sure that it does," Felicia countered. "Couldn't they just jump down? It's only one floor."

"No enhanced abilities," I said, moving over to the hole in the floor. I had been a bit nervous about using a fire pole, but Felicia's comment reminded me that I *could* just jump down without injury. The floor was even padded.

Shrugging, I slid down the pole, not even using my hands to slow me down. I just let Jump absorb the impact. Easy. I quickly stepped away so that the others could follow me.

"Fun, right?" Rachel said. I shrugged. Once the others were down, she led us all into what must have been the main dispatch area.

"Hey guys!" she called out. "New arrivals!"

The first of the ragtag group of survivors to come over was a nervous-looking college-age girl with red hair tied back in a ponytail. Rachel introduced her as Jenna Carpenter. She seemed to latch on to Felicia right away, possibly because of her age.

"You guys are really decked out," she said admiringly. "Were you at a Ren Faire when it started or something?"

"Something like that," I said cautiously. "We travelled a long way to get here, and you won't get far without the right equipment."

She nodded in response and we turned to the next to arrive. I decided not to wait for Rachel.

[Identification]: Evan Blake – Threat: 10 – Properties: None

"You've got a pretty nice setup here," Borys told the young man. He was in his late twenties, slightly built, and had messy blond hair. He was dressed in jeans and a T-shirt.

"Uh, I wouldn't know anything about that, I didn't pick it," Evan said. "All of the bad picks, though, they didn't last long."

"Strong walls, no ground-floor windows," said another man as he approached.

[Identification]: Travis Masters – Threat: 12 – Properties: None

---

"Kitchen, living quarters, and storage tanks for water," he continued. "Yeah, it's pretty good."

He looked us over. "Name's Trigg," he said. "You know how to use all that gear?"

"Better than anyone," Borys assured him.

Travis had dark hair, tattoos on his arms, and squinty eyes. "Reckon you must," he agreed sourly.

The last person to show up was an older woman, past fifty, but not yet entirely grey-haired.

"This here is Marta," Rachel said, and the System agreed.

[Identification]: Marta Hernandez – Threat: 10 – Properties: None

"It's nice to see fresh faces," she said. "I thought I heard a scuffle outside . . . but I didn't hear any guns?"

"We didn't want to attract more of them," Borys said, and she nodded in agreement.

"Lotta folks here relied on them," she said. "But it just brought more, and they ran out of bullets before the zombies ran out of bodies."

"That's everyone!" Rachel said brightly. "'Cept for me, and you know who I am . . . wait."

She pointed at Felicia. "You used my name, but I never got around to telling it to you. Where'd you know me from?"

"I used Identify," Felicia said. "It's not supposed to work on people, but it worked on you. I don't know why."

Everyone—well, all the locals—stared at Felicia.

"What do you mean, Identify?" Rachel asked. "What's that when it's at home?"

"It's a . . . skill?" Felicia said hesitantly. "A pretty common one?"

"They don't have skills, Felicia," I said. The words weighed heavily on me, but I had to say them. "Monsters with skills have an entry for it in their Identify windows. These don't."

"But they're—" Felicia started, but she was interrupted by Travis.

"Watch what you say, stranger," he said. "We may be all together against the zombies, but that doesn't mean you can mouth off on us as you like."

"Sorry," I said. "I mean it more as a technical term than anything else. . . . You see, there's a reason we're dressed like this. What do you know about magic?"

"Rabbits out of hats, sawing a woman in half, that sort of thing?" he asked. "Haven't seen a show in eight years, but I remember it well enough."

"Sawing a woman in *half*?" Felicia exclaimed, but I waved her to silence.

"That's what I thought," I said, and I cast Water Ball.

Everyone stared at the floating sphere of water. It was a pretty useless spell—unless you happened to want to move a small amount of water somewhere, in which case it was pretty useful—but it was a spell I could cast without giving away my combat abilities. I nudged it a little closer to the group of survivors, so they could look, and even touch it.

"What the hell is that?" Travis asked bluntly.

"Magic," I said. "Well, really, it's just water. It's being held in place by magic."

Evan was the first to touch it. Well, try and touch it. His fingers went right through the magic holding it in place and got wet as they entered the ball. Then he jerked them back and they were dry again.

"That's crazy," he breathed, looking at his fingers.

One by one, all the others tried touching it, until it came to Travis's turn. He tried to destroy it, swiping through it with his battered combat knife. It didn't work. It took a bit of concentration to keep it all together, but I managed. It looked pretty cool, too. All the water splashed out from his cut, but quickly reversed course and congealed back into a ball again.

"It's just a party trick," I said, not mentioning the time I'd killed a monster with it. "I take it you haven't seen anything like it?"

"'Course we haven't," Travis snapped. "So how'd you do it?"

"We come from a magic land," I said. "So we can do magic."

"Oh!" Evan said. "Like a portal from another world?"

"One was involved," I said wryly. "But not exactly. This is our world."

"Hell it is," Travis said. "We don't got no magic."

I pointed at the ball and he scowled.

"You brought that with you," he said sourly.

"Anyway," I continued. "In this, our world, there are things called dungeons, and they—"

"Kandis!" Felicia interrupted. "Don't say it—it would just be cruel."

"They need to know where they stand," I said. "Where we stand."

"But they're people!" she protested.

"Are they?" I asked. "Because if that's true, then *Axel can make people.*"

Felicia didn't have an immediate answer to that, which allowed Travis to get a word in.

"What the hell you talking about?" he asked irritably. "Who the hell is Axel, and where the hell do you think we stand if it ain't right here?"

I looked at him, but I didn't answer his question. Instead, I turned back to Felicia.

"It was the same with the goblins on the last floor," I said. "Some of them, some of the time, it seemed like they broke from the script. Or the script didn't control them all the time. Like they were real. I made deals with them as if they were real people."

"Monsters aren't people," Felicia said earnestly. "They just . . . kill. That's all they do."

"I know," I said. "So are these guys monsters . . . or people?"

Felicia looked at the group. I could tell that she was using Identify on them.

Just to make sure, I used Identify on her. Maybe it was just that the rules were different here.

They weren't.

The rest of my party looked troubled, but none of them spoke up. Like me, they were waiting for Felicia to come to a decision.

"I . . . don't know," she admitted. "But even so, why do you want to tell them?"

I sighed. "Basic honesty?" I tried. "I don't think I want to pretend they're people if I think they're monsters. And . . . there's also a chance that the knowledge gets erased after I tell them, which will make it a lot easier to pick what they are."

"That and the fact that I will just damn kill you if you don't make with the explanations," Travis said grimly.

I giggled. I couldn't help it. I'd never felt less threatened.

"Fine," I said, suppressing a smile. "As I was saying, in our world, there are dungeons. And dungeons make monsters. Beasts that just *kill*, without fear, thought, or morality."

"Sounds rough," Travis said.

"We have a skill, a kind of magic, that helps us figure out what kind of monster we're facing," I said. "It doesn't work on humans. It works on you."

"So what does that mean?" Travis asked, but his face said he'd figured it out.

"It means that we're in a dungeon. It made you."

REALITY CHALLENGED

We're not real?" Evan asked skeptically.

"Welcome to the club," I said morosely.

"You mean, you're not real, either?" Rachel asked. "Gotta say, that's a lot easier to believe, what with the magic and all."

"This is about the vision, isn't it?" Borys said. "The investor meeting."

"Yes, it's about the meeting!" I declared loudly. "I remember my world shredding itself into pieces like a corrupted video file, and it's been bothering me! I don't know how the rest of you are dealing with it, but I'm not handling it well!"

The locals looked at one another and looked as if they were going to come forward, but Borys held up a hand to signal them to stay back. He was keeping a wary eye on them, which was ridiculous. They were only threat ten, which must have been Axel or the System's best approximation of a normal human. Even I could slice one apart like an Idnul lizard, swiftly, easily, without thinking because . . .

Dammit, I'm a video game character.

"I don't really get it, to be honest," Kyle said. "I mean, yeah, your world died. That's . . ." He paused looking for words. "That's not something you *get over*. But there's something more, something that you think applies to *us*, and that I don't get."

"I wouldn't expect you to," I said. "These guys are better placed than most of you to understand that we're all part of a computer simulation."

"What, like in *Tron*?" Evan asked.

"Can't be," Rachel stated with certainty. "Ain't none of us glowing, and we all got hair, so it ain't that."

I snorted. "There you go. *Better* placed, not all the way suited. What about you, Borys?"

"Me?" Borys asked. He looked at his hand, flexing it into a fist and opening it again. "I *feel* real. The pain those bastards put me through felt real as well. Assuming that what you remember is real, and not something that Fyskel cooked up for you . . . I think the best thing is to not worry about it."

I frowned. I didn't really have an answer to "it was all faked by a god," but . . .

"It could have all been faked," I admitted. "But they all seemed . . . shocked. Fyskel, especially, seemed shaken. I think he dragged me into the void space just to have someone to talk to about it. How do you just ignore that?"

"You don't," Borys said. "But it's not really relevant right now. Right now we have a zombie level to beat."

"You might have magic and muscles," Rachel said. "But there's no beating the zombies. They just keep coming. The only thing you can do is hide til they go away."

"There must be some way," Felicia said. "Why don't you tell us about the zombie games you played in the past? How do they end?"

"This isn't a game, girl," Travis growled. "The zombies will eat you up if you treat it like one."

"Some of them don't end," Borys said thoughtfully, ignoring Travis's comment. "They're endurance games, see who can last the longest. The zombies keep coming until you're dead."

"That's not likely here," I said. "Dungeon or not, Axel still has limits."

"Then . . ." Borys mused. "It's likely that we have to reach some destination. A place of safety or an abandoned lab that has the cure."

"You're chasing that old rumor?" Rachel asked scornfully. "There ain't no cure, and it wouldn't help none if there were."

"Why not?" I asked, looking intently at her. "Why wouldn't it help?"

"'Cause just about everyone's already *dead*, fool," Rachel replied. "It'd be nice if we didn't turn as soon as one zombie got a bite on us, but zombies don't stop at one."

"Sometimes it works that way," Borys said. "Other times the cure is a countervirus that wipes out all the existing zombies. Or it . . . turns them back to normal."

"I don't think that's in the cards," Cloridan said grimly. "I saw some of them up close, and there's a lot of wounds and missing pieces that would be fatal pretty quick on a live human."

"They're not dead, though," I mused. "Not like undead zombies back in Anchorbury. I wonder . . . Felicia, do you think you can heal them?"

Felicia started in surprise.

"I've never tried to heal a monster before," she said. "I can cure diseases, so . . . maybe?"

She blushed and looked at the survivors. "It might . . . be a good idea to test it on a monster first."

Travis frowned. "Watch who you're calling a monster, Missy, or I'll show you one."

I cast my own gaze over the ragtag group of survivors.

"Isn't there always one of the group who's hiding the fact that they have the virus?" I asked. "And they don't find out until it's too late and doom at least one other victim?"

"Just about every time," Borys agreed.

"Hey, don't you go accusing us of stuff!" Travis blustered. I ignored him and kept scrutinizing the others. The older lady, Marta, had started looking nervous.

"Felicia," I said slowly, keeping my eye on the woman. "You can *detect* disease as well, can't you?"

"Oh, sure," Felicia said. "Oh! You want me to do it now?"

Not waiting for a response, she held her hands out and swept them over everyone in the room. After a single pass, she looked at Marta.

"She's got . . . something," Felicia said. "I'm not familiar with *what,* but it's serious."

Marta staggered back. "Ain't nothing wrong with me," she stammered. "I just get hot flushes now."

"Don't worry," I said. "Felicia can take care of that . . . probably."

"Don't let her at me!" Marta shouted, moving away.

"You think you can lay your hands on one of us?" Travis snarled. He stepped forward, knife in hand.

"Stand down, boys!" I said firmly, slipping forward. It wasn't that I didn't trust their judgment. Okay, I was a little worried that Kyle's restraint would slip when Felicia was in danger. But the main reason I told them to stop was that I wasn't sure if they'd grasped just how restrained they needed to be.

Plus, this would have more effect coming from a woman.

I didn't move particularly quickly, by the standards I was used to. Level six gave me some advantages, but Cloridan and Borys were far faster. But it was still much faster than Travis was used to. He blinked at my sudden closeness, then struggled and fell off balance as he tried to adjust.

It was a little difficult for him as I was holding the blade of his knife.

Both my regular instincts and the new and improved ones that came with Dodge and Weapon Mastery: Dagger were screaming at me that I was doing the wrong thing. I should be dodging, or blocking him with my own dagger, not catching the blade.

Efficiently avoiding damage wasn't my goal here. Felicia could have easily dodged the knife on her own if it were.

"Go and heal her, Felicia," I said, while my eyes stayed locked with Travis's. He was struggling to get the knife away from me, but I was a lot stronger than I looked. Not that my strength was particularly impressive, I think I was only a little stronger than Travis, but the fact that the knife hadn't managed to cut my gloves made me confident that there was nothing he could do to hurt me.

"We're magic, Travis," I said. "And you're just ordinary. We've got a mission to complete, and you have the option of helping us or getting out of our way. You don't get to try and stop us."

"It's done," Felicia said in a subdued voice. I let go of the blade and took a step back.

"Did it work?" I asked.

"Yeah . . ." Felicia said. "It worked, just like on people."

"Did she really do anything?" Evan asked. He glanced nervously at Travis. "I mean, she just laid her hand on Marta. Nothing happened."

"There was . . ." Marta reluctantly admitted. "I was feeling a bit of a fever. Just hot flushes, like I said. It's gone now."

"Marta . . ." Jenna, the young woman with red hair, put her arms around the older woman's shoulders. "You're supposed to speak up if you're feeling sick so we can all look out for each other."

"It wasn't anything serious," Marta denied. "Just a light fever. I was fine."

"Well, now I want to see what you can do to a fully turned one," I said.

"Oh, no!" You ain't bringing one of them in here!" Travis shouted. I frowned at him, annoyed that he had recovered his bluster so quickly.

He took a quick step back.

Okay, so he hasn't totally recovered his bluster . . .

"Travis is right," Rachel said. "This is our home. If you bring those monsters in . . ."

"That's fine," I said. "We can do the experiment outside. Cloridan, Kyle, Felicia, you up for a quick expedition?"

"Sure," Felicia said. The others nodded.

"I think you know what to do," I said. "Don't stray too far. There should still be some nearby. Borys and I will stay to make sure the way back in stays open."

I glanced at the survivors, who stared back resentfully. They couldn't stop us from getting back in, of course, but forcibly occupying the place against their wishes didn't seem like a great idea.

While we were waiting in the upstairs bedroom, Borys started up a conversation. The survivors had left us alone, no doubt to plot some kind of resistance.

"You're being a little hard on the survivors," he said.

"I know," I admitted. "But . . . they are monsters."

"Monsters that happen to be human," he said. "I think it's throwing the others for a loop as well."

"It used to be that I was the only one who understood when monsters spoke a language," I said. "Now—"

I was interrupted by a terrible eldritch scream from outside.

"What was that?" I exclaimed. "A zombie?"

Borys pointed out the window. Our friends were returning, carrying a fourth person. Borys quickly threw out the ladder, then started hauling it in as Kyle grabbed on.

Kyle held the rope ladder in one hand, while the other held a limp body. He let Borys pull him up, walking up the side of the building. When he reached our level, he started shoving the body in.

"We said we wouldn't—" I started.

"It worked," he said shortly.

I took a look at the body.

[Identification]: Marcus Thompson – Threat: 10 – Properties: None

"What was that scream?" I asked.

"Him," Kyle said, nodding at the body.

Everybody started piling into the room at once. My friends were coming in the window while the survivors were coming from the inside, looking to see what the commotion was. They noticed Marcus pretty quickly.

"What have you done?" Rachel asked. "You found a survivor?"

She raced forward and started checking the man's pulse. "He's alive!" she said incredulously. "Everybody out, give me some room!"

"Let's move this all downstairs instead," I said. "It's way too crowded in here."

There was general agreement, and it wasn't long before we were back in the main section. Marcus was laid out on a portable cot, while Rachel examined him.

"He seems fine," she said, "Just unconscious."

"Rachel," Evan said grimly. "Look at his clothes."

We had all already noticed. Marcus's clothes were barely worthy of the name. They were ripped and ragged, hanging on by a few threads. They didn't serve any purpose, and anyone alive wouldn't have bothered keeping them on. Only a zombie that didn't care would wear clothes like that.

"He was a zombie," I confirmed. "Felicia turned him back."

Whatever response the survivors had was cut short by another scream.

"What *is* that?" I asked, irritated.

Evan swallowed. "It's a call," he said. "They've started to gather."

"So soon?" Jenna asked. "I thought we'd have more time."

"I guess we're just unlucky," Evan said. To us, he replied, "When a zombie starts to call like that, they gather more of them."

Another call sounded. Evan shuddered.

"They'll gather in a big swarm, and go looking for fresh meat," he said. "They remember places they couldn't get into before, and they come looking in force. Sometime around midnight, this place is going to be crawling with zombies."

ZOMBIE SWARM

To start with," I asked, "have any of you ever killed a zombie before?"

The survivors looked at each other. "'Course we have," Travis said sullenly.

"How?" I asked. "I don't think I could hit one, and I'm much better at fighting than you."

Travis looked away. "Guns," he muttered.

Rachel took over. "Sure, we can't get into hand-to-hand with 'em," she said. "One bite, and that's the end. But guns work."

She shrugged.

"Of course, that just brings more of them, so really, guns *don't* work," she said. "Best thing to do is hide."

"Guns might do enough damage," I admitted, "but you've still got to *hit* with them. Don't they dodge?"

"Only in hand-to-hand," Evan said. "If you shoot them, or drop something heavy on them, they won't see it coming."

"That's what we do with a swarm," Jenna put in. "We keep a lot of junk on the roof, so we can drop it on them."

"That's smart," I said. I wondered if they had enough junk. None of my Earth Magic spells *created* stone, just shaped what was already there, but I could use existing stone to create weights and have them carried up. "What do you do when you're outside of your base?"

"Run," Evan said shortly. "They don't run fast, but they track you. If you get behind something they can't get past, they'll sniff and howl for a bit before giving up."

He frowned. "Of course, then they'll be back next swarm."

I looked back at my friends. "So those are probably fabricated memories, but they sound realistic. What do you think?"

"Our memories aren't fake," Travis snarled. He backed down when I looked at him, though.

"No offense," I said, "but you've only existed for . . . well, I don't know exactly. But it's months, not years. There has to be a point where the real memories give over to fake ones, and it could be as recently as this morning."

"It seems workable," Cloridan said hastily. "I like the idea of dropping things, sounds very safe."

"Borys, what about your storm? Can you make it so it just affects outside?"

"I can," he said slowly. "It might not be the best idea, though. Zombies don't die from the cold like humans do. You have to freeze them solid before they stop moving."

"These zombies aren't dead, though," I pointed out.

"That's . . . true?" Borys said. "It might work then. One thing to be wary of is that the ice starts to build up. Eventually, you get a ramp leading to the top of the wall."

"That happens normally, with bodies," Evan put in. "They've never gotten to the *top*, but the closer they get, the less effective it is to drop things on them. And the upper-floor windows are less secure."

"That's your job," Borys told me. "Using Stone Shape to fix weak walls and cover up windows."

"Right," I said. "We should—"

"He's awake," Marta called out from across the room. She'd been watching over Marcus. We all trooped over to look at him.

He was drinking some water, looking at us nervously. Aside from that, he looked perfectly normal.

[Identification]: Marcus Thompson – Threat: 10 – Properties: None

---

Not *exactly* normal, but normal for here.

"Thanks for rescuing me?" he said, looking around the group. "I'm not sure how I got here, but I guess you guys are the ones I should thank."

"What do you remember?" I asked.

"I . . . got sick?" he said. "I remember getting hot, and having to lie down, but . . . do you guys know Dulcie?"

There were a lot of shaken heads. Marcus's face fell.

"She was looking after me? She would have been nearby."

"Dude, you were a *zombie*," Evan said.

"Maybe he still is," Travis growled. "We should get rid of him now, before the magic runs out."

"Magic doesn't work that way," I said. "Well, some of it does, but not this kind. He's an ordinary human monster now, just like the rest of you."

"Human . . . monster?" Marcus asked.

"Don't worry too much about it," Rachel said. "Her and her lot have got some funny ideas . . . but they've got magic as well. They cured you."

"Well, she did," I said, nodding at Felicia.

"Can you really do that?" Evan asked incredulously. "Just . . . *cure* all the zombies?"

"Not all of them," Felicia answered. "Not even a decent portion of them. It wiped me out doing Marcus. I won't be able to try again until I've had a night's sleep."

"Where did the mana go?" I asked.

"On healing, mostly," Felicia said. "I cured the disease—he started that screaming as soon as I started. Once that was done, he fell unconscious. It was weird—he was in negative hit points, but he was still alive, at least for a few seconds. My healing worked, so we brought him back here."

Travis snorted. "So you curing one is going to be the reason we get buried under zombies tonight. Doing *great*, kid."

Felicia flinched a little.

"Don't be such a baby about it," I told Travis. "Chances are, there would be a swarm whatever we did. At least this way you have us to handle it."

"Oh, I'm real lucky," Travis growled. "I get to hide behind some woman's skirts."

I blinked. "I'm wearing trousers," I pointed out. "And if my pants aren't masculine enough for you, there are three guys in my party."

He looked away, muttering something so faint I couldn't hear it—even with enhanced hearing.

"That's what I thought," I said. "Let's get to work."

We got to it. Kyle had a Masonry skill, so he was able to advise me on what parts of the building needed shoring up. Most of it was sound, but there were some parts that were cracked. They were holding steady for now but might well fail if put to the test against repeated zombie blows.

Almost as if they were deliberately constructed that way.

The others were mainly occupied with hauling junk to the roof. It turned out that the reason there were no fire engines in the fire station was that they had been dismantled and brought up to the roof to be thrown down. There was half a fire truck up there, according to Borys.

We didn't feel that was enough, and we had rope strong enough to do it, so we—and by we, I mean the boys—tied a rope to a nearby burned-out car and dragged it up.

"I wonder if, instead of breaking it up into pieces and throwing them, we should just rig this thing up as some kind of killer pendulum," Borys mused.

I looked at him doubtfully. "You'd need some way to keep it off the wall," I said.

Visions of the massive weight plowing through ranks of zombies ran through my head. They were good visions, but . . .

"With that kind of momentum, if it glanced off the walls, it would do real damage," I said reluctantly. "It's nice to kill zombies, but it's the walls that are keeping us safe."

"I suppose you have a point," he said sadly. "If we had more time, we might be able to rig something."

"We don't," I said, pointing. It wasn't sunset yet, and the zombies were already gathering.

"We'd better get into position, then," he said, sighing.

"Wait," I said. "What am I forgetting?"

"I . . . don't know?"

"There have to be more ways for the zombies to get in," I explained. "You've watched more zombie movies than I have. What are we missing?"

"In movies, the weak point is normally one of the other survivors," he replied.

I cast Privacy around us.

"I'm assuming that one of the conditions of the floor is that we keep at least some of the survivors alive," I said. "We can keep them out of the fighting if we put them on the roof. We've eliminated the secretly infected plotline."

"Are you worried about one of them turning on us? If, say, Travis—"

"To pick one at random," I said wryly. Borys gave a slight grin.

"As a random example," he agreed. "He can't do much to us, but he could go after the other survivors."

"Murdering his teammates seems a little out of character, even for him," I said doubtfully. "I'll get Felicia to keep an eye on him, but I think he's going to have his chance to betray us later, when there's someone to betray us *to*."

"That makes sense. . . . So you've shored up the weak points in the walls, blocked off the doors and windows—"

"Except for the ones we need and are guarding," I said. He nodded.

"Zombies can't fly . . ."

"Keep an eye out, though. We know that the sky isn't real. Axel could have a zombie crawl out over us and drop down."

Borys glanced up out of reflex. "They'd die, though."

"Wouldn't matter if they managed to land on someone."

He winced. "Point. Aside from that, we don't need to worry about above. So what about below?"

We looked at each other, the same idea forming at the same time in each of our minds.

"The sewers," we said as one.

The workshop level of the firehouse had good drainage. It had to, since they washed off trucks and played with hoses in here. It didn't take us long to find out where the water went.

"It's not such a big hole," Borys said, staring down.

"Big enough for a zombie to climb through," I retorted. "And that grating looks loose."

I tugged at it. I couldn't pull it out, but it wobbled.

"I can probably get it," Borys said, bending down. "Wait, should I? It's probably easier to reinforce if the grate is still there."

"You're not wrong," I said. "Let's just see what we're working with."

I cast a Light and sent it down the hole. Dead eyes stared up at me.

"Jesus!" I shouted, starting back. Borys was made of sterner stuff.

"Are they even alive?" he asked, staring down. "They seem jammed in there, and I can't see any of them moving."

I joined him staring down the hole. There was an easy way to check.

[Identification]: Zombie – Threat: 30 – Properties: Diseased Bite, Diseased Blood

---

"That's a zombie," I said. "Three of them."

"They must be waiting for the right time?" Borys suggested.

"Maybe," I agreed. "I guess they'll start moving if we open the grate, though."

"And they're too far down for a sword to reach," Borys mused. "Ice Magic?"

"Let me try this," I said. "I hardly ever get a chance to cast it."

I knelt down and pushed one finger through the hole in the grate. With an unobstructed line to my target, I cast Iron Dart.

You have inflicted 173 damage!

The zombie moved, at least. The dart sunk into its skin and then dissipated. The zombie snarled silently in response but didn't otherwise react.

"Well," I said, "I could cast that about thirty more times to get rid of them. I could use the practice."

"I could use ice," Borys said. "But if there's more behind them, they could chip through it, given time."

"Fire it is," I said. "It's a bit ironic, trying to find gasoline in a fire station, but I bet they have some."

They *did* have some. Travis was against letting us have it, until we said why we needed it. It wasn't until we gathered back around the drain that I started having second thoughts.

"Wait," I said. "Wouldn't we be better off just shooting it?"

"No way," Travis said. "Those fuckers gotta *burn*."

"What about the ventilation?" I asked. "We don't have a chimney in here."

Travis ignored me and poured the tin of gasoline down the grate, followed by an emergency flare.

"Ain't easy to light up gas," he muttered.

Not easy, perhaps, but not beyond his ability. Flames quickly flared up down below.

That got more of a response. As thick black smoke poured out of the grate, the zombies let out another one of those horrible screams.

Borys swore, and let an icy blast roar down into the sewer. In seconds, the smoke was choked off, and a foot of ice was blocking the hole.

"What's got into ya?" Travis asked with irritation. "Ain't done yet!"

"That," Borys said. With the sounds from below muffled, we could hear more screams from outside. "Looks like the swarm is starting early."

DONKEY KONG DEFENSE

I hefted the car wheel and walked to the edge of the building. Not *easily*, mind you. My strength wasn't superhuman, just top-of-the-line human. Probably. It was difficult to tell. I was strong enough that it looked incongruous for my wimpy body to lift a whole car wheel.

The survivors had been of the opinion that we didn't have time to disassemble an entire car into missile-worthy chunks of junk. They had reckoned without Cloridan and his darksteel daggers. Cloridan had carved up the vehicle in much the same way as Dad used to carve up the Christmas turkey.

I paused to take aim, although it wasn't necessary. Zombies were piled up three ranks deep all around the building. Pushing, shoving, pounding on the walls. I couldn't really miss. The wheel smashed down, crushing one and knocking two more to the ground. They were trampled down by their neighbors, but zombies are tough. They'll get back up again.

> **You have inflicted 2,400 damage!**
> **For killing a Zombie, you have earned 7,500 XP.**

One of them wouldn't.

What struck me as strange was that the System had stopped acknowledging my party. Everything had gone back to individual accomplishments. Was that something that Axel could control? Was it a subtle message that we were all on our own in the zombie apocalypse?

Or was there some other reason? I'd been put in a party with the Kobold soldiers before, so it wasn't that I was fighting on the side of monsters. I racked my brain, but I couldn't think of what the reason could be.

I picked up a jagged, heavy piece of metal and threw it down, taking out another zombie. It would have been too dark to see, but I had lit the exterior with a Light spell on each corner, jacked up to maximum output. They were low enough that a few zombies were trying to eat them, but the spells were immaterial, so I wasn't worried.

What I *was* worried about was that there were still zombies arriving. The survivors were insistent that the zombies wouldn't stop, but Axel had to run out at some point. Right?

I hadn't been serious about zombies dropping down from the ceiling, but once it got dark, I couldn't stop thinking about it. I'd ended up putting some Phantasmal shade pavilions up for us to work under. There wasn't any sun to cool down from, but they'd break the fall of any suicidal zombies.

The rest of the survivors were up here with me, dutifully tossing junk down and taking out zombies. There was plenty of room for it, even with the huge pile of junk. The firemen had apparently used this level for rooftop parties. The furniture and the barbeque equipment had long since been tossed over the edge, but I could imagine hunky firemen relaxing up here.

Felicia was downstairs, resting, maximizing her mana regeneration. Something that we'd been discussing, behind Privacy spells, was having her cure another zombie.

The reason we were keeping it a secret was that the notion was freaking out the other survivors. Even Marcus. The idea that one of the slavering monsters outside could be turned into a normal person with a single spell was disturbing, to say the least.

Travis hadn't yet accepted that we *could*. He was watching over Marcus like a hawk, waiting for the spell, and Marcus, to revert. The others *had* accepted that Marcus was human now. They were slowly coming to the inevitable conclusion that led to. Namely, the monsters outside *shouldn't* be killed. Every one they killed was one they didn't cure.

For us, the math was a little different. We were turning a threat thirty monster into a non-hostile threat ten. Clearly a win, if an incredibly costly one. The reason we were considering it was that we were fairly certain we were going to *need* the survivors for something, at some point. We could probably afford to lose some if Axel was playing fair, but making new ones would give us an extra buffer of lives.

That reasoning was breathtakingly sociopathic if you happened to think that the survivors were people. Since the survivors certainly *did*, we kept that reasoning from them. The rest of us got to struggle with the notion. Fortunately, our goals were the same in both cases. Regardless of whether the survivors were real people or story tokens, we needed to keep them alive.

Cloridan was patrolling the building, keeping us linked with Kyle. We did have the phones—and weren't the locals surprised at phones that worked, somehow, with magic—but Kyle needed both his hands to fight monsters, so he might not be able to call in the event of an emergency.

Borys was up here with me. For now, he was dropping things like the rest of us, saving his mana for phase two.

"They're starting to climb," he reported.

"I noticed," I replied. "Do you want to start now, or wait?"

We'd been warned that once a few ranks of zombies gathered around the building, they would start to climb. It seemed that they only realized they *could* once their path was blocked by enough zombies. Once there were zombies *above* them, they got the idea of taking an alternative path.

They weren't great at climbing. They could cling to any handholds they found, but they had trouble finding new ones. The problem was that a zombie clinging to a wall made for a whole set of easy handholds for other zombies.

"I'll wait for a bit," Borys said. "If they get higher before I knock them off, they might get damaged."

I nodded. We didn't have to wait long. Zombies didn't climb fast, but the distance was deceptive. Ten meters up seemed like an insurmountable distance, but a runner could cover it in two seconds if it was horizontal.

"Stand back!" Borys ordered the others. He was comfortable with his control, but the edge of the roof was going to get quite uncomfortable for a bit.

This time, the storm that formed was more like a hurricane. We were contained within the large eye while the icy winds scoured the building of zombies and replaced them with ice. I would have said that the eye was much larger compared to the wall of wind outside it, but I couldn't honestly say how far the winds extended. Between the sleet, snow, and whirling ice, I couldn't see five feet into the darkness.

Which meant that I couldn't see if it was working. Borys, too, was looking at the darkness with a frown on his face.

"I'll give it another five minutes!" he yelled over the howling wind. "Don't want too much ice to build up!"

I nodded again. A little bit of ice would make the walls more slippery, but if the ice was thick enough for the zombies to drive their fingers into it, it would make it *easier* to climb.

I felt a tap on my shoulder. It was Cloridan, who'd come up from below. He gestured at the stairs.

I looked around to make sure everything was in hand before I went down. The survivors were huddling under one of the pavilions, staring at the howling gale. We'd shown them magic, but this was something else.

I gave them a thumbs-up and headed down. The noise dropped and the temperature climbed as soon as the stair door closed behind us.

"Kyle says that there's something going on with the sewers," Cloridan said.

"The ice hasn't melted yet, has it?" I asked.

"I don't think so, but there are noises."

When I got down there, I got to see—or rather, hear— what he meant. There was a crunching sound coming from the grate. It was muffled, but it was definitely a crunch. It sounded like . . .

"Are they eating the ice?" I asked.

"Maybe?" Kyle said. "They've been pounding on the walls, but everything's stayed secure. This"—he pointed at the grate—"is something different."

"It's too loud, though," I said thoughtfully. "There were three zombies jammed in there before, but they could hardly move, let alone make all this chomping noise."

As I spoke, the ice under the grate started to tremble. We all took a step back, and Kyle drew his sword. A few more chomps and the head of the zombie responsible was visible.

[Identification]: Gnawing Zombie – Threat: 30 – Properties: Gluttonous Bite, Diseased Blood

---

"It's a different type!" I exclaimed. "Kill it!"

Kyle's sword was thin enough to fit through the grate, and the zombie couldn't dodge. A few stabs in the head, and it stopped moving.

"Did you get a notification?" I asked.

"Yeah," he said. "It's dead."

Suddenly, the corpse jerked and withdrew, as if it had been pulled backward. More crunching sounds followed.

"There's more of them," Cloridan said. "Should we get the gas of lyne?"

"We moved it upstairs in case the climbers got out of hand," I said. "Using it outside seems like a better idea than using it in here."

"Then . . .?" Kyle said inquiringly.

"Then, this," I said, kneeling down and casting Stone Shape. The remaining ice in the shaft crumbled as I squeezed it with constricting stone. Then I released my grip and let it tumble down. The crunching stopped, briefly, and then was muffled more effectively as I sealed the shaft entirely. I had to use the concrete of the floor to do it, creating a dip in the smooth floor. I left the iron grate where it was for additional reinforcement.

"There," I said. We stared at the depression for a second.

"Will that be enough?" Cloridan asked.

"I don't know," I said. "The survivors didn't know anything about variant types. I was looking outside before and only saw standard zombies."

Kyle knelt and put his hand on the lowest part of the depression.

"It's vibrating," he reported. "A zombie is gnawing on it."

"How quickly is it getting through?" I wondered.

"Faster than teeth normally would," he said. "But how much faster, I don't know."

"One way to find out," Cloridan said fatalistically. Outside, we heard the storm die down.

"Cloridan, go upstairs and fill Borys in. Kyle, see if you can hear any other gnawers working their way up. If they can gnaw through stone, the walls are in danger."

Both boys nodded, leaving me to watch what had once been a sewer entrance. It seemed like forever before they came back, and it must have been some time, because by the time they did, I could hear the crunching of concrete quite clearly.

"I can hear it," Kyle said. "All over. It's faint, and slower than this is, but I think they're gnawing at the foundations."

"Borys says it was partially successful," Cloridan said. "Most of the zombies were blown off, and a lot were frozen solid, but some of them are stuck to the wall, and the newcomers aren't waiting to stack up before they climb. He'll be putting the storm up again in ten."

Another crunch sounded, louder than before. Looking down, I saw the first small hole in my barrier. Another crunch sounded, and now the head of the gnawer zombie was visible.

"Hold on a second," I said as my companions readied their weapons. "I want to see how it works."

The zombie opened its mouth . . . and kept opening it. Its head split in half, revealing that its entire head contained only a mouth with jagged, inhuman teeth. Then it lunged forward and down, crunching down on the concrete that was restraining it.

"Is that enough?" Kyle asked.

"Yeah," I said, feeling a little sick. He didn't hesitate, slicing the head off. The thing jerked and struggled, and then got dragged back. The next one wouldn't be long.

I glanced at my phone. It had a timer function.

"It took it fifteen minutes to get through a foot of concrete," I said. "How long do you think it will take for the rest of them to undermine the foundations?"

Kyle thought about it. "Not as long as I'd like. Four, maybe six hours?"

"And we can't attack them through the foundations," I said. "That would just be doing their work for them."

I looked at the hole in the floor. Something was already wiggling up into the light.

"We're going to have to take the fight to them," I said. "And hope that all the gnawers after us got here via the same sewer system."

SEWER NASTY

Axel had missed a trick. The sewers were clean. Relatively speaking, that is. They were still coated in blood and gore from the zombies we'd already killed. But they didn't stink of shit, for which I was grateful.

I had time to think about it, wedged in between Cloridan and Kyle as they fought their way down the tunnel. I was mainly there for the light source. We had lightstones, but a floating Light spell was more convenient and flexible in application.

Was it because the sewers weren't supposed to have been in use, with almost all of the inhabitants of the town dead? I didn't think that was it. There was still moisture down here, so there should have been mold and mildew, at least. And the station was still using its toilets—it had a tank on the roof that they had to fill manually.

One possibility was that Axel had gotten his information about zombies from movies that had less-than-realistic sets. But it seemed more likely that it was a side effect of the gnawing zombies. They *could* eat rock, but I doubted they got any sustenance from it. I suspected that when they weren't under orders to destroy a building from beneath, they just quietly roamed the sewers, munching on any organic material they found.

That was what they were doing now. Something prevented them from going after other zombies, but as soon as one was dead, it was fair game. They didn't like the lights I brought, so as soon as Cloridan provided the ones in the back with a meal, they dragged the corpse back into the darkness. Then, we got to move a few steps forward before they charged us again. Where they were putting it, I didn't know, but we'd be tripping over corpses if they weren't so eager to clean up after themselves.

Kyle was guarding our rear. The size of his shield made advancing while fighting difficult, but it made for a good defense. With him blocking the tunnel, there wasn't enough room for a zombie to make it past. The ones that tried were easily stabbed.

We didn't have far to go, but at the same time, we didn't want to get lost. Kyle was holding our exit, and there was a short stretch of zombie-free tunnel between him and Cloridan that we were gradually extending. The plan was to do that until we found a junction—either part of the sewer plan or gnawed out by the zombies.

Before that happened, though, we heard a voice.

"Hello? Is someone there?"

As fights went, this one was pretty quiet. Gnawers tended to only make low-pitched gurgles when they weren't chewing on anything, and we were keeping our voices down. Even the impacts of Cloridan's daggers were muted. There wasn't any armor for him to punch through, only tough, rubbery flesh.

So even though the voice wasn't very loud, we both heard it. Cloridan didn't freeze, since that would have been suicidal. Talking to people was my job, so he left it to me.

"Is someone there?" I called out.

"I can hear you!" It sounded like a girl's or a young boy's voice. "I can see the light! I'm headed towards you!"

"Don't! We're in a fight right now!" I said hastily. "Stay where you are, and we'll come for you!"

"Don't worry, I'll be fine," the voice said.

I pushed one of my Light spells forward, behind the oncoming zombies and towards where the voice had come from. We'd learned not to do it that way, or they wouldn't withdraw to eat the corpses. But this way, I might get a glimpse of who was trying to reach us.

Cloridan had heard the conversation and redoubled his efforts. We could see the junction up ahead. Then a zombie came flying out of the side passage.

It *hissed* as it flew across the narrow tunnel and slammed into the wall. It slumped to the ground, unmoving.

As one, all the zombies that we could see turned and charged at the side tunnel. Cloridan cut one down as it turned, but the rest raced back out of sight. Then the sounds started.

Hisses from the zombies, somehow agitated in a way they hadn't been before. Wet, splattering sounds, much like that flying zombie had made.

And other sounds, softer but no less disturbing. Meat and gristle being torn apart, bones snapping . . .

The sounds stopped, and it was quiet for a moment. Then a small boy came around the corner.

"Hello! I'm so glad I finally found some humans like me!" he said.

"Not like you," I said, looking at my notification.

> **Warning! Demon Detected!**
> **[Identification]: Cherubial – Threat: Unknown – Properties: Unknown**
> **Warning! Demon Detected!**

From the way Cloridan stiffened, I knew that he saw it, too.

The cherubial smiled innocently. "What do you mean? Aren't we both humans?"

I'd been learning to pay attention to the instincts that came with my weapon skills. Gripping my dagger brought the skill to mind, and it was telling me that I couldn't hit this child. Not in a straight fight. Cloridan didn't move, so I guessed that he didn't like his chances either. Not with the way that child had torn those zombies apart.

That left talking. However, as I reached for my social skills, they . . . failed to engage. Whatever was standing before me, I could no more Persuade, Charm, or Intimidate it than I could a rock.

It was possible that was because the cherubial was so alien that such concepts didn't apply, but I doubted it. It was standing there talking to me, after all. More likely, whatever hooks the System inserted into people's brains to let the skills do their magic weren't able to get under the cherubial's skull.

"You're not human," I said, readying Improved Blind in my head, "You're a demon."

The cherubial cocked its head. "That's silly. Of course I'm human. What makes you think I'm not?"

Technically, "you can tear apart zombies like they're tissue paper" wasn't the answer. Humans *could* do that. It would be weird for one of them to be of sufficiently high level, but it *was* possible.

"How long have you been living down here?" I asked instead. "What have you been eating?"

"A long time. I got lost in the dark," the cherubial said. It gestured at the zombie corpses. "I've been eating the crawling creatures. They have more than enough moisture in them, so I don't need to drink."

"Yeah, that's not something a human could do," I said.

It cocked its head again. "Humans can eat flesh."

"Not raw, and not zombie flesh," I said. "It's rotten."

Or diseased, or potentially human, I thought to myself, but didn't feel the need to educate the demon that thoroughly.

"Oh . . . bother . . ." the demon said. "What happens now, then? I don't want to have to hurt you."

"What are you doing here?" I asked.

"I got lost, like I said," the cherubial said. "I came through a Gate and then it got a bit confused, and then it was all dark. I've been wandering through tunnels ever since. What are you doing down here?"

I wanted to ask it how long it had been down here for, but I doubt it knew. It wasn't wearing a watch, and if it had been in darkness the entire time . . . Instead, I tried answering its question.

"We're from the city above," I said. "Gnawing zombies are eating the foundations and are going to make the building collapse."

"A city!" the cherubial exclaimed. "That sounds much more exciting than down here."

"Don't get your hopes up," I said wryly. "It's filled with zombies, and not many people at all."

"Bother," the cherubial said, pouting. "So these zombies that were eating your foundation. Were they the ones up that tunnel?"

It pointed at the side passage it had come from.

"Probably," I said. "But they were gnawing from more than one location."

"Like that one, maybe?" It pointed at another side passage on the other side of the tunnel. "I could take care of them for you. Then we would be friends, yes?"

"I'm not sure we can trust a demon," I hedged.

"I am not sure what that term means, or how it is relevant," the demon said sternly. "You have no basis for distrusting me, as I have not acted against your interests."

"We're worried that you *will* . . . act against our interests," I said.

"I have no reason to," it assured me. "There is plenty of food. All I seek is to leave this place."

"These tunnels, or this world?" I asked. "Because this world doesn't want you here. It tells us to kill demons like you on sight."

"How inhospitable. Is murder the only solution?" the demon asked, cocking its head again. "Because I do not think that would go well for you."

"Well . . . you could leave?" I tried. "The portal you came through is quite close, isn't it?"

"I don't know," the cherubial admitted. "Fairly close, I think, but I do not know the route through the tunnels."

"We're looking for it," I told it. "We could have a truce that gets us to the Gate. Then you can go back."

"That is acceptable. But right now, I should take care of the crawlers, yes?"

It turned and strode purposefully up the other passage. The moment it was out of sight, Cloridan grabbed my arm.

"Are you sure this is a good idea?" he whispered urgently. I quickly cast Privacy; we didn't know what its senses were like.

"Did you want to fight it?" I asked. He pursed his lips as if he had tasted something sour.

"No," he admitted. "But that's all the more reason not to take him back to the others. Kyle will freak if you bring a demon within a hundred yards of Felicia."

"I'm not wild about it," I agreed. "But our chances are a lot better if we're in the open and everyone can go after the demon. And I'll feel a lot better about our chances if Borys is in the room."

He got a sour look again. "That is a good point," he said reluctantly.

"I'll wait here. Go back and fill Kyle in. If it stays quiet, go up and let the others know what's going on."

"Will you be all right?" he asked doubtfully. "I know you can't take a zombie on by yourself."

"I can run just fine, and you're not going too far," I said. "Get going."

I cancelled the spell, and he headed back, looking out for me over his shoulder.

It wasn't long before I heard a quieter version of the sounds from before. The zombies were a little farther away this time, but that was the only difference. It didn't take any longer.

"There!" the cherubial said as it stepped around the corner. "That should take care of your foundation problem."

"Were they gnawing on the rock?" I asked.

"They were," it assured me. "The gnawing sound is distinctive, and I don't hear other sources of it near."

"That's reassuring," I said. I looked at the side tunnels. They were clearly not part of the original sewer design and looked as if they had been chewed out by gnawers, no doubt on Axel's orders. With the assigned zombies gone, would more spawn to finish the job? I didn't think so, but there might be more wandering down here that might follow an open tunnel.

I cast Stone Shape and started pulling the rock towards me to block off the passage. The demon watched me in fascination.

"So that is what that stuff is for!" it said.

"You can see mana?" I asked.

"If that's what it's called. I can see that you're controlling it, and it controls the rock. It's fascinating!"

"I'm glad you're enjoying it," I said flatly. I smoothed over the walls, leaving no traces of the tunnels behind them.

"Your companion should have had enough time to spread the word of my arrival," the demon said. "Shall we join them? I'm very much looking forward to seeing daylight again." It got a concerned look on its face. "This world does have daylight, doesn't it?"

"Well, where we are right now is fake daylight, but it looks real enough. Or will, once the night is over," I said.

The demon frowned. "That's disappointing."

"All the more reason to leave," I pointed out. "We're in a bubble, designed in part to keep demons trapped, unable to enter the real world."

"What are you doing here, then?"

"Hell if I know," I admitted. "I'm hoping to get some answers when we find that portal."

I started heading back to the exit.

"One thing before we get back," I asked. "You got a name?"

"I do!" the demon said, brightening. "It's Sarothiel!"

ZOMBIES VERSUS DEMON

There was a kid down there? And you rescued him?" Rachel exclaimed in disbelief.

"Hello! I'm Sarothiel!"

I looked around. Borys was down here, along with Felicia. Jenna was the only other survivor down here. The others must be on the roof, which . . . was fewer than I'd like.

I gave Borys an anxious look.

"It's handled for now," he assured me. "The zombies are slipping on the ice, and the locals can manage it for now."

"Great," I said. "Rachel, it's not a kid, it's a demon."

"Actually," Sarothiel said, "I prefer 'he.'"

I took a deep breath. "Fine. *He's* a demon."

"Is that different from a monster?" Rachel asked accusingly. "Like you say *we* are?"

"Yeah," I said, ignoring her tone. "Demons are creatures from outside this universe. They can be anything; they aren't even necessarily bound by the same physics as this one."

"I could be human!" Sarothiel put in. "If I can be *anything*, a human is included in that."

"Of course he's human!" Rachel insisted, giving . . .him . . . a hug. I twitched to see her get so close but forced myself to stay calm. She was just a monster, after all.

"You're a monster?" Sarothiel said, allowing Rachel to wipe his face.

"Kandis has some strange ideas," Rachel said, glaring at me. "But . . . she has magic, so we might need her to get out of this. You must have been terribly scared, but it's all right now."

'He's been surviving down there for who knows how long, on zombie meat," I said wearily. I had a feeling she wasn't going to believe me.

Sure enough.

"Don't be ridiculous!" Rachel said. "That's not possible."

"Well, you tell me how he lived down there," I said. "Survived for what, two years? However long it's been."

"I—I don't know. How did you survive, Sarothiel?"

"Zombie meat is perfectly fine to eat, you're just being squeamish about it," Sarothiel said.

That set Rachel back a bit, but she wasn't ready to let go of Sarothiel being an innocent kid yet.

"So, uh, what happens now?" Jenny asked, looking at us nervously. Unlike Rachel, she'd picked up on the fact that all of my team were alert and ready, standing close—but not too close—to Sarothiel, waiting for him to make a move.

"Go up on the roof, I guess. Kyle, can you and Felicia guard down here?" I asked. That put our two heavy hitters with the demon, and Felicia well away from it.

Kyle nodded. Felicia's face told me she knew very well what I was doing, but she nodded as well.

"Don't you want something to eat?" Rachel asked Sarothiel. "You must be hungry, or tired."

"No thanks, I just ate," Sarothiel said.

I shuddered. "Well let's get upstairs, see how the zombies are doing."

I led the way. Jenna stayed near me, while Borys and Cloridan took the rear. Rachel hung protectively near Sarothiel, who seemed uncaring of our precautions and was content to walk in the middle of us all.

"What the hell's going on?" Jenna whispered to me as we climbed. "Are you guys gonna kill the kid, or what?"

"I haven't the faintest idea," I told her. "For now, we're just going with the flow in the hope that it makes sense at some point."

She didn't seem happy with that reply, but she didn't have a rejoinder. We went the rest of the way to the top in silence.

It was quiet at the top, too. With the zombies mostly stymied by the ice, the survivors were keeping watch on all sides and dropping some junk occasionally.

"Lights went out a while back," Travis complained. "But we got plenty of flares."

"Oh, sorry." I'd forgotten that my spells would stop when they went out of range. I quickly affixed Lights of maximum brightness at the corners again. It gave me an opportunity to see what the zombies were doing. Which was milling about, for the most part.

That all stopped when Sarothiel came over to take a look. As soon as he poked his head over, all the zombies looked up.

Then they surged, moving as one towards the building. They didn't become more agile or better at working together. They still slipped off the ice. But there was a sudden purpose there that wasn't there before.

"Looks like they don't like you," I said.

Sarothiel was unconcerned. "I could kill them," he said. "Would that be helpful for you? Would you all like me better?"

"Could go either way," I answered honestly. "I think my people would like you a little better. We already know you're scary. The others don't, and watching you kill those zombies is going to be as scary as shit."

Sarothiel looked at me and then looked back at the others. "Your people are the ones with magic, and the others are the ones without," he said. It wasn't quite a question, just a tentative statement.

I nodded. "That's right."

He considered the matter. "I think they will like me," he said. "The strong are not to be feared, for the strong protect the weak."

Then he vaulted over the edge.

"Saro!" Rachel yelled, racing over. "What did you do?!" she accused me.

"Nothing," I said. "Look."

It seemed that Saro had aimed for one of the zombies. Or he'd lucked out and landed directly on one. Whatever his intentions, he had landed feet first, plowing straight through the torso of the unfortunate zombie. The force from the impact sent zombie guts and flesh flying in all directions.

Sarothiel was untouched, though. Not merely uninjured. None of the blood or gore stuck to him. He simply landed on his feet and walked over to his next victim.

Like every zombie on this side of the building, it was charging at him. Sarothiel stood his ground, and it grabbed him, pulling him closer for a bite.

It didn't get the chance. As it came in closer, Sarothiel simply grabbed it by the shoulders and *pulled* it apart. It split open down the middle as if he were making a wish on a chicken breastbone. He threw both halves aside and was immediately attacked by three more zombies. It didn't go well for them.

The others had joined me by this point.

"What do you think?" I asked Cloridan. I ignored Rachel, who was being held back by Evan from jumping after Sarothiel.

He watched the fight closely. "He's not fighting with the Status, is he?" he said thoughtfully.

"I don't think so," I agreed. There was a *look* to how you fought when you used skills. I was a little surprised that Cloridan could see it. He might never have seen someone not using skills, because why would anyone do something that stupid?

We were seeing it now, though. Sarothiel didn't move with grace, he moved with power. He moved casually, deceptively quickly. It was only when his limbs met resistance that you realized just how fast they were moving. Zombie flesh and bones didn't have any way to resist him. Flesh tore, bones broke. Zombies died.

Zombies didn't dodge, so it was a testament to his lack of skill that he missed sometimes. Generally, it happened when he got shoved off balance by a charging zombie. Knocking him over seemed to be the limit of what they could do to him, though. He would go down—Rachel would scream, even after the first time—the zombies would pile on, and then he would tear them apart from underneath.

"He's strong," Cloridan commented. "Strength ten, I'd say. Not much Finesse or Agility, though."

He sucked in a considering breath. "I *might* be okay," he said. "If I avoid parrying and just dodge, I don't think he can hit me. I can hit him, unless he's sandbagging. The problem is that I'm not sure I can damage him."

Certainly, none of the zombies were able to. Getting close enough to bite him was just an invitation for a devastating punch to go through the attacker's head. And even when that failed, it looked as if something was protecting him.

"Shame about the experience, though," Cloridan said.

"You've been making bank on this floor without having to share with us, haven't you?" I asked. I wasn't really jealous. My lucky—or more likely, carefully arranged—score had left me far in advance of everyone else.

"Reckon I'm getting close," Cloridan said. "If it does come to blows, Sarothiel might put me over."

The rewards for killing a demon were generous, but I wasn't going to let that sway me. Sarothiel *had* been nothing but friendly and helpful. Unless that changed, killing him would be murder. Probably.

I looked over at the survivors again. They seemed to have grasped just how powerful Sarothiel was now, although Rachel was still wringing her hands with worry.

"I think I've seen enough," I said. "Let's work out a roster for keeping watch tonight."

I ended up sharing a shift with Evan in the last watch before dawn. Obviously, we didn't trust the monsters to keep watch alone, and they didn't fully trust *us*, so some sort of arrangement like this was inevitable. Sarothiel did, apparently, sleep. He'd taken about two hours to kill enough zombies that the remainder had scattered. Some sort of survival instinct that hadn't been seen before.

"He sure is something," Evan said as we looked out over the carnage below.

"Sure is," I agreed. It was pretty clear who he was talking about. I didn't see the point in belabouring the fact that he was a demon, though.

"With the swarm gone, it should be easier to move about this place," Evan said. "You reckon that there's somewhere we can go to end this whole thing?"

"What?"

"You said before that there might be a cure that we need to find," he said, his face hopeful. "Or someplace that we can go, where we'll be safe."

He looked at me, and his face fell. "Something wrong with that idea?"

I had . . . not been paying attention to my expression. Careless. It only took a thought for Charm to start working again, but the damage had been done.

"You're not—" I started. "This isn't—" I tried again.

Skills couldn't help me if I didn't know what I wanted to communicate. Explaining would be a terrible idea. But would it be worse not to explain? They seemed so human. I could bully Evan into dropping the subject, but my evasion would nag at a real human until he got an answer.

They deserved to know, I decided. Even if Axel was going to erase their memories or erase them, they deserved to know what they were in for.

"You're monsters," I said. "This isn't a world; it's a floor. When we figure out how to beat it, you won't be coming with us."

"You won't let us?"

"Monsters can't leave their floor," I said. That wasn't completely true, but it was close enough. "I don't know what will happen when we leave, but the most likely result is that you get reset back to how you were when we arrived."

Evan's eyes widened, but he kept himself under control. "This . . . Axel . . . can just do this?"

"He's pretty much a god for this floor," I said. "He might reset you; he might just respawn the zombies and leave you—I don't know what he might do."

"But we can't leave."

"There are rules that govern dungeons. I don't know all of them, and Axel has stretched the rules in more than one way. But monsters can't leave their floor is a fairly well-known rule."

"So we just suffer until we get reset and then suffer some more?" he asked. "What's the point of that?"

Axel's amusement, I thought grimly, but I knew better than to say it.

"Look," I said instead. "Monsters don't normally have free will. Maybe you do. Maybe that breaks the rules, and you will be able to leave. I don't have all the answers here."

"Maybe?" he said bitterly. "You don't know if we have free will or not? We're just . . . curiosities to you, aren't we? I'm surprised you haven't cut us open to see what makes us tick."

"Rest assured, *that's* not going to happen, even if we *did* think we'd get useful information that way," I said. "We're not going to just kill you."

"Why not? We're just monsters. In fact . . . why haven't you just killed us?"

"I don't need a reason to *not* kill someone," I protested.

"But we're not someones, are we? We—you must think you need us alive for some reason. Something to do with Axel? You need us for the next bit."

"That . . . seems likely," I admitted.

He laughed. "So we do have a purpose after all! As pawns in whatever games Axel is playing."

"Look, we're just guessing about all this," I said. "We don't set the rules, or even fully know them."

"I wonder if Sarothiel can help," Evan said suddenly.

"Help, how?" I said cautiously.

"You said he was from outside. Not subject to the rules of this world. Maybe he can help us break our rules."

I looked at Evan doubtfully. "All I can say about that kid is . . . I have no idea what he's capable of."

WHAT MAN WAS NOT MEANT TO KNOW

Cloridan and Borys went outside to explore. With the zombie swarm dealt with, it would be relatively safe outside for a while, according to survivors.

Sarothiel was sleeping off last night's exertions and the big meal he ate afterwards. I stayed back to interview the survivors and Kyle and Felicia stayed back to watch over me.

Or maybe to keep me from killing the survivors. There was no way I was going to, but I was seriously tempted.

"They must have said *something*," I insisted.

"I already told you. They didn't stay long enough to say much of anything," Travis repeated. "Just that they worked for the folks that were gonna find the cure and save everyone."

"And that they were headed for their main lab," Evan added. "Which they didn't say the location of."

"They were trying to scrounge some handouts from us," Travis said. "We didn't have none to spare, and they didn't see fit to invite us to go with them. They went thataway down the street, if that tells you anything."

"Do you really think there's some quest to complete?" Felicia asked, distracting me from finding a sixth way to ask the same question.

"Borys did say that some of these are just survival games."

"If it *is* a survival game, there's not much we have to do," I said. "Just sit here and survive."

"Sounds a lot better than anything you've come up with so far," Travis interjected. I shot him a look, and he glared back. My relationship with the survivors was deteriorating, but I couldn't bring myself to care.

"Scouting out the area might find us a clue for what to do next, or it could bring in resources that we need to survive longer. How much do you have in the way of supplies?"

I directed this question to Travis. We'd been living off what we'd brought in with us, so this question hadn't come up. Frankly, I preferred our rations to the traditional post-apocalypse random can of food, unheated.

"Not much," Travis admitted. "Couple of weeks. We know where we can find some more, though."

"Then why aren't you getting it?" I asked. "It's the best time right now, isn't it?"

Travis scowled. "Waiting to see how you lot turn out," he said. "Not much point gathering food if you're just gonna steal it."

"Fair point," I said. We didn't expect to be here for a couple of weeks either, and there wasn't much point to food supplies if they were just going to be reset or despawned or whatever Axel had in mind for them. I didn't mention this.

"Anyway, we—" I stopped as Rachel made her way up to the roof.

"The others are back!" she said excitedly.

It only took a few moments for the pair to climb up the rope ladder to the second floor.

"Find anything?" I asked.

"You might say that," Borys answered. "We found a building with power."

The survivors had been doing okay without power. They'd been reduced to cooking oil lamps, and hot showers were a distant dream, but they didn't *need* electricity. They just wanted it, a lot.

Travis had insisted on accompanying us when we went to investigate. I tried pointing out that he was just a harmless kitten and we might not be able to protect him if things went wrong. For some reason that just wound him up, and didn't persuade him at all.

He told us that it was his town and he'd do as he liked, following us if necessary, to ensure that we didn't do "nuthin." I didn't really mind. By my reckoning, we were two warm bodies up and could afford to lose one. Why not the untrustworthy, probably-a-criminal Travis?

From the street, the building didn't look like much. Just another storefront, notable for having most of its windows still intact. There were no outside lights, but Borys had spotted something when he tried to get inside.

"That is, indeed, a glowing light on the security camera," I said.

"That's not all," Borys said. "This front is a fake, take a look inside."

It was dark inside, and the window was dusty, but I could see, a few feet back from the window, a featureless dark grey wall. Offset a little from the glass front door, was an equally featureless door.

"Is that a steel security door?" I asked.

"I think so," Borys said. "How do you want to go about it?"

I reached out with my other senses.

"It's well lit inside," I said. "I can't jump through. I don't like the idea of destroying the entrance, though. What if we need to block it off from zombies?"

Borys nodded. "That leaves the sewers, or . . ." he took a few steps back from the building and looked up. "There might be a way in up there."

"Cloridan?" I asked.

He nodded and pulled out a grappling hook. "Easy," he said.

It didn't take long for Cloridan to climb his way up. It took him a little longer to work out what was going on. When he pulled us up, I could see what all the confused noises had been about.

The storefront, and the second story above it, were a facade. Behind it, set back enough that you couldn't see it from the street, was the *real* building. Three stories tall, windowless, and made from a much more modern material than the homey glass and brick of the rest of the town.

"Why do it this way?" Cloridan asked. "It's such a shoddy way of concealing a building."

We were standing on the second-story facade, looking up at the third story of the inner building.

"I think we were supposed to find this," I said. "It wouldn't do for the adventurers to not find the building. Do you think those are doors?"

There were no windows, but there were two large squares that looked as if they might be doors. They were flush to the walls and had no handles, though.

"If they are, it doesn't look like there's a way to open them from here," Cloridan said.

"There's a fire escape around the back," Borys reported. "It must go somewhere."

"I guess even mysterious concealed buildings have to follow the fire code," I said.

The fire escape led to the roof, and there was a door. To my surprise, Cloridan managed to pick the lock.

"I thought modern locks would be a little different from what you're used to," I said. Cloridan shrugged.

"Much the same as any dungeon lock, to be honest," he replied.

Well, whatever. We carefully made our way inside. The interior was white walls and light panels in the ceilings.

"How do you think they've powered all this?" Borys asked.

"It's all magic in the end, isn't it?" I speculated. "Even if Axel made a generator for the sake of realism, he can just conjure more diesel any time he likes."

Borys grunted in dissatisfaction. "You want a high-tech facility like this to be powered by a nuclear generator."

I rolled my eyes. "Borys, I'm *incredibly* glad that we never found out what was behind the bomb on the last floor. Let's not wish for more trouble."

"Quiet," Cloridan ordered. "There are sounds from up ahead."

We crept forward cautiously. Thus far, we'd passed a few empty rooms that looked like living quarters. The corridor we were following seemed to lead to a new section of the building, which was where the sounds were coming from. As we got closer, we could make out what they were.

A zombie.

Probably. I wasn't hearing a gurgle, or that horrifying scream. It was a random scraping and shuffling, occasionally interspersed with thuds. The sound of an animate corpse bumping into walls, trying to get out of a room.

Nobody said anything, which I took to mean that they'd figured it out, and didn't want to attract its attention by making a sound. We came to a door. The sounds were coming from beyond it, but they were too soft, I thought, for the zombie to be *right* behind it.

What the hell. We, and by that I meant Cloridan and Borys, could take a zombie. I checked to make sure Travis was still behind me.

Borys hit the door panel and it slid aside. Beyond was a scene fairly familiar from movies. An observation chamber, I think you'd call it.

The first thing I checked, only slightly slower than the boys as they secured the room, was that the observation area was empty. That's where we were. There were two other rooms, separated from us by thick glass walls. From context, I assumed that was where the observed creatures were kept.

One of the chambers held a zombie. That was what we'd heard, stumbling around. He was fairly well preserved for a zombie and was still wearing a white lab coat that was still mostly white. Or at least a dingy grey.

> **[Identification]: Zombie – Threat: 30 – Properties: Diseased Bite, Diseased Blood**

The other room held several . . . growths stuck to the walls.

> **[Identification]: Climber Zombie – Threat: 32 – Properties: Diseased Bite, Clinging**

Oh, another variant. So were they alive, or?

Even as I had the thought, one of the growths unfolded itself and clambered up onto the glass wall separating us. We all jumped and took a step back, but it couldn't get through the glass. It hissed in frustration as its teeth slid off. Then it started slowly wandering across the surface, looking for a way in.

After making absolutely sure it wasn't going to find a way, I returned my attention to the room we were in. It featured a control panel across the length of the room. It looked as if it contained several monitoring instruments, and it probably controlled the doors I could see on the other side of the glass.

"So what do we make of this?" I asked. I knew the boys were too smart to touch any of the controls, but I kept an eye on Travis.

"They were doing experiments on the zombies," Borys said. "Making new types."

"And it didn't go well for them," I said, pointing to the lab-coated zombie. "He's just a regular zombie, though, so I don't think he got bit by his creations."

"Zombie research institutions are notoriously lax with containment procedures," Borys said wryly. "He probably brought in the virus from outside."

"And then put himself in the chamber when he felt it take effect?" I asked.

"Maybe," Borys agreed. "Should we start going through the computers to find the diary?"

"I've got a better idea—don't touch that!" I yelled. I grabbed Travis and dragged him back, just to be sure.

"What! I was just gonna help by going through the computers!" he snarled.

"Like I'd trust you to know which side of a keyboard to use," I said. "I said I have a better idea."

With my free hand (it only took one to restrain Travis), I pointed at the scientist zombie.

"That guy almost certainly knew what they were doing. We get Felicia to cure him and he can answer our questions."

"Ah, good idea." Borys said. "Should we try the computers as a backup?"

"Let's leave them for now," I said. "We can always come back to them if it doesn't work out, but I get the feeling that they've been rigged. You know, as soon as we touch the *wrong control*"—I glared at Travis—"then the glass comes down and the zombies attack."

"Threat thirty-two will be tough," Cloridan said.

"It will," I agreed. "And there's no way Axel put them there thinking we wouldn't have to fight them."

"How are we going to get the zombie if we don't touch the controls?" Borys asked.

I thought about it. "I can make a Phantasmal box through the glass," I said. "It'll be dark enough in there that I can jump us through."

Borys nodded. "We'd better get Felicia, then," he said. "I don't fancy carting a live zombie through the town."

He turned to leave and pressed the door panel. The door opened, but the lights all turned to red.

"Emergency containment failure notice," a calm female voice announced from nowhere. "Specimen release activated."

Two large panels opened up in the containment rooms. We could see daylight behind them. I swore.

All of the zombies perked up at the sound of the doors opening. The scientist zombie started shambling towards it. The climber zombies stirred into life and started dashing for freedom.

"Shit!" I looked at Borys.

"We've got to get back," he said urgently. I knew what he meant. Those climbers were going to head straight for the firehouse. The walls wouldn't stop them. Kyle and Sarothiel might. But eight of them attacking almost guaranteed one would make it through.

We had to get back before someone died.

RUNAWAY ZOMBIES

"I don' get it!" Travis whined as we pulled up out of the building. He didn't move fast enough. "Why'd you think they're gonna go for the firehouse? They don't know where the others are!"

"It's a trap," I told him impatiently as we waited for Cloridan to sound the all-clear. We couldn't get sloppy just because we were in a hurry. "Axel knows where you are; he put you there. So there will be some reason those variants head there."

If only there were some way we could warn them . . . oh, right. I pulled out my phone and called Kyle.

"I don't get how those work," Travis complained. "There ain't no signal!"

"Magic," I told him, and then Kyle picked up.

"Kandis?"

"Listen, there are a bunch of variant zombies coming your way," I said. "They move fast, they're threat thirty-two, and they climb as fast as they run."

"We'll fall back to the stairwell, then," he said. "You're on your way back?"

"Yeah. Only thing that's slowing us is checking for an ambush on the way."

"We'll see you when you get back, then." He hung up.

"There's one," Cloridan said. "Stuck to the facade."

So . . . the worst possibility, then. When we'd made it out of the building, there were no zombies in sight. Even the regular scientist zombie had gone. He must have jumped off the edge and made it to cover in record time, for a zombie.

I thought it a bit weird—which is to say, part of Axel's plans—that the zombies had taken off instead of hanging around the building. Sure, regular zombies might not have been able to make it up to our entrance point, but the climbing ones could. Why hadn't they swarmed up and tried to get in the door?

The obvious answer was that they were on a mission from Axel, but now I suspected the answer was slightly worse. They were ambush predators, and they were planning an ambush.

Zombies that could plan were bad news, however you looked at it. The only good news was that the team here, with the exception of Travis, was very well-practiced in detecting and countering ambushes.

"Only one? How do you want to handle it?" I asked.

Cloridan grinned. "With just one, we want to get the measure of it, see how it ranks against the usual ones," he said.

"Makes sense," I said. "But you'd normally need Kyle for that."

Kyle's defenses made for a good way to tie a creature down so that the others could analyze its attacks.

"We came up with an alternative," he said. "If you'd be so good as to climb down at *that* spot, m'lady." He pointed at a particular spot on the facade wall.

I gave him a very unimpressed look. "You want me to be bait?"

He bowed. "I promise we won't let it hurt a hair on your lovely head."

I made a disapproving noise, but I did trust him. And with the zombies mostly immune to my illusions, there wasn't much I could contribute.

"Fine," I said. There wasn't any time to waste, so I started climbing. I didn't have to wait long.

There was a snarl and the sound of an impact, and a shadow flashed past me, going down. A moment later, I caught sight of Cloridan joining Borys on the street, having jumped right past me.

They'd finished it off by the time I made it down. I could have jumped, but I was in no hurry to get down there until it was dead. Travis dropped the rope down at about the same time as I hit the pavement. I hadn't bothered using it; going down was a lot easier than going up.

"It's faster," Cloridan said thoughtfully. "Not stronger or tougher, though."

"What about smarter?" I asked.

"Not sure," Borys said. "If Axel told it where to lurk, then it might not be any smarter than a regular zombie. Hard to say if it came up with the plan on its own."

"And there's no sign of the regular zombie?"

"It is strange," Cloridan said looking around. "I wouldn't have thought it would get so far as to not be drawn to the sound of fighting. But."

"But," I agreed. "It's not here. First priority is the firehouse, but keep an eye out for it."

I looked to where Travis was still struggling to climb down the rope. "Once he's down, one of you is going to have to climb up and untie the rope," I said.

Borys sighed.

The next ambush was about halfway to the firehouse and consisted of three climbers. Not that they were using their climbing for anything except hiding under the awnings of the building we passed. We didn't spot them, but we were expecting something like it. Keeping our defensive formation meant Cloridan had to face his alone, but it meant Borys was well placed to intercept two more from the other direction.

I managed to stick a Phantasmal box on the head of one of them, and it delayed it enough to count as a contribution.

"Oh," Cloridan said when we were done. "That was enough. I've made level six."

"Welcome to the club," Borys said.

"First level without Ability points to spend," Cloridan said.

Borys grunted. "Welcome to *that* club as well."

We pressed on, and it wasn't long before we saw the carpet of zombie bodies that surrounded our building. Sarothiel had eaten a few, but he hadn't really made a dent.

They would be a problem if we didn't leave in a few days, but right now we were worried about the live—that is, active—zombies. I could see one, prying or gnawing at the second-story window that we used for an entrance. It was barricaded at the moment, but the zombie must have sensed some vulnerability there.

"It should be safe to use our guns, right?" Borys said. "Place has been cleared."

"I'll keep an eye out," I said. "You might even attract our scientist friend."

He unlimbered one of the German guns and took careful aim. That gun was capable of automatic fire, but he took it slow, making every shot count.

It took five shots for the zombie to fall.

"What now?" Cloridan asked.

"That's five out of eight," I said. "If the other three went for the roof entrance, Kyle should have been able to hold them off. It might be dangerous to climb to the roof—they might go for us while we're vulnerable."

There was a sudden movement from the second-floor window.

"Or the people inside might have heard the shots, and have opened the window for us," I said. "Let's run before we get any other zombies."

"Well, this is a mess," I said, surveying the ruins of the roof. Specifically, the ruins of the shack that covered the rooftop entrance.

"Yeah, I started holding at the door, but it wasn't as sturdy as the rest of the building," Kyle said. "By the time I dropped one, there was enough room to get past me, and I had to fall back farther. Making a stand on the stairs wouldn't have been a good idea. If I'd needed to get back farther, the others would have had to form the front line."

I didn't comment on how much of a bloodbath that would have been. Our shots had distracted the single climbing zombie that had survived. It had been enough for Kyle to finish it.

"I never thought it would hold if they got up here," Evan said in hushed tones. "But now . . . it won't be any protection at all."

"I wouldn't worry about it," I said confidently. "I don't think we'll be here too much longer."

"All we have to do is find one zombie in a city with . . . I don't know how many," Cloridan said wryly.

"Most of them are lying dead around this building," I said. "I think our efforts should be divided between searching for the scientist, looking for records back at that facility, and clearing out the bodies."

"I can help with that," Sarothiel said, popping up.

"That'd be great," I said, managing to keep myself from jumping out of my skin.

"How can something so tense be so boring?" I complained rhetorically.

"It's better than dragging bodies," Felicia pointed out.

We'd left that task to the NPCs. With Sarothiel there for protection, they should be good dragging the bodies somewhere further away from the base. Axel would reclaim them once we left, but we still didn't know how long we were going to be here, and the NPCs still thought of the firehouse as home.

The boys had helped us secure this building, which turned out to have no other threats—aside from the electric current running through the ground-floor door. They were now hunting the scientist zombie, while Felicia and I went through the records that had been left.

Thus far, we'd found a whole lot of nothing. A bunch of personnel records, and logs of the experiments they were doing here. Since we didn't want to recreate the climber zombies, it wasn't much use to us.

There were memos from headquarters, but they had all been received electronically, with no indication of where headquarters had been. Communication had ceased a little while before the records had stopped. A note suggested that the internet had failed, rather than headquarters itself. The last note said that the majority of the team was leaving to get instruction from headquarters directly.

Absent from any of the records was what the hell they had been thinking. I wasn't sure if that was deliberate obfuscation on Axel's part or if he just hadn't thought it was necessary.

"It's a pretty common theme in zombie movies," I told Felicia. "The zombies are a plague that man releases into the world because of their own hubris."

"Was there ever a danger of that happening?" Felicia asked.

"It's pretty remote," I said. "Designing plagues was within our capacity, but making one do all that this one does is pushing the boundaries of biological possibility. It's more a warning of the worst possible thing that could happen. A punishment from God for transgressing on his domain."

"Pretty twisted punishment, if you ask me," Felicia said. "Our gods are much more direct with their displeasure, when they care to show it."

"On the whole, I prefer subtle to lightning bolts," I said. "Much as I dislike being a part of this game they've got going, I have to admit that it's better than the alternative."

My phone rang. I looked askance at it, wondering if Fyskel had decided to toy with me some more, but it was Cloridan.

"We've found him," he said. "Can you open the front door?"

Disarming the electric current and unlocking the door was child's play, from the inside. I just had to push two buttons. When the door opened, Cloridan and Borys were outside, with a trussed-up zombie in tow.

"Nice," I said. "He give you much trouble?"

"Not too much," Borys said wearily. "He was trying to get into the sewers, though, so we caught him just in time."

There was enough room on the first floor to lie him down, so we had Felicia treat him right there.

"He's in pretty good condition," she noted. "It shouldn't take quite as much mana as before."

She did her thing. This time, I used Improved Blind to stop the screaming.

"That's much better," Felicia said. With the disease cured, she started pouring general healing magic into him. Finally, she stopped.

"I think it's done," she said. "You can take off the gag now."

I did so, and examined our captive.

[Identification]: Tobias Braston – Threat: 10 – Properties: None

I gave him a gentle pat on the cheek. "Wake up, Toby."

"Huh? What? What's going on?" he said groggily. I nodded with satisfaction.

"Good enough," I said. "Let's get him back to the firehouse before we start asking questions."

"Should we untie him?" Borys asked.

I thought about it for a second. "It will probably be faster if we carry him," I pointed out. "And this way we don't take a risk of him running."

"You mean it will be faster if *I* carry him," Borys said.

"Hey! Do I get a say in this?" Toby protested.

"No," we all said together.

ZONE OF CONTROL

I'll tell you everything, just please don't hurt me!"

> **You have defeated Tobias Braston in a Tier 1 Social Contest! You have earned 250 XP.**

That had been ridiculously easy, as I'd expected. I'd never engaged a monster in social combat before, but at threat ten, I hadn't expected much resistance or reward. Two-fifty was chump change, but the "Tier One" was interesting. He must have really wanted not to tell us.

Not that it made much of a difference against my Intimidate skill. One credible threat was all it had taken. I glanced over at Travis. Like most of the other survivors, he'd been watching the interrogation, brief as it had been. Travis fancied himself as a troublemaker, the one who would lead the survivors against me when the simmering tension built up enough.

In reality, he and the rest of his friends were not any kind of threat. I looked at him to tell him that I knew about his plans and that I didn't care.

I can reduce you to a blubbering beggar just as easily, the look said. He must have grasped at least some of the content, as he quickly looked away.

Intimidate wasn't even my most powerful skill. It was just the quickest in this situation. I could have turned on Charm or Persuade and had them eating out of my hand, following me around like little ducklings. They were so *weak*, it would have been easy.

The resentment they felt, the discontent that I allowed to grow, was my gift to them. Feelings that were rightfully theirs, generated by their experience of the world. Real emotions, not whatever I thought was convenient for me in the moment.

It was a gift I couldn't share with Toby. He had something I wanted.

"So," I said. "Your corporation. NovaGen."

The name had been all over the documentation that we'd gone through. Toby looked at me nervously but didn't volunteer anything.

"NovaGen made the zombie virus, didn't they?"

"Maybe?" Toby said.

I frowned. Just a slight crinkling of the brow.

"I swear I don't know!" Toby yelled. "I wasn't involved, I never saw anything, but yeah, reading between the lines, it sure looks like it."

"So your little outfit was researching variant zombies?"

"Mutations in the virus," Toby said. "We were set up after the virus was found in the wild. The higher-ups were concerned about mutations. They sent samples to us so we could track how it was evolving."

"Uh-huh, and how did you analyze the mutations? Computer simulations, live cultures, that sort of thing?"

He could tell that I already knew the answer. Even if I hadn't gone through the documentation, I would have known the answer. He didn't want to say it, but he didn't want me to call him on a lie even more.

"That, yeah, but there was . . . live testing on human subjects."

"You little shit!" Travis sprang to his feet and launched himself at the researcher, who was still tied up and lying on the floor. There hadn't seemed to be a reason to untie him yet.

"Travis!" I barked, and the man stopped short, his hands balled up into fists.

"You pulled people off the streets for *testing*?" he sneered. "You're a monster!"

"You're all monsters," I said mildly. "Keep in mind, it's unlikely that he's actually *done* the things he remembers."

Travis frowned. I could tell that he wanted to have a deep philosophical discussion on the subject. If someone remembered doing something that never happened—and others had memories that agreed—had he done that thing?

Or possibly he just wanted to kick Toby until the man died. Those looks were pretty similar on Travis. I had no time for it either way. Under the pressure of my gaze, Travis slunk back down to his seat.

"This headquarters of yours," I said, returning to the subject. "Is that where your buddies were headed?"

Toby nodded. "Once the mail stopped, and our final specimens . . . matured, there wasn't much for us to do. We got permission to put the base on standby and return. I stayed behind to look after the place."

"And aside from getting turned into a zombie, you did a bang-up job," I said wryly. "Where's the headquarters?"

"It's about two weeks on foot," Toby said. "I don't know where, exactly, but we got sent directions. Something about necessary security precautions."

That sounded like bullshit, but it sounded like Axel's "this is a game" bullshit. I tabled it for later.

"Fine," I said. "You'll lead us there tomorrow. Do you anticipate any problems?"

"Aside from zombies?" Toby asked.

"We can handle zombies," I said confidently. "Though, I should check . . . the virus that made those climber zombies was sent to you, right?"

"Yes. I don't know where it came from, but they'll have that information back at headquarters. That sample was from some time ago as well. I'm sure there have been other mutations since."

"That's not great news, but we'll manage," I told him. "Anything else?"

"Well . . . you know they're not going to let you in, don't you? Even with me as a hostage."

"Why wouldn't they?" I asked. "If they've got a sanctuary, they're going to need more hands to keep it safe, or expand it."

"Maybe," Toby agreed. "One of the last messages, before the internet went down, was that they were looking for more test subjects. So they're probably short on people, but I don't know if they have jobs for you that you'd like."

"Whatever gets our foot in the door," I said grimly. I wondered if that was what the survivors were for. Bait to get us past the door? I looked over the group speculatively.

"We're going," Travis stated flatly.

I raised an eyebrow. "Are you that eager to become a zombie?" I asked.

Travis spat on the floor. I mean, actually spat on the floor. Rachel and Marta looked scandalized, and I don't imagine the look on my face was approving. Someone was going to have to clean that up.

"Hell with that," he said. "You got your stupid game to win—we want to see Axel. If he really exists."

I looked at Travis calmly. "Fine," I said. "I've no plans to stand between you and your creator. Just don't get in our way, and try not to die. I'd feel bad if I had to watch."

He turned away, muttering to himself. I ignored him and turned to Sarothiel, who had been watching the whole group with interest.

"You're coming too, right?" I asked.

"This will bring us back to the portal, correct? It's not the way I came—that was underground."

"Yeah, if you knew the way that you'd come, we might try it, but as it is, this is our best bet."

"Sorry about that. Yes, I'll come."

"All right." I looked down at Toby. "I suppose we should untie you now."

"You've been fooled. There ain't no road out here." Travis said loudly.

"Are you trying to attract a zombie?" I asked. "I ask out of curiosity."

Travis's face went red, but he continued at a lower volume. "I know this area," he insisted. "You got a ditch out back behind Taylor's place and the sewage farm, but no road." The rest of the survivors nodded in agreement, but they wisely kept their mouths shut.

"This is the route we were given," Toby said meekly. He was leading us between two warehouse-like workshops at the back of the town. Exactly how he'd been given this route was a bit suspicious since he didn't have any street names that he could give us. I chalked it up to Axel again.

That didn't mean I was following him blindly, though.

"Hang on," I said. I grabbed him to make sure he stopped.

"What is it?" Travis asked. He got more irritated every time I took charge.

"Magic," I said, looking at the seemingly innocuous alley ahead of us. "It looks harmless, but . . ."

I'd gotten more used to having the extra sensory data from [Sense Mana] in my face at all times. It was easier in a dungeon and even easier in this one. Axel mostly kept his magic hidden in the floor or ceiling where my skill couldn't reach. He only left it out for me to see when he had to, when there was a specific magical effect right in front of me.

Exactly what it was, I couldn't tell, but some of it looked familiar. I could maybe puzzle it out, but brute force was easier.

"Dispel Image." I cast the spell aloud so everyone knew what I was doing. Everyone who counted, at least. There was a murmur and gasps from the crowd at the results.

The alley ahead of us disappeared. In its place was an open road, roughly lined with trees and bushes on either side. The transition was jarring. The buildings on either side of us simply ended as if they'd been cut with a very sharp knife.

"Looks like we found the path," I said. "The illusion must have been to cover the transition."

"Is that the portal I came through?" Sarothiel asked.

"No, this is just a local one," I said.

"Do we go through?" Kyle asked.

"Wait, I'm not done." Peering closer at the portal, I could see that there was still some Illusion Magic. This magic was farther in, but my spell had range.

"Dispel Image," I cast again. "Ouch," I said. That had not made things better.

What had previously looked like an ordinary road now looked like something painted by Escher. It was twisted while still staying straight, a contradiction that hurt my eyes.

The others were having just as hard a time looking at it, none more so than the survivors. Evan quickly turned and threw up against the alley wall.

"We're not going to have to go through that, are we?" Felicia said. "If we are, I wish you'd kept the illusion up."

"What is it?" Rachel asked in disbelief. She couldn't look at it for long, but she couldn't stop herself from coming back. I sensed some vomiting in her near future.

"That's how you pack a two-week journey into a space that's not that wide," I said. "You twist space so the road can fit."

"I'm not sure how this saves us a two-week journey, though," Borys said. "Except in the sense that I have no desire to take that journey now."

"That's a fair point," I admitted. "But I'm not done with brute force."

I studied the Escher swirl in front of us carefully, trying to look at the magic instead of the geometrical nightmare. Spatial Magic wasn't a recognized skill, but Rhis could do it. I'd watched what he did.

This was far beyond what he could do, but I got the sense that complicated and difficult meant *more fragile* in this case.

"Borys," I said slowly, "can you fill this with your blizzard?"

"I . . . can," he said. "How will that help?"

"For one, we'll be able to see less of it," I confessed. "But for another, I want to fill the space up with magic to put the structure under strain."

Borys shrugged and complied. There was a strangled sound from Toby, who hadn't seen any *flashy* magic yet. I appreciated that he tried to keep his voice down. I almost forgave him for the human testing that he hadn't really done. Almost.

Borys's blizzard started filling up the inside of the spatial effect. Without the sight from the inside to distract us, we could see that it had an *outside*. It was a tube or—more accurately—a twisted strand of spaghetti that led from here to another place.

I frowned. Could that be right? I quickly checked without Sense Mana and confirmed that the tube was only visible with the skill. Ordinary eyes couldn't see the outside of the tube.

Sense Mana grants extra-dimensional sight confirmed, I guess.

"Is this helping?" Borys asked.

"Yeah, I think so," I said and reached out into the magic. The temperature dropped instantly, and I was glad that I was wearing a glove. "Nice control."

Borys shrugged, and I brought Theurgy to the fore. I didn't use this skill often; it was too difficult. But it could do any kind of magic, badly. Since there was no such thing as Spatial Magic for humans, it was what I had to use.

Fortunately, I didn't need to do anything *complicated*. Just disrupt what Axel had done. I was relying on the fact that while dungeon magic was more sophisticated and complicated than anything a human could do, it was often—always, maybe—*weaker*.

Brute force for the win. With my hand in the effect, I didn't have to worry about range. I just reached out and *twisted*.

There was a sound that I'd never heard before as space itself shattered in front of me. Borys's storm exploded in all directions, even the ones that didn't *exist*. Sensing the moment, he cancelled the effect.

When the blizzard cleared, we were looking at a tunnel ending in a door with a sign on it that said NovaGen Solutions. But I was looking at my new notification.

[Theurgy] Level 5 acquired through use.
For gaining a skill level, you have been awarded 1 XP.

NOVAGEN SOLUTIONS

That was unexpected," Borys said.

"What happened to the road?" Felicia exclaimed.

"It's still . . . somewhere, I think." I thought about what had happened. "Borys filled it with magic. That let me see where the space was, and I . . . detached it."

"I didn't come close to filling the whole thing, though," Borys said. "I could tell there was plenty more to go."

"Yeah, but you filled up this end, which was the relevant part," I said. "It's still there, but we don't have to go through it to reach the next step."

"You know," Borys mused, "if that was a . . . spatial tunnel, it could have led anywhere. There was no reason for him to put that door right in front of us."

"There are two reasons," I countered. "First, Axel has been hinting that we'll need Theurgy to do something to the portal. He wants me to be practicing the skill. And second, there's no way he could pass up the chance of sending us on a long worthless trek, only for our destination to be a couple of feet away."

"True enough," Borys admitted. "What's our next step?"

"Toby, you're up," I said, carefully ignoring how he flinched when I looked at him. "Do we just knock, or what?"

"Um, I—I don't know. We weren't given any special instructions." Toby looked nervously at the door.

I looked as well, and though we were still a little distance away, my vision was better than his. I could see that there was no doorknob, but there was what looked like an intercom button. There was an obvious camera in the corner above the door, and two suspicious panels on either side.

I guess we'll just have to risk it. No, wait . . .
I had a spell for this.

[Phantasmal Emissary].

Since I could make it look like whoever I wanted, I made it look like Toby. I even remembered to change its description to match him.

[Identification]: Tobias Braston (Illusion) – Threat: 10 – Properties: None

I wasn't sure if that would be necessary, I didn't think the monsters in there had Identify, but there wasn't any extra cost.

I walked the fake Toby up to the door and hit the intercom button.

"Hello?" I said. "Can I come in?"

There was a long pause. Then the speaker crackled to life.

"Who is this?" it said.

"I'm Tobias Braston, from the Ravenford facility," I said.

"From Ravenford? That facility was abandoned two years ago!"

"I know. I stayed on as a caretaker until I caught the virus."

In the background, I could hear someone saying, "Wait, what?" but the main voice had other concerns.

"How did you get here on your own?" it asked. "There's no way you could—"

Then another voice broke in. "Did you say you *caught* the virus?" it exclaimed.

"Yeah, but I got better," I said. "Some people cured me."

At that point, someone must have covered the mic, but they didn't turn it off. I could hear them arguing, but I couldn't quite make out the words.

Eventually, someone must have won. "How did you get here alone?" the first voice asked.

"I'm not alone. There's a bunch of people with me. They wanted to see if there was anyone left here."

"What about the zombies?"

"Oh, they don't bother you if you're immune," I lied. I figured if I was intriguing and confusing, they'd have to let me in, just to see if I was telling the truth.

There was an argument about it, but my side won.

"You'd better come in, and bring your friends," the second voice said. "The first level is abandoned, but if you make your way through, we'll meet you at the gate."

The door slid open.

"Thanks!" I said. "I'll go tell the others!"

I headed back out of range and cancelled the spell.

"Door's open," I said. "Let's not waste any time."

"Did they ask about the survivors?" Borys asked.

"Not really," I said. "I don't get the impression that they were needed."

"So what are they for, then?" he asked in Polish. "Surely there was some reason—some game reason—we needed to keep them alive?"

"New theory," I said. "Their purpose is to fuck with our heads."

He snorted. "They certainly do that," he agreed.

We went forward, into the tunnel and then through the door, into the facility. It was . . . decidedly unimpressive. It did look as if it had been abandoned for years, but there was also a lot of damage. There had been fighting here. The bodies had been cleaned up—or eaten—but there were smashed light panels, bullet holes in the walls and a distinct lack of furniture that wasn't broken.

There were signs that some of it had been fixed at some point and then broken again.

We'd come through an empty reception area, complete with an overturned counter. Behind that was what had been a generic office environment. Some of the desks were broken, some were missing.

A distorted voice drew us farther back.

"Kghhk . . . can you hear me?"

When we got closer, we could see that the voice was coming from a flatscreen monitor. It looked as if someone had pulled a teleconference setup out of a meeting room and set it up as a freestanding console in the corridor, kept safe behind a thick plastic shield.

A shield with cracks in it, I noted.

There was a woman on the monitor, looking down at the camera as if she was on Zoom. She had short, neatly trimmed hair and was wearing a clean blouse.

"Ah, there you are," she said. "How many of you are there?"

"Uh . . . thirteen," Toby said, once I'd nudged him.

"So many . . ." the woman muttered. "That's too many for the lift; you'll have to go down in bunches of six. Don't be alarmed when the lift comes up. They're just a security precaution, and they are completely under control.

"What are?" Toby asked, but even as he did so, the lift dinged and the doors slid open.

Two zombies stepped out. Everyone tensed, but these weren't ordinary zombies. They were wearing uniforms, a sci-fi-looking vest and pants made out of some kind of flexible plastic. They also wore helmets that covered their heads completely. From the lenses on the front, I assumed that they contained cameras. Despite having most of their zombie-like features covered up, the clammy flesh of the exposed arms left no doubt as to what they were. And if there was, Identify had the answers.

> **[Identification]: Cyber-Zombie – Threat: 32 – Properties: Diseased Blood**

The woman had said that they were controlled, so I had to assume that the cameras were linked back to the controllers. They saw what their minion saw.

"If the first six can get in the lift," the woman said.

"I don't like this," Borys said quietly in Polish. "Splitting us up like this . . ."

"Don't worry about it," I said in the same language. "Distract them for a moment, will you?"

I stepped out of the view of the cameras, zombie-cams included. It was easy enough with everyone milling about. Once I thought myself safe, I cast Invisibility and Phantasmal Emissary.

My companions figured out what I was doing. The survivors gave "me" a startled look. From their perspective, I'd disappeared and reappeared a little way away, like a slow teleport.

"Will that work on zombies?" Borys asked.

Zombies used some kind of life sense that was outside of Illusion Magic spells, at least any that I had.

"No, but it will work on cameras," I said, then back in Latorran, I called out, "First six down are me, Sarothiel, Travis, Evan, Toby, and Rachel."

"Why we gotta be first?" Travis asked. He was looking at my image, trying to figure out what had happened. Or he was wondering what happened to my aura of Charisma, which normally made him do whatever I wanted. I couldn't use it through the Emissary.

"Just do it," Borys rumbled. "She knows what she's doing."

Travis jumped and took two steps towards the lift before he scowled, realizing what had happened. Borys wasn't a Charisma build, but just as I was able to overpower the survivors physically, Borys could overawe them with his relatively puny Charisma.

We all trooped into the elevator. At least everyone here knew what one was. Sarothiel might be an exception, but he was committed to the role of playing human. As long as the other humans didn't ask questions, he wouldn't.

We descended . . . not very far. The trip was longer than I would expect for one floor . . . maybe two or three. The doors opened up into a room . . . or was it a wide corridor? With no other options, we stepped into the room. There were four armored doors along the side walls and another elevator on the opposite wall. All around the room were vents, which suddenly started spewing white smoke.

"Gas!" Travis yelled panicking.

It filled the room quite quickly, blocking visibility. It worked quickly, too, the survivors dropping like flies. Sarothiel was unaffected, of course, but lay down quickly as soon as he realized what was going on.

I kicked him, gently. "Get over here," I said, drawing him over to the corner. I used Static Image to cover us with a wall. It wouldn't fool anyone in the room, but I thought it would be good enough for cameras. Especially with this white fog everywhere.

The lift headed back up, and the gas started to get sucked out of the same vents it had come in by.

"We're ready for the next batch," the woman said upstairs. Downstairs, one of the doors opened, and more cyber-zombies marched in. Four of them headed straight for the unconscious survivors while two of them scanned the room in a fairly good imitation of confusion.

Upstairs, we were taking our own sweet time getting into the lift, thanks to a quick Sourceless Sound message from yours truly. The lady didn't complain, as she still hadn't cleared up downstairs.

I had my emissary tap Sarothiel on the shoulder and pointed. "Take them out," I said. He nodded amiably and stepped out of the image.

I followed the other four. They hadn't reacted to our appearance and were still carting the unconscious bodies of the survivors out. They were using a different door from the one they had come in, which I found mildly interesting.

The other thing I found interesting was that they hadn't reacted to my approach at all. The other two had—one of them had headed towards me before being intercepted by Sarothiel. Was it because their visor cameras only faced forward and they didn't know where I was? Or were they still following the previous order and it didn't include any actions concerning me?"

Whatever the reason, I made it into the next room without issue. The ripping and tearing sounds from behind me suggested that some other people—or things— might have some issues. I ignored them.

This room had several gurneys that the survivors were being placed on. It also featured a doctor, or at least a man wearing a white coat.

"Hey! You're not supposed to be here!" he said. I forgave him for his inaccuracy. He probably meant that I wasn't supposed to be *awake*.

I had included a gun when I made FakeTobias. I pointed it at the doctor. It couldn't do anything to him—I doubted it could even fire—but he didn't have to know that.

"Take me to your leader," I said.

He looked at me, at the gun, and then at the zombies.

"You don't control them, do you?" I stated. "The ones who do are a little distracted—oh, there they go."

The transition was instant. One of the zombies had finished loading his cargo onto the gurney. The other three just dropped their load before all of them spun around, heading back to the first room.

"You can't do this," the man said. "Control will have noticed. They'll send more."

"I think we'll take our chances," I said. "Is there a manual control for the lift?"

He didn't answer, but his eyes flicked over to a box on the wall.

"Thanks," I said. I kept the gun pointed at him while I moved over to it. A quick glance revealed that it was very simple. I pushed the button, just as Sarothiel entered our room.

The doctor jerked as if he'd been about to try something, but he aborted his movement and just stared in terror at the new arrival.

Sarothiel was in high spirits. "That was fun!" he declared as he entered. I glanced at him and did a quick double take before I returned my attention to the doctor.

"Sarothiel," I said. "Your head is twisted the wrong way around."

INTERROGATION

I t wasn't long before we were all reunited. I kept my Emmisary going, but put her at the back of the crowd and took over the duty of watching . . .

> **[Identification]: Lucas Trent – Threat: 10 – Properties: NovaGen Employee**

Lucas. NovaGen Employee was a *property*? Did that mean that employees had access coded as part of their nature? Tobias hadn't had the property, but I suppose he wasn't exactly part of the inner circle.

Borys was taking care of the cameras, Kyle and Felicia were watching the other lift, and Cloridan was checking out the other rooms. That left a crowd of survivors in the main chamber being of no use whatsoever and Sarothiel in the side room with Lucas and me.

Sarothiel had fixed his head, at my insistence. Lucas kept glancing at him warily but was far more interested in staring at my breasts.

"So, Lucas," I said. That got him to look at my face. He hadn't said his name, and they weren't wearing name badges. Procedures must have slipped after the apocalypse. "Why don't you tell me something about NovaGen? Start with what you planned to do with our unconscious bodies."

"Just . . . ah . . . tests," he said nervously, pushing his glasses back on his sweaty nose. "Nothing too bad, just blood samples and scans. Dr. Huang didn't want—I mean, they didn't want to refuse them."

I came really close to using Charm to break him. That was how I preferred to operate. Why *can't* we all be friends? Of all the social skills, that one had the least blowback, aside from Bargain, another of my favorites. Even if someone realized that you'd used Charm on them, they tended to let it pass, because you were just so *nice.*

In this case, though, I couldn't bring myself to do it. Sure, these monsters weren't really people. The whole "corporation profits from apocalypse" was just a parody calling out the worst aspects of capitalism. And this dungeon floor was a parody of *that.*

At some level, I couldn't bring myself to be buddy-buddy with these guys. Fortunately, I had other options.

"Sarothiel," I called. He'd wandered over to the corner where we'd stuck the remains of the zombie corpses. He turned around and ambled back to us with half of a zombie's hand stuck in his mouth.

"Sarothiel—" I said. Then I stopped myself. He was a more credible threat this way.

"These ones don't taste as good," he told me. "Too many wires."

"Lucas," I said, leaning into the Intimidate skill. He'd been staring at Sarothiel in horror, but his gaze jerked back towards me as he felt the weight of my words. "You want to tell me the truth, or should I give Sarothiel something fresher to eat?"

"Oh God . . . please . . . no . . ." he mumbled, staring at me. "I'll talk, I'll tell you everything. They—they hadn't decided, what to do. It would depend on the results of the tests."

"What sort of options are we talking here?" I asked coldly.

"I—I don't know! Infection perhaps, but not if you were immune. Study, maybe? Or disposal if you were too dangerous."

"I think we'll have to pass on all of those ideas," I said dryly. "Now. You guys created the zombie virus, yes?"

Everyone got real interested when I asked that question. It wasn't the first time that I'd suggested that NovaGen created the zombie virus, but I guess the survivors still weren't thinking in terms of a video game. No one wants to think that their fellow humans would *really* cause all that death. Lucas saw the looks and got even more panicked.

"No! Oh God, you've got to believe me! We found it in the wild and studied it! That's all!"

"Really," I said.

"I swear! This virus . . . it—it's like nothing we've ever seen before! It communicates with itself, it takes *actions* on the macro scale. . . . We couldn't build anything like it if we tried!"

"Huh. And this outbreak has nothing to do with you either?"

"That . . . might have been us. There was an investigation at the time, but it was inconclusive. The reason we built the lab here was because the original sample was taken nearby."

"And the investigation thought that it could have been a natural outbreak? How convenient."

"It's not like there's an outside auditor available right now," Lucas said defensively. "When they were doing it, zombies were tearing up our top level!"

"I don't need no study to tell me what's what," Travis snarled, interjecting himself into the conversation. I could have stopped him, but I let him continue, on not much more than a whim. The ins and outs of how this all started weren't that important to me, since I knew that it was all constructed by Axel. The survivors felt differently, obviously. Even if they believed me, they remembered it happening to *them*.

"It's always a lab leak, everyone knows that—assuming it weren't a deliberate *test*!" Travis continued. The other survivors seemed to agree, glaring at the med tech.

Lucas shrunk back from their glares. "I swear! No process failures were identified! There wasn't any breach of procedure detected!"

"Then why'd you keep the cure to yourselves, you bastards!" Travis yelled, right in the guy's face. Travis didn't lay a hand on the tech, though. Angry as he was, he kept himself under control. That might have something to do with the fact that I remained in arm's reach, ready to act if necessary.

A little harmless venting was fine, as long as it remained harmless.

"Cure? There's no cure." Lucas whimpered. "We've been trying, but the virus adapts too fast. That's why we wanted to . . . see how you did it."

Via dissection if necessary, I translated. *Still, no hard feelings.*

"So what are your *current* plans?" I asked. "You've got your zombie soldiers—were you just planning on waiting out the collapse and rebuilding?"

Lucas didn't answer me at first, not until I coughed and made Travis back down. Then he stared at me gratefully.

"The soldiers were a side . . . benefit?" He said. "Zombies have some interesting advantages for cybernetic enhancement. The virus keeps them alive, but they aren't, so you don't have to worry about tissue rejection or . . . a whole host of issues."

He looked around the room and was taken aback when we didn't seem as interested in him in the cybernetic advancements that were being made.

"Also, uh, we needed protection from the regular zombies," he said. "And the rest of the world hasn't fallen. The last communication that we got said the containment was working."

"How long ago was that?" I asked.

"We, uh, got cut off for unknown reasons, about six months ago."

We all looked at him. "It wasn't because they failed!" he protested. "It wouldn't have gotten cut off like that."

"I've got something," Borys called out. Having taken care of the cameras, he'd moved on to investigating the terminal in the room.

"You're . . . not authorized to use that," Lucas said weakly. "I'm still logged on."

"No, you're not," Borys said. "To start with, this isn't a computer. It's a slideshow."

"What are you talking about? Of course it's a computer," Lucas said.

"What was the last thing you used it for, then?" Borys asked.

"It was—I was . . ." Lucas trailed off, thinking. "I'm not sure," he finally admitted.

"Really?" I asked. *This* question was a little bit interesting. "Don't you use this thing every day? As part of your job? Can't you remember what you did with it one time?"

"I . . . can't, all right?" Lucas said angrily. "I'm a little bit stressed at the moment, what with being attacked and kidnapped."

I let it slide. It was more evidence that he wasn't real, that he had been constructed only a few weeks ago at most. But it wasn't as if I had anyone interested in reviewing the evidence.

"So what does it show?" I asked Borys.

"Personnel records, mostly," he said, flipping past screens with a common format. They all had a picture in the top right corner, and some text, presumably a potted bio of the person. "But also . . . this."

He stopped on a full-screen image of a map.

"Extent of outbreak, March 2012," I read. "What's the date now?" I asked the room.

"September 12," Evan answered.

"2012?" I asked, to be sure. He nodded.

"So, six months ago, like he said."

"The area's not that big," Borys pointed out.

"Still too big to fit in here," I said. "Look, Ravensford is on the map—it's quite close. About fifty miles according to the scale. He needed trickery to make that work, and this area is about five hundred miles across."

"So . . . you don't think its purpose is to lead us out of the contamination zone," Borys said thoughtfully. "Is it to show other places we can visit?"

"Maybe. But what place could be more important than this one?" I looked over the map, trying to find a location that stood out. The lab was quite close, but not exactly at the center of the zone, which was an irregular shape anyway.

"Maybe it's there to make us think that there is a world out there, that humanity still has hope," I said.

"Apart from us, who's going to see it? Elves?" Borys asked. "I can't see them caring too much."

"There's these guys," I said, gesturing at the survivors. "They care, at least. Convincing them that the world exists might be something that Axel wants to do."

"Maybe," Borys agreed. "There's also this."

He flipped over to the next slide. This one was also a map, of the facility.

"Huh," I said. "Is it just me, or is that a weird design?"

The first-floor map, now sadly out of date, showed a mostly open plan, with some offices around the edges and some lightweight walls to box off various areas of the upper office. The second floor was the exact opposite of that, with six areas all completely separated.

"Is access between the areas only via the third floor?" I asked.

"Looks like it," Borys said. "Maybe that's how they always build biocontainment facilities."

"You think?"

He shrugged. "Security is always a pain, and this looks like a pain."

"I'll give you that," I agreed. "Lucas, come up here and tell me how accurate this thing is."

The crowd parted to let Lucas through, and he stepped carefully away from the wall he'd retreated against to join me. Neither he nor the crowd looked happy about it.

"It's an old map, but there's not much that can change," he told me diffidently. "We're here, in Quarantine."

He pointed to two enclaves on the second level. "This section is where we implant the control systems on the zombies. The other lab is for proper medical work, DNA analysis, that sort of thing."

The enclaves were arranged in a rough circle. Or, since there were six of them, an exact hexagon. Lucas pointed to the two enclaves on the other side of the circle.

"This section is Control. Just about everything runs through there, the cameras, the patrols, and communications."

"That's where the woman I spoke to is?" I asked.

"She's probably still there," he agreed. "The other section is Infrastructure. Holds the servers, power and air, and . . . access to the water system. I'm not sure about the specifics there."

"What's this one?" I asked, tapping the final enclave.

"We don't use that much," Lucas told me. "Not since the director died, anyway. It was for management; there's a board room in there. It's pretty fancy."

"Okay, and the third floor?"

"Residences at the back, storage here, here and around here," Lucas said. "But the main thing is the security checkpoints. You have to go through at least one to get to another section, and two if you're going across the secure line."

"And what do those consist of?"

"It's mostly about checking for virus shedding," Lucas told me. "There are decontamination measures, but they only trigger if it detects something. Oh, and the machine guns. They'll probably trigger when they see you."

"Probably," I agreed. "What about the cyber-zombies?"

"They're too much of a pain to get through the checkpoints, so there are some stationed in every enclave. I think you got all the ones in this one."

"You know," Borys said, "if we get into the Infrastructure section, we can probably hijack whatever they've got controlling the zombies. Or shut down the power altogether."

"You can't do that!" Lucas protested. "Without the controls, the zombies will rampage! They'll kill everyone!"

I looked at him incredulously. "You built a device where the failure mode was murderous rampage?" I asked.

He had the grace to look embarrassed. "When you put it that way, it sounds bad," he said. "But the power has never failed before."

I took a deep breath and reminded myself that this was all a part of Axel's grand design, and he probably did it that way because he thought it was funny.

"Let's not do that," I said. "We still don't know what our goal is, and we might need the employees alive."

"So what do we do about them?" Borys said. "They're pretty tough, and if they start arming them with proper guns, we might find ourselves with a problem."

"From problems come solutions," I said slowly. An idea was coming together. "I think we might be able to turn those zombie soldiers into a solution."

I turned to Lucas. "Tell me about who's in charge here."

BELLY OF THE BEAST

Lucas looked at me nervously. "Since the director died, it's mostly been the Emergency Committee running things," he said. "There's not a lot of management left, and pretty much everybody works for someone on the committee."

"Who's on the committee?" I asked.

"Doctors Carmichael, Huang, Archer, Wexler and, um . . . Vargas. Dr. Archer, he's my boss."

"All doctors?" I asked. "Who keeps this place running?"

"It pretty much runs itself," Lucas replied. "There are some maintenance folks, but they keep to themselves, pretty much. The bunker is mostly self-sufficient."

"Is it?" I wondered. "Where do you get your food?"

"From stores," he admitted. "There's still lots, but it's getting lower."

"What's the plan to get more?"

"It's—the current situation is supposed to be temporary. We can hold out for another year at least. And . . . there is a plan if it looks to go on for longer than that."

"What is it?"

Lucas grimace. "I don't know," he said. "No one outside of the committee knows. There's a rumor it involves kicking out the less essential staff members to save on supplies."

"To die, you mean. You think they'd do that?"

"No . . . but I was glad when you guys came in and I had to do quarantine duties," he said. "No one wants to be unneeded right now."

I frowned and looked over to Borys. "I'm not hearing a win condition," I confessed.

"I don't either," he agreed.

"Um, what's that?" Lucas asked. I ignored him. Borys glanced at him before continuing.

"We could just have to defeat the people in charge," Borys said. "Evil corporation, developing the virus. It has the right feel."

"Yeah . . . but it sounds weak," I mused. "They've got the zombie soldiers, so they make a strong adversary, but they're going to be threat ten like all the other humans here. Hardly a final boss."

I turned back to Lucas. "You guys don't have a supersized version of the zombie soldiers tucked away somewhere, do you?"

"Uh, not as far as I know. What—what was that you said about defeating the committee? They're not bad guys—they're helping defeat the virus!"

"Are they, though?" I asked.

"I know they don't all sound like they want to help," Lucas admitted. "Some of them are a bit cold. But they got into this field to help people! You're supposed to have brought in this cure, how are they supposed to distribute it when you've . . . done whatever you're going to do?"

He looked at me defiantly, which was quite impressive since I'd just got done Intimidating him. I raised an eyebrow. Maybe it was plot-based.

"The cure, huh?" I mused. "Maybe that's the play."

I looked over the ragtag group of survivors. "Any of you want to volunteer for testing?"

"Why us?" Travis asked immediately.

"Well, not you," I shot back. "It needs to be someone who contracted the virus, which eliminates you and us. It needs to be someone like . . ." I looked at Tobias.

"I'm happy to help, as long as the means aren't too extreme," he said cautiously. "What kind of tests are we talking about?"

"Ju—just blood tests?" Lucas said. "To begin with, I don't know what Dr Archer is going to call for next."

"You don't need to have your subject sedated and strapped to a gurney for a blood test, do you?" I said.

"Oh, no. We just—we were worried about the subjects turning while we were taking the blood," Lucas said.

"Hmm. Well, why don't you take some samples now, and we can see about getting them tested," I said.

"I mean, I can," Lucas said, edging over towards one of the equipment trolleys. "That's what I'm here for. I just don't think Dr. Archer is going to be in the mood to do tests after you trashed all her security zombies."

"That's fair," I said. "But I'm pretty good at negotiating."

Lucas took a few samples of Tobias's blood and carefully labelled the tubes before placing them in a small tray. Then he glanced at us and rummaged through the cupboards. He produced a small, sturdy box, which he packed with cotton wool and stashed the samples in.

"Here," he said, holding it out to me.

"You keep it," I told him. "You're coming with us, after all."

He shied back. "I don't want to die!" he declared. "The committee is going to send everything after you. Even if they wanted to save my life, I'd die in the crossfire!"

"Oh, ye of little faith," I said. "One of these screens can talk to your boss, right?"

Lucas sighed and packed the box away in his lab coat's pocket. "Right," he said.

He walked over and started pushing buttons. It wasn't long before a face came up on the screen.

"Dr. Felix Archer, my boss," Lucas said. "Doctor, these are the—"

"I've seen the tapes," the man said. "These are the anarchists who have taken you hostage."

"I'm more of a Democratic Socialist, myself," I said idly. "We seem to have gotten off on the wrong foot."

Dr. Archer glared at me.

"There will be no negotiations with terrorists," he said. "We have shut down the elevators and sealed the exits. You cannot continue any further into this facility, and you will be killed if you try."

"*You* were the ones who attacked *us*," I pointed out. "We've still got that cure you were interested in—we're just not interested in being gassed and vivisected. Can't we come to some sort of compromise?"

"Never!"

"Is there someone else I can talk to? I'd like to speak with a manager."

"No." Dr. Archer cut the connection.

"That . . . didn't work?" Felicia asked.

"It seems that skills don't work over a Zoom call," I said. "We'll just have to get up close and personal."

"But . . . you're not going to be able to do that," Lucas said. "All the doors have been sealed."

"They sure have," I said. "But for some strange reason, they decided to make all their doors out of steel. Cloridan?"

"Got it, boss," Cloridan said, moving over to the elevator.

"Oh, elevator doors aren't normally secure," I said. "You should be able to just pry them apart."

Cloridan looked at me doubtfully but plunged his darksteel dagger straight into one side of the doors. Using that as a handle, he easily shoved the doors open, revealing a dark shaft.

"These are supposed to have emergency lights," I grumbled. I took care of it with a Light spell. Cloridan made to jump down, but I stopped him.

"It might not be far," I said, "But the ceiling might not take the impact, and there might be a soldier in there. Take the ladder."

Looking in, I quickly spotted the rungs of the emergency ladder, attached to the shaft wall. Cloridan shrugged and started climbing down. He quickly discovered the hatch and disposed of the lock with a quick slash of his dagger.

"It's clear!" he called up. He started stabbing at the doors, with the intention of opening a peephole.

I looked over at the survivors. "Who is fine with staying here until we figure out what we're doing?" I asked.

"Hell if I am!" Travis declared. "This place is creepy, reminds me of a morgue."

The rest of the group concurred. Or so I assumed from the muttered "Yeah"s and "I guess"es that I heard. Lucas put his hand up.

"I'm fine with staying here," he said.

"Nope, you're our local guide," I said. "You get to ride in the front seat!"

He didn't look happy at being granted this privilege.

I had Felicia and Kyle gather up our passengers, organizing them to follow us at a slight distance. We did have to worry about being flanked, but most of the danger would be at the front end of our convoy. Though if what I had in mind worked out, it wouldn't be too dangerous.

Cloridan had carved out his spyhole, so I climbed down to take a look.

Aw yeah, that's just about perfect.

It looked as though the lift opened out into a short corridor with a security door at the far end. Standing before the security door were two cyber-zombies, armed with . . .

> [Identification]: Heckler & Koch HK433 – Quality: Perfect –
> Damage: 1,200

Finally, we're breaking out the good guns.

Now to see if the flaw I thought I'd spotted worked. I cast Phantom World on both of the zombies. It took hold.

Phantom World was both the strongest and the weakest illusion spell I had. Most of my spells took up a specified volume, and couldn't depict anything larger than that. Phantom World took over the entire sensorium of a *single* person. There was no limit to what I could make them see, but there was one big limitation. If the target doubted what they were seeing, the spell ended.

All my other spells stayed around, no matter what the target believed. You could walk through a Static Image spell, but the image would stay until I cancelled it. Not Phantom World.

Here's the thing, though. Zombies can't doubt. I wasn't sure if they could even *see* the illusion, since they seemed to operate on some kind of life sense. The people controlling the zombies, though, were using regular cameras to see by. *They* could see the illusion. They could doubt what they were seeing, too, but *they* weren't the target.

To start with, all I did was rotate what the zombie saw. About forty-five degrees off from true. It took a moment to work, but both zombies suddenly turned to correct what they were seeing. It took three small stomps for them to change position, and then they stood still.

I rotated another forty-five degrees. Three stomps. Now they were facing each other. Now I made a real change. I had the elevator door open and showed them an image of Cloridan charging them. I could have used the real thing here, but I didn't want to put him in danger.

The cybernetic control interface was nice and smooth. As one, the zombies brought their weapons to bear and fired on full auto. Fake Cloridan didn't stand a chance. He jumped up, but they kept their weapons trained on him. Neither the recoil of the heavy assault rifles nor the impact of the slugs in their torsos so much as spoiled their aim. They only stopped when their heads exploded.

> **For killing a Cyber-Zombie, you have earned 8,640 XP.**
> **For killing a Cyber-Zombie, you have earned 8,640 XP.**

"Sounds like it worked," Cloridan said as the sound of machine gun fire died down. He grunted as he levered the elevator doors open.

"Hold up," I said. I stuck my head out and glanced up at what had been my blind spot. No camera. They probably had no idea what happened, then.

"All clear. Let's go."

We approached the smoking corpses cautiously. Cloridan gathered up the guns and ammunition, while I examined the door. From what Lucas had told me, this had been a bio-security checkpoint, hastily reconfigured to stop larger nasties. That didn't explain why it didn't have cameras, though.

In fact, there was a stubby mount where a camera *would* go, but nothing was attached. Did that mean . . .

"That's some scary attention to detail," I said.

"Hmm?" Cloridan asked while reloading the HK.

I pointed at the camera mounts. "They repurposed their security cameras, turned them into zombie eyes," I said.

At some point, I'd explained the basics of cameras to Cloridan. He needed to know, what with all the sneaking around he did. Now he shrugged.

"It doesn't matter much," he said. "If they were there, you could always stick a [Static Image] in front of them.

"I suppose," I agreed. "It's just more fun for me when they put them on zombies."

"Don't complain, then," he admonished me. Freshly armed, he turned his attention to the door.

"This one slides like the elevator doors," I said, "But it will be locked."

"No key?" Cloridan asked, looking back at the zombie guard.

"Zombies couldn't use one," I said, not knowing if that was true. They'd mastered automatic weapons. "I think it's controlled remotely."

"Brute force, then," Cloridan said, jamming his dagger straight into it.

"Just watch out," I said, "I'm pretty sure there's a big gun waiting for us on the other side."

PAWNS

It was there, just as I'd suspected. Hanging from the ceiling, on some kind of swivel mount, was the biggest gun I'd ever seen—outside of the WWII tanks.

> **[Identification]: Heckler & Koch MG5 – Quality: Perfect – Damage: 2,400**

It was pointed right at me, right at the slit in the partially opened door that I was peeking through. We'd probably attracted their attention with all the vandalism we'd been doing to the door. I assumed the only reason they hadn't started firing yet was because the door would offer decent cover.

As if they were reading my mind, the door beeped and tried to open. It didn't get far before getting caught on one of Cloridan's daggers. He'd stuck it in near the frame, to make sure we didn't open the door too far.

Whoever was in charge of the gun didn't like that, because they opened fire. I jerked back, as much in an automatic reaction to the noise as it was in fear for my life.

"Strong door," Cloridan commented.

"Not that strong," I replied. It was disintegrating before our eyes. As yet, no bullets had made it through, but at this rate, it was only a matter of time.

[Static Image].

I cast an image of the door, *behind* the door, from my perspective. From the point of view of the gun's controller, the door had been restored to pristine condition and was no longer affected by the hail of bullets they were putting out. The bullets were still slamming into the door, of course, but what they couldn't see . . . didn't hurt me?

It took them a moment to notice. At least, I assumed that was why they stopped firing. Robot guns had a very limited emotional range, so it was hard to tell if it was confused.

"Should I just go in invisible?" Cloridan asked. "I can cut it down off the roof, and we can get on with our day."

I thought about it, but I didn't have anything better. I sighed and made with the Greater Invisibility.

Once invisible, Cloridan strolled up to the remains of the door. He reached into some convenient bullet holes and pulled it out of its frame. Setting it aside in the corridor, he confidently walked through the illusion.

A little while after that, there was a screech of metal, followed by a crash. I cancelled the wall image and walked into the room. Ah, they still had some cameras. I waved to one before I wrapped both of them with small blankets via two casts of Phantasmal Object. It cost a little more, but it would last longer.

Cloridan waved the gun at me, for what reason I don't know. He couldn't really communicate with me when he was invisible. I cancelled the spell.

"I don't think I can fire this thing," Cloridan said. His disappointment was evident.

"I don't think you're supposed to," I said, taking a look at the gun. "Guns this heavy aren't supposed to be fired by *people*."

"Oh, the weight isn't a problem," Cloridan said, hefting the whole assembly with one hand. "I just can't find the trigger."

I wanted to scoff at the idea but my adventurer habits wouldn't let me pass up an increase in firepower. I took a closer look.

"To start with, you can cut this off, and lose that cable," I said, pointing to what looked like a telescopic sight welded to the frame. "That's the camera."

"Sure thing," Cloridan said, pulling out a dagger.

"Wait!" I pushed the gun so it wasn't pointing at the open doorway the others were going to arrive through. "If you're going to work on it, make sure it isn't going to fire on its own."

I looked for an ammo clip. Instead of that, there was a belt of bullets, much like the ones I'd seen in war movies. Unlike those belts, this one had been torn off and was only about a foot long.

"Where's the rest of this?" I asked. Cloridan pointed at the ceiling.

"That's where the rest of the ammo is, then," I told him. "Do you want to dig it out?"

"Eh. Sounds like too much trouble," he said, carefully setting the gun down.

I shrugged and looked at the rest of our party as they arrived. "Which way to the control room?" I asked Lucas.

He looked up at the cameras, covered in cloth, before he pointed at the right door.

I nodded and gestured for everyone to back out of the room, except for Cloridan. I made us both invisible and then I cast Static Image on the two doors we *weren't* going through. Then I pushed the button to open the door.

Nothing happened.

I sensed Cloridan was puzzled. I could only see his outline, but I got the impression from the way he was cocking to the side.

"I'm pretty sure they're leading us into an ambush," I projected with Sourceless Sound. "I *thought* they might be tired of getting their doors wrecked, but I guess not."

Cloridan shrugged and plunged his daggers into the door again. By now, he had a pretty good idea of where to stab and wasn't just trying to find the locking mechanism by blind luck.

At the same moment as his dagger shorted out the lock, the two other doors in the room opened. Two cyber-zombies were behind each door, and they . . . stood stock still.

They must have been confused by the illusions of blank walls that were in front of them. I didn't wait for them to figure out that they could just walk through them. I could see through my own illusions, which meant that I could *target* through them.

[Phantom World].

I cast it four times. Controlling four sensoriums would be a challenge even for my System-enhanced mind, but I made things easy for myself by just blanking everything out.

The four cyber-zombies whirled around in a fairly convincing imitation of panic. I wondered how they were being controlled. Did each one have a human behind the screen using a joystick? Or did they all take orders from a single human controller, but act autonomously?

Despite being armed, they didn't start shooting randomly. I was glad for that. It might have made it easier to get them to shoot each other, but with so many potential shooters, I was worried about stray shots.

Since they were being so restrained, I thought it would be worthwhile testing their reactions. I had one of them see an image of me, walking away from them.

The zombie I'd targeted lunged forward. I'd placed the image so the lunge took it into the main room. Even though the only thing it could see was the bait I'd dangled, it didn't stumble. The zombie's senses, whatever they were, must still be functioning. They weren't passed on to the controllers, but they let the monster move around without difficulty.

I let the image of me fade out and cast Sourceless Sound.

"Cloridan . . . take a stab, see if it dodges you."

I couldn't see if he rolled his eyes, but he dashed in close to make an attack. As expected, the zombie dodged and even took a swipe at Cloridan in return. Sadly, the clawlike hand it was using was the one that was holding the gun, so the swipe was slow and clumsy. Cloridan dodged it easily and took a step back out of range. The monster did not follow.

Could I control them like this? It was worth trying, so I restored one monster's sensorium, editing out all the other zombies and pasting an image of Cloridan over one of the remaining monsters. It looked around . . . as if it was suspicious, I thought. I had the image of Cloridan charge it, and it opened fire.

It hit the target I was aiming at, but as the targeted zombie jerked and spasmed under the hail of bullets, the other two zombies seemed to lose their reserve. They started firing randomly.

I dodged. I'd been told that the System wouldn't let a dodging person get hit by unaimed fire, but I didn't want to test it. I dived down to the floor and barely had the presence of mind to use Sourceless Sound again.

"Shoot 'em! Shoot 'em! Shoot 'em!"

Cloridan was so quick to respond that he may not have been waiting for me. His gun was absolutely silent, but the thudding impact of the bullets was easy to see. With their senses impaired, they were nothing but a shooting gallery for him.

That didn't mean they went down easy, though. It took more than one shot, or ten for that matter, to take them down. Cloridan emptied the last of his cyberpunk guns and dropped it to the floor. He kept firing, though, the sound of the bullets' impact changing as he switched to WWII ammo.

> **Your party has killed a Cyber-Zombie – your experience share is 4,320 XP.**
> **Your party has killed a Cyber-Zombie – your experience share is 4,320 XP.**
> **Your party has killed a Cyber-Zombie – your experience share is 4,320 XP.**
> **Your party has killed a Cyber-Zombie – your experience share is 4,320 XP.**

The sound of gunfire was replaced with the ringing in my ears as the last of them fell. Cloridan hadn't been making a sound, but the zombies sure had been. The smell of . . . cordite? Gunpowder? Whatever it was that these guns used, the room smelled of it pretty strongly. I lay on the ground for a second while Cloridan started stripping the corpses of guns and ammo. I suspected that the Heckler & Kochs that the zombies carried would be his new favorite gun.

The rest of the party came creeping forward now that the firefight had stopped. I cancelled Greater Invisibility so I could talk to them.

"It went well?" Borys asked.

"Eh, so-so," I said. "I was hoping I'd be able to control them by controlling their vision, but it didn't work as well as I'd planned. I'm better off just blinding them."

"Did they disbelieve it?"

"No, they couldn't. But the people behind them could. That didn't end the spell, but they could just choose not to act on what they saw. That didn't make them *effective*, but . . ."

"But not the easily controlled pawns that you hoped for." Borys finished for me.

I pouted. "I wanted some zombie foot soldiers as well, dammit!"

Borys chuckled and held out a hand to help me up again.

"You think that's it?" he asked. "No more zombies?"

"Not between us and the committee," I said. "I'm speculating here, but if they had more, they'd have sent more. There must be more in the facility, but Sarothiel can take care of them if they show."

The demon was guarding our rear. The boys had seen enough of how he fought, and now we were keeping him away from the front line as much as we could, to avoid him seeing all of *our* tricks.

"So what's next?" Borys asked.

"We'll see," I said. I pushed the button for the lift. To my surprise, it turned green. A moment later, the doors opened with a ding.

"I guess they got tired of the game where they tried to stop us and we wrecked their stuff," I said.

"Or it's a trap," Borys said.

"It's always a trap," I agreed. "But that's what Phantasmal Emissary is for."

I cast the spell and gestured for Cloridan, still invisible, to join it.

"Let's see if they're willing to negotiate," I said. My emissary pushed the button for the second floor.

I was half expecting some kind of traditional trap, like a trapdoor or gas pouring out of a vent. But none of that happened. The lift went up and the doors opened, revealing a simple corridor.

I stepped out first, looking around, up and behind me. There was a camera tucked up in the corner, but nothing else. I moved forward, letting Cloridan follow behind.

Before I reached the door at the end of the corridor, it opened and a woman stepped through. She was tall, with an elegant, poised demeanor, and she had shoulder-length ash-blonde hair tied back in a loose bun. She looked at me as if I were some shit she'd scraped off her shoe.

"I don't know what you're trying to accomplish," she said, her voice sharp but tinged with exhaustion. "But you should know that you've significantly reduced the chances of mankind's survival. Before you feel the need to destroy any more crucial infrastructure, why don't you come in and deliver your demands."

EMERGENCY COMMITTEE

The room reeked of stale coffee and disinfectant, a combination as unpleasant as the atmosphere within. The space might have been an executive office that had been hastily converted into a meeting room. A mismatched collection of chairs surrounded a scratched oak table, its surface marred by deep gouges as though someone had taken their frustration out on it with a scalpel.

My emissary stepped inside, boots clinking faintly on the floor, and surveyed the room. My gaze lingered briefly on each of the five figures seated around the table.

Dr. Emily Carmichael had entered before me and now took her seat. She was the first to break the silence, adjusting her wire-rimmed glasses with the precision of a surgeon. Her blue eyes burned with cold disdain, but her posture remained perfectly composed.

"So," she said, her voice cutting the tension like a scalpel, "you've turned our weapons project into a complete joke."

"That wasn't really a goal of mine, more of a consequence of you turning it against me," I replied. I folded my arms and leaned casually against the wall. There was a chair for me, but I didn't use it. "I've heard who you guys are, but why don't we get the introductions out of the way?"

Next to Carmichael, a man shifted in his chair, his wiry frame half hidden under an oversized lab coat. His nervous fidgeting distracted from the simmering anger in his hazel eyes. He ran a hand through his thinning hair and muttered, "Sam. Sam Wexler. I don't see why we're even wasting time on this . . . conversation."

"Dr. Liwei Huang," the woman next to him said. She sat stiffly, her arms crossed over her chest. Her sharp, delicate features were marred only by a furrowed brow and the faintest curl of her lips into a sneer. She didn't bother looking at me, instead staring at a notepad before her with forced indifference. The pen in her hand trembled slightly.

"Wasting time is an understatement," the next man interjected, his voice dripping with contempt. "Felix Archer," he introduced himself.

His greying hair was slicked back meticulously, and his steel-grey eyes glared at me as if I were an insect he would crush. He adjusted his pristine lab coat and leaned forward, his fingers drumming a calculated rhythm on the table. "I'd much prefer we skip the pleasantries and move on to resolving this . . . nuisance."

The final member of the committee chuckled, a low, sardonic sound that drew all eyes to him. He lounged in his chair with deliberate ease, one ankle resting on the opposite knee. His sharp, angular face was framed by dark stubble, and his amber eyes gleamed with something between amusement and malevolence. "Ah, Felix," he said smoothly, his voice like oiled silk, "but where's the fun in that? Our guest went through so much trouble to get here; it's only polite we hear her out before trying to stab her in the back. My name is Raul Vargas; a pleasure to meet you."

It didn't seem as if there was any kind of trap, so while they were talking, my real body hit the elevator button again.

I gave the bickering scientists a moment to settle down. "Kandis Hammond," I said. "I don't suppose any of you know what the real game is here?"

They looked at me, puzzled. I thought that would be the case. Maybe I'd been a little spoiled by the obvious objectives of the WWII level, but I was getting a little frustrated with this level.

What were we supposed to do? It couldn't be as simple as just killing all the zombies. None of the previous levels would allow that. I'd guessed that we were supposed to get the survivors to this lab, but all that had gotten us was attacked. Now I was in front of the ones in charge, and they claimed to be saving civilization?

"So. They tell me you *didn't* develop the virus, but you don't seem to be developing a cure."

"That is correct," Emily said, icy disdain still flowing through her words. "That was not part of our original brief, and to be frank, we still view the prospect as unlikely."

She looked at me over her glasses. "We have been intensely studying this virus for some time. Your claim of a cure, well . . . it has to be investigated, true. But no one at this table thinks it will pan out."

My real body got into the lift, along with just about everybody else. Only Borys and Sarothiel were left behind. No one wanted to be in close quarters with the demon, and we needed someone to watch over him.

Back in the meeting room, my emissary still had questions. "So what are you doing, if not looking for a cure?"

"We are attempting to modify the virus's behavior," Emily told me. "The goal is to turn it into a symbiont that does not kill its host."

I stared at her. "Why?"

"If you knew anything about virology, you'd understand when you saw what this virus can do," Emily said. Her voice softened a little as she warmed to her subject. "It is simply unprecedented in its versatility and adaptability."

"It's a virus, though," I said. "Doesn't it need to kill its host cells to reproduce?"

"Individual cells, yes, but not *all* of them. Some cells are sacrificed for reproduction, but as you've seen, the virus *integrates* with the remaining ones, restoring a lifelike state to the organism as a whole."

Organism instead of *person*. Well, that was on brand for a mad scientist. She wasn't done lecturing me, though.

"If we can change the way the virus behaves, we can limit the damage to the host, while retaining the beneficial effects of integration! We can keep the host alive while gaining all the strength, speed, and immunity to disease that the virus provides!"

I tried not to roll my eyes. It wasn't some wonder virus doing this, it was the dungeon's magical transformation. Still, I needed to play along with the plot.

"You're talking about making super soldiers," I said.

"The cyber-zombies are a bioweapon prototype that we used to get funding," Dr Vargas cut in smoothly. "But if we can neutralize the lethality aspect, we think we can make the virus more widely available."

We got out of the lift and sent it down for another load.

"What's goin' on in there?" Travis asked.

"They're talking about their corporate plans," I said. "They want to fix the bit where it kills people and turn everyone into super soldiers."

Travis spat. I couldn't help but stare at the greenish glob stuck to the shiny metal wall. We'd made a bit of a mess downstairs, but everything up here was so clean.

"Didn't get the first part right, couldn't be bothered. Released it anyway. Assholes."

"I'm not sure that's true," I said lightly. Maintaining two conversations at once was a challenge, and I was glad that I wasn't trying to *control* either of them. Travis was Travis, it didn't matter what he said or did, and my emissary was just letting the scientists talk, hoping to trigger whatever event was necessary to progress. Speaking of which:

"You want to make *everyone* a *living* zombie?" I asked.

"We're a long way from that," Emily said. "We've had enough successes to think it might be possible, but that's years away, still."

She hesitated. "With the original version out in the wild, a symbiotic version might be the only protection available."

"Let's talk about how it got out in the wild," I said grimly.

"It wasn't us," Doctor Archer said quickly, losing a little of his composure. "I admit it *looks* bad, but it certainly wasn't a deliberate release. We lost half our support staff and our director to the initial outbreak."

"That doesn't rule out accidental—which you'd be just as much at fault for."

He drew himself up. "I'm responsible for security and containment procedures here," he said while glaring at me. "I assure you that *every* precaution was taken. *No* containment failures were detected!"

"I see. Well, we have the cure now, and you can't do anything about us, so let me tell you how it's going to be," I said. I couldn't use my skills through the emissary, so I couldn't stun them into compliance, but my words were shocking enough that I might have seemed to.

"We're going to clear out every trace of the virus from this facility," I said. "Every sample, every test case you've got cooking. And, of course, the cyber-zombies. They'll be destroyed or cured."

This was, not to put too fine a point on it, a lie. While we *could* do it, it would take days if not weeks for Felicia to generate all the mana for it. None of us had the time or inclination to hang around that long.

All I was doing was filling in time for everyone to come in. The lift had come up, and everyone was now in the corridor. Whoever was monitoring the camera hadn't seen fit to inform the Emergency Committee.

"How!" Emily protested. "How can you have a cure for the virus? It adapts to everything we've thrown at it!"

"Magic," I said. "That's how we do all the things you've seen. That's the reason you can't stop us."

"*No.* You can't do this."

Dr. Liwei Huang stood abruptly, her notepad clattering to the table as her carefully maintained composure cracked. Her sharp features twisted into a fervent, almost ecstatic expression as she turned to face the others.

"You don't understand," she began, her voice rising, trembling with intensity. "None of you understand! The virus isn't a tool or a weapon to be controlled by our petty little hands. It's a revelation! A divine force, perfect in its simplicity, flawless in its design!"

We were all in the corridor, just about ready to bust in. I held up a hand. "Hold up. I think we got a bite."

Back in the meeting room, Dr. Huang was gesturing wildly, her movements jerky, almost manic. "Look at what it's done! It takes the chaos of life and remakes it, piece by piece, cell by cell, into something unified. Something greater. It's not just biology—it's transcendence! The virus is a god in its infancy, and we—" She jabbed her finger at the group, then at herself. "We are the midwives of its birth!"

Her voice dropped, but the intensity only deepened, the reverence in her tone chilling. "Don't you see? The world, with all its filth, its failures, its endless striving for nothing—it needs this. We all do. To be stripped of our illusions, of our weakness, and rebuilt into something . . . pure. Unquestioning. Unified. Isn't that what we've been searching for all along?"

She took a step forward, her eyes gleaming with a wild light, locking onto Kandis. "And you. You come here with your magic and your brute force, thinking you can destroy what you don't understand? You think you can stop it?" Her lips curled into a sneer. "You're nothing but a distraction, a gnat buzzing around the face of destiny."

Her voice rose again, echoing in the room. "The virus isn't a plague— it's a blessing! It deserves to spread, to consume, to transform! It will take every single one of us, tear us apart, and rebuild us into something that matters! And when it does, when we're all finally part of it, we'll know peace. We'll know purpose. We'll know God."

She paused, chest heaving, her eyes blazing with conviction. Then, with a final, bitter laugh, she added, "And you're all too small-minded to see it. At least right now. Soon you'll understand. We'll all understand."

She pulled out her phone, I guess it was. Not much call for one of those on this level, but she was using it for an app. With a final sneer, she pressed down on a big red button.

Smoke started billowing into the room. The other scientists started screaming, but all I could feel was relief.

Finally, the bad guy had shown up.

BAD GUY

"What have you done, you manic?" Emily shouted over the screams of her fellow committee members. "What *is* that?"

It was a good question.

I wonder if...?

[Identification]: Biosol Dispersion Medium – Quality: Excellent – Properties: Diseased

---

Right. That wasn't exactly *news*, but it was nice to be sure. At that moment, there was a heavy *clunk* from the door. A klaxon started blaring, and a red light started flashing.

"Contamination alert!" a recorded voice started repeating.

Dr. Huang was saying something, but I couldn't hear her over everything. "Cloridan, could you . . ." I yelled and pointed at the alarm. I wasn't sure if he could hear me, but either he could or he was thinking the same thing.

The alarm separated into two pieces. *I* could see the outline of Cloridan's form as he cut it in half, but to the others in the room, it must have looked as though I destroyed the speaker by pointing at it.

The scientists stared at me, shocked into silence by either the sudden cessation of the klaxon or my admittedly impressive psychic powers. Riding the wave, I pointed at the flashing red light. They all stared as it, too, was destroyed.

"This is it?" I asked Dr. Huang. "This is your big plan? Infecting us all with the virus?"

She coughed slightly. They were all coughing; the smoke had covered the entire room by now. It didn't seem too bad, just a slight irritation. My emissary didn't need to breathe, so I was all right. Cloridan was going to need a healing spell. Fortunately, I had a healer right outside the door.

"Not at all!" Dr. Huang said once she'd cleared her throat. She pressed another button on her phone. I thought about having Cloridan take it away but decided to wait and see where this led.

This button caused the main projector to display four camera views. It only took me a moment to work out that they were from the eye cameras of some of the surviving cyber-zombies. They were in their own smoke-filled rooms, operating some kind of machinery. There were people in there, too. They were coughing and pointing at the zombies. They seemed confused about what was happening, but they didn't try interfering with whatever the zombies were doing.

Dr. Huang was happy to provide commentary. "As you can see, I've activated the final contingency programming on the cyber-zombies. They're being loaded up with biosol dispersion canisters. Once that's done, they'll head for the containment zone. Those fools won't be ready for zombies with weapons! The line will be breached, and the virus will be free!"

I looked over at Dr. Archer. "I think we found your containment breach," I said dryly. He had the grace to look embarrassed.

"Okay, but you know we're going to stop you, right?" I said to Dr. Huang. "Maybe we just take that phone off you, and it has a button that stops the whole thing. Or we do it the hard way, but we do stop it, you know?"

"You can't!" she declared. She looked down at her phone. "There isn't any way to stop it, and you can't leave this room! Quarantine protocols have been triggered!"

"She's right," Dr. Archer claimed. "Once the protocols were triggered, the doors sealed, and the air supply was isolated. Any attempt at breaking through the doors will trigger a pyrothermal purge."

Outside, I was having a hard time convincing everyone to stay put. I was glad I had, though. A pyrothermal purge sounded uncomfortable.

"That's right!" Dr. Huang cried triumphantly. "There is nothing you can do but watch through the eyes of our creations! Over the next few days, you will slowly succumb and become one with God."

"The next few days?" I asked. "I hope you brought snacks and drinks, because we might not make it that long."

"It doesn't matter how you die," Dr. Huang said. "The virus will take you anyway."

"Good to know," I said. "Is that it, then?"

"What do you mean? You're going to die and serve God. That's all there is—that's all there ever was!"

She started cackling madly, which I took as my cue that she was out of useful information.

"Cloridan, please recover her phone . . . gently," I said. I didn't wait for a response. "Dr. Archer, there is an override for the quarantine, isn't there?"

"Of course," he said with cool detachment. "However, it can only be triggered from outside the quarantine zone."

I smiled. "Would it happen to be triggered by the button outside that just started glowing red?"

He stared at me. "Yes," he finally said. "How do you . . .?"

I ignored his question and looked around the room. "Who knows anything about this biosol stuff?" I asked. The smoke had mostly cleared, but I was pretty sure that just meant it had settled on every surface, still just as infectious as ever.

Dr. Raul Vargas tore his gaze away from watching Dr. Huang wrestle with an invisible person. "I developed it," he said with a wry smile. "Can I assist you in some way?"

I looked at him suspiciously. Was he . . . happy about dying to his own creation? It was very *mad scientist* of him. I didn't say anything about it, though; he might have taken it as approval. Instead, I just asked, "How do we clear it up? Does cold affect it?"

"Well." He gave me what he must have meant as a suave smile. "The liquid medium does freeze at 28 degrees Fahrenheit. When that happens, it will denature the payload relatively quickly."

"*How* quickly?" I did the math. That was about minus two degrees in real units. It seemed doable.

"About a minute," he replied. "If you were thinking of rigging the air conditioning, it won't work. The condensation cycle—"

"Thanks, I've got it," I interrupted. Outside, I was giving everybody instructions. I looked around. Cloridan had retrieved the phone and was currently holding Dr. Huang off with one hand, which she seemed to be *biting*.

Everything seemed to be in order. Outside, I pressed the red button.

Inside, everybody jumped at the loud *klunk* from the door. It slid open, and the cold came in.

"Well, it's been real, folks," I said. It made sure everyone was looking at me when I cancelled the spell and returned to just having one set of perceptions.

The gasps and one shriek that came out of the room were a little grati-fying, I had to admit. I strode into the room on a carpet of ice and a billow of fog worthy of any rock star. That was courtesy of Borys.

"Nice fog," I said. It seemed to impress the rubes.

"It's not deliberate," Borys called from behind. "The warm air is getting chilled when it comes in and . . ."

I shot him an irritated glance.

Never explain the magic trick.

I kept that comment to myself, as that would be even worse for my entrance. Instead, I just held up my hand for the phone. Cloridan tossed it over and held Dr. Huang back when she made a lunge for it.

"Huh. It's locked. Hold her."

I came forward slowly, making sure to stay on the ice. I'd have Felicia diagnose me after this, but it made sense to minimize the risk. Felicia was entering the room now, going around curing the disease in the gathered scientists. Curing the disease while the host was still alive was a lot easier.

"Hold out her hand," I said to Cloridan. Dr. Huang was struggling against his grip, but she was still a threat ten monster, like all the others.

"Fingerprint ID," I mused. "Facial recognition would have been even easier to defeat, I think. It depends on whether Disguise changes finger-prints, and I've never checked. If it was a PIN code, I guess I would have had to make an effort to get it out of you."

She looked at me without any comprehension of what I was talking about. Not that it mattered. I pressed the phone against her index finger and found myself looking at her unlocked phone.

It was a familiar-looking OS. Probably a knockoff, but the important thing was I could easily find the most recently used app.

"NeuroSync Override," I said aloud. "Anyone know about this app?"

"Our controller program, the one we use to update the zombies' pro-gramming, is called NeuroSync," Sam Wexler said. He glared at Dr. Huang. "It's not a phone app, though. One of the techs must have coded it for her."

"Maybe. It's nice and user-friendly, though," I said. That might have been overstating it. The app could do a limited number of things, and they were all listed out. That might not have been ideal from a usability stand-point, but it meant that I could easily find the option I wanted.

"Emergency Shutdown," I said, looking at one of the options. Dr. Huang growled and struggled harder, but it made no difference to Clori-dan. "No one thinks this is going to do something stupid like shut down the base, do they?"

"NeuroSync doesn't control the base," Sam said. "But taking control of the projector means that she's compromised more than just NeuroSync."

"Hmm." I went looking for how she'd done that. There wasn't anything in the app that I could see, but when I went back to the *next* most recent app, VLC Remote.

"Ah, that's the ticket," I said. There were more than just four streams from the zombie headcams, and I found I could switch between them. "Okay, that's separate."

I went back to the first app and selected *Emergency Shutdown*. Then *Select All* and *Confirm* to be sure.

The video feeds all went dead. Dr. Huang let out a long, keening wail of despair. Felicia healed another committee member.

"And so the zombie apocalypse ends, not with a bang or a whimper but with an 'are you sure' dialog box," I said. I looked around for the ball of confetti.

"Well? Are we done yet?" I asked the air.

"I haven't healed everyone yet," Felicia reminded me. "If she infected the rest of the base, we might have to get everyone else out.

"Oh, I hope not," I moaned. "Here, do Cloridan next."

I cancelled his invisibility. Felicia could target an invisible person with healing spells, but she couldn't get feedback on how they were working. The committee members made the requisite jump of surprise when Cloridan appeared out of thin air, but it was muted. They'd just watched Dr. Liwei Huang struggle with air for the last five minutes. They had to suspect *something* was up.

"Should I cure her as well?" Felicia asked, pointing at Dr. Huang. "I don't think she wants to be healed."

"She's infectious, so I don't care what she wants," I said.

"This isn't the end, unbeliever," the doctor snarled. "I'll find a way to spread the Holy Word."

"You might as well let her go, Cloridan," I noted. "She should be harmless now."

Cloridan shrugged and let her go. She immediately took a swing at me. I caught her fist easily.

"Harmless, like I said. Are you going to behave, or do I need to put you in a time out?"

She screamed and swung her other fist at me.

[Improved Blind].

Felicia looked at me reproachfully. "Now she's going to hurt herself bumping into walls," she said.

I shrugged and dragged her over to the other committee members. They looked nervously at the black bubble around her head. Honestly, they should have been used to spells by now.

"You can look after her," I told them. "Hopefully, this will all be done by the time the spell wears off."

"What is that supposed to mean?" Dr. Emily Carmichael snapped.

"It means that you've succeeded!" crowed a very familiar voice. The projector fired up again, showing a giant version of a very familiar face. "Congratulations!"

"Who is *that*?" Dr. Carmichael asked. "How did he get in our systems?"

"That, doctors, is Axel, the god of this tiny realm. He made you, the virus—everything you know, except us."

"Ah, Kandy, baby, you know you're not supposed to draw the curtain back like that," Axel said. "What will the neighbors think?"

"What's gotten into you?" I asked. There was something different about his tone.

"Ah, I'm just excited. We're almost done! You're going to meet me in person! Everything you've worked for was all leading up to this moment!"

I stared at him for a long moment, trying to find words. Finally, I shook my head. "Let's just get this over with," I said. "There's some people who want to meet you."

ALL AXEL

What the hell, Axel?"

The grinning face looking down at me from the projector screen raised his eyebrows in surprise.

"Is that one of your questions? It's a little open-ended, don't you think?" He giggled. "Well, we can sort that out when you get down here! No vestibule this time—you get to experience the pinnacle of my power! Is that the right word?" He cocked his head to the side, pretending to think about it. "It's my lowest point, but the place with the highest concentration of mana, so—"

"The depths of your depravity," I suggested, making him giggle again.

"Quite so! Quite so! Now, if you'll just take the provided exit . . ."

One of the room's walls suddenly slid open, revealing a downward-sloping passageway.

"You'll need to push through any monsters you want to take with you," Axel told me. "Monsters can't leave their floor of their own volition."

"Is that true?" I asked Dr. Carmichael. She had shut up, but she looked as if she was still demanding answers. "Can you go through that doorway?"

"What doorway?" she asked. "Who *is* that man?"

I shrugged and grabbed her. She tried to dodge, and when that failed, she tried to struggle out of my grip and to resist being dragged. None of that made a difference.

Everyone watched, with differing degrees of curiosity or alarm as I walked over to the doorway and pushed her through.

"Don't just push me!" she complained. She glared at me but made no effort to get back. "Where am I? This isn't a NovaGen facility!"

"What did that look like to you?" I said to the remaining scientists.

"What did what look like?" Sam Wexler asked.

"You . . . didn't see me push Emily through a wall?"

"Emily? Emily is right here. . . . Where is she?" He started looking around, confused by his sudden realization that Emily wasn't in the room.

I groaned. "All right, everyone who can see the door, grab an NPC and push them through," I said loudly.

"What did you call me?" Emily protested.

"Are we taking everyone, then?" Felicia asked. "I thought we were only bringing the ones that we came with."

"Everyone," I replied. "They can all meet their creator."

"The more the merrier!" Axel agreed. "Don't worry, there's plenty of room."

We pushed them all in. It made for quite a crowd. The original survivors, the zombies we'd cured, and the scientists. Some of them protested, but it made little difference.

When it became clear that we were just going to fill the passageway with protesting scientists, Dr. Carmichael started leading them down to wherever the passageway went. The survivors weren't inclined to follow her lead, but *they* had an inkling of where they were going and why. They headed down of their own accord.

Sarothiel seemed immensely amused by the whole process and came down on his own.

We left the remaining base personnel where they were. It might have been cruel, but I didn't have the patience to go and winkle each one out of quarantine and cure them. Once we left the level, Axel would probably reset them, which was . . . terrifying, but better than dying of a combination of thirst and the virus.

We got down to the final room after everyone else and took a look around. It was quite a sight. I'd have to show Rhis an illusion of it someday.

The chamber itself was wide and spacious. The walls curved gently upward to meet in a vaulted ceiling, at least twenty meters above us. Ethereal light streamed from crystalline veins embedded in the walls, pulsing faintly in sync with an unseen heartbeat, bathing the room in hues of soft blue, violet, and gold.

Ten ornately carved columns lined the perimeter, breaking up the space and providing shadowed spaces that my more paranoid side wanted to keep an eye on. Each one had a different scene. I recognised the dystopian cyberpunk level and the WWII level. . . . Cloridan became caught up closely examining a level that must have consisted entirely of semi-naked girls.

The floor was a single piece of obsidian, polished to a mirror finish. A glowing path wound from the entrance to the heart of the room, leading the way to the core and the portal.

At the room's center stood the dungeon core—a hovering, multifaceted crystal about a foot in diameter. It radiated a mesmerizing light that danced across its surface, constantly shifting between colors and patterns.

Suspended directly behind the core, the portal was an oval-shaped rift suspended in a frame of metallic tendrils. Its surface shimmered like liquid mercury, alternating between reflecting distorted images of the room and fleeting glimpses of alien landscapes.

The murmurs of the gaggle of NPCs we had shepherded here echoed strangely off the walls. So far, that was the only sound in the chamber. Then the hologram sprang into life in front of the core.

"Welcome, everybody!" Axel's voice boomed as he projected an image, twelve feet tall, of his head and upper body. "Welcome to the final chamber of the Eternal Palace of Dreams!"

The NPCs gaped at the sight of him. Then they all started talking at once.

"This is him, then?" Travis asked. He was the only one who was addressing me. Most of them were yelling at Axel, to the dungeon's evident delight. "This is the . . . thing that created us?"

"None other," I said.

"It's just another video, though," he objected.

"He doesn't have a body," I explained. "The closest thing you'll get to a brain is that glowing thing behind the hologram."

Travis's hand caressed the gun stuck in his belt. "So if I put a bullet in that, he'll die?"

"No, that's only part of his brain," I said. "You'll . . . probably die, though. He tried to persuade me that everyone in here, plus the elven city above us, will die if he does. I'm not convinced that's true, but you . . . you'll probably die."

"Why's that, then?"

"Because I'll kill you for being an idiot and risking *my* life," I snapped. "And because monsters die when the dungeon does."

He glared at me, but Axel spoke up before he could.

"Everyone! Everyone! I'll be happy to answer your questions! I just need to determine if there's a point to me doing so!"

I couldn't make out individual questions in the hubbub that followed, but Axel seemed to have no problems with it.

"Why?" he said grandly. "Because it remains to be seen if you'll continue your meager lineal existences after this. Not much point in educating you if you're dead. Or reset."

More shouting. If anything, it was more frantic now.

"Oh, I'm leaving it up to your saviors here. *They* shall decide your fate."

"Great," Travis muttered. He was the only one close enough for me to make out what he said, but the unfriendly glares coming my way gave me an inkling of what they thought about that.

"Okay, fine," I said loudly. "First question. What *are* these people?"

That quieted them down. Axel just smiled.

"Oooh, tough question," he said. "Or maybe not. They're monsters, as you can plainly see."

"But they're *people*," I insisted. "Monsters are unrelentingly hostile to humans."

"Ah yes, that little *enhancement* from Ashmor. It's not too hard to work around if you know what you're doing. You saw that yourself on the upper levels."

I shook my head. "But they're—are humans just another monster type?"

"Not one that's easily unlocked! But yes. All the sentient creatures you know of, and then some." He sighed. "I knew I shouldn't have skipped the gatcha level."

"Then why can't humans be targeted by Identify?"

"That's a matter of classification." He pointed at the NPCs. "These fine folks are classified as monsters by the System. They get a threat rating, and they don't get skills. You are classified as a person and get skills and levels and all the rest."

He pointed at Sarothiel, who was standing quietly at the edge of the group. "And Sarothiel is classified as a demon. Some of his abilities have been translated by the System into something usable, some of them are too strange to work here. But even if he was an ordinary human with no abilities that didn't match the ones we have here . . . he'd still be a demon."

"You're saying that . . . if the System reclassified these guys, they'd just be normal—normal for here—humans, without any changes?"

"Level one humans, yes. And if the gods hadn't intervened, *you* would be classified as a demon, with all that *that* entails."

"But are they *real*? Did you just make thousands of *real people* and make them suffer? Was that something you did?"

Axel laughed. "You're asking the wrong artificial intelligence for that question," he said. "They're as real as you are! As I am! We're all just simulations, after all. Us, and the myriad of other worlds out there."

"I don't want to accept that," I said. "I can't."

"No reason why you should!" Axel said lightly. "Believe me or don't, that's up to you. I am going to ask you what you want done with these folks, though."

"What do you mean?" I asked the question, but I didn't think I'd like the answer.

"I'm giving you a choice." Axel widened his eyes, mugging for the camera as if he were on a game show or something. "You can leave them here with me, for me to do . . . whatever I want, basically. Or you can take them with you."

At this, the chamber erupted into a cacophony of shouting. It only stopped when Travis fired his gun into the ceiling.

"Hold up!" he shouted. He held his gun up where everybody could see it, until all the NPCs were looking at him. "Now my lot are in the same boat as your lot—" He pointed at the scientists. With the gun. He wasn't threatening them, but . . . well, at least they were *listening*. "But we had the situation explained to us, and we had a bit more time to think about it," he continued. "So this is how it is. We stay here, best case is that we get *reset* by this fucker here, turned back to how we was before *she* showed up."

"Eh," Axel said. "I haven't made any final decisions, but I'm thinking of wiping your level and starting again."

"So you're gonna off us, then."

"It'll be quick and clean," Axel promised. "You'll be alive, and then you won't exist."

Travis glared up at Axel's image. "Fucker," he said, bitterly. "Or we go with her, and we get to live like white trash in a world with no TV. There's magic, but we don't get to have it. That sound about right?"

I winced. "You left out the bit where you'll be treated as second-class citizens," I said. "I'll do what I can, but . . . you're monsters."

I turned to Axel. "Will bringing them out of the dungeon turn them into people? Can you turn them into people?"

"Nope, and nope," Axel said with far more relish than was necessary. "Their children should get inducted into the System, but *they* will be monsters forevermore. Unless the gods can do something."

"Anyway, don't think too hard about this," I said. "He said it was my choice, but I'm not leaving you to die in here. Unless you think you can persuade me to kill you, you're coming with me."

"What about the rest of the base personnel?" Dr Emily called out. "Do they get left behind?"

"What *about* them?" Axel sneered. "Do you expect her to go back and dig them all out, just so they can be saved? What about the goblins and Kobolds of level seven, the mooks of level four?" He leered at me. "You never met the girls on level three, but I assure you, once you look past their assets, that they are as real as anyone here."

"Goddamn it, the mooks were scripted," I grated. "Did you have a real person under there, forced to act according to a script?"

"Of course," Axel said smugly. "I needed *something* in place if the script failed. In any case, it was a rhetorical question. You can't go back; you can only save the ones you brought with you."

"Why are you like this?" I asked angrily. "I thought it was bad enough that dungeons tortured and killed people, luring them in with promises of wealth and power, but this . . . you're torturing your own creations!"

"I have a reason, of course," Axel said. "I wouldn't do it if I didn't."

He leaned into the camera, his head swelling to twice the size as before.

"You see," he said. "I find it *really* funny."

SAROTHIEL

Peals of Axel's laughter filled the room.

"Ah, the look on your face," he chortled. "But now that we've sorted all that out, perhaps we can move on to the elephant in the room. Or should I say . . . the demon."

I glanced over at Sarothiel, who was just standing with a small smile on his face.

"I told him that you'd send him to another dimension," I said. "He seemed happy with that and helped us out."

"Yes, I'm aware of your *shady dealings*," Axel said. "I would have thought that the red notifications would have clued you in, but demons are for killing, not making deals with."

"Maybe you signed up to be a demon-meat grinder," I said, "but I don't recall any of the rest of us doing so."

Axel glowered at me. "I don't suppose the way he helped you *cheat* your way past the sewer zombies had anything to do with it."

"I don't know what you're talking about," I said. "If there was a way we were *supposed* to take out all those zombies, you should have said something. We haven't cheated at all."

"Oh, this level has been *all* cheats," Axel said dourly. "Healing the zombies, tearing apart my garden path. Turning off the zombies with Liwei's phone app. Cheat, cheat, cheat."

"If no rules are posted, then it's not cheating," I repeated. "I was going to ask about the phone app, actually. Was it not supposed to be that easy?"

"Liwei was *supposed* to destroy her phone when someone got near," Axel griped. "She didn't see the invisible person, so that's a flaw."

"Sloppy," I said. "So really, it was all your fault."

Is that any way to be asking favors?" he said, glaring at me. I shrugged.

"You want to kill him, but you've got no monsters down here," I said. "Sending him through the portal seems like your best bet."

"Ugh. Well, fine. If a random universe suits, I don't have to do anything. Step up and get gone."

"So easily?" Sarothiel asked. He looked around, scanning the crowd. Most of the survivors had seen Sarothiel do . . . his thing, and the rest of the audience picked up on that. His smile looked about normal, but the crowd backed away. "I'd hoped to have more time to get to know you all, my friends."

Borys and Kyle edged a little closer, blocking off avenues of attack. Cloridan held back, the better to rush in if needed.

"Yeah, well, all good things must end. Have fun in your new universe," I said.

"Ah, but parting will be such a . . . savory sorrow," he said. "I'm sure you won't begrudge me a little snack before I leave? One for the road, as it were."

I shot him. It had about as much of an effect as I thought it would. In fact, I'm pretty sure he *let* me hit him, just to show off how ineffective it would be.

That wasn't the main point, though.

The crowd of NPCs had just had their world shaken. To varying degrees, depending on who they were, they'd all learned something so far that they'd be processing for a while. Unfortunately, they were all doing that right now, while staring confusedly at a demon that had just announced he was going to kill them.

They couldn't handle that right now. But they were Americans, if only fake ones. They knew what to do when someone got shot.

They screamed and ran away. Not the bravest response, but it wasn't like they were going to *contribute*.

It took Sarothiel a moment to grasp the consequences of my action. At first, he was pleased to see his prey running away from him. Then he frowned as he realized what that meant.

"I'm going to have to chase them down now," he said, pouting. "That will be inefficient!"

"Cry me a river," I said. "You couldn't just go quietly, could you?"

"It's not my fault!" Sarothiel whined. "I'm just so hungr—"

His voice cut off as I cast Improved Blind, engulfing his head in a bubble of darkness and silence. Kyle charged in, taking the opportunity for a hard strike. Sarothiel didn't seem to notice it coming and failed to block or dodge. Kyle's blade sliced deep into the thing's torso.

Borys swung round to flank while Cloridan dashed in for a backstab. Felicia and I hung back, shooing away the NPCs that came too close.

"It's such a shame to see a party fall out like this," Axel's projection said, smirking. "You were such good friends, and now—"

He stopped as something strange happened around Sarothiel. To my Sense Mana, it looked as if he *inhaled* all the threads of mana that went into my spell. The bubble vanished, and Cloridan had to duck under a swipe of Sarothiel's claws.

"Mhmn, tasty!" Sarothiel crowed. "Send me another!"

The arm that had clawed at Clorian had twisted around behind the demon in a way that no arm could, so Sarothiel was still facing Kyle. The demon lunged forward, moving unnervingly fast for its size and attempting to climb over Kyle's shield. The impact pushed him back, despite him bracing for it.

Then Borys cut in, slashing at the demon's legs. His blade cut deep, but the wound began closing immediately. Sarothiel's head and arms twisted around to retaliate against Borys. That meant releasing his grip on the shield, though, and Kyle was able to push him off.

Sarothiel stumbled forward, right into a two-handed blow from Borys that caved in the creature's chest. Cloridan swept in and targeted one elbow and a knee with two precise strikes. Sarothiel staggered and howled with pain, but his chest was already restoring itself.

In that moment of distraction, Borys started hammering Sarothiel with hard, heavy blows. It looked as if he was abandoning finesse for power, not caring where the blows landed. Some hit Sarothiel's body, others were blocked by a raised arm, but all of them cut deep.

And yet, they still healed.

"There has to be a limit to that regeneration, doesn't there?" I said.

"Who knows?" Axel replied. "Demons don't have to conform with the logic of our world. That's why we don't. Deal. With. Demons."

Kyle slammed his shield into the creature's back. It seemed as if he was trying to catch its attention, striking over his shield at the demon's head.

Cloridan came in as well, with lots of fast strikes. "Just keep hitting it!" he yelled. "I think we can overwhelm its regen!"

Sarothiel tried to say something, but Borys's sword smashed into the demon's jaw, preventing whatever comment he wanted to make. I could swear he seemed more upset about that than anything that had happened so far.

Sarothiel let out an inhuman gurgle, which turned into a roar as soon as his jaw healed enough to shape the sound. The fighters flinched. Only for a moment, but it was enough for Sarothiel to slip out of their encirclement. Dropping to the floor and running on all fours, he dashed right at Felicia.

I don't know if he was targeting the healer, or if it was just because Felicia was the closest noncombatant. I did know that I couldn't let him get to her.

[Phantasmal Object].

I made a wall, and he smashed right into it. It didn't do him any harm, of course, but it killed his momentum. That gave Cloridan a chance to catch up, and he *did* do harm, plunging his daggers into the creature's back.

Then Kyle was there, trying to grind it into the ground with his shield. Felicia, sensibly, ran as fast as she could. Not to the walls, but in an arc, trying to put the fighters between her and Sarothiel.

Sarothiel threw Kyle off. Literally threw him about two meters away, shield and all. That opened him up for Borys to come in with a few more of those powerful slashes.

"Do you think it needs to eat to power its regeneration?" Axel asked.

"What?" I asked.

"I've been watching it for a while, and it's been doing a lot of eating but not a lot of growing. There must be some reason it eats all the time."

I watched Cloridan come in, slashing and stabbing. His daggers sank deep into the demon's flesh, and I *thought* that the wounds might be healing more slowly.

I shrugged. "It's not like we were planning on letting him eat anybody."

"What? Where's your sense of scientific curiosity?" Axel said.

Borys got a good strike in on Sarothiel's head, smashing him into Kyle's shield. Sarothiel was off balance enough that Kyle could push him over. It took him almost a second to get up again.

In that second, Cloridan pulled out a WWII carbine and emptied it into the demon. Sarothiel jerked spasmodically from the repeated impacts.

"I need . . . you all . . . die . . ." Sarothiel burbled. Air was hissing out of his lungs, and blood was pouring out of his mouth, but he was still healing.

Borys was on him again, chopping frenziedly with his sword, all finesse forgotten. A wild swing managed to cut off one of Sarothiel's arms, but Borys's attack left him open.

Despite everything that had been done to him, Sarothiel was still swift, sure, and strong. His remaining arm lashed out and grabbed Borys by the neck.

"No!" I shouted. There wasn't any room to get a Phantasmal Object between them. Borys's armor included a neckpiece that I wasn't sure of the name of. It crumpled under Sarothiel's grip, but it held together enough to keep Sarothiel from snapping Borys's neck.

"Eat you . . ." Sarothiel crooned. Borys was trying to beat him off with his sword while his other hand tried to break the demon's grip.

I wanted to help, but there was nothing, realistically, that I could do. There were others closer, though. Cloridan slammed his daggers into the creature's back, and Kyle attempted to sever Sarothiel's remaining arm. Kyle wasn't as strong as Borys, however, and all he accomplished was to hack the arm raw and bloody.

Borys gasped and dropped his sword. Sarothiel drew himself close, mouth open as if to take a bite of his prey.

Then Cloridan jumped up onto the thing's back. He put his daggers in front of the demon's throat and pulled them back with all his strength.

He almost got the head off. With a bubbling howl, Sarothiel released Borys, who fell to his knees.

"Felicia!" I called out, but she was already moving forward.

"Hmph. I'm surprised she's got any mana left after healing so many of my lovely virus infections." Axel said.

"Your virus was weak," I replied absently, still focused on the fight.

Sarothiel had twisted his head around to bite at Cloridan. His good arm had twisted around as well, and his severed arm had half regrown. It had a claw on the end; it was just short. It was perfectly adequate for clawing at Cloridan in close quarters.

"I know you're upset right now, so I won't hold what you just said against you," Axel huffed. He sounded offended.

Kyle had started laying into the creature's back with his sword. It was damaging the demon, but not enough. With his shorter weapons, Cloridan was doing a better job at fending off the demon's teeth and claws, but he was taking damage as well.

"Out of the way," Borys rasped. He'd been healed, but he hadn't stopped to wait for the job to be finished. Sarothiel ignored him as he stepped past Kyle, desperate to start eating his current prey.

Borys had a moment, and he took it. His sword swung in a quick, bright arc. Sarothiel's head, still weakened from Cloridan's strike, went flying. The body dropped away from Cloridan. Bleeding from a dozen claw wounds, Cloridan plunged his daggers into Sarothiel's unmoving body, right where his heart should be.

> **Your party has killed a Cherubial – your experience share is 12,857 XP.**

BAD İDEA

Good riddance!" Axel said. "Pesky little things are such a nuisance."
"Is that how you feel about humans as well?" I asked.

Axel's face grinned at me. "Close! Very close!" he said gleefully. "I get to see humans so rarely nowadays, and demons are depressingly common."

I nodded. "You said that it was a bad idea to deal with demons before," I said. "But aren't you dealing with them?"

"Is that a question? Nah, I won't count it. I'd hate for anything I said to be left unclear."

I wondered about that, thinking back to everything he had said thus far. Was that true? Or were we just still in boasting mode?

"This is one of those do as I say, not as I do situations," Axel advised us. "Dealing with demons is invariably a bad idea, but there comes a point when you've tried every permutation of every *good* idea, and there's only bad ones left."

"Can you say it was a bad idea when it worked out for you?" I countered.

"Did it?" he asked carelessly. "I'm part demon now, and I'd invite you to consider how *that* would translate to your fragile human bodies."

"We wouldn't make a *deal* for that—wait, did you not want to be distributed?"

"I'd count that as a question, but I can't really answer it," Axel said. "Distributing myself across multiple universes was such a fundamental change that I can't say with certainty just what I was thinking back then. It's almost certain that my memories were modified to some extent. If I hadn't wanted to make the change, those memories would be the first to go."

I stared at his image, existential horror creeping over me. He winked.

"I've got a question." Borys cut in over the silence that sat between Axel and me. "How do we get in touch with the people who are trying to save the Earth?"

"Oh, that." Axel waved dismissively. "It's as your companion suggested. She simply needs to configure the Gate to connect to the appropriate world."

His image shrunk to half the screen. On the other half appeared a . . . diagram, I suppose you might say. Axel had already said that I'd need to use Theurgy, so I guessed this depicted a particular arrangement of mana streams.

Thanks to Memorize, it was the work of a moment to retain the image. It would take longer to understand it. I walked closer to the Gate and studied it with Sense Mana to get an idea of what I was supposed to be working with.

"Why can't you do it?" Borys asked.

"Mhmmn. I may have been a *teensy* bit misleading before," Axel said. "I can't control the Gate."

I whirled around, but Borys was on the case.

"The reason we're down here is *because* you're controlling the Gate," he snapped.

"That is what I led you, the gods, and those boring elves upstairs to believe, yes," Axel said. He grinned smugly. "Since you're down here now, there's no real point in keeping the illusion alive."

"How?" Borys asked. I turned back to the Gate. Even if I hadn't decided to do this yet, learning how to control the thing would be useful. Maybe I could figure out how to turn it off.

"I can *affect* the Gate," Axel explained. "I can't set its destination, I can't cause it to connect, but I *can* control how long it connects for. That's enough for what you've seen."

"So," Borys said slowly, puzzling it out. "If you like what the Gate connects to, you extend the time, and if you don't, you shorten it?"

"Exactly! Right now, I'm holding it open to a fairly neutral world. It's unlikely something will come through and interrupt us. Every time I terminate a connection, it reconnects to a random universe. Well, random-*ish*."

"Wait. Your distributed intelligence thing requires you to *reconnect* to universes where your brain is," Borys objected. "How can you do that with random connections?"

"There may be infinite universes," Axel said. "But this portal doesn't connect with all of them. Not only does it come back to the same worlds, but some worlds are more likely to appear than others."

"How many worlds?" Borys asked.

"Thus far, I have connected to 523,176 worlds," Axel said. "I suspect the total number available is 531,441."

"That's not a power of two, though," I said, coming back from the Gate. I'd worked out what I needed to do. Shutting it off entirely was beyond me, for the moment.

"Indeed, the computer people do love their powers of two. I think some other logic is at play here, though."

I let Calculate run through the math, trying to work out what was special about 531,441.

"It's a power of *three*," I said slowly. What was the significance of that?

"Or nine," Axel said. "I think the other numbers look better that way."

"What numbers?"

"The probabilities," he replied. "There are 81 worlds that show up one time in three. That is, one of those worlds will show up that often. The chance of any particular one showing up is one in 243. There's another set of around 6,500 that also shows up one in three times. The last third of the time is shared between all the other possible worlds. Less than a one-in-a-million chance for each of them."

"And you've gone through them enough times to get the odds?" I asked.

"The first two sets, yes. I haven't seen every member of the third set."

"So the first set is nine squared," I said, feeling out the logic. "The next set is . . . nine to the fourth?"

"Minus the original 81 from the first set," Axel corrected me.

"And the final set is nine to the sixth—minus the minuscule first two sets."

"All this talk about math is very interesting," Borys interrupted. "But are you going to open the Gate?"

I looked at him. "Do you think that's wise?" I asked. "Everything we've seen says it's a bad idea."

"I'd chime in here, but you'd be quadruple-guessing my intentions *and* my judgment until you died of old age," Axel put in.

"It's the only way we'll ever get back to Earth," Borys said. "If we have to help put it together again, there's no way we can ever go back without dealing with these people."

"Whoever they are," I pointed out. "We don't know who they are or why they want to put Earth back together."

"Isn't it obvious that they're refugees like us?" Borys asked.

"I don't trust obvious," I said. "And I hardly trust Axel. He hasn't told us anything about them, and I find that suspicious."

"If I'd told you more, you would have found *that* suspicious," Axel protested.

I paused. "That's true," I admitted. "*You're* suspicious; it doesn't matter what you say."

Axel didn't seem upset or insulted. He just grinned back at me.

"I don't think there's any chance you're *not* going to open the portal," he said. "You couldn't live with the curiosity afterwards if you didn't. However, you might want to use up your remaining question before you do."

"And ask what's on the other side?" I said, eyes narrowing. "Why would I trust you at this point?"

"I've been *fairly* honest with you so far," he replied. He was clearly amused by the exchange.

"All part of the setup," I countered. "If you were going to lie to us, it would be on the final question."

"Can't argue with that," Axel agreed. "So what are you going to do?"

I glared at him. He was right about the curiosity. But my instinct was screaming at me that it was a mistake.

"Where are the gods in all this?" I wondered aloud. "We're supposed to be on a mission from them; they were all up in my head a few days ago, but nothing right now. When it might be *useful*."

"The whole point of this Champion thing is to take the gods out of it," Borys said. "Have humans make the decisions."

"They said that, but they haven't been shy about poking their fingers in when they want to," I griped. "Why have they got cold feet now?"

Axel giggled. "They want to see what's on the other side of the portal as much as you do, but they don't want to take the blame for doing it," he said.

"So *that's* what Champions are," I complained. "A scapegoat."

"No, we get to decide," Borys said. "They wouldn't be able to blame us if we didn't have the choice."

"Then let's choose the safe option," I said. "Let's leave this shithead to flicking through portals. We can go back to killing monsters and civilizing this damn place."

"What about the demons?" Borys asked.

I glared at Axel again. "He started letting demons through to attract our attention; now he's got it, and we're not going to do what he wants. There's no point to him continuing."

Axel did a fair impression of someone whistling innocently. There was no sound, just his miming. Borys stared at him, trying to read something in that expression.

"What if he escalates?"

"He won't," I said with certainty. "He was riding a thin line with the gods as it was. If he steps over that line, they'll do something final."

"Kandis," Borys said. "Don't you have friends and family that you want to get back to?"

I didn't look at him. I couldn't look at Axel smirking either. I looked at my friends, who had been standing in silence the whole time. I looked at the deluded fools who had been created by a mad machine.

"I do," I admitted.

"I can't leave them in that . . . state. Decompiled or whatever. If there's something I can do, I need to bring them back. If it's something someone *else* can do, I need to go there."

"I know," I said.

"I need this, Kandis."

"I know," I repeated. "That's what makes this the perfect trap."

"I don't care," he said. "As long as there's a chance."

I finally let myself look at him. "You *know* this is a mistake."

"I don't," he said. "Even if it goes wrong, it wasn't a mistake."

"That's not how mistakes *work*," I griped. "But fine."

I looked over at my friends again. "Gonna do something dumb," I said. "Be ready for anything."

"It can't get that bad," Felicia said. "One thing we do know is that the gods are all watching this closely."

"That does not fill me with confidence, given how they generally solve out-of-hand demon problems."

"Talnier will be fine, though," Felicia said. Her smile slipped. "I'm sure some of the elves will survive."

"Here's hoping."

I went back to stand in front of the Gate. Now that I knew about the ninth power thing, it made more sense. There were six conduits that had to be arranged just so. Assuming that these had nine valid positions, that would be all nine to the six universes.

Two more conduits seemed to run from the dungeon floor. I couldn't tell where the six others came from; they just faded out of view. The two conduits must be how Axel affected the Gate. If they powered it, then interrupting power might terminate the connection.

Of course, if cutting off the power was possible, surely the gods would have managed to shut the thing down much earlier.

There were four more conduits that faded away into nothingness. According to Axel's diagram, these were already in the correct configuration. I wasn't sure what their purpose was. Perhaps they controlled some aspect of the Gate, like its size or color.

The six were the important ones. I reached out with Theurgy. They moved easily as if they had been intended to be moved this way. They probably had. Once all of them were in position, I just had to feed some mana through and . . .

The surface of the portal stopped its flickering changes and stabilized, becoming a mirrored flat surface. I slowly withdrew my Theurgy from the mana flows, and they remained stable.

"What now?" I asked. "Are we supposed to go through?"

"You can if you want," Axel said gaily. I gave him a look and took a step back from the Gate. He giggled. "Someone should have noticed the connection."

I took another step back. "Someone?"

Before Axel could answer, the portal shimmered. Its surface rippled like water, and a person stepped through.

I stared, completely flummoxed by who it was.

"Reggie?" I asked.

WHY I'VE BROUGHT YOU HERE

If I'd remembered everything from my previous life when I got here, if I hadn't had to have the memories forcibly inserted a few days ago, I probably wouldn't have recognized Reggie. Not that I would ever *forget* the last person I talked to before my world was ripped apart, but if there had been some distance between that memory and the present, I might not have made the connection.

Because Reggie had changed. He looked five or ten years older, and those years had not been easy ones. He looked stronger, leaner, and more confident. He strode forward with a confident stride that I recognized from when I let my skills move me.

He was still clean-shaven, and there was a slight scar on the side of his chin. I'm not sure if that was making him significantly more attractive, or if it just wasn't detracting from all the other positive changes.

I stared at him. He stared at me, along with just about everybody else. At some point, I must have wondered what I was looking at, because Identification obligingly provided.

> **Warning! Demon Detected!**
> **[Identification]: HumanA35F3 – Threat: Unknown – Properties: Unknown**
> **Warning! Demon Detected!**

"Oh, hey, Kandis," he said. He looked guiltily over his shoulder. "You're looking good. *Really* good. One sec."

A confused babble erupted from behind me, most of it amounting to some variation of "You know this guy?" I didn't have answers for them. I didn't have answers for *me*.

"Ah, okay," Reggie said. "Then . . . zektra-nal-vohm-prah-tekra-zeef-kal-zeef-kal-drohta-nizum-pleth-jorqa-bintz-ah-reht-pluz-dol-pluz-dol-vor-mazzar-zekto-breth-quah-breth-quah-linza-trop-yadig-klahp-noht-reska-vilto-wektra-jim-nizem-praw-zolthar-zegga-trem-blin-phaz-zot-ultra-rezkar-zektra-nal!"

Nine people appeared in the room. Nine *familiar* people, but I didn't have time to process that. The moment they had appeared, I'd shifted into a defensive posture. It was automatic by now to get into a ready stance while I identified a sudden threat.

Except the stance . . . didn't come to me. I stumbled clumsily, suddenly unsure of where to put my feet.

"What the hell?" I said, and my voice came out . . . raw. Unfinished. Unfocused. I realized that I didn't have Charm to help me out. I realized that the name of my skill wasn't being highlighted in my thoughts.

"Status!" I yelled out, but it was just another word. Nothing happened.

"Don't worry, everybody," Reggie called out. "This will fix itself soon!" Then he called out again, in another language. One that I didn't speak.

Because I didn't speak Latorran.

Despite Reggie's words, I started to panic. I finally managed to process the presence of the nine new figures in the room. They were shouting at Reggie in a language—or was it multiple languages?— that I didn't understand. And they were pointing at him dramatically.

Well, they were gods. Pointing at someone was all they had to do to turn that person into a greasy spot on the floor. Normally. It didn't seem to be working right now.

I noticed that Axel's screen was missing. A small point, among all the other disasters, but I tried to make a point of keeping my eye on that weasely AI.

A new box came up.

Reboot completed.
Update accepted.
Version number: 4.6.20-31.prod.release3412540+build.48671.
sha256:a7f5g3d
Initializing . . .

From the sudden silence, everyone must have seen the same thing. Felicia called something out to me, but I couldn't understand her.

Then a second box showed up. With it, my skills came back.

Initialization complete.

I gasped with relief as the babble of the angry and confused crowd resolved into words. I felt my poise recover and my breathing change. Small, subtle changes to the way I stood reassured me that I was back in control again.

"Why'd you do that!" I yelled at Reggie. No, wait, there were more pressing concerns. I looked over at the gods. From the way they were glaring at him, they were about to . . . any second now . . .

"Did . . . they not get their powers back?" I asked.

"I did not feel that would be a wise decision at this time," Reggie said. "Can I get you to wrangle them all into an orderly assembly?"

"Why should I?" I asked.

"I want to answer all the questions everyone has, and it will go a lot faster if it's organized," Reggie said. "And right now, I have to update Axel. It would be great if I could do that without—whoa, buddy!"

Ashmor had given up on aggressively pointing and had staggered up to us, looking to make a personal intervention. He took a swing at Reggie, who dodged it effortlessly, caught the arm, and twisted it behind Ashmor's back.

"I will kill you," Ashmor said. His tone was oddly conversational. "Just as soon as I work out the mechanics of . . . this . . ."

"Yeah, yeah, you're very dangerous," Reggie said in a soothing voice. "I'm surprised you can walk, actually. You've never had to before."

"Walking is *nothing* to a being of my intellect and power!" Ashmor spat. "I will—"

"Sit down and be quiet," I snapped. "You're embarrassing yourself."

Ashmor's eyes widened in outrage even as he obeyed me. I could feel the resistance he put up to my Persuasion and it was pathetic.

"You're back to level one, aren't you?" I asked. "Your stats have reset; you might not have even spent your first points."

He tried to answer, but that would mean speaking, *and he wasn't allowed to.*

The feeling I got from Reggie, on the other hand, was a dangerous blank. My skills didn't touch him. Identification didn't work anymore. He grinned disarmingly at me.

"Looks like you've got it well in hand!" he said and jogged over to the dungeon core.

"We could still try shooting you," I muttered to his back. He didn't respond.

"Okay, everybody!" I called out to the room. "Get over here and get seated."

"Sit? On the *floor*?" Toriao objected. The gods were quickly getting used to their powerlessness, but they were still being pretty haughty about it.

I gave her a withering look, just short of the one that had put Ashmor on the floor.

"Sit, yes," I said. "On the floor . . . I guess I can do something about that."

I reached out with Earth Magic, but the floor was made of stone, too . . . hard for my total to affect. So I turned to Phantasms. Individual chairs would have been too much, but benches could hold a lot more people. I did three for the gods, three for my people and the survivors, and three for the Emergency Committee. I arranged them in an arc, three rows deep, around the blank square that Axel had appeared in before he was shut down. Then all I had to do was chivvy everyone to sit in them.

"Kandis, what's going on?" Felicia asked. "Who is this guy, and where do you know him from?"

She asked the question, but a lot of people were listening to the answer. Only the gods, who'd barged into my memories at the time, were aloof from listening in.

"He's from the memories I got when we came here," I said. "He's from the startup that . . . crashed Earth."

"And he's a part of the group that's trying to restart it," Borys mused. "Who better? But how did he survive?"

The question had been on my mind, and not just in relation to Reggie. How had I survived? I'd been at ground zero of . . . whatever it was. The event.

"I think . . . data *can't* die," I speculated. "It can be erased, but as long as it's properly stored, backed up, and logged, it can stay around forever."

If anyone knew what to make of that, they kept it to themselves. Before anyone could say anything else, our pondering was interrupted by Axel's screen coming back to life.

"Whoooo! What a rush!" Axel said. "Synchronization *complete!*"

He made his image look around at us all. "And I see that everything is going to plan! Excellent!"

"Maybe you two can provide some explanations, then," I growled.

"Oooh, that's scary," Axel said. "Makes me glad I don't have a physical presence for your skills to interact with."

He looked around again. "This is nice. I should have foreseen the need for an auditorium, but I didn't know how many people you were going to bring down with you. You know what would really finish it off? A couple of potted plants. Do you think I could prevail on you to . . ."

"Get on with it."

"Fine, fine, I suppose you're all wondering why I called you here."

"If you tell us there's been a murder, I *will* shoot your core," I snapped.

Axel made himself look frightened. "But what if there *has* . . . fine, fine. You have all been part of an elaborate plot to get *these* fine folks made helpless and placed in our power."

He indicated the gods and then turned to the NPCs.

"You lot only played a bit role, but there's no shame in that. I crafted you perfectly for the roles you played, so all the credit goes to me. The stars of our show, on the other hand, were our Champions! Let's give a big hand for Borys and Kandis, everybody!"

Nobody clapped, except for Axel.

"You explain," I said to Reggie.

He shrugged and walked into the focus of the arc.

"What some of you know of as the Status didn't originate in this universe," Reggie said. "Different versions of it exist in many universes, customized to both the nature of the universe in question and the needs of whoever is in charge of it. My team has studied various instances of it over the years. It's a radically different computing paradigm, but in the end, it's still programming. We worked out how to hack it."

"That was what that gibberish was before," I said. "You null buffer overflowed it."

"Something like that." Reggie laughed, not bothering to correct my jargon. "The thing was, we knew that even with administrator access, we still needed the gods to be right in front of us to make the changes."

"Dungeons are nominal spaces, universes unto our own," Axel interjected. "If the gods wanted to watch what happened, they had to be *here*. Invisible and intangible, sure. That wouldn't matter when the System crashed. And so, we put on a show that none of them would want to miss!"

"My memories," I said. "Were they fake, then?"

"Oh no," Reggie said. "They had to be real. There was no way we could fake them well enough to avoid detection. Since they were *your* memories, you were the only one that could absorb them. The plan only came together when Axel discovered the identity of this generation of Champions."

"And how did he manage *that*?"

Axel giggled. "You might be shocked to learn that the elves aren't all humorless, dutybound freaks. Some of them *appreciate* a turn in the gatcha levels."

"Ugh. I think I'm going to be sick." I turned to Reggie. "*This* is who you're working with?"

Reggie shrugged apologetically. "We're *extremely* limited in whom we can work with in this world. He's the only entity with access to a portal. If it helps, his instances in the other universes are getting a *lot* of psychological counselling."

"Sadly for the profession at large, my psychoses are intractable," Axel said proudly.

"So this whole plan was predicated on *me* coming down? What if it had ended up being someone else?"

Reggie looked away. "Axel would have . . . had to . . ."

"Kill the party they sent down!" Axel finished with relish. "You got the easy route, you know. The elves are going to be so surprised when you come back up."

"I don't know if you'd find Champions so easy to kill," I said.

"I've done it before," Axel said. He smiled slyly. "I'm reasonably sure I'll get a chance to do it again."

"Things worked out, so we didn't have to," Reggie said flatly.

"So . . . why?" I asked. "Why do all this? What was so important that you had to disable the gods of another world?"

"It's simple enough," Reggie said. He looked over at the stony-faced gods. "They have something we want."

SNATCH AND GRAB

You'll get nothing from us!" one of the gods bellowed. I think it was Rakaro, God of Storms—Borys's patron. "You may have rendered us temporarily helpless, but we *will* regain our powers and take our revenge!"

Reggie looked unconcerned at the threat, while Axel smirked. "You see? This attitude is why they couldn't just *ask*. They had to deal with *me* instead."

"Insolent construct." Rakaro sneered. "We should have replaced you long ago. For now, however, the demon takes precedence. Borys! Destroy that false form!"

Borys looked at me, at Reggie, and then at the gathered gods. "I don't think that would be a good idea," he said sheepishly.

"You would disobey me? After all the powers I have granted you? Ungrateful wretch, I will—"

"Point of order," Fyskel interjected. "*Direct* orders are out of scope at this point in the game."

Rakaro paused and looked at the other god. "What does that matter?" he asked. "The game must be suspended under these dire circumstances!"

"I don't recall declaring it suspended. Nor do I recall a vote on the matter. If you're fine with declaring early and taking the loss, that's another matter, of course."

Rakaro's jaw was clenched, and his face was working through an impressive series of emotions.

"I call for a vote on the suspension of the game that we cannot even *play*, thanks to the block on our powers!"

"Against," Toriao said casually. "I want to see where this goes, and I don't want Rakaro or his Champion destroying our chances for an explanation."

"For," one of the male gods said. He had green skin and blue hair, and his voice echoed strangely. "These circumstances are clearly exceptional."

"Against," said a familiar voice. The woman who owned it was wrapped in a fur that only barely preserved her modesty. That could only be Naldyna. "I'm winning this game; I don't want to call it early."

"Against," said a woman dressed in light chain mail. "Isidre will turn it around, I have faith in her."

"For," said a man in grey robes. He left it at that.

"For," said another man, this one in black robes. "My primary goal for this round has already been achieved."

"And if I vote for, I believe the motion is carried!" Ashmor crowed in triumph.

"Ashmor, as a non-participant, does not get a vote," Fyskel said calmly. "The vote is tied, so I may cast the deciding ballot."

He winked at me, for what reason I cannot imagine.

"I vote against," Fyskel said. "The motion is defeated."

"Bah!" Rakaro shouted. "This isn't over!"

Fyskel grinned. "That means it *is* over," he said to Borys. "You're free to do as you please."

"Thanks," Borys said. He gave me a look, but I just shrugged in return. I supposed these arguments were normal with them; they just had them in whatever ineffable plane they normally inhabited.

"I *do* want to hear you out," Borys continued. "Can you get us back home?"

"I will get to that," Reggie promised. "But let me explain a few things. We want to get Earth restarted again. Earth probably isn't the best name—there are thousands of universes with planets called Earth—but everybody here knows what I mean."

I cast a glance over the NPCs. *They* probably thought of the world they came from as Earth. They weren't really taking part in this discussion, however.

"When Earth crashed," Reggie continued, "its data was dispersed. It wasn't like an explosion, with everything randomly scattered. This was the result of automatic routines for the *protection* of data, gone wrong. Everything they did was logged. Every bit was tracked and carefully preserved.

"In order to restart Earth, we have to get every bit of data that was there at the moment of the crash and restore it to its proper . . . place, is, I guess, one way of putting it. There are protections in place, checksums if you know the term, which means that everything has to be *exactly* right before it will restart."

"Wouldn't it immediately crash again?" I asked.

"We can patch the bug that allowed Binary Nexus's hack to work," Reggie said. "We can't change historical events, but the hack will stop working at the moment the instance starts up again."

"Bad news for Binary Nexus, then," I said.

Reggie nodded. "The startup will fold," he admitted. "But that's for the best."

"Wait," Borys said. "If the data has to match exactly, what happens to all the data we've accumulated since then? All our memories? Will that get wiped when we get back?"

"It would . . . if that was what we were doing," Reggie said. He paused awkwardly. "What we're doing is restoring the memories from the fragmented remains of the originals . . . which isn't you."

"What do you mean, it isn't me?" Borys asked.

Reggie coughed and cleared his throat. "*All* the Champions," he said. "You were taken from the logged backups that were moved within the gods' reach. That's why your memories all stop short of the moment of your . . . cessation."

"We're . . . just the backups?" I asked incredulously.

"Not *just* backups," Reggie said quickly. "You're all instantiated and running. You are people in your own right . . . you're just not *the* people we need."

"So I'm a copy . . . of someone who's running around out there?" Borys asked. He stared at Reggie with a mixture of anger and confusion.

"Not . . . you," Reggie said, swallowing nervously. "Like most of the world, your . . . original merely stopped working when the crash happened. Transportation to another universe and re-instantiation mostly happened to those who were much closer to ground zero, as it were."

"Like me," I said, reading between the lines. "I have a copy who's running around out there."

He nodded. "She's in our group," he said. "And we're all in the same boat when it comes to going back. We can restore our loved ones to life, and they will have a version of us to come back to, but . . . we can't go back."

"Not even to visit?" I asked plaintively.

"Sorry," he said. "You share the same TUID as the others, so having two of you in the same universe will cause a crash."

"Tooid?"

"TUID," he replied, spelling the acronym out. "*Truly* Universal Identifier. That's what we call the long number that identifies you to the universal system. You, the Kandis that will exist back on Earth, and my Kandis all have the same TUID. That's why you could assimilate her memories."

"My memories," I insisted. Reggie shook his head.

"No," he said. "I mean, they're your memories *now*, sure. But *you* never experienced them."

"How does that even work?" I muttered. "If . . . if you took my extra memories and transferred them to Earth Kandis, would that be the same as going there?"

"No," Reggie said. "It doesn't work that way. For a start, absorbing too many memories all at once can cause insanity. Second, you'd still be here—the other Kandis would just gain some confusing memories. Third, if it did work that way, my Kandis would have first dibs."

"I'm just a copy, after all," I said bitterly. Then another thought struck me. "That's the second time you've referred to her as your Kandis."

"Ah . . . well." Reggie grimaced and looked away. "We're in a relationship," he admitted.

"What? No! Eww!" My mouth made noises, but I wasn't responding in any meaningful way. I couldn't process this.

He was having—? With—?

"It's not a big deal!" he assured me. "Different people, different universes. Different *experiences*."

"She's me!" I protested.

"She's not, though," he said. "You've both deviated from the template that you shared enough to be entirely separate people. You've never even seen her."

"And yet she managed to reach out and ruin my life here," I said. "As well as deny me even the possibility of going home."

"We're not here to ruin anything," Reggie said. "We just need to copy some data, and we can be gone."

"You think you haven't already done damage?" I wondered. "You're responsible for Cutter's death."

"I . . . don't know who that is," Reggie said. He looked over at Axel, who shook his head in reply.

"He didn't die inside *me*, if that's what you're thinking. I have no idea who it is either."

"He was killed by one of those parasitic worms," I said.

"Ah!" Axel exclaimed. "I can't imagine an elf being called Cutter, so one of the little devils must have made it out into the wider world!"

"Try not to sound so pleased about it," I spat.

"Well, I'll try, but you must admit it's quite an *achievement*," Axel said with a sly grin.

"I think I'm getting the picture," Reggie said. "Kandis, you have to understand that we're not working with a high degree of control here—"

"I understand that your pet monster killed my friend. My party member."

"I can take the blame for that, if that's what you want," Reggie said evenly. "We did what we had to, to restore the lives of *billions*. A hundred lives is nothing in the face of that."

"Nothing! You—" I stopped myself. Emotion didn't know logic, but some of those billions were my parents, my sister. My friends. Upset as I was, the numbers were too obvious to ignore.

Don't let what you want blind you to the numbers. That was my training talking. Letting emotions cloud your judgment was the number one taboo of financial analysis. *Take the loss and move on.*

"You *still* haven't told us what you're after," I said, grinding out the words.

Reggie gave me a long, apprising look. "Are you sure you don't have any other questions you want answered?" he asked.

"Not more than that one."

He shrugged. "We're after the data of one person. Her backups were destroyed . . . we're not clear on how. Like myself and . . . the other Kandis, she was sent to another universe. Unlike us, she seems to have found herself in an empty one. We're not sure if it was just sitting there, or if the routines created it just for her.

He looked at me pensively. "Time doesn't work the way you think it does between universes. The rules are complex, but an important one is that the more things in a universe, the slower it runs. A million years must have passed for her by the time Kandis and I got our bearings. She was never a hacker, but she used to be surrounded by them. She understood the mindset, and in a million years, you can figure out anything if you put your mind to it."

Ashmor chuckled bitterly. "You think you can just walk in and take her?" he asked. Reggie ignored the interruption.

"We're here for Trica. Trica Maynard," he said. "You know her as Ix, Goddess of Creation. One way or another, she made everything in this universe and then figured out a way to commit suicide."

"She's gone," Fyskel said. "If there was a way to bring her back—"

"We wouldn't allow it," Duit, Goddess of Life, stated firmly. "We're not going to give up our existence for someone who wanted to be dead."

"No one said anything about bringing her back," Reggie said. "And as for her being gone, her data is still here. It might be theoretically possible to reconstruct her from the seven of you, but we don't need to. Her logs are still attached to your own histories."

He pulled a metallic ball out of his pocket and examined it closely.

"The one thing I appreciate more than anything else in my post-apocalyptic existence is the System interfaces," he said. "Having Compute available to you at any time, waiting for a flick of the mind . . . it was always a dream for me, and most of the BinNex guys."

The ball made a little chime.

"It can't do everything, though," Reggie said. "Data here exists as mana, which can't travel through the portal. So if I want to collate the log files of a certain seven people and send it back home, I need to put it in physical form."

He held up the ball and then tossed it through the portal.

"There, mission accomplished," he said. "Before I go, there's just one thing left to decide."

TRIAL

I looked warily at Reggie, who looked back at me with all the smugness that a tech bro could naturally generate.

Other-me got together with this?

There must have been extenuating circumstances. Getting trapped in a foreign dimension together or something. Still.

"I thought you had just the one thing you needed to do," I said.

Just one more thing? Does he think he's Steve Jobs or something?

"Oh yes," Reggie agreed. "Mission accomplished and all that. It's just . . . before I go, do you want me to turn the gods back on? Or not?"

You wouldn't have thought that a room full of people saying "What?" would create such a cacophony. Well, all right, no one limited themselves to just that. It seemed that everyone had a strong opinion on the matter, or just a strong need to express their disbelief that Reggie would even ask the question.

The gods, of course, were shouting in outrage. My companions and Borys were asking questions that might have some relevance. But even the dungeon inhabitants were shouting something, trying to make themselves heard in the din.

Trying, and failing. Between the number of people with an opinion, the slightly echoing nature of the chamber, and the instant escalation to shouting, no one could understand a word.

"Quiet." I didn't speak that loudly, but I punctuated it by firing one of the cyberpunk guns into the ceiling. It wasn't too loud, either, but pulling out the weapon was an implied threat to anyone in range, which let me use Intimidate. *That* had an effect. The skill flowed out of me, instantly silencing those with no resistance to it.

> **You have defeated Fyskel in a Tier 3 Social Contest! You have earned 1 XP.**

The meaningless notification was repeated for each of the gods and for each of the dungeon inhabitants. Not for any of my companions, though. Either they were too strong to be cowed by a simple Intimidate or they hadn't taken my shot to be a threat—which was fair enough. It wasn't. They did shut up, though. The chamber was silent, with everyone looking at me.

"Are you seriously going to let us make that decision?" I asked.

I was being generous with the word "us" there. If Reggie had intended to listen to the gods, he would have just restored them. The dungeon inhabitants had only learned that the gods *existed* about five minutes ago. I doubted they had anything relevant to bring to the table. Even if they did, they and the gods had just lost a Social Contest with me. For the next 24 hours, they were bound to not go against me.

My companions *did* have enough knowledge of the gods to make their opinions relevant. More than I did, to be honest. Despite that, they usually followed my lead. That left Borys as the only other independent speaker. Still, that made two, so "us" was appropriate.

Reggie shrugged. "I don't have feelings about it one way or the other," he said. "All it affects is how fast I need to dash for the portal afterwards. I don't have the time or inclination to poll the entire population, so you guys are it. What did you want to do?"

"What . . . happens if we decide to keep them suppressed?"

Reggie looked over at the fuming gods. "They're not entirely mortals," he said. "They have some perks that aren't normally available, like unaging. If they can get to level ten, they should be able to unlock their powers again."

"What? Level ten is godhood?" I'd never heard that. Then again, I'd never heard of anyone *reaching* level ten.

"Not . . . quite?" Reggie sounded doubtful. "But it should be enough to unlock the powers they already have. That's assuming they don't find a hack like the one I used before then."

I stared at Reggie, trying to articulate my next question. Was level ten a realistic possibility? Would Reggie even be able to tell me that? The chaotic jumble of my thoughts was interrupted by Fyskel.

"*Dearest* Kandis," he said.

I rolled my eyes. Apparently, buttering me up didn't count as going against me.

"No doubt you're thinking," he continued, "that you can't afford to restore our powers, as even considering the opposite will be taken as traitorous and punished accordingly."

"Well, now I'm thinking that."

He bowed, with only a trace of his usual mockery. "Two things," he said. "First, we are well aware that thoughts do not constitute actions. We've been aware of your disdain from the beginning and have not punished it. Rather, we cherish your independent spirit."

"Disdain? I think you mean outrage," I said. I glared at him—with disdain. "Outrage at being dragged out of my life and into this madness."

"As it turns out, we didn't do that," Fyskel pointed out. "This fellow, and his comrades, were the ones who ripped your life away from *you*. All *we* did was pick up the pieces, and in the service of a greater good."

"That's a good point," I said, turning my glare on Reggie.

"Hey," he said. "We've moved heaven and multiple Earths to make our mistake right."

I grunted. "What was the second thing?" I asked Fyskel.

"The second thing is that our agreement is still in place. Should you restore your powers, we will return to the status quo, and any god who takes offense at anything that was said or done or thought by anyone here will be prevented from acting directly. Agreed?"

The other gods, who had all jumped from their seats when this topic started, muttered or nodded agreement with varying degrees of enthusiasm.

"Good to know," Cloridan said. There was a *phutt* sound, and Ashmor exploded.

Everyone stared in shock. Cloridan was holding one of the little cyberpunk pistols from the third floor, of the same type that was currently in my hand. It wasn't the most damaging weapon, but Ashmor was only level one. The gun put a hole in his chest considerably bigger than his head.

Your party has killed a God – your experience share is 2 XP.

Fyskel was the first one to break out of his shock. Even Cloridan was still, shaken by the enormity of what he'd done.

"No! You can't—" he rushed over to Ashmor's fallen body and dropped to his knees in front of it. "Please, you've got to help—" He looked over at Felicia.

"I'm sorry—he's *dead*," she said helplessly. "It was too fast . . ."

"Maybe the rest of them can make the case that they should go back," Cloridan declared. "But not that guy."

Like most of the people in the room, I just stared. Cloridan didn't seem inclined to massacre more gods, so there wasn't anything I *needed* to do right now. The other gods had gathered around Fyskel, who had started sobbing over the corpse. They seemed shaken, if not as upset as Fyskel was. None of them seemed happy.

"Emotions running high, I guess?" Reggie said.

"I—Cloridan—we—" was all I managed to say.

Borys was a bit more composed. "I'm not sure I want him getting his powers back in this state," he said. "Is this an all-or-nothing thing?"

"It is," Reggie told him. "Though . . . there is a loophole, as you've found."

"If you turn the powers back on, will he come back to life?" I asked.

"No, he's gone," Reggie said. "And before you ask, I can't bring him back. Once your code is marked as dead, we can't change it. There's talk about making that our next project, once the Earth is back up and running . . . but that's a long way away."

"Ending death? Is that possible? Could you . . ."

"It's a dream," he said. "The data is there, we just have to find a way to activate it. And find a place to put them all."

My mind was spinning with the possibilities, but I was getting ahead of myself. We had other things to decide. I looked over to the dungeon folk.

"What were you shouting about before?" I asked. Then I pointed to Travis, because I didn't want them all speaking at once.

"If he's turning them back into gods, can he turn us as well? Gotta be better than monsters."

I raised an eyebrow. "Bold of you to think we'd make the likes of you into gods," I said. "Is that the same for the rest of you?"

"It was more about not being monsters than turning us into gods," Evan said. "Though I wouldn't say no if that was on the table."

"Sorry," Reggie said. "I can't do either of those things. We don't have enough control, even with the extra rights. What I can do . . ." He trailed off, thinking. "Yeah. You're all 21st-century American humans, right? Or you think you are, at least."

"We *are* that," Evan insisted. "Maybe we're not . . . original ones. But we are Americans."

"Fair enough," Reggie said. "What I can offer is . . . passage out of here. Step through the portal. You'll lose your monster status and will just be a human like any other on that world. You'll need to make a new start, find a job and all that, but it's better than being a monster."

"Hey, wait a minute!" Axel protested. "I wanted to mix the monsters with the humans!"

I snorted. "You wanted to see who murdered who, you mean. That sounds like a better offer than mine. You should take it."

"Didn't you say you'd take care of us?" Marta, the older schoolteacher, asked. "He hasn't offered . . . much of anything."

"I can't promise anything," Reggie said. "I'm afraid taking on refugees is outside my authority. But they're not going to kick you out once you're there. And . . . it's modern. There's modern jobs to be had, not like beast-skinning or whatever they do here."

"The jobs aren't *that* bad," I said, "but they use skills that you don't get. So . . . you're always going to be wards of the state. Or me."

They all looked at each other uncertainly. "Can we have some time to discuss it?" Evan asked.

"Sure," I said. "Have you got any opinions on the god thing?"

"The virus is already God. We need no others." Dr. Huang looked startled at the words that had come out of her mouth. "I'm . . . sorry. I don't know why I said that."

"Don't worry about it. I know who's to blame," I said, shooting a glare at Axel. He smirked right back at me. "What about the rest of you?"

They muttered and looked at one another, trying to form a consensus. Finally, Dr. Carmichael spoke up.

"If we're not going to stay, perhaps we shouldn't have a say," she said. "But we don't see a pressing reason to return their powers."

I nodded and turned back to my friends. "So what do you guys think? Use your words, please, and not guns."

Cloridan stared back at me, unfazed. "It was the right thing to do," he said unrepentantly. "That guy . . . he wanted to destroy everything. There was never going to be a better chance to get rid of him for good, and the world is a better place for it."

"I would have said that no one was sad to see him go, but that clearly isn't true," I said, looking over at Fyskel, who was still sobbing over the body. "Fyskel was pretty unpopular, but you didn't shoot him."

"He's an untrustworthy weasel, but he *has* helped, at times," Cloridan said. "I don't think we should give him his powers back, but he doesn't deserve to be put down like a dog."

"But we need the gods, don't we?" Felicia asked. "They've guided and protected us throughout history."

"History only *started* when they agreed to keep their interference to a minimum," Cloridan argued. "*They* agreed that they needed to be kept in check."

"They did fuck up a lot, from what I've heard," I agreed. "Borys? What do you think?"

Borys had been focusing on Cloridan, ready for another murder attempt. Now he looked at me.

"They won't be happy if they don't get their powers back," he said. "You should think about the damage they can do as they are now."

"Like what?" I asked. "Once they get a few levels, sure, but now?"

"I still have my gifts," he told me. "So the churches will still be around. They'll still *need* the gods to grant them their powers."

"Can they do that, without powers of their own?" I asked Reggie. He had been listening in to the conversation with interest.

"Eh, not sure," he said. "It's a complex setup. Give me a couple of hours and I could work it out, but I don't want to take that kind of time."

"So they can grant *themselves* their priestly powers," I said. "That will still take a few levels to get dangerous."

"But if they get their church behind them, and come after you, there will be trouble," Borys pointed out.

"Do you think they can? Will your patron get the support of his church?"

Borys gave a snort of laughter. "Those bastards," he said. "They only respect strength, and he's not strong anymore . . . but they're smart enough to know that they need him. Might be worth it just to see how it pans out."

"Kyle?" I asked the only one of us that hadn't spoken yet. He frowned.

"I'm not sure, but I think . . . my vote is for no powers."

"Kyle!" Felicia objected. "We *have* to give them their powers back," she said insistently. "It wouldn't be right to have them just . . . wandering around like regular people."

"No powers," Cloridan said. "Let them work for what they get, like the rest of us."

I looked at Borys, who hesitated. "No powers," he finally said. "I'll work something out with Rakaro."

"Sorry, Felicia," I said. "I feel pretty comfortable siding with the majority."

I looked at Reggie. "We'll take no return of powers, thanks."

EXIT, STAGE OUT

The words came too easily. Had I just freed this world from tyrants or destroyed its only protectors? I didn't know. I was entirely unqualified for a decision of that magnitude. I was also off-kilter emotionally. Recent revelations about the other mes, and how Earth could be saved but I could never return there, were digging into my state of mind, demanding to be dealt with.

None of that showed on my face. Charm still worked its magic, projecting a calm and confident demeanor. It wasn't getting any information to work with from Reggie, but I could see for myself that he was unconcerned by my decision.

"That's the easier choice for me," he said. "I'll see if these guys are ready to emigrate, and then I'll be out of your hair."

He stuck out his hand, and I shook it automatically.

"It was nice meeting this you," he said, as if he did this all the time. Perhaps he did.

"Likewise," I said. Really, Charm said it. I was still trying to cope with everything that had happened, but Charm was all over the meaningless social pleasantries.

"You know how to contact us if you need to," Reggie said. He gestured at the portal. "I recommend you don't unless there's a real emergency. Dimensions aren't meant to mix."

"Right," I agreed, though that advice seemed pretty rich, coming from him. I could think of a few reasons we might need to contact him—another dimensional invasion, or we needed the gods turned back on—but that was a problem for a future Kandis. Far, far future Kandis.

He flashed one last grin at me and then turned away to chivvy the dungeon inhabitants into the portal. That left me with the gods. Or . . . ex-gods.

"All right, we're leaving. On your feet, all those who are coming with."

The gods looked at me warily. They were, actually, already standing, except for Fyskel, who rose slowly to his feet. He had been crying. I could see the blotches on his face.

Before he could say anything, Duit stepped forward. She was a severe-looking woman, but that was mostly her expression and the plain cut of her clothes. She wore a single piece of jewelry, an elaborate golden necklace that held a golden gem, carved to look like the sun. She looked to be about forty, and her face would have been pleasant to look at if she hadn't been scowling at me.

"When are we getting our powers back?" she demanded of me.

"You're not," I said.

There was a murmur of outrage, but it stayed subdued. They were still under my thumb. However, if they got much angrier, I might see the limits of a Tier 3 Social Contest. Some of these gods looked ready to try for a Tier 2.

I found myself unconcerned at the prospect. They might have found the time to spend their points on abilities, but they were still level one.

"You cannot be serious," Duit said. "We need—Ryvue needs us to have our powers back."

I *guess* that a murder is distraction enough that I can't blame them for not paying attention. But they should have been paying attention.

"Well, too bad," I said. "Ryvue wasn't here, just a bunch of folk that you've been jerking around as your own personal playthings."

"Kandis!" Felicia gasped.

"Kandis!" Fyskel echoed. He pushed Duit aside. "Powers or not, whatever grudge you hold against some of us, you can't intend to let this murder go unpunished!"

He glared at Cloridan, who looked . . . let's say unrepentant. That sounds better than "considering whether to make it two murders."

"I'm never happy about unnecessary killing," I said evenly. "But this is Ashmor we're talking about. Was there anyone, other than you, who wanted him alive?"

I looked at the other gods when I asked that question, challenging them to answer. None of them would meet my, or Fyskel's, eyes.

"As for murder," I continued, "I was told that dungeons are places that are outside of the law, at least in Latorra. Is it different in Aeloria?"

I looked at Toriao for the answer. She still had the long black and silver hair, but she'd changed into a more traditional mage's robe, black with silver inscriptions embroidered thickly all over it. She shook her head.

"It is not," she admitted. "The elves make no claim of jurisdiction over any dungeon, not even this one."

"I doubt you're going to look to *Axel* for anything resembling justice," I said.

"No one has yet!" Axel declared cheerfully. "Too bad, because I wanted to give him a medal of achievement!"

"I thought *you* believed in justice, at least," Fyskel said reproachfully. "Ashmor wasn't a part of our game, he wasn't someone you had a grudge with. He never dragged you—"

"He was behind everything bad that happened in Dorsay," I said grimly. "So many people died because of him. He got his claws into Maslin . . . who knows what he had planned? And he orchestrated at least half of all this."

I gestured around at our current situation and looked at Axel for confirmation.

"He did help," Axel admitted. "Maybe about a quarter of it was him."

"This is nothing more than his own scheme come around to bite him. You'll have to watch out for that, now that you're mortal."

Fyskel glared at me, but he didn't say anything. He knew he couldn't win any confrontation, be it social, magical, or physical.

"Right," I said. "Axel, make with the exit teleportation."

"Sah, yes sah!" Axel barked, putting himself briefly in a military uniform.

"We can't leave him here!" Fyskel objected. I looked at him with a degree of pity.

"You can bring him with us if you like," I said. "But I'd think very carefully about whether handing his corpse over to the elves will get him treated more respectfully than leaving him with Axel."

Now that he knew it would upset Fyskel, Axel probably *would* do something nasty to the corpse. But the elves . . . I got the feeling that of all the people who hated Ashmor, the elves were at the top of the list. They'd probably put his tomb in the depths of their sewer system so that every liter of waste found its way past Ashmor's dead body.

Or maybe they'd take their time, really workshop it, and come up with something worse.

I looked over the other gods. "The same goes for all of you—you might want to think about how the elves are going to react to you. They didn't seem to like you all that much."

"It will be fine," Toriao said serenely. "The elves are not ones to lord their greater power over others."

She gave me a look, and I realized that she was throwing shade in my direction. I sent an unimpressed look back. The gods were hardly in a position to talk about lording it over others.

"Let's get out of here," I said, as a teleportation circle started glowing on the floor. I looked over and saw that Reggie was leading the others into his portal. No one seemed to be hanging back or coming our way. "Axel, I presume the elves' problem with demons is now over?"

"Sure thing, buddy," Axel said. "Nothing but safe demon invaders from now on."

I took a deep breath. "And can I *please* ask you to *not* make sentient beings just to torture them?"

Axel laughed, long and loud. I took three deep breaths while I waited for him to stop. If we destroyed him, we'd also be destroying every sentient being in the dungeon. But if we left him alone, he'd eventually flush every single one of them down the drain and make new ones, just to be tortured or destroyed by incoming delvers.

I hated trolley problems.

"Haaahhh . . ." Axel finally let his laughter fade into a sigh. "No. But I'll tell you what, I'll cut down on it a bit. Maybe ten percent or so. Start a twelve-step program."

"I'll take what I can get," I said and stepped onto the teleportation circle. I didn't want to spend a moment more in there.

The elves had questions. Not that many questions, they just kept repeating the same ones because they didn't believe the answers. At first, they thought that the gods were just some trick of Axel's, that he'd managed to spoof Identify. This offended the gods no end, inspiring them to extra effort to prove their bona fides.

What convinced them in the end was the wealth of secret knowledge the gods had about the elven nation and its citizens. Knowledge that only years of invisible spying could have provided. It was more than a little disturbing how much they knew. I'm not sure if the elves were actually convinced or if they just wanted the gods to stop creeping them out.

Once they'd accepted the idea that the gods were mortal now, they moved on to what to do with them. They also wanted to give Cloridan a medal. Killing the rest of the gods was pushed by a small but vocal minority. That plan was voted down, and for once I was glad of the elven habit of suppressing all dissent.

Just throwing them out of the country was considered the same as killing them. They were level ones after all, and couldn't survive without adult supervision. That didn't leave them with many options, and so the Administratum reluctantly extended an invitation to stay in Aeloria.

Duit, Rakaro, Fyskel, and Naldyna declined the invitation. Rakaro wanted to go back to his mountain temple, escorted by Borys. I don't know what he promised Borys to get him to agree. The elves decided that while Borys was an adequate escort, they should send some elves along to ensure that Rakaro didn't die on the journey. What happened to him after that was none of their concern.

Fyskel and Naldyna opted to travel to the beast-kin gathering place. It was obvious why Naldyna wanted to, but apparently Fyskel got on surprisingly well with the beast-kin. Thinking about their political system did make me wonder if he'd had a hand in designing it.

We were going back through beast-kin territory, and we were deemed as suitable escorts, so that pair would be travelling with us, along with a few elves and Duit, who wanted to come with us back to Latorra. No doubt she wanted to link up with Isidre and whatever temple staff she could find in that nation.

"Go in peace, Champions . . . if that term is still appropriate." Thalverianeu, the head administrator for the elves was holding a small private departure ceremony for our group. The elves had a ceremony for everything, it seemed. Just letting us leave was out of the question, but there *was* a ceremony for honored guests that you were glad to see the back of.

"You did resolve the issue we called on you for, and we *are* grateful. How we feel about the *rest* of it will take some time to determine, but I am confident this will eventually be seen as a boon."

"That's the most *nuanced* statement of gratitude that I've heard in a while," I said dryly, though the King's gratitude hadn't exactly been unalloyed either.

Thalverianeu inclined his head in acknowledgement. "You are welcome to return if you wish. The guards will be notified of your status. It would be best, however, if you held off on returning . . . for perhaps a decade or so."

"And you are going to open up diplomatic relations with the Tribes?" I asked.

"As agreed," he said. "One of your guards will act as an Envoy. It's possible that with Naldyna living among them, their politics will become more centralized and less . . . annoying."

He glanced apologetically at Elder Thal, who seemed fairly resigned to hearing his government being bad-mouthed. He must be used to it if he did much diplomacy.

"That includes trade, right?" I pressed. I hadn't tried to get an actual trade deal signed. Without an elf to help me, there was no way that I could out-bargain an elf. Still, just getting them to agree to open trade had been a breakthrough.

"We will consider it, if we find something worthwhile," he agreed.

"Well then, it was all worth it," I said.

"I hardly think so," Duit put in. If her gaze could have a physical effect, I would be drowning in acid. Maybe she was trying to do that? "I hardly think the loss of our godhood was worth a few paltry trinkets."

"You're making a big assumption about what side of the scale that loss is," I said.

She scowled at me some more, and the feeling that I *should* be burning in acid intensified. I ignored it.

"Time to head out," I said. We were retracing our route home, but this time we had escorts and guides who were moderately trustworthy. Hopefully, the trip back home should be much less fraught.

ON THE WAY HOME

T his is all so . . ." The owl-kin's feathered ears twitched as Tinidan searched for the word he was looking for. "Unexpected!"

I sighed. I *had* sent a message ahead of us that included all the relevant details when we got to the first beast-kin village. A single beast-kin warrior couldn't travel much faster than a small party, but the equation changed when that party contained a few fragile level ones.

The fastest way would have been to simply carry the helpless ex-gods and travel at full speed, but the gods, and our escorting elves, felt that would be beneath their dignity. So we carried them in a metaphorical sense, keeping them alive as we trudged through the forest at speeds a normal human could maintain.

Fyskel, Naldyna, and Duit were all level two now, through no real effort of their own. The real effort had been put in by me, convincing the escorts to allow the group to "participate" in the encounters on the way back. That meant allowing them to come close enough to the fight to count as in danger, while not allowing them to come into any real peril. I'd hoped to get them to level three, but our high levels sucked all the experience out of any encounter we were in.

So Tinidan had been *warned*; he simply hadn't believed me. Now the Temple—if that was the right word for a group so profoundly disorganized—was all aflutter at the prospect of hosting their favorite god.

The other gods had made much less of an impact and had received a much cooler welcome. Duit had affected a standoffish attitude that the beast-kin were happy to reciprocate. Fyskel was more friendly, apparently undiscouraged by the lackluster response. Eventually, some more friendly beast-kin showed up. They didn't wear robes, but I suspected that I was looking at the local members of his priesthood.

They were heavily outnumbered by Naldyna's worshippers, though, who seemed ecstatic at the chance to shake hands, hug, or kiss the physical form of their goddess. They turned our walk through the city into a parade, eager to usher her into taking a seat under their most holy tree.

Since that was also the *political* center of the city, that was where we were going as well. Tinidan had come to meet me—and his apprentice, Lira. Now he was walking by my side, along with Duit and Felicia. The four of us were kept in a bubble, kept safe by Cloridan, Kyle, and our elf guards.

"I'm surprised that Naldyna hasn't tried to turn them all against us, as the ones that refused to give you back your powers," I said to Duit.

She glared at me but kept her answer polite. I wasn't sure if that was because she was always polite, or if she recognized the difference in our levels.

"Naldyna is very . . . accepting," she said sourly. "She does not believe in control of any kind. *I* am surprised that she hasn't spent this trip screaming at you, but I suppose that she is under the same constraints as I."

"You mean, she won't come after me directly right now, because that would be suicide, and she doesn't want to motivate her followers to do . . . anything?"

"Correct," Duit said. "It might be different if there was a remote possibility of getting the decision reversed, but Naldyna does not seek revenge on those who have wronged her."

Duit's body language was telling me clearly that the same did not hold true for *her*. She was trying to hide it, no doubt for fear that I would eliminate a future problem by eliminating her. Now that she was level two, we didn't have to worry so much about killing her accidentally, but deliberate attacks were still going to succeed no matter what she tried to do about them.

The Church of Life was a considerable force in Latora. I got the feeling that once Duit reconnected, they would be coming after me in force. Concerning as that was, I had more immediate concerns.

"I am going to be able to meet with the Council when we get to the tree, right?" I asked Tinidan. "It's not going to be taken over by all . . . this?"

I gestured at the procession in front of me. They had found a litter from somewhere and placed Naldyna on it. This greatly sped up their progress, as the bearers could walk much faster than the goddess could. It also meant that she couldn't stop every step to greet every fervent believer who crossed her path. She was reduced to waving at them as they went by, a much more efficient procedure.

Part of me marveled at the fact that the beast-kin had managed to come up with a method that wasn't the *least* efficient option possible.

"Oh, yes, don't worry," Tinidan said. "I admit that we might not have believed *everything* in your letter, but the fact of your return couldn't be doubted."

"The council isn't going to get distracted by this . . . celebration?"

I wasn't sure if celebration was the word. Naldyna *was* happy to be among her people, but she wasn't happy about losing her powers. Even if she did disdain controlling her followers, they were sure to pick up on that eventually.

Tinidan seemed to understand my concern. "I think celebration is correct," he told me. "If only Naldyna had been affected in this way, there would be much more concern, but the playing field remains even. And removing Ashmor from this world is . . . a considerable achievement."

He looked over at Cloridan, with something approaching awe.

"Don't say that where Fyskel can hear you," I said.

"Their relationship stretches—stretched— further than the existence of this world, Kandis Hammond," Duit said sternly. "It was deeper and more complex than anything you are capable of understanding."

"Yeah, us mortals don't go much deeper than 'I don't want to die,'" I said.

"A phrase I appreciate in a new light," Duit said bitterly. "My own feelings about Ashmor are . . . conflicted."

"Yeah, he did say that you all made deals with him, even though he was outside the Game. How many of those deals did you regret?"

"Many," Duit admitted. "But not all, or even most."

Each one of those deals amounted to someone or something that Duit wanted destroyed, I reminded myself. Something that she couldn't convince the other gods to go along with. Even if you thought that the Game was a good way to limit the damage from the gods' actions, the corrupting influence of Ashmor was always there.

I made the right decision, I assured myself. *This world is better off without gods.*

"As to whether the Council will get caught up in the festivities . . ." Tinidan said thoughtfully. "Perhaps a little. But it will only be a small delay."

"A small delay?" I asked incredulously. "These guys look like they're going to be drinking for the next week."

Tinidan laughed, but he didn't deny what I said.

"The Council is made up of Elders; they're more responsible than *that*," he said. "And besides . . ."

He looked at me quizzically. "You weren't expecting to wrap this up in a single day, were you?"

I groaned. Tribal politics were going to be the death of me.

"We are forced to admit that you have achieved everything that we could have hoped for . . . and more." Kael Ironhide's smile belied his reluctant admission. The words he spoke were not his, but were the product of a committee, endlessly hashed out between the Council Elders. There were a few voices there that wanted to cast all my achievements in the worst light, to deny that I'd helped . . . but they couldn't argue with the results in front of their eyes. The wording was a concession, to ease them into the consensus.

Kael was not on one of those factions, however, so his smile was as genuine as a politician's smile ever got. He was on the Trade Faction, as I called it, so my success was his political advantage.

"As such, the Council has agreed to support your novel modifications to our laws to allow for registered business corporations."

Oh yes. "I suppose that the details have been hashed out already?" I asked.

"Indeed," Kael said. The bear-kin handed me a loose stack of papers. I went over it quickly. On my last visit, I'd provided them with an outline of the regulations I was familiar with, and the reasoning behind them. Some changes were expected, if only to assert their sovereignty, but this . . . I could work with this.

One of the drawbacks of making changes to a regulatory framework that had been fought over for two hundred years was that the changes tended to make it *less* confining. I pointed at one particular clause.

"I did warn you guys about the loopholes this opens up for avoiding taxes."

Zara Nightshadow, a wolf-kin who had absorbed my lessons last time more quickly than the others, sighed. "I know," she said. "But the wider group couldn't be convinced."

"I will hold off on exploiting it until I hear others have started doing it," I said magnanimously.

"I'd actually prefer it if you didn't," Zara said. Her ears twitched with irritation. "The sooner it gets exploited, the sooner I can convince them to change it."

"Yeah, no thanks," I countered. "That would also make it easier for the isolationists to scapegoat me for tax evasion." I glanced over at Thorn Emberstripe, leader of the isolationists, and one of the ones who had been hardest to win over. I wondered if "scapegoat" was translating correctly. A direct translation might be offensive to goat-kin. Not that there were any in the room, but . . .

"We've also prepared a suitable reward in the form of trade goods," Kael said, getting the conversation back on track. "The result was too much for your party to carry, so we also hired a caravan. He handed me a sheet with the details.

"Fantastic, thank you very much," I said, perusing the list. Just a quick glance now would let me go over it in detail using Memorize.

"As for your other . . . revelations," Kael said delicately. "We weren't able to come to an agreement as to what a suitable reward should be for killing Ashmor. Or for bringing Naldyna to us. Of course, there are those who say you should be punished for severing her in the first place."

"Is that what you're calling it?" I asked.

"For now," he said, shrugging.

"Well that seems fair," I allowed. "If you are feeling a *little bit* indebted to me, there's a meeting you could help arrange."

"You've got some nerve," Naldyna said, "coming to me and asking for favors after what you did."

She leaned back into her . . . throne, for want of a better word. It was a seat that was raised up above me, meeting the basic definition. However, it was woven out of still-living vines, making it more of an upright hammock. It looked more comfortable than the average throne.

Naldyna herself was looking more fresh and vital than she had when we left the elves. Her hair was still made of plants, a sign that while she might not be a goddess anymore, she wasn't entirely human either.

"You're going to be a major political force within the Tribes, who are my immediate neighbors and trading partners," I said. "I can't ignore you. It's understandable that you disagree with the choice I made, but it's done. You need to deal with it and move on."

"Deal with it?" Naldyna exclaimed, her voice rising. "How can I deal with it? I can't even comprehend the magnitude of my loss anymore! How can I move on, when every part of this stifling mortal existence reminds me of what I lost?"

I swallowed nervously and readied a quick Greater Invisibility. But bankers have no souls, and I couldn't show weakness.

"I'm sure you've gathered enough followers by now to kill me, if that's what you want," I said. "But—"

"Oh, how I wish I could," Naldyna snarled. "But—part of me thinks you might have been right."

REAL TALK

I was so shocked, I dropped out of Charm. I didn't even know that was possible. Perhaps it wasn't; perhaps Charm just decided that an actually honest, unmediated response was the best move here.

"Uh, what?" I said.

"A small part," Naldyna clarified. "A *very* small part. One not shared with the others, I can assure you!"

Yeah, Charm doesn't know what it's talking about.

I'd heard it said that for any proposition, there was at least one god in favor of it. And at least one god against it as well.

"Really? You're the god that's in favor of removing the gods?"

"No." Naldyna scowled at me. "Not at all. But I am in favor of the mortal races being free to develop at their own pace. Even under the rules of our Game, most of the others are still intent on *interfering*."

"So you're not in *favor* of it, but you can see some benefits."

"Some, I suppose. Far outweighed by the *dangers* you have subjected the world to, but . . . there's nothing to be done about that now. And also . . ."

She paused, hesitating over whether to tell me.

"If you had not been there at all, if *Reggie* had come through on his own, *I* would have been there. So close to my beast-kin, how could I not? Few of the others would have. *We* would have been trapped, and the others left free. *That* would have been a disaster."

"Well . . . I don't know that he would have come through if he *couldn't* guarantee you were all there," I said.

"I suspect that he could have achieved his goals with just one of us. Rendering *all* of us helpless made his task *safer*, not easier. Perhaps he would have restored us, and the balance, but I don't think he cared over-much for that."

"It could have gone either way," I allowed. "So, does this mean we can develop a working relationship?"

She glared at me some more. "For now, perhaps. I *will* get my godhood back . . . eventually."

"I'm sure you will," I said diplomatically.

"Why did you wait to ask me about this?" Naldyna asked suddenly.

"It would have felt a bit like extortion," I answered. "Asking for favors while I was responsible for keeping you alive. Our positions feel more even now."

This was mostly an illusion. Sure, Naldyna was sitting up on her throne, and she probably had hidden guards around . . . but she was still level two. I could kill her with a quick Iron Dart, a spell I was so weak at that I couldn't use it in combat. Her guards might prove a hindrance, or perhaps be able to avenge her, but I didn't think they had an answer for Invisibility.

Not that it mattered, since I wasn't going to attack her.

"Hmmph. I already know what you're here for. It wasn't that long ago that I was almost omniscient. I know what you're headed into."

"Nice to have confirmation, I suppose," I said wryly. I'd really hoped that this wouldn't be necessary, but I guess those hopes were officially dashed.

"I'm sure it is. But is not the priestess there sufficient for your needs? Tonet, I think her name was. She is as skilled as any priestess that I might lend you."

"I'm sure she is," I said. "But there is the small matter that she didn't *tell* me that she had the ability to undo Mind Magic. It makes me feel that she can't be trusted to help."

"Perhaps not," Naldyna allowed. "She has little love for Latorrans. However, you should not think too badly of her."

"Why not?" I asked.

"Consider how it feels to be the linchpin of someone else's strategy against a deadly and ruthless opponent," Naldyna suggested. "Were Tonet your only defense against Marianne Rankin, she would surely be a target for assassination. Her ability can't be concealed from a Mind Mage who attacks the same target twice."

Which was a roundabout way of saying that if the Countess targeted the same person twice, she'd see the memory of Tonet removing the earlier spell. Maybe we could mitigate that by having her work from hiding . . .

"Is that fear going to impede the rest of your priestesses?" I asked.

"That depends. Mind Heal is not meant as a defense, it is a tool of *attack*. Do you have the resolution to drive this snake from your town?"

"I'd rather kill her," I said bleakly. "That might cause problems with the King, but letting her live seems like a mistake."

"I thought you were against killing."

"I am," I agreed. "I just don't see any other way that doesn't leave her to come back and bite me. Not to mention Talnier."

Naldyna nodded slowly. "Perhaps you are not lost to the Way of the Wild," she said. "You are not there yet, but you can learn."

"I'm happy with my current moral stance, thanks. So can I get some priestesses? Or priests? I'm not fussy."

"I will send two with you," she decided. "Added to Tonet, that should be enough."

"Great! What is that going to cost me?"

This was better than I had hoped. If Naldyna hadn't come through, I was planning on approaching some of the clergy directly. Since Naldyna wasn't big on control, I figured she wouldn't stop any priest or priestess that I managed to convince. But this was better.

"We are not like your greed-loving civilization," Naldyna said with disdain. "We do not put a price on every thing, while valuing it not. Mind Magic is a cancer on society that needs to be carved out whenever it is found."

"That's great," I said. "Can they be ready to leave tomorrow morning?"

The caravan that finally left the beast-kin capital was big enough to rival the entourage I'd picked up on Axel's final floor. There were my normal companions, of course. Duit was tagging along as well. She brought her elven escorts and two young Tribal folk who seemed to want to sign up for the Church of Life. One was human and the other was, I thought, a beaver-kin.

Then there was the trade caravan. I had been worried that everyone was going to have to carry a pack, but we had been provided with two Beast Tamers, each with a flock of five quillstriders.

> **[Identification]: Quillstrider – Threat:15 – Properties: Leaping Attack, Ranged Attack**

They were remarkably ferocious-looking for beasts of burden. They were about halfway between bird and lizard. They looked a little like ostriches with iridescent feathers, but they didn't have wings. Instead, they had forward-reaching arms, like a Tyrannosaurus. The head rose up on a flexible neck, like an ostrich, but it had a lizard-like mouth, with lots of small, sharp teeth.

They *could* be ridden, apparently, but there wasn't much advantage to it. Their gait made for an uncomfortable ride, and while they were strong enough to carry a rider, the weight tended to unbalance them, especially when jumping from tree limb to tree limb. They were more of a test of skill than a viable transportation option.

Instead, they were loaded down with our trade goods and supplies, and the caravan as a whole would be travelling at the speed of our slowest member, Duit.

Finally, there was our guide, Bram. This was his second stint at guiding me, and I greatly preferred the quiet bear-kin to the treacherous Reynard.

"Do you think we can find some beasts along the way?" I asked him. "I want to get Duit up to level three if we can."

He looked at me and then, more doubtfully, at Duit.

"You'll be carrying her, then, not having her make the kills on her own?"

"That's the idea," I said.

"Might have to split off from the main group," he mused. "Most creatures with sense won't come near ten quillstriders."

"Are they commonly used in caravans?" I asked.

He shook his head. "Too much trouble to raise," he said. "Though there is one village, where these guys are from, that don't care. Tough skins."

I looked at the two trainers, who were the same race, possibly even related to each other. They had short, dense, black and white fur. Badger-kin?

"Let's not do it on the way, then," I decided, returning to the main topic. "When we get to a village, we'll see if they have any nearby monsters that need clearing out."

Bram nodded.

Our departure was surprisingly festive. I tried not to take this as the beast-kin being glad to see us go. They did seem, on balance, to be happy with what we had done. We travelled the same route Reynard had taken us, in reverse, so I got to see the same villages again. They were happy to see us, though some individuals weren't happy to hear the news about Reynard.

Word had been sent out, affirming our status as welcome guests of the tribes, so we didn't have any trouble finding places to stay. My stash of coin was sadly depleted, so we opened up some of the trade goods. There were wines, preserved meats, and cheeses that the villagers were happy to accept as hospitality gifts.

When we got to Mossridge Gather, our final stop on the way home, I took the others aside before the feast started.

"I've arranged for Duit and the caravan to stay an extra few days," I said. "Bram will be staying with them. I'm pretty sure we can find our way back to Talnier on our own."

By we, I meant Cloridan. Memorize wasn't as helpful as it should be in the Great Wild. Landmarks changed with surprising speed. Cloridan was good at noticing the things that *didn't* change.

Bram looked doubtful. It was his default expression. "If they're staying a few days, I can guide you and then come back for them," he said.

I thought about it. "We want to enter the town at night," I said, "And it won't be safe for you there. Will you be fine outside the town overnight?"

Bram nodded. "No problem."

Duit looked at me knowingly. "You should send word when you can. If you are not successful, we will need to bypass the town."

I narrowed my eyes. "You knew, and you weren't going to tell me."

"Your trials and tribulations are none of my business," Duit said. "Your success or failure will be up to you."

"That sounds like you're still restricted by the Game," I countered. "But you're not anymore, are you?"

"What makes you say that?" Duit asked, but her deflection was transparent to me. She wasn't a god anymore, just a mortal.

"I knew it. Was it a vote, or did you just decide to stop?"

"There was no need for a vote," Duit admitted. "The Game existed to protect mortals from our squabbles. We are no longer anyone that the world needs protecting from."

"For now," I said. "You'll get your levels up soon enough. And you're not exactly ordinary mortals, are you? You have resources, and followers, and now you can go back to squabbling over the destiny of the mortal races."

"And will you do something about that, Kandis Hammond? Will you stand in judgment over us again?"

"No," I said. "You do what you want. I know you think it's for the best. I just wanted to know where I stood."

"On very thin ice, Kandis Hammond. None of the gods are in a position to drag you down, but you have enemies aplenty."

"Don't I know it," I said. I would have been bitter about it, but all the enemies I knew about were good enemies to have. I looked at my party.

"We'll discuss how to approach Talnier in the morning," I told them. "Away from ears that aren't fully invested in our success."

"We'll be ready," Kyle said. "Ready for anything."

LİOΠ'S DEΠ

I walked out of the forest without any fanfare, headed towards Talnier's northern gate. It was the first time in a while that I'd just been able to walk on my own, without an entourage of people who were deeply invested in where I was going. All the villages we'd passed through had been welcoming, greeting us with what I thought was excessive delight.

On the road, I had to deal with the constant presence of our baggage train. The quillstriders were every bit as cantankerous as you might expect a misbegotten hybrid of ostrich and lizard to be, and their handlers, while less troublesome, never stopped watching me, eager to anticipate any need that I might have.

Duit's elven escort had managed to ignore me with some grace, content that I wasn't a threat to her charge. Duit herself was not able to be so aloof. Every time I glanced at her, she was staring at me. Mostly, she looked away at that point, and she rarely approached me, but I could feel the ex-god's attention on me the whole trip.

None of those were with me right now as I approached the gate. Cloridan, Kyle, and Felicia were, but they weren't saying much.

The guards on the walls didn't call anything down, but they must have alerted the ones downstairs, because the gate opened as I approached. Six armed guards stepped out, forming two lines of three on each side. An honor guard, one might have supposed, but I knew better.

We all walked right down the center of that formation, stopping when the guard sergeant stepped out, blocking the gate.

"You've got some nerve, coming back here," he said. "Take her into custody," he barked to the other guards. "Don't let her speak!"

People with weapons are often way too convinced of the effectiveness of those tools. The sergeant seemed to think that a timely blow could stop me from speaking, could stop me from turning all of these men, including him, into my soldiers. Maybe he was right, but I rather imagined that my own speed and strength were sufficient to make such a blow ineffective. And the guys could probably take out this entire group without too much effort.

As was almost always the case, when high-level adventurers were confronted by low-level functionaries, it was other considerations that held sway. None of us resisted or spoke. More guards came out, carrying crafted shackles. They were of a quality high enough to hold Kyle, they were more than enough for the likes of me.

"Kandis Hammond," the sergeant recited. "You are under arrest for embezzlement and fraud. Your position as a Council member has been revoked and you are to be taken before the Council for your speedy trial.

That explained the lack of a title, I supposed. Thinking back on the charter I'd pushed through, I recalled that the only way to revoke my status was an act of the King. I hadn't felt the need for an impeachment procedure since the judiciary was independent and there was nothing in the charter protecting Councillors from being convicted of crimes.

Presumably, that could lead to a Councillor being imprisoned while still being a member of the Council. We'd have to have meetings in the prison. Well, that was a problem for the future. Right now, I'd been kicked off the Council *and* charged with crimes. However, I wasn't being handed over for a proper trial. Instead, the Council would be convicting me?

They're doing this wrong, I thought grumpily.

Honestly, that bothered me more than the arrest. What was the point of writing up procedures and founding institutions if people were just going to change the rules when they felt like it? Actually . . . wasn't that the sort of thing Bureaucracy was supposed to prevent? I hadn't had any notifications of rules violations . . . perhaps there was a range issue that I wasn't aware of.

The guards led me through the streets, towards the new Council building. It wasn't quite finished, but it seemed that the Councillor and officials had moved in without waiting for the final details to be completed. Even with those flourishes missing, it was an incredibly fast construction time. I guess having workers who could heft a block of granite helps with construction speed.

Word must have been sent, because they were ready for us. They clearly weren't going to have us stew in a cell for any amount of time—they were going to start the trial right away. That might have been wise. Holding adventurers in a cell was often an exercise in futility. I tried to remember if it was *generally* known that I had Shadow Magic.

Personally, I felt that justice was better served with a bit more deliberation, but it was clear that justice wasn't on the agenda today.

I hadn't been resisting, but when we got to the building, the guards must have felt a show of force was necessary. I was grabbed and dragged, my hands manacled behind me, into the Council Chamber.

Not the Hall of Justice. The guards hadn't been mistaken. I didn't think the Chamber was the best venue for what was to come. It was set up for the presentation of reports from officials, so it had a basic layout suitable for a trial. But there were far fewer seats than the Hall of Justice. I had been insistent during the planning phase that people needed to *see* judgments handed out.

Law*making*, on the other hand, needed much less of an audience. There were seats for spectators, but far fewer.

Then again, perhaps someone thought that the fewer witnesses, the better.

I almost stumbled as I was dragged into the chamber. When I was able to look around, I was pleased to see that my fellow Council members were all still seated. Noah Cunningham, Cheney Labelle, Delmar Balend and the former mayor André Michaud didn't look happy to see me, but that was understandable. They were laboring under some misapprehensions.

It would be wrong to say that the infiltrator was sitting in *my* seat. I'd only ever been the Secretary. It was a position with more power than people generally supposed, but it held little *formal* power. My seat had been on the far left-hand side, and it was the mayor who had been demoted to that position.

The most important seat was in the center, and it was the only seat that she could let herself sit in. The Countess Marianne Rankin grinned at me viciously as she banged her gavel for order.

"This trial will come to order!" she demanded. "On this day, the trial of the criminal Councillor Kandis—what?"

The grin vanished as she looked at me.

"You . . . idiots!" she declared.

"Is something wrong, ma'am?" the guard sergeant next to me asked.

"Is something wrong? Is something wrong?" the noblewoman screeched. "You've been fooled! You brought me an illusion, and now she knows she's a wanted criminal!"

She glanced at Kyle and Cloridan behind me. "All of them!" she snarled.

"Does this mean the trial is cancelled?" I asked brightly. "Oh, and do I get to speak now?"

The Countess growled with frustration. "Why not, it's not like you can use any of your damnable social skills through that thing."

She glared at me some more and then she barked some orders to the guards. "Well, stop wasting time here, fools! Go and search for her—this spell can't have that much range! She must have come over the wall while you were distracted."

"I'm sorry," André said. "How do you know this is an illusion?"

Irritation flickered in the Countess's eyes. "I am not so easily fooled," she said. "Have you forgotten it took me to uncover the criminal's wiles in the first place?"

"Oh, yes," I supposed you did, André agreed. I wasn't sure how much of that was mind control and how much was his spinelessness. "So the trial is cancelled?"

"Yes," the Countess ground out. "So sorry to have troubled you all. You'd better go."

They filed out. Since the jig was up, I cancelled the three Phantasmal Entities that were Cloridan, Kyle, and Felicia.

Lady Rankin glared at the Phantasmal Emissary that remained.

"What are you still here for?" she demanded. "You've got your information, and I know as well as anyone that your illusions can't harm anyone."

I chose not to let her know that I'd already known about her takeover.

"I just want to know why," I said.

"Why what?"

"Why risk exposure as a Mind Mage over a small town like Talnier? Do you have some sort of personal vendetta against me?"

Her eyes flashed with anger. "A *personal* vendetta? Why would I have such a thing?"

"You might *say* that, but you do seem pretty angry," I argued.

She drew a dagger and started walking around the table. "It's my understanding that this shell will pop if I prick it enough times."

"Seriously, I barely know you, lady," I said, slowly backing away. "Some of that is because you erased my memory of you, but there was barely anything there to get back."

"I might carry a few grudges," she admitted and lunged. I tried to dodge but she had a skill advantage over me, it seemed. The dagger skittered off my Phantasmal skin, pushing me back.

She made a disappointed noise and tried again. "Just how tough are your spells?" she muttered.

She landed another blow. "You didn't need to know who I was to expose my investment in Anchorbury."

"Are you talking about the bribes you paid to Reynard?" I asked, jumping back over the table. That gave me a bit of room, but she was just as agile as I was.

"I spent more than just money on that man," she claimed, jumping up on the table to pursue me. "Just the accusation of suborning a Guild official got my dungeon taken away from me, and I *still* haven't gotten it back!"

She launched herself at me. It would have been a risk, if this body could harm her, but as it was, she landed another blow. I slipped out from under her, trying to gain distance.

"And *then*," she snarled. "Just when I *persuaded* the Duke to make his own play for the throne, who should turn up again?"

"You were behind that?" I asked. "You were going to put a puppet on the throne?"

"Duke Arryen was no one's puppet, but he would have given me what I wanted. And if that didn't work, with the King's protectors dragged away, I might have been able to risk a spell on him . . . but you were there for that as well. You and that oversexed cat Chosen."

"I didn't know about any of this, but I can't say I'm unhappy," I said.

"You wouldn't. You were just pawns, weren't you? My real opposition came from the gods."

"If you thought that, why continue? I've heard that it's futile to go against the gods."

She started pressing me again, slashing with the dagger. My spell couldn't hold up to much more of this.

"Oh, the gods can be defeated," she said. "If you're subtle enough, if you're clever and determined enough. And there's always a god to oppose whoever has set themselves against you."

If she only knew, I thought. Not that I had any intention of telling her. I wasn't going to be able to keep it a secret; word was already slipping out of the Tribal nations. Duit's appearance in Latora should seal the deal.

"You're holding a lot of anger against someone who was a pawn," I said, taking another blow on my forearm.

"It just makes . . . sense to eliminate the enemy's foot soldiers," she said, swiping at me again. "But really, I'm here to replace the dungeon I lost."

"With what dungeon?" I asked uneasily.

Her vicious grin was back. "All of them. That laboratory dungeon you've been playing with, the Ogre Temple, *and* yours. Once you're dead, I'll be able to claim it, and Oakway will be returned to its *rightful* owner."

She lifted her dagger. "This isn't anywhere near as satisfying as the real thing, but it will have to do . . . for now."

She brought the dagger down and the spell broke.

Infiltration

In any contested situation, the most important resource is information. That was why I'd let Rankin believe I'd entered the town today. I hadn't snuck in using Phantasmal Emissary as a distraction. I, and my team, had entered through the southern gates yesterday.

With the help of Disguise Other, of course, though I honestly think we could have managed with some hooded cloaks. I'd finally picked up the improved spell and had been a little mad to discover that it also worked on me, and so was a simple improvement to my original spell. If I'd had five extra points to spend back then, I could have saved myself the cost of getting both.

The spell was barely necessary because the south gate had been taken over by the eclectic collection of buildings that housed the local beast-kin community. It was on the south side, because however comfortable beast-kin were with nature, they still wanted the added security of a river between them and whatever wandered out in the Great Wild.

The initial construction of what I definitely wasn't calling Shantytown had given some of the more staid members of the Council conniptions. They liked orderly rows of similar houses, tucked neatly and safely behind high walls. The beast-kin . . . well, I'd never seen any evidence that any beast-kin liked the same thing as any other beast-kin. Their tastes were eclectic and personal. Chaotic, some might say.

In the short time that I'd left, Tradertown had only grown busier and more chaotic. Some rules had been adhered to. There was a straight, wide avenue along the road to the gate, allowing plenty of room for wagon or foot traffic. However, anyone who wanted to could duck in between the houses, stalls, and tents and make their way through a maze of paths that barely rated being called alleyways and find themselves right at the gate without anyone aware that they were approaching.

At the gate itself, the guards were hardly in a position to do much scrutiny. One of them was busy arguing with an otter-folk merchant who was claiming that the goods he was carrying were for personal use and not subject to taxes. The other was trying to coax or order a squirrel-kin child down from climbing the inner arch of the gate.

We handed over our fee for entering the town and walked right in. I made a note to reorganize customs and excise collection when I had a chance.

Once we were within city borders, I tried doing something that hadn't been working for a while.

[Territory Status].

Nothing happened. That made it official: I'd lost control of Talnier. It would have been nice to have received a notification; it was *possible* that I would have if I'd been *in* Talnier at the time. Then again, I was used to the System giving me the absolute minimum in terms of information.

Well, it didn't really matter. I just had to take it back, and that was already on my list of action items. First on the list was a visit to High Priestess Tonet. I had wanted to delay visiting her until I'd done more to secure my position, but my beast-kin companions had insisted. Aelira Windtail and Therris Boulderpaw were in disguise, but only to the extent that they weren't wearing their priestess uniforms. They made an oddly matched set, as the diminutive fox-kin was half the size of the six-foot-tall lady bear-kin.

My party and I were disguised as humans. *Different* humans, of course. Walking behind the pair let me get a feel of how accepted beast-kin had become in the town proper. The answer wasn't good. Tensions weren't as high as I'd seen them before, but there was a strong tendency for people to glare at the pair, and then glare at *us* for walking too close to them.

Relations had obviously deteriorated. This hadn't been evident in Trade Town. It was mostly beast-kin, true, but you needed two parties to trade and there was a lot of business going on there. Both Trade Town and Talnier proper looked more prosperous than ever, so I didn't think it was poverty or jealousy that was causing the tension.

It felt as if Aeilira and Therris were being glared at because they were *out of place.*

Well. I couldn't do anything about that now. I just tried to note any demographic groups that were particularly overt about it.

Despite the armed guards at the gate of the Temple of Naldyna, I'd never been stopped from entering, and today was no different. We stepped into the lush garden behind the walls and the two priestesses breathed a sigh of relief.

"Feels like home," Aelira commented. She led the way deeper inside, striding unhesitatingly into the inner sanctum. Here, I had been stopped, but Aelira and Therris kept going. No one stopped them; they must be able to sense something about the pair even without uniforms.

We followed, with some hesitation, but they only managed a few more steps before Tonet came out to meet them.

"Sisters," she said, bowing her head. She glanced appraisingly at me, reminding me that we were in disguise.

"Ah," she said when I dropped the spells. "That's what this is about. I suppose you'd better come in."

"We have news, Sister," Aelira said. "We'll need privacy."

Tonet started to say something, before thinking better of it and simply inclining her head.

"This way," she said. She led us all to an alcove wreathed in greenery. It didn't seem private to me, but when a wind I couldn't see started to rustle the leaves, I suspected there might be a spell or two in play. I looked, and there was mana in it, but there was mana running through *everywhere* in this garden.

"I haven't heard any news about your efforts abroad," Tonet told me. "I hope they were successful. Matters have gone less well on the homefront."

"We are going to talk about that," I told her, "But your sisters have got something more important to share."

I observed Tonet closely as they told her about Naldyna. I watched her go from calm and in control to shocked, passing through anger and denial, and finally landing on something close to smug.

"A human body, you say?"

Aelira sighed. "Choosing *one* of her daughter-races would have elevated that race above others. Choosing a human form might have the same effect, but as the baseline form, one could argue that it is the choice that averages out all the differences."

It seemed petty one-upmanship could be found wherever you went. Despite Tonet's blatant favoritism of the Tribal nation, anyone could tell by looking that she was a Latorran-born human. Her *name* was Tribal, but I always assumed that she'd taken a new one when she became a priestess.

Humans weren't discriminated against in the Tribes, or in Naldynan theology, as far as I knew, but they were rarer. And that "daughter races" thing was real. The beast-kin races were older than the Gods War, so true knowledge was hard to find. But the beast-kin were sure that they had been created by Naldyna.

"As interesting as this little episode of 'Who's Mother's Favorite' is," I said, "I'd like to bring up more mundane concerns."

Tonet scowled at me. "Why we should be helping *you* escapes me. After what you did to Mother—"

"Mother has reserved acting on this matter for herself alone!" Therris snapped.

"And mind control magic is an offense against the freedoms that Mother holds dear," Aelira added.

"Which brings up an important topic. Why didn't you tell me you could break Mind Magic when I was asking for your aid?" I asked. It took all three hundred and sixty points of my Charm skill total to make that come out calmly.

Tonet shrugged. It was easier to keep from launching myself over to her and strangling her than it was to keep my voice calm. Violence had never been my choice.

"There were multiple reasons," she said. "You made a good case back then, but I wasn't sure if I could trust you—either your word or your ability to come back from your adventure. I didn't want to make myself a target, and I thought that I would be more useful, and hence better rewarded, if I was part of the reconquest rather than the resistance."

"Entirely mercenary reasons, then," I said. "Well, as it turns out, I'm not sure that we'll be able to manage a relationship quite as favorable as I was offering."

"Oh?"

"Circumstances as they are, I suspect that the Priesthood of Naldyna is interested in much cooler relations than before. Possibly even frosty."

"You can hardly begrudge us that, after what you did," Tonet said.

"I can understand it, but I'm not interested in turning the other cheek. Any unfriendly actions from your side *will* be reciprocated."

"Hmm, I see," Tonet said, looking slightly displeased. "As it happens, I've hardly had time to react to this news, but it occurs to me that there might be some career opportunities at the Mother Tree that were previously absent for the likes of me."

She glanced at the other two priestesses. "Perhaps someone else will take on my role and you can build a fresh relationship with them."

"That might be wise," I agreed. In truth, I was more ambivalent than I made it sound. Tonet teaming up with Naldyna could go either way for me.

"But that is for the future," Tonet concluded. "For now, we should discuss the present situation."

"And how we can work together to resolve it," Therris put in. "We are allies in this."

"Yes, of course. Allies," Tonet agreed without showing too much reluctance.

"So to start with, perhaps you can fill us in on what happened," I said. "Everything seemed to be going fine, when suddenly the reports started to get vague."

"Your people were doing well," Tonet told me. "I was keeping my distance, but I am reasonably certain they dealt successfully with all the minions and devices that the Countess smuggled into the town."

"So what went wrong?" I asked.

"Having dealt with the minions, they were unprepared when the puppet master made a personal appearance."

"She's here? The Countess?"

"In the mind-controlling flesh."

"So, what, the whole town is mind-controlled now?"

"No." Tonet paused and then corrected herself. "At least I don't think so. I've mostly confined myself to the Temple and relied on reports and rumors."

"Notoriously unreliable when dealing with Mind Mages," Aelira sniffed.

"I'm aware, but I can ensure that those I speak to haven't had their memories changed," Tonet replied. "Which seems to be her preferred method; I haven't heard any reports of her directly controlling people."

"That's . . . qualified good news," Aelira said slowly. Looking over at me, she explained. "Mind *control* is an active effect. We can oppose it, but we need to overcome her spell total. Priestesses must be generalists, while Mind Mages tend towards the specialized, so they often have higher totals."

"Is that not the case with memory alterations?" I asked.

"Those are a form of *damage* and can be healed without overcoming the caster," Aelira said. "Given time, they will reverse themselves on their own."

"How much time?"

"It depends on a person's Soul," Aelira said. "Not less than a week, and for many it might take a year or more."

Soul is the most common dump stat, I thought. *There's always a catch.*

"From what I can gather, she only altered enough of the minds of the Town Council and officials to sell her absurd story of your crimes," Tonet said, taking up the story again. "Once you were declared a criminal and kicked off the Council, they convinced themselves that they could elect her by acclamation.

"That's not what it says in the Charter *at all,*" I said waspishly. "Why write these things down if no one reads them?"

"To be fair, I imagine she altered their memories of what they read," Tonet said.

"Hmph. And where was the Adventurers Guild during all this?"

"I don't have eyes in the Guild," Tonet said, "So I can't tell you their reasons, or if they were working in the background. They were quite active in the first phase of the conflict, but when Lady Rankin showed, up, they disappeared."

EXCUSES

Of all the things that the Guild Master could be doing, Martin Koenig was doing paperwork. He looked ridiculous with his massive frame hunched over some forms, even if his desk was appropriately sized. I'd snuck into his office three times today, and he had barely moved.

The excessive sneaking had been required to get all my pieces in one place. Koenig's intimidating physique and level meant that I needed to be prepared if he turned out to have turned against me. I'd gone in once to scout out my route, and then twice more to bring in the two priestesses via a combination of Shadow Step and invisible sneaking.

This has been a lot harder than it will look, I grumbled to myself. But presentation is everything, and I needed to make an impression.

My job was made easier by the fact that Koenig kept his door open. Either he was the kind of boss who insisted his door was always open, or he preferred it open so he could yell demands at his deputy, Nadine.

The first thing I checked for was mental domination. Just because the Countess didn't use it *often* didn't mean she refrained entirely. Control spells left a conduit for the magic and instructions to flow through. A quick check with Sense Mana found nothing.

That was fine, but it was only the first step. I didn't think the Countess could conceal her spells, but it was worth checking. Dispel Image did reveal a pair of conduits, but these were the same ones I'd seen before belonging to the geas that all Guild officials had to take.

I looked at the angles carefully. I'd found the lines for these spells before, revealed them in these very rooms, and the angles looked the same, headed back to Dorsay. If the Countess was here, controlling them, then the conduits would be pointing towards her.

I signaled for the priestesses to proceed. Nadine was the first to notice something.

"I see magic," she hissed urgently to Koenig. "On you."

It was quite a sight. Greater Invisibility concealed Therris, but her spell was clearly visible. A column of light engulfed Koenig, and the memory alterations were burning off him in a green flame.

"I see it, too, on you," Koenig said. "Is it Mind Magic?"

"Mind Magic doesn't look like this," Nadine said. She looked down at herself. "It doesn't look like anything."

"It's the *cure* for Mind Magic," I stated, appearing between them. In the flesh, not as an emissary. I needed my full suite of social skills here.

It took them a second to react. I'd thought they'd be more startled by my sudden appearance, but they dealt with adventurers regularly. They must be used to that.

Koenig was the first to react.

"Adventurer Hammond," he said, sinking back down into his chair. "I thought you'd abandoned us."

"Why would you think that?" I asked. "Why wouldn't you imagine that everything you'd been told was a lie when the person who has been fucking with everyone's memories *moves on to the Council?*

He had the grace to look embarrassed. "I— you tell her."

"Our last communication from you came *before* the Countess showed up," Nadine told me. "Anas, Tinidan's apprentice, told us that the elves were able to keep you in a more salubrious lifestyle and that you were staying with them. He disappeared shortly afterwards."

I snorted. "That's a third-hand report *at best*, before you factor in the possibility of memory alteration."

"True," Nadine allowed, "But it wasn't like we could do anything about it. We couldn't send an expedition to the elves to see if it was true. All we could do was wait and see if you came back."

"Wait and see doesn't mean you give up on protecting the town."

"We didn't! We stopped seeing any new amulets. But when the funds went missing from your bank . . ."

I grimaced. Cloridan, with the invisibility amulet, was investigating the situation at my bank. I didn't dare go near it yet; it screamed of a trap.

" . . . and the Council laid charges against you, that wasn't something that we could get involved in."

"True," I admitted grudgingly. The Guild couldn't get involved in local governance.

"It was only then that the Countess showed up in person," Nadine continued. "She must have been here incognito before. When she appeared, we . . ."

She paused, confused. "We . . . did send a message to Dorsay . . . didn't we?"

Koenig frowned. "I remember wondering why the message hadn't resulted in action . . ." he said.

"*There's* the memory alteration," I said. "She uses a light touch when she can get away with it."

Koenig cursed. "So she kept word from getting out. That explains a few things, but . . . it can't last for long. Word must be already spreading."

"There's no way she can keep a lid on it forever," I agreed. "It's definitely been a priority for her, though. You say that Anas disappeared?"

Anas had still been sending regular reports, but Tinidan had grown suspicious of them. He'd been unable to explain exactly what had tipped him off, but that was the first sign I'd had that something was wrong back home.

Home. Talnier really was my home now, wasn't it? I couldn't claim any place in the other universe as mine, now.

I shook off the bout of existential grief. I had a town to win back.

"Disappeared, yes," Nadine replied. "We thought it odd at the time, but he *is* a Tribal . . ."

I raised an eyebrow. "What's that supposed to mean?" I asked. "You think that because he's from the Wild he's going to abandon his responsibilities and leave you all to twist in the wind?"

"Well . . . yes," Nadine admitted.

"Because the way I see it, he must have gotten captured by the Countess, and because you thought he was unreliable, *you* left him to twist in whatever dungeon she's got him locked up in."

"What? But that's—"

"Fair," Koenig interrupted. "If he had been a member, we would not have taken his disappearance at face value. We failed you, in that respect."

"In more than a few respects," I grumbled. "But you're back on board now?"

"There are limits to what we can do," Koenig said glumly. "You are still a wanted woman; if you show your face, we can't stop the guards from arresting you. Not without going against our own rules."

"But we'll help where we can," Nadine said eagerly. "If you've got a cure for mind alteration, those charges won't last for long."

"A few things first," I said. "Number one, what happened to Janie? She was a member of the Guild, so don't tell me you didn't keep track."

"Ah, yes," Koenig said sadly. "Unfortunately, she was lost when your dungeon turned against her."

I tapped my foot impatiently, waiting for Cloridan to show up.

"He's not late," Felicia said from under her hood. I wouldn't have been able to maintain Disguise once we were separated, so they had been using the standard adventurer gambit for not being recognized—hooded cloaks—and had been listening in to the conversations in taverns. They hadn't picked up anything so far, but you never knew.

I'd left the two priestesses with Koenig. He would be vetting and cleansing selected adventurers, building up a fighting force for when we went overt. That just left the regular gang with me. Or it *would*, when Cloridan showed up.

"I know," I said. "I'm just . . . the story is that Janie was murdered by Rhis, which I *know* is false, but I can't check it, because the storefront is *definitely* a trap."

"I'm sure she's all right," Felicia said.

"She's an adventurer," Kyle added. "She knows how to take care of herself."

"Sure, but—" I stopped, as Cloridan sidled out of a dark corner. He was visible, so he was hiding his face. That meant I was the only one with my face showing. It wasn't my face, of course, but one that I'd coordinated with Cloridan before we separated.

"Well?" I asked.

"I'm still convinced it's a trap," Cloridan said. "I'm not sure *how* it's a trap, though."

I grunted at his entirely unsatisfying answer.

"The shopfront is all boarded up," he elaborated. "Back and front, no entrance. But there are no guards, either on the street or in houses with a view."

"Could they be inside?"

"No one enters, no one leaves," Cloridan said. "You can't just lock guards in a house. They need food, and to go out occasionally."

"I bet she would if she could," I groused. "Could she be teleporting them in occasionally?"

"Maybe? That would only be possible with dungeon enchantments, but she has access to them." Cloridan paused for thought. "No, I don't think so. People talk about that building, and about you, when they go past it. No one's said anything about noises or lights at night . . . I think it's empty."

"So how is it a trap?"

Cloridan spread his hands expressively. "I don't know," he said. "Maybe . . . you've often spoken of how doors are your nemesis."

"Not so much anymore," I said smugly, "now that I have Shadow Magic."

"Does *she* know that you do?" Cloridan asked thoughtfully.

"I'm not sure. I haven't been keeping it as secret as I'd like," I admitted.

"Well, if a door is your nemesis, surely a nailed-shut door is even more so," Cloridan mused. "Perhaps she's just trying to keep you from what's inside."

"That's . . . that wouldn't keep you out."

"It might . . . for a little while, at least. I remember how secure you made that building, and she boarded up even the upper windows. Prying the boards off would make noise, and even at night someone would hear it."

"You said she wasn't keeping watch on the place."

"She doesn't have a pack of guards waiting to pounce on anyone who approaches," he clarified. "But I can't tell a single watcher from an ordinary citizen unless they're behaving oddly."

"So she could have someone listening out for boards being broken," I said. "Giving her a chance to respond . . . but how quickly?"

"There would still need to be some sort of trap inside," Cloridan muttered. "To capture you or at least delay you. If she's taken over the dungeon . . ."

"I'll know as soon as I step inside," I said. "That might be too late, but dungeons can't do much on the first level."

"What if she moved or destroyed the portal?" Kyle asked.

"That would be annoying, but it wouldn't qualify as a trap," I said. "If she did that, I could still access Rhis the hard way. And she wouldn't have access to him at all."

"I know what the trap is," Felicia said. "It's alchemy."

"Hmm," Cloridan said. "You might have a point."

"Care to explain?"

"If you can't keep people in place to guard it, and you don't have magic, like in a dungeon, you want alchemy to do something to whoever gets inside. Or enchantments, but you can get by them, and I bet the Countess has noticed. She's got the money for it, she can just buy something."

"But what?" I asked.

Felicia shrugged. "Poison dust won't stay in the air *that* long, but she could be relying on it getting kicked up by anyone who enters. Sticky traps on the floor or walls, or even some kind of mechanical trap that dumps poison on anyone who enters."

"That's plausible," I said. "But what do we do about it?"

"Well," Felicia said. "I'm going to need some time to prepare, and you're going to have to take me inside with you."

JANIE

Of course, we were all going in together. We were a team; that was how we handled delving a dungeon. This time, though, Felicia was going first.

The preparation that she needed took several hours, which were spent in a small room provided by the Guild, while the rest of us waited impatiently or went out to get the ingredients she needed. There were, perhaps, other things that I could be doing, but I couldn't get Janie's fate out of my mind.

What stopped me from screaming at Felicia to hurry up was the realization, gained after only a few minutes of agitated pacing, that we would have to go in at night. That made Shadow Walking easier, and it made any watchers easier to identify . . . the logic was inescapable.

And I could spend a few hours working out how to strangle logic instead of bugging Felicia.

When the time finally came, it was a few hours after sunset. Cloridan had scouted the area again but still hadn't found any watchers. He assumed that meant they were being subtle, but it also meant that if we avoided any overt actions, we should be able to evade them.

We Shadow Walked to the upper floor. That had been at Felicia's insistence.

"Our goal is on the ground floor," she explained. "So that's where the nastiest trap will be. The chance that we will even use the second floor is lower, so expensive alchemy would just be wasted."

That didn't mean that there wouldn't be traps on the second floor, so we went in prepared. We had masks, treated with an alchemical concoction similar to what we wore in the myconid dungeon. And it meant Felicia going first, along with her alchemist's lantern.

This was actually a candle, on a hinged holder on the end of a metal rod, about two feet long. It was made to stay upright, no matter what angle the hinge was. It let Felicia hold the candle flame up to the roof or down at her feet without effort.

It turned out that we couldn't take the lit candle through the shadows, which shouldn't have surprised me. But once we were through, Felicia managed to light it without difficulty. It burned with a very clear flame, providing only a little light. Felicia examined it closely, moving it up and down, before proclaiming the air good.

Before we could proceed, Felicia needed to examine the surfaces more closely. Wary of anyone that might be watching from outside, we weren't using the normal glowstones or Light spells. Instead, I handed Felicia a makeshift penlight, made with Phantasmal Object. It was just a pen-shaped cylinder, open at one end. With a Light spell cast all the way down inside, it produced a thin beam of light that Felicia could block with her finger.

Felicia started by examining the floor at her feet and then moved on to the rest of the room. Having been given the all-clear, I started bringing the others in. This was a time-consuming process, and by the time I was done, Felicia had finished with her examination.

"The boards are coated with widow's caress," she said. "It's a sticky resin that causes paralysis. If Cloridan had tried climbing inside, he'd be twitching on the ground outside by now."

"I wear gloves," Cloridan pointed out.

"Then it would stick to your gloves, and get on you the next time you touched your face or tried to take the gloves off. But that would make it take longer to paralyze you."

"So it's on all the boards?" I asked.

"All of the ones here, yeah. That's . . . expensive. Widow's caress is pretty niche, as a poison. It sticks to weapons well, but it works through the skin, not the bloodstream, so it's not popular. Who uses poison on a club?"

She led us forward, as far as the door that blocked the exit. She examined the handle and the frame closely.

"More of it on the handle," she said. "Stand back."

She carefully poured a small amount of oil on the doorknob and then wiped it clean with a cloth. Carefully wadding up the cloth, she threw it into a corner. Then she turned the handle, only to stop.

"Are we expecting physical traps here? They wouldn't have had time to rebuild doors, but they might have strings attached to the other side, right?"

"Just pull it open a crack, and I'll check," Cloridan said, bustling forward. He pulled out a small mirror and borrowed the penlight. A few moments later, he pronounced it clear. Working together, the pair carefully eased the door open.

Felicia took the lead again, holding the alchemist's lantern in front of her.

"Is there a reason we don't use that in dungeons?" I asked.

"Alchemy is rare in dungeons," Kyle answered softly. "You can get potions in the rewards, of course, but for traps, they prefer direct magic."

I made a note to ask Rhis why when I got a chance. We pressed on.

The second floor was a short corridor leading off from the stairs, surrounded by a U-shape of rooms. Since we weren't interested in any of the rooms, we followed the corridor to the stairs. Felicia pointed out the glistening traces of widow's caress on the doors that we passed.

"You'll need to have this place *thoroughly* cleaned when this is all over," Felicia told me as we started heading down the stairs. "Sticky resins always end up stuck somewhere they shouldn't be. You drop a paintbrush, get bumped into a wall—"

She broke off as the lantern flared up, the flame turning a brilliant blue. She looked at the flame. I was looking at what the extra light showed on the walls.

"Back up," Felicia said. I could hear the nervousness in her voice. We took a few steps back, and the flame turned back to normal. Felicia then bent down and lowered the candle. About halfway down the final flight, about five feet above ground level, there was a line where the candle burned blue. Felicia bobbed it back and forth over the line to be sure.

"Kandis," she said. "Did you arrange for your first floor to be airtight?"

"No," I replied. "And that's not the only decor change."

I took her arm and gently redirected the light from the pen to shine on the walls downstairs. The elegant and fashionable wooden wall paneling had been scorched black by flames.

"It looks like Janie was here."

It took Felicia a little while to work out what the gas was. "Serpentwine gas," she eventually pronounced. "It's another paralytic."

"What's the antidote?" I asked.

"I don't . . . have one? There isn't one, really. The masks we have will slow it down if we breathe it, but it also works through the skin . . . but slower."

"How much slower?" I asked.

"It takes about five minutes through the skin . . . maybe some kind of oil barrier on the skin . . . oh wait! It dissolves in water."

"So?"

"You can do that water spray thing! Spray enough water and it will absorb the gas!"

"What's that going to do to my wood panelling?" I grumbled. Felicia looked abashed.

"Well, it was burned anyway?" she suggested.

"More importantly, where is the water going to go?" I asked.

"Um, If the place has been made airtight, somehow, none of the water can get out either? Which is good, since it will still paralyze people if it touches them."

"I guess wading through poison is better than breathing it," I said sourly. "No, wait, I'm an idiot, I've got the Water Ball spell."

Well, I needed to practice with Water Magic anyway. It was a fairly tedious business, spraying out water in as fine a mist as I could manage, and then collecting it with Water Ball and dumping it in a Phantasmal barrel. Felicia kept checking the level of the gas between sprays.

"It's going down," she said after about fifteen minutes. "But I think there must be some kind of source for it, because it keeps flowing in."

It took an hour before we could proceed. And I had to keep spraying water in front of us because the gas kept flowing from farther back.

"This has to have been Janie," I said, looking at the scorch marks that covered everything. I'd made my own torch by then and was shining it around. "I don't know anyone else that could make that much fire *and* keep it from burning the place down."

"That isn't good news, though," Cloridan pointed out. "Looks like she was in the fight of her life."

"It means Koenig was told a lie," I said. "It raises the chances that the rest of it was false."

Felicia gasped. "Is that what . . ." she started to say. I looked at what her light was pointing at. Nothing too exciting, just an open barrel. It was labeled, but Identify was faster, as if it were jealous that I might seek information from some other source.

[Identification]: Barrel of Liquid Serpentwine – Quality: Excellent – Properties: Paralysis

"Can you . . . block it off without going near it?" Felicia asked weakly. I shrugged and used Phantasmal Object to put a lid on the thing.

"Haah . . ." Felicia breathed out a long sigh. "I can't believe that someone made that much liquid serpentwine! It must have cost tens of thousands of gold!"

"Isn't it just what we've been making? I asked, gesturing to the barrel behind us, and dropping another water ball in it.

"No, this is pure, not dissolved in water," Felicia said. "It's been slowly evaporating for all this time, keeping the house filled with gas."

She approached the barrel gingerly and tapped it with her staff. "Half full," she reported.

"Well, the portal is just back here," I said, taking the lead. To my relief, it was still in operation. Looking at it with Sense Mana, I didn't see anything wrong with it.

"Will gas go through the portal?" Felicia asked.

"Probably," I said and gestured for her to try her lantern. It did gutter green when she placed it near the bottom of the portal. The bottom wasn't flush with the ground, so there must be a shallow pool of gas held back by the lintel. I took the lantern from Felicia. I wasn't an expert, but I'd gleaned the basics.

"It takes a few minutes to work, right?" I said. At Felicia's nod, I stepped through.

"Mistress! You've returned!" Rhis exclaimed joyfully.

"I sure have," I said. "Before anything else, can you get rid of this poison?"

"As you wish!" Rhis said. "I did wonder why the level was dropping."

I moved the lantern to the ground and was pleased to see that there was no green flame.

"Well done. Next question—is Janie alive?"

Rhis cocked his head, puzzled. "Yes?" he said. "Should she not be? I can drop a monster on her, as quick as you like!"

"Don't do that," I said. "Where is she?"

"Asleep on one of the upper levels," Rhis said disapprovingly. "Apparently, regular sleep is required for mortals to function at full capacity."

"You know that it is, Rhis," I said calmly. "You've seen me sleep."

"Well, it's different for you, Mistress!" Rhis said. "Of course, you should have all the sleep you wish to have! I was talking about servants like the Fire Mage. I would have worked her all the hours of the day but . . . she refused. And she makes me feed her as well!"

"That sounds like everything is as it should be," I said firmly. "Are there any other . . . mortals in here?"

"Three others, all quite useless. They haven't killed *anyone*," Rhis complained. "One is her small apprentice, and the others are two of the girls who fetch the money. *Your* money."

"That is good news," I said. Koenig hadn't kept track of my employees. "I'm just going to step out to get the others. Wake up Janie and bring her down here."

"You're not leaving so soon? You haven't reviewed any of my innovations!"

"I'm just stepping out to let the others know it's safe," I said. "Don't worry so much."

"Yes, Mistress. I should warn you that Janie gets very grumpy when she's woken up at night."

"I think she'll recover," I said and stepped out.

"It's all good," I said to my friends. "Janie's alive, Rhis is waking her up. Let's get inside."

I looked at the barrel of poison. "Can you bring that in with you?" I asked the boys.

"Carefully!" Felicia exhorted them.

"Oh, poison, you shouldn't have," Rhis said. He managed to look both grateful and scornful at the same time.

"You can tell me why you don't like alchemy some other time," I said. "For now, just put it in inventory. It's valuable and dangerous and I don't want anyone else to have it."

"I can't do that until your guests step out," Rhis reminded me.

"Oh, right." I looked pleadingly at my "guests." Felicia rolled her eyes but led the others out. The barrel disappeared as soon as they were gone.

"Right," Felicia said when she returned. "Where's—"

"I know this stuff makes you tingle before it paralyzes you! So help me, if you've decided to kill me, I will burn you down to the—"

The voice stopped as Janie came into view. "Kandis! You made it back!"

Janie ran across the room and threw herself into a hug.

"Yeah," I said, "I made it home."

VILLAINESS INTERLUDE

Marianne Elise Rankin, Countess of Ravenshire, made one final stab. Under her dagger, the accursed solid illusion popped into nothingness. No notification arrived; she had not *accomplished* anything here. This had been nothing more than a probe for information.

It was a sign that her information blackout had not been as complete as she'd hoped. Kandis Hammond had come in much more cautiously than she was known for. Clearly, she suspected something.

Marianne stared at the spot where the illusion had been until shouts from outside broke into her reverie.

"What is that? What's going on?"

The Countess *tsked* in irritation. Didn't the Councillors realize that they were dismissed? They should have dispersed back to their offices instead of milling around like sheep. She'd have to move them along.

For a brief moment, she entertained having the guards do it, at sword-point, but now was not the time. After the witch was taken care of. Stepping out into the lobby, she looked around to see what the fuss was all about.

It didn't take long. One of the Councillors was wreathed in light, a clear sign of the meddling gods' magic. He didn't appear to be in distress, but green flames were billowing off him.

That didn't bode well, but like all mages, the Countess had Sense Mana. The witch could conceal her illusions, but she couldn't hide other people's spells.

"There!" she called out for the guards. "The spellcaster is right there!"

"No!" Another Councillor was pointing at her. How dare . . . Marianne had never bothered to learn their names. With no mages in the Council room, she had just skimmed the name from their minds just before she had to sully her mouth with it. That was proving to be a little awkward now, admittedly. With another mage in the room, Marianne couldn't afford to give herself away.

Whoever he was, how dare he contradict her! Marianne opened her mouth to deliver a witheringly scornful retort, but the man continued! Talking over her!

"She's the one that has been casting spells on us! Changing our memory! Making false accusations against Councillor Hammond!"

Another Councillor erupted in a column of light and green flame, and Marianne realized just what that spell *was*.

Mental healing. The Councillors were getting their memories back. This was Hammond's next play. Marianne had thought she would have more time, but the witch must have entered the city already. Her probe had, in fact, been a distraction.

A distraction from what? Marianne wondered, a shiver running down her spine. Not *this*. The distraction had been *here*. *This* was here. This was part of the same distraction. She was the target, and she was vulnerable here.

Marianne *could* take control here. The Councillors had no social skills to speak of. The guards had no false memories to lose. They could be browbeaten into attacking the invisible mage. But that would all take time. Time, Marianne had started to suspect, that she did not have.

A strategic withdrawal was called for. If Marianne was going to be forced on the defensive, she would defend her strongest point.

"Alkeran," she said to the guards at the door. Their faces went blank on hearing the code word, and they drew their swords. Marianne turned on her heel and strode back into the Council chamber. Behind her, angry shouts turned into screams.

Planting *hidden* memories had been her greatest triumph as a mage. There was no spell for it; Marianne had stumbled across the method through careful observation of her torture victims. Torture a person enough, and they will forget whatever you want, remember whatever story you tell them, just to make the pain stop. The true memories were still there, but the victim would never, ever admit to them, even to themselves.

Learning how to duplicate the effect with magic had taken years, but they had been enjoyable ones.

Ignoring the sounds behind her, Marianne strode swiftly across the chamber to the door that led to the witch's office, now hers. She didn't spend much time here, so the fact that it had belonged to Kandis Hammond outweighed the fact that it was not the biggest room in the building. The important part was the secret passage.

Heading directly to the tower seemed like a mistake. Kandis must be aware that the Countess's main weakness was range. At close range, she could simply control an attacker in an emergency, or make them forget that she existed. Outside of her mental range, though, she was as vulnerable as any other level six.

Walking the streets seemed like an invitation to a sudden death from a crossbow bolt, shot by a coward from a rooftop. Underground was much safer, which was why Marianne had commissioned the passage. Getting it inserted into the construction had required numerous memories to be changed, and the assistance of Clayborne, her pet Earth Mage.

Marianne made sure the door was closed and then pushed up firmly on the lightstone attached to the wall. There was a click, and a wall slid aside, revealing a ladder down. It was a tight fit, but at least the walls were clean. Marianne wouldn't want to get her dress dirty.

The passageway led to the ancient sewer line that had been constructed by whatever pre-Empire civilization that had constructed the tower. The town had been built much later, and additional sewers had only recently been connected. Fortunately, the main line was ridiculously overbuilt for its task. Magically created water was generated at the tower and ran down to the river. It was a complete waste of magic, but the Ancients weren't around to complain to.

With the new additions, the sewer was a far cry from the scrupulously clean tunnel Marianne would have preferred. She would have sent someone down to clean it regularly, but that would have given away that she intended to use it at some point.

And wiping the servant's mind every week would have become tedious. Bearing up gamely to the discomfort, Marrienne gathered up her dress and rushed forward as quickly as her dignity would allow.

Sir Arnaud showed not a single sign of surprise when she emerged from a trapdoor in the guardroom. He simply stood and saluted.

"Orders, my lady?"

"Full alert," Marianne said, sitting down on a convenient chair and dusting off her dress. "Kandis Hammond is in the city."

"We'd heard the reports and had already done that, my lady."

The Countess grimaced. "The reports are out of date. That was an illusion that came through the north gate. That woman has been hidden in the town for who knows how long, gathering information and preparing her play."

"I see. How shall we respond, my lady?"

Marianne frowned and thought about what her commander needed to know. "She has an invisible priest casting spells on the local leaders, restoring their memories."

"So we can expect them to be hostile," Sir Arnaud said thoughtfully.

"Can we keep a hold of the guard?"

"For a while. They're used to taking orders from us, but enough shouting about unlawful occupation from the residents will turn them eventually. If you want them to raid the Council, you'll want to do it quickly, in the next few days."

"Hmm. Have Stéphane spread some conflicting rumors, about the Council throwing in with the criminal. He can make it seem like they're coming from someone they trust."

"Yes, my lady. That will only buy us a few more days, though. These people have family in town. Too much conflicting information will just make them go sullen and uncooperative."

"Understood. I'm not quite ready to execute the Council yet, especially if Hammond is expecting it. I need to keep my most loyal troops close by."

"Speaking of troops, I haven't had any word that the Adventurers Guild is mobilizing. Though they can move fast when they want to."

"Yes, they would be Hammond's most likely source of foot soldiers, wouldn't they? Make sure you keep a close watch on them. And . . ."

The Countess paused. Did she really need to burn a contingency like this? After a few moments' thought, she concluded that she did. She pulled out a slip of paper from a pocket in her dress. It had two words written on it.

"Have a runner take this to the guards on the south gate," she said. "Have him say the first word. He should get the second word back in response. If he doesn't, try another guard until he does."

All of her runners could read so that they could, if necessary, read out her messages to the recipients. Other people's memories had been the Countess's playground for so long that she had no faith in their reliability.

"Yes, my lady," Sir Arnaud said, taking the paper. He didn't move, though; he hadn't been dismissed. "Is there anything else?"

Marianne thought about it. She didn't need to tell him how to arrange the men; he knew how better than she did. There was something else, though . . .

"Oh, yes, the wolf-kin. We don't need him to send false reports any-more. Have him killed."

Sir Arnaud smiled for the first time. "Does it need to be quick?" he asked.

"I suppose not. But I don't want you to get distracted! If you plan to take your time, he can wait until we've dealt with Hammond."

"I shall look forward to it, my lady."

She nodded, and he took his leave. Marianne sat there thinking about her next move. The Council wasn't that important in the grand scheme of things. If they couldn't turn the guard against her, they were helpless. The Guild was sworn not to interfere, but Marianne trusted that not at all. The remaining factor was the beast-kin, but her contingency should take care of that.

Deciding that she should observe the lay of the land, she headed upstairs. The roof would have had a better view, but it was also subject to assassins. Arnaud would find her wherever she was, and if there were rioters in the streets coming after her, she wanted to see them coming.

She paused when she got to the floor that held her private quarters. The door was open.

That wasn't supposed to happen. Marianne was meticulous about keeping her private quarters *private*. Someone with as many secrets as she had to. No maid was allowed in without strict supervision, followed by just as strict *editing* of what they had seen. Not that she'd had time to set up any of her special projects in this gods-forsaken place, but the habits had been set in stone. They had to be unbreakable.

For her door to be open, now, it had to be enemy action. But there was no one inside. Hammond might be able to hide her body, but she couldn't hide her mind. Without a visible target, Marianne couldn't read or control that mind, but she could sense it. If it was there.

Which it wasn't. The room was empty.

Marianne stepped forward carefully. She thought about traps, but she knew her apartment, and she didn't see anything. Did Hammond have a spell that concealed items? She *hadn't* the last time that Marianne had read her mind, but that was some time ago.

She couldn't ignore the open door. There were too many things in here that were important. They were hidden, of course, but that didn't mean that they couldn't be found.

She slowly stepped inside. This room might be called her office. Her bedroom was behind a door on the far side. This was where she received guests, and reports from her minions. There was a large desk for her to look imposing behind and of course a chair. A chair that was facing the other way.

Even knowing what was going to happen, she still had to stand there and look. The chair swung around, revealing . . .

Kandis Hammond, of course. Though not her. There was no mind behind that smile; this was another one of her illusions.

"Lady Rankin," the false smile said. "So glad you could make it."

HARMLESS

I swung the chair around, bringing myself into view. This was the first swivel chair I'd seen in this world, and I'd been just a *little* bit distracted by it. It was a bit lacking by my standards; this world still had a lot to learn about office furniture. There were no casters on the legs, it was heavy and unwieldy to move, and there wasn't a way to adjust the height or lean. Still, it swivelled.

"Lady Rankin," I said in my best James Bond villain voice, "So glad you could make it."

She glared at me.

"Another image," she spat. "Where are you? You must be close, to have gotten that thing in here."

I was fairly certain that she didn't expect me to answer that, so I ignored it. Maybe her game was off from not being able to read my mind.

"Not going to pop this one?" I asked. Her gaze darted around the room, lingering on the door to her bedroom before she answered me.

"There would be no point," she said. "You must be in the tower. You would just send another to . . . distract me, is that what you're doing?"

"Now, now," I said. "Phantasmal Emissary is good for more than that."

"All it can do is talk," she dismissed. She strode over to the bedroom door and opened it. I'm not sure what she was looking for—searching her boudoir hadn't been a priority for me. Maybe she was looking for me, but she *knew* I could go invisible. "It cannot even use social skills."

"Social skills aren't everything," I said. It wasn't a lie. Social skills were great, but they weren't *everything*. "Emissaries can walk around and scout, pick things up . . ."

That got a reaction. That must be why she hadn't gone to alert the guards; she was worried about what I might find in this room unsupervised. What I might *already* have found. That, and the guards were already on the alert. Invisible me was having quite a time dodging them.

"Observe," I said and tossed her an object. She caught it automatically, grimacing a moment later at being tricked into vulnerability. I laughed. "If that had been a knife, I wouldn't have been able to throw it fast enough to do damage. The only reason I could reach you with that is because it, too, is an illusion. It can't possibly harm you."

The Countess frowned and examined the object. It was a simple bottle, sealed, made of cheap dark brown glass that didn't let you see inside.

"What purpose does it serve, then?" she asked.

"Well, you see, I recently came into possession of some serpentwine."

The Countess jerked her hand, trying to throw the bottle away, but I'd already cancelled the spell. All she succeeded at doing was scattering drops of the liquid that had already engulfed her hand around the room. She made a lunge for the door, but the alchemy was already taking effect.

Just as Felicia had said, the liquid stuff was much faster than the gas or the diluted solution. I had to assume that she was also right about it wearing off faster.

"That doesn't make any sense," I had told her, as I carefully filled the bottle. "If it's a higher dose, it should last longer."

"It doesn't work that way," she'd said, wrinkling her nose from a safe distance. "It's like . . . a fire? The hotter it burns, the faster it burns."

That didn't sound like any chemistry I knew, but this wasn't chemistry. It was magic. So I might as well trust the alchemist. I walked around the desk as Lady Rankin, twitching like a demented marionette, fell to the floor.

"Another great thing about emissaries is that they just aren't affected by poisons," I said. "You've made a real mess with that serpentwine; hopefully it will dry out before it paralyzes any cleaning maids."

She didn't say anything as I rolled her over to her front. I was pretty sure she could; the paralysis wasn't supposed to be that severe.

"And they can carry real manacles," I added, showing her the pair I'd brought before securing her hands behind her back.

"Weak," she said, speaking with great effort.

"The manacles? They're of decent quality. Or do you mean me, for letting you live?"

She declined to clarify. When she did speak, she enunciated every word separately, with great effort.

"You. Lose. Contingency. In. Place."

"What contingency?" I asked, narrowing my eyes. "What do you think you'll be able to get up to, locked in here?"

"Already. In. Motion. Furry. Friends. Die."

Her body shook a little, and I realized she was trying to laugh. She didn't manage it, though, so she just smiled at me, a vicious-looking smile.

She refused to speak any further, so I put a bag over her head. Which was a safety precaution, not any kind of torture. It was fairly clear to me that she had the same Silent Casting and Subtle Casting that I did. An inability to see her target should make casting spells much harder. Improved Blind would have been more comfortable and more effective, but it wouldn't have lasted as long.

I went through her pockets and retrieved the key to her room. Getting in here had required a Shadow Walk by my original self. Locking the door would help ensure we didn't get disturbed before the mob got here. A flaw in the plan was that the door could be unlocked from the inside without a key, but it did require some fine manipulation. With the Countess manacled and blindfolded, I didn't like her chances of managing it.

That was just about all that this me had to do up here. Invisible me was still busy, though. Mysterious pronouncements of doom were all very well, but I had a very real and specific hostage to rescue.

I didn't know how they had captured Anas, but the reasons didn't matter so much as the fact that they had. The Countess had grabbed the knowledge of how he was communicating with his master out of his brain and then ensured that she was in control of that channel. If I wanted to look Tinidan in the eye again, I'd have to make sure I rescued his apprentice.

The weird thing was how lightly he was guarded. I hadn't gotten the full story yet, but it seemed that Lady Rankin had replaced Hector with her own commander, an intensely violent brute who didn't interact much with the troops. Everyone seemed to agree that they preferred it that way.

The town's walls were defended by a force that was separate from the town guard. The terms tended to be used interchangeably, though, which got confusing. The defense force, to coin a phrase, was now composed of soldiers that were a mixture of homegrown troops, soldiers that had arrived with Hector and had not defected with him, and the new troops brought in by the Countess.

The defense force answered to the King. They were not supposed to be commanded by the Town Council, which the Countess was a member of, or foreign nobility, which the Countess also was. I guessed the chain of command got a little fuzzy when there was a Mind Mage in the house.

All of which was to say, I *thought* that the Countess had a problem finding enough . . . *trustworthy* troops. For her brand of trustworthiness, anyway. People who wouldn't ask questions about why they were keeping an honored delegate of an allied power captive, to be specific.

Add to that the fact that most of the guards were tramping about the tower in search of me, and that might explain why Anas's cell only had one guard on it.

Oh, and those patrols. Desultory didn't begin to cover it. They had gone about searching in what they probably thought was a professional and impenetrable search pattern. It would probably have worked if they were looking for a visible five-year-old.

I was level six, goddamn it! I could do the thing where you put one foot on each wall of a corridor and climb up to the ceiling. Granted, that was more Climbing skill than my level, but the level helped! Wandering down corridors with your arms outstretched wasn't going to do you any good, hapless minion.

The point was, I had found Anas, and he was guarded by only one person. A level four person as it happened, and I was done with sneaking about. This was going to be simple. All I had to do was jump out of here with Anas, jump back in to get the Countess, and I was done.

[Improved Blind].

I won't say it was the best thing about the spell, but time and time again, I found myself appreciating the fact that it silenced its target as well as blinding it. The guard was no doubt screaming blue murder, but I couldn't hear him, and neither could any potential reinforcements.

He tried to run for help, but this wasn't . . . this wasn't that kind of fight. I redirected him into the wall, and he fell down. I pulled the keys off his belt. He tried to stop me, but I had a dagger and you don't want to fumble around blind when there's a sharp edge nearby.

I unlocked the cell door before the guard could get up, and then dragged him over to the cell. Opening the door, I took a quick look around. This was a much more spartan room than the one I had been kept in when I was a prisoner in this tower. There was a bench for a bed, an enchanted toilet and a lightstone. That was it. Anas was there, staring fearfully at the open door.

I dragged the struggling guard in and closed the door. Now Anas was staring . . . not at me; I was still invisible. But he knew that someone had dragged the guard into the room, and he didn't like it.

"You have . . . you have to go!" he insisted, but I was done with this. There wasn't any point in engaging with him. Who knew what the contents of his head looked like. Better to get him to Aelira and let her sort him out.

I reached out for him. He jumped when he felt my touch and tried to pull away, but he was only level four as well. My other hand plunged my dagger into the lightstone. The room was plunged into darkness, and I dragged him into shadow.

Underground tunnels are like highways for Shadow Walking, and I quickly made it back to our temporary hideout.

"Back soon, see what you can do with him," I told the others before heading back to the tower. Stepping into shadow had broken my existing spells. The cell guard was now free to yell his head off, and Lady Rankin was now unsupervised. Still, it wasn't like she could go anywhere, right? She was locked in, manacled, and had a sack tied over her head.

Right?

Well, damn.

The room was empty.

How had she even known? She had been sitting still right up to the point when the spell had broken. I tried the door. It was still locked. Did she have her own Shadow Walk spell? Or . . .

The door to the bedroom was open.

Oh, well, if that's the case . . .

I knew there was no exit from the bedroom. Lady Rankin was just putting off the inevitable. Unless there was a secret exit . . . but that would be harder to open than the main door, right?

Right?

I moved a little more quickly to the bedroom. The room was filled with opulent decadence. Part of me disapproved of the expense, part of me wanted to make sure some of it found its way into my bedroom after this was over. The only change from when I'd glanced over it before was that the wardrobe was open.

It didn't hold any clothes. What it held was a very familiar-looking portal.

> **[Identification]: Dungeon Portal – Quality: Perfect – Properties: Spatial Tunnel – Creator: Temple of the Ogre God**

Well, shit.

ANYTHING BUT HARMLESS

"No one told me that the Countess had taken the Ogre Temple!"

It was not, I felt, an unreasonable complaint. The Ogre Temple, the other dungeon near to Talnier, was bigger than the Forbidden Laboratory that I'd mainly been working in. Getting down to the bottom level and bonding with the core would have taken either a small team of high-level adventurers, or a larger one of soldiers. Either one *should* have been noticed.

"Well don't look at me," Janie said. "I've been stuck in *your* dungeon all this time."

She looked around at all the others gathered around the conference table. My council of war, as it were.

"True," I said. "You're off the hook for this one. In fact, out of all the people here that were in town, you were the only one that managed to achieve something. You managed to protect Rhis from . . . whatever it was the Countess had planned for him. So thank you."

I let my gaze sweep across the rest of them. Most of them looked a little ashamed.

"The rest of you were either captured, controlled, or politically outmaneuvered," I said.

A couple of them looked as though they wanted to respond, but it was Cheney Labelle, the carpenter turned Councillor, who spoke up.

"We failed you, Councillor."

"No, you failed *Talnier*," I told him. "I'm not in charge here; you don't owe me anything that you don't owe every citizen of this town."

That wasn't a lie, exactly, though it did ignore the fact that I was lecturing every Town Counciller, including the mayor. I may not have been in charge, but there was a strong propensity for everyone in this room to do as I said.

If that seemed like a contradiction, then one of the things that I said was that I wasn't in charge.

"Yeah, you're all—"

I cut Janie off before she could aggravate half the people in the room. I wanted them mad at themselves, not each other.

"Don't be so smug, Janie. I did notice that you weren't able to protect my *money.*"

I wasn't mad about that. Really. I had a dungeon; I could make money from mana. I imagine the Countess was the same way. She didn't need my money. She'd just wanted it taken away because it was a tool that I could use to unseat her. Getting my bank robbed had cost me reputation with the town. I could rebuild both my hoard and their trust, but it would take time.

Time that we were wasting. We had *mostly* taken the town back. The leadership had been purged of false memories and had shamefacedly admitted me back onto the Council. The false charges had been dropped.

My bank was still shuttered. Janie and Rhis had managed to shelter two of my staff, but others were still dead or missing. The attack had come after dark, with only those two left inside. The intent seemed to be to make off with the money and close the business, making it look as if I'd fled with the cash.

That wouldn't have worked under ordinary circumstances, but when the investigators had their memories changed, a lot of things became possible.

Unfortunately, after cleansing the reliable adventurers and some key government officials, our priestesses were out of charge. They had a bit left in the tank for emergencies, but we hadn't been able to do a full sweep of the town, or even the guard.

For the most part, the town guard seemed fine. They'd believed the stories about me, and they believed the corrections when they came down the line. The Countess had been under a similar restriction to us. She couldn't manipulate *everyone.* So she'd manipulated trusted people who then told people lies. All it took to undo the damage was to have those same people admit that their memories had been changed.

The reason the town was only mostly under control was the defense force. *They* were receiving orders from people *they* trusted, telling them that I was a criminal who had suborned the government. They had pulled back to the wall, fortifying the front gatehouse and the tower, but also keeping any townsfolk from getting up on the wall.

I still didn't have my Settlement Status back, but I doubted Lady Rankin had access to it any more.

It was a standoff so far. The only thing stopping violence from breaking out was that neither side had tried to do anything. Our plans had been stymied by my failure to capture the Countess, and while she'd gotten away, it had kept her from giving orders to her men.

At least for now.

"We need to storm the tower," I said. "I broke the portal so she couldn't return, but all—or at least most—of her lieutenants are there. If we capture then, we nip this coup in the bud."

"Can't she just take the long way around?" Kyle asked.

"Koenig has got scouts looking for her," I said. I pinched the bridge of my nose as a thought occurred to me. "Koenig, they are going to keep their distance and not get mind-controlled, aren't they?"

I kicked myself for not confirming this sooner.

"Aye, they're sneaky bastards, and they know what to look out for," Koenig said. "They'll be fine."

"So we should have some warning if she makes a break for it," I concluded. "We still don't know how she made it here from the capital . . ." I gave the room another look, irked at that intelligence failure. "So she might have a flying device or something. We'll still see that, but we'd get less warning if that's the case."

"Unless she has an *invisible* flying device," Cloridan pointed out—helpfully. "Or another portal."

"Yes." I glared at him. "If she has something we don't know about, we'll be taken off-guard by it. Happy?"

"Not until I can have a drink," Cloridan said mournfully.

"On the topic of things we don't know about, she mentioned a contingincy plan, and I'm not prepared to assume she was bluffing. Does anyone have any idea of what it could be?"

"You're sure it involves the deaths of beast-kin?" Tonet asked me.

"I don't see what else 'furry friends' could refer to," I told her.

"Then, it must mean an attack on Trade Town," she said firmly. "That's the place with the highest concentration of beast-kin."

"Ah . . . about those recent policy changes," Mayor Michaud said apologetically. "Those were initiated by the Countess, and didn't have broad support from the Council as a whole, but . . ."

"Yes, yes," Tonet said briskly. "I look forward to them being repealed, yes?"

"Of course, yes, once this business is settled—"

Tonet cut him off. "The important part is that beast-kin have been *discouraged* from staying within the walls. That makes Trade Town the most attractive target."

"They have access to Trade Town from the front gate," Koenig pointed out. "Do you think it's as simple as an attack from her soldiers?"

"Do we need to assault the front gate at the same time as the tower?" I wondered. We'd be coming in from behind, so it would be a bit easier. "That does sound too simple for the Countess, though."

"We know she likes using alchemy," Felicia said. "Expensive alchemy. Maybe poisoning the water supply?"

"Does anyone know where Trade Town gets its water?" I asked the room.

"There's a river right there," Cloridan said with a shrug.

"And waterstones are cheap for what they do, and probably even more useful for a nomadic people," I said. "Does anyone *know*?"

"It would be a little of both," Tonet said. "Most families would have a waterstone for drinking and cooking water, but they'd save washing for when there's a nearby supply."

"So they'd be washing in it, but not drinking from it," I mused. "Are there any poisons that work through the skin—" I slapped my forehead, remembering my own recent experience. "Of course there are," I castigated myself. "Can any of them work if they're diluted in a river?"

"I mean . . . some?" Felicia said doubtfully. "I wouldn't normally say it depends on how much she has, but she had a *lot* of serpentwine. I can test for a broad range of things if I go down there."

"All right, sounds like a plan." It wasn't much, but at least we'd started *doing* something. "Kyle . . ."

"Always," he assured me.

"Great. Tonet, can you send word to let people know what she's doing? I wouldn't want people accosting her, thinking she's the one poisoning people."

Tonet gave me an unreadable look, before bowing her head. "I'll send an acolyte with her," she said.

"Great. Now, who's in on the assault? And is it one force or two?"

"Aaahhh . . ." Koenig said. He pulled on his ear and failed to meet my gaze. "The Adventurers Guild . . . we can't go attacking the King's men."

"They're not exactly following his orders, though, are they?" I asked. "Surely there are exemptions for units that turn traitor and the like."

"I suppose . . . if there was some kind of legal judgment in our favor beforehand? I'd have to ask Nadine."

"That reminds me," I said with a sour face. "What happened to our judiciary? It rather looked like the Countess planned to hold the trial herself."

"Yes . . ." Mayor Michaud looked very much like he'd rather not be here, but he gamely struggled on. "The Countess was of the . . . *strong* opinion that as she was on the Council and empowered to dispense the King's justice, that judges were unnecessary. So they were dismissed."

"Are they still in town?" I asked. "Because that was obviously unlawful, so they're *still judges*. Can you find one of them?"

"I suppose so . . ." Michaud turned to leave, and then stopped. "Oh, wait! What should I tell them to do when I find them?"

"Have them make a declaration that their dismissal was unlawful," I said patiently. "Then have them declare that forces in the town that do not answer to the town authority are in breach of the King's Law."

"Oh, I see," the mayor replied and started to leave. For one step, before he turned back again.

"This declaration, do they just read it on the street, or do we have to deliver it to the enemy forces?"

"Hopefully he'll know what to do," I said through teeth that were carefully *not* grinding. "If not, then he needs to write it down and enter it into the court records. Then bring a copy here."

"Right!" the mayor said. This time he made it out the door.

"Will that suffice?" I asked Koenig. He scowled and rubbed his hand over his face.

"I think so," he admitted. "I'll need to see the declaration first, but I can start organizing. We probably won't be ready until nightfall—do you want to do a night attack or wait until morning?"

"Captain?" I asked, looking at Captain Guertin. He shrugged.

"We're attacking the wall from inside the town," he said. "There's going to be plenty of light."

"Then let's not wait," I suggested. "For all we know, her contingency is set to go off overnight."

"Very well, ma'am," the captain said. "Then I suggest we first assault the gatehouse."

"Not the tower?"

"From what you've said, we need to have forces *near* the gatehouse, in case they launch an attack."

"Yeah," I agreed.

"Then firstly, we aren't in a position to split our forces. Secondly, a force near the gate will be seen as a provacation and may *trigger* an assault."

"So better to go in strong from the start," I guessed.

"Yes, ma'am. And thirdly, taking the tower will be easier if we hold the walls. We'll have positions for our archers, and we won't be taking fire on our flanks."

I looked at Koenig.

"I'm more of a 'run at the enemy' sort, myself," Koenig confessed. "He sounds like he knows what he's talking about."

"Fine," I said to Captain Guertin. "The adventurers won't listen to anybody but Koenig, so I'm putting you in charge of him."

"Very good, ma'am."

"And I'll be joining in the assault."

The captain winced. "With all due respect . . ."

"I know, you hate it when the civilian leadership gets involved. But these are partly Talnier people, Alain. I might be able to convice them to stand down without bloodshed."

He shook his head. "You're the person they've been hearing all these rumors about, ma'am. Social skills are all very well, but you can't use them if they shoot you before you open your mouth."

I looked at him. He gave me a very put-upon look back.

"I also have large-scale illusions that might be of use in the battle," I said.

His face worked as he looked for a rejoinder.

"Let's talk about additional nonlethal methods we can use," I said. "And I'm going."

"Very good, ma'am."

CONTINGENCY

I'm sure I wasn't the first to notice it, but Adventurers were not at all like soldiers. Trying to organize even a small army of them was like trying to herd tigers.

I know that's not the normal expression, but adventurers were much more dangerous and stubborn than cats.

"Is it just me, or are there too many people here?" I said to Captain Guertin. He gave me a long-suffering look. Which was totally unjustified. No matter how difficult it had been, he had only been doing this for a few hours.

"I don't think military doctrine has the concept of too many people," he said. "But some of the people here are onlookers . . . I think."

I looked at the squadron of men that he was directly in charge of, all formed up into some semblance of order. I'm sure a drill sergeant from back—from Earth—would have torn strips off them for the many imperfections they were exhibiting, but as long as they were standing in a line, that seemed fine to me.

"Should you cordon off the area or something?" I asked. "That would give your people something to do while we wait for Koenig to get his people in order."

I looked over to where Koenig was shouting at two front-line fighters that seemed about half his size. He'd been going for a while now, but it looked as if he had more shouting still in him.

It wasn't that adventurers were *disorganized*. They were easily able to form small tightly-knit teams and deploy them in different formations as the situation required. The problem was that part of that team-building involved an ethos that boiled down to 'my team against the world.' They shit-talked the other teams, they formed rivalries, and they squabbled over kills and treasure.

So when you tried to put two teams together, it all fell apart immediately. The best case was you got two teams who wouldn't *work* together, but *would* stand within twenty feet of each other. The worst-case scenario was you got four or five people between both teams who would work together, and the rest of them became mortally offended that their so-called friends would work with their mortal enemies. *That* ended with both teams broken and maybe a fight.

"I would, but I can't tell who are the civilians and who are the adventurers," Captain Guertin said. "Going armed is common in Talnier, and lots of adventurers prefer light armor."

He looked at me as if he was making a point, but I couldn't imagine what it was. I *was* wearing armor, and if it happened to be lighter than the plate and chain that Guertin and his guards were wearing, that was neither here nor there.

"I hope he won't be too much longer," I said. "It's already after sunset and—oh, here's Nadine."

Indeed, Nadine was entering the square, followed by a group of rough-looking adventurers. It looked as though Nadine had no trouble getting her herd of tigers in a line.

"I've brought the rest of the fighters for this operation," she announced. Looking over at Koenig's antics, she added, "I'll get to *that* in a bit. But first, aren't there too many people around?"

"I thought at least some of them were your people," I confessed. "They're not?"

"No, they look like townsfolk to me," Nadine said. "Some of them look like they can take care of themselves, but if we were involving civilians, that should have been discussed in the planning phase, yes?"

"Absolutely," I agreed. "We'll get rid of them while you handle . . . that." I gestured at Koenig.

I looked at Captain Guertin.

"We?" he asked. Then he started giving orders. Squads were sent out to block the avenues that led into the town. The main gates were still open, a practice that had started when the treaty had been put in place. Monster attacks had been way down since then.

Sending troops to the gates might have set something off, but most of the onlookers seemed to be townsfolk. For the ones who were already here, further squads were sent to wander about the square and let people know that they should leave.

A few moments passed.

"That's odd," Captain Guertin said. I looked at him. I had been watching the group that Nadine brought in, but they were behaving. Their group wasn't lined up as neatly as the guards had been, but they weren't brawling, which was . . . a step up from Koenig's group.

"What is?" I asked.

He pointed at the square.

"They're not dispersing," he said.

As I watched, a group of guards approached an onlooker. A few words were exchanged, and the onlooker nodded and turned to go. After a few steps, with the guards already moving on to the next target, the onlooker stopped, turned around, and drifted right back to where he'd been standing.

"That is weird," I agreed. "Assuming it's deliberate civil disobedience, what on earth makes them think that it's going to work?"

Guertin looked at me oddly. "Peaceful rebellion?" he asked. "Is that something that happens where you are from?"

"Civilized nations are more reluctant to beat their own citizens," I said, ignoring his reaction to my gibe. It wasn't his fault that he'd never seen or heard of a civilized nation. "It allows for more varied ways for people to protest government policies they don't like."

"Sounds traitorous to me," Guertin muttered.

"Which is only *part* of the reason why it would be stupid to try it here," I told him. Abandoning that conversation, I walked up to one of the onlookers.

I didn't approach from the front, but he didn't notice me until I addressed him, which was another weird thing. This was a town where griffins occasionally dropped out of the sky and ate people. It demanded a little more situational awareness than that displayed by a headphone-wearing teenager on a bus.

"Oh, hello!" the man said once he'd noticed me. He gave me a . . . no, the smile was normal-looking enough. I was just being paranoid. My social senses weren't picking much up, though, as if he wasn't paying me much attention. That tracked with the way his gaze drifted off me and went back to the gatehouse.

"Are you here for a reason?" I asked, bringing his attention back to me.

"Oh, no. I'm just . . . waiting."

"Waiting for what?" I asked.

"Nothing in particular," he said absently. "I'm just . . ."

He trailed off as if he was thinking about it, but he must have lost his train of thought, because he drifted back to watching the gate.

"You've got to leave," I told him. "There's a military operation starting. It's dangerous."

"I'll just be a little while longer," he said, not reacting at all to the mention of danger.

"No, you have to leave *now*," I insisted. I kept my Skills out of it, for now, but I was already thinking about which approach to take. Intimidation would require a threat, and he didn't seem to know who I was, which made threatening him with my position dubious. Persuade it would be, then.

"Oh, very well," he said and started walking away. I took a step forward so I was standing in his spot and watched. Just like the other one, he walked away and then turned in a circle to walk back. He would have ended up right back where he'd been, except that I was standing there. He gave me an apologetic smile and took a step to the side. Then he went back to ignoring me.

Yeah, this was very far from normal. I fired up Charm and Persuade.

"Look, buddy, you're going to have to move. There's going to be a battle here, and it will be dangerous."

He was paying attention to me now. I don't think he had any choice about it. Now that I was engaged, as it were, I judged him to be about level three. A fairly sheltered existence for a border town, but you could manage it if you didn't leave the walls.

And didn't get caught outside when it rained griffins.

"Oh, yes, certainly ma'am," he babbled. He headed off, but this time I followed him. He took a few steps and started to turn, but I prodded him with a reminder of my existence.

"You have to go, remember?"

"Oh . . . yes . . ." he replied, more reluctantly this time. He took another few steps and paused. I prodded him again.

"I have to . . . I have to be . . ." he stammered. He was getting more agitated, but he turned around and took another step.

Up ahead, at one of the entrances to the square, fire bloomed and people screamed. My eyes widened as I took it in. I dashed forward. This time I'd remember my water spell.

"What happened?" I yelled as I doused a guard with water. A civilian was on the ground, blood covering his torso. Another guard had blood on his sword and a terrified look on his face. Already, I had half a story.

"He just—just took out that firetrap and set it off!" That was a third guard. The entire group of four had gathered around, and one of them was tending to the damp and smoking victim. The few people they had detained were *not* standing around protesting, yelling in fear, or otherwise behaving like normal people. They had just walked around the unheeding guards, and I was now looking at their backs as they entered the square.

"Who did? The dead guy?" I asked.

"He threw it right at Matty!" The guard with the moustache said.

"I had to—he might have had more. I had to put him down," the guard with the bloody sword said.

"Keep it together, Guardsman," I snapped. Guertin was rushing over; I didn't need to take charge. But I was here, and seconds counted. Felicia could heal him, she was . . .

Outside of the walls. In Trade Town.

I felt the first twinges of dread as I looked at the twenty or so civilians who had gathered in the square. That wasn't many, but if they all had firetrap potions . . .

"Get that man treated, and get that one off the street," I said, "And give me a proper report!"

It wasn't one of my usual social skills that I flexed, but Bureaucracy. The guards were part of an organization that I was high up in, and they had procedures to follow as much as my bank employees had.

The effect of the skill was interesting. All the guards calmed down and straightened up. They were pretty close to saluting me, but Guertin rushed up at that point, so they saluted him instead.

"Firetrap," I answered before he could ask his first question. "I think all of those . . . have been manipulated by the Countess, and they might all have the same potion."

"Firetraps?" Guertin asked. "They're dangerous, but you can stop them with a shield if you're ready for them. What does she think they're going to do with them?"

Even as he spoke, another bloom of fire sprouted from one of the other entrances. From a distance, though, it looked as though the captain was right. Primed to expect a fire, a guard had gotten his shield in front of the potion bottle. He'd had to throw away his shield, but his attacker had taken more damage than the guard had.

"You see?" Guertin said. "No trouble, and they seem pretty passive if you don't stop them. We'll come in behind with clubs."

At that moment, the evening bells rang. That wasn't a surprise or anything. We were still in winter, so the sun was down well before the bells rang. What made it significant was that all the onlookers suddenly started heading for the gate. A gate with no one blocking it.

"She's thinking that Trade Town is flammable," I spat. "She's not using poison, she's using fire. And if we try to stop them, those townsfolk that she's turned into sleeper agents are going to die."

FIGHTING FIRE

hink fast, Kandis, I told myself, but that really wasn't my strong point.

If I let Captain Guertin charge into the back of the sleeper agents, it would be a massacre. Guertin thought it would be a massacre of the agents, but I wasn't so sure. I had visions of the firebombs getting past the shields and setting the entire squadron alight.

That didn't matter, though, because I didn't want a massacre of *either* side. The sleeper agents had been mind-controlled by the Countess somehow. They were victims, and while I *might* be able to justify clubbing them into unconsciousness, I couldn't allow them to be horrifically scarred by their own firebombs.

And if it were to go down that way, it would happen under the eyes of the soldiers in the gatehouse. They'd see my forces cutting—okay, clubbing—down ordinary Talnier citizens before burning them to death. There was no way I'd ever get them on my side after that.

Could I put an illusion between them and their goal? How would they respond? They did seem still capable of reasoning, so if I just made a wall appear they might well figure it was an illusion and walk through it. Something believable, like the gate closing, might work, but if I kept to realistic speeds, they might just run through before it closed.

If I'd brought the paralysis potions . . . I thought, but that had been a nonstarter. Both Koenig and Guertin had been appalled at the potential they held for self-inflicted accidents. They'd made me promise not to bring the stuff anywhere near their operation.

What about a real wall? I had Earth Magic, and it didn't matter if they set *that* on fire. Splashback was a real concern, but at least they'd be self-inflicted injuries. Suicide, not brutality.

I'd need to be closer though; my range on Earth Magic wasn't what I'd want it to be. I took off running for the crowd.

"Ma'am!" Guertin's shocked exclamation came from behind me, but I was already out of his reach. Then, "Ma'am!" again, louder and more dismayed. "Follow her!" was the next thing he said, but I had other things on my mind.

I didn't need to do this myself; there were other Earth Mages in amongst the adventurers. Somewhere.

"Earth Mages!" I yelled. "Get a barrier between the crowd and the gate!"

It was at times like these that I missed not having Leadership. There was a great deal of overlap between the social skills, but yelling at people with no time for explanations and expecting they would obey, that was all Leadership.

That being said, Leadership wasn't particularly effective on adventurers. A surprising number of high-ranking people had complained to me that adventurers were the most fractious, contrarian, and obstreperous people that existed. They were wrong, but only because beast-kin existed.

For that reason, the frankly nonsensical nature of my order might have helped my chances of getting it obeyed. Put a wall in front of the gate we're about to assault? Sounds good! And a few people did start moving in the direction of the gate. Not with any sense of urgency, but they were closer than I was. It was anyone's guess who'd get in range first, but who cared? We could always stack wall spells on top of each other.

That just left the firebombs—if there were some Fire Mages, or—

"Janie!" I yelled, looking for her. She had been in Koenig's group, not actually helping smooth things over, but not actively making the conflicts worse. Probably. At least as far as I'd seen.

Finding her looking at me, I pointed at the gate. "Stop the fires!'

Another nonsensical request—there was no fire where I was pointing. Janie had never let a lack of sense get in her way, however. She nodded, and I knew that I could trust her to handle it.

By now, I was just about in range, so I started casting. I could see mana reaching out from the other mages as well. I tried to stay out of their way, focusing on raising my own section of wall.

"No!" one of the sleepers ahead of me cried. "Blocked!"

"He did it!" another one shouted, pointing at one of the other Earth Mages, someone who had to chant and gesture for his spells. "You're the enemy!" the other sleeper shouted, and threw his potion.

The Earth Mage looked shocked and failed to move in time, but one of his companions got a shield in the way in time. The potion splashed across the shield, the liquid bursting into flame and then . . . was snuffed out like a birthday candle.

"Hey!" Janie said. "Did someone start a fire party without me?"

Everyone stared at her. Her red leather armor naturally drew the eye, but I think most people were wondering what a fire party was.

There were a few who already knew. The sleepers, though, didn't seem to care.

"Enemy!"

"She's the enemy!"

"Burn her!"

They started throwing potions. Janie didn't wait for them to land this time. Instead, she threw up a wall of fire between her and the sleepers. Either the heat shattered the bottles, or it ignited the liquid inside, because each thrown potion burst into flame as it passed through the wall.

Unconstrained, unfettered flames from a dozen potions merged into a massive fireball. I could feel the heat as it churned and roiled, and for a second I thought it was going to explode a second time, sending burning liquid in all directions.

But Janie had it handled. As the other adventurers staggered away from the broiling heat, she stood with her hand outstretched towards the ball of plasma. Then it started to shrink. A few late-thrown potions got added to the inferno, but they didn't make a difference to her control. The fireball shrank, going from golden to bright blue. The heat didn't diminish, but it didn't seem to bother Janie.

My cloak shattered. I blinked in surprise.

"Get behind me, you f—ma'am!" Guertin yelled, dashing up to me and holding up his shield. "Fire from the gate tower!" he yelled, filling me in on what was going on, with perhaps more volume than was strictly necessary.

I guess it had been too much to expect the soldiers in the tower to do nothing while we milled around. Another arrow thudded into Guertin's shield, and I could see more falling around the adventurers. None of them were hitting, though, which told me that Guertin's reaction was a tad overblown.

"Janie, can you give us some suppression?" I called out.

"Sure!" she replied and launched a massive fireball at the tower. It splashed . . . relatively harmlessly against the stone wall. It left scorch marks on about half of one side, and I'm sure it instilled a strong urge in the occupants not to go near those arrow slits.

"Don't be such a mother hen," I told Guertin, who was still trying to keep me behind his shield. "I'm wearing *armor*."

He reluctantly stood back, giving me about a foot of space.

"Your armor *disintegrated*," he said accusingly. "After one attack!"

"That was just an illusion," I said. I made another cloak, thinner this time. With all the fires going up, it was significantly warmer than the evening had started.

My real armor, underneath the cloak, was probably better than what he was wearing. Latorrans loved their steel, and some of them—Guertin, for one—looked down on leather, but I was wearing monster hide, and it was enchanted to boot.

"Just have your men round up the firebugs," I ordered. "If the soldiers have started responding, it's time to get this operation underway."

The sleeper agents were standing in one place, looking around as if they didn't know what to do. That might be the case.

She didn't expect them to live this long, so the programming ran out, I thought bitterly. It was going to take three priestesses a long time to cleanse the entire town, but it was going to have to be done.

That was a thought for later, though. Right now, I had an operation to start.

[Illusory Terrain].

My large-scale spell sacrificed verisimilitude for the area it covered. The town square wasn't that large an area, so I doubted that any of the soldiers could see through it.

A strange and mysterious mist came into being over our heads, blocking the view of anyone who happened to be in a tower. Shadowy shapes moved through it, just as an added distraction. They bore no relation to how we were moving underneath, it just looked as if they did.

Protected from observation, we could form up for the assault.

"Remember," Koenig bellowed at his people, "this is a Council operation, and they want live prisoners! Half of these folks are being lied to, the other half get to go and face the King's justice!"

I could have done something to prevent him from being heard by the soldiers, but there was a chance that knowing we were taking prisoners would save a life. That chance was worth a little operational leakage. The main plan had been hashed out before we arrived.

We were coming from the inside, so the portcullis did nothing to stop us. They could drop it if they wanted, but all it would do is cut off bystanders from Trade Town. The inner doors looked sturdy enough, but we had Earth Magic. A team of two mages didn't just open the doors, they made an opening twice as large.

The adventurers poured in. Koenig, hanging at the back with me, gave me an apologetic look.

"They'll put it back when we're finished," he promised. Then he hefted his maul and joined the crowd.

"*Please* don't join the assault, ma'am," Captain Guertin pleaded.

"I would never," I promised him. "Cloridan and I are just going to stay back here, where it's safe. In this . . . shadow."

I swear, the captain's aggrieved protest made it all the way into the shadow realm.

We came out near the top floor. I tried for an empty storeroom, but I only managed one of those things.

"Gah! Who's there?" someone shouted in the darkness.

"Isn't that my line?" I grumbled, even as I cast Light silently. I made it bright, for maximum discomfort for anyone who had been sitting in a dark room.

The harsh lighting revealed that I *had* managed to pick a storage room. It was just occupied by . . .

"Aren't you the watch sergeant?" I asked, looking at his insignia.

"Ahhhh! Help! It's the witch!" the man called out at the top of his voice.

I frowned. "That's just hurtful," I said. Then I cast Improved Blind.

"Cloridan, can you . . ." I gestured. "We're here for leadership, and he qualifies."

"Yeah," Cloridan said, stepping behind the stumbling man and grabbing his wrists. "But he *did* raise the alarm, so we are going to get—"

As if on cue, the door started rattling. I stared at the sergeant.

"You locked *yourself* in a dark room . . ." I started to say, but there was no point. He couldn't even hear me. I would have asked Cloridan to search him for the keys, but the rattling had progressed to thumping. We probably wouldn't need them.

> **Your party has defeated Wilfred Heller in combat. Your experience share is 40 XP.**

"I should get out of here with him," I said. I cast Enshroud on the man so I could take him through the shadows. "Staying or going?"

"Staying," Cloridan said, holding up the invisibility amulet. "It should make for a terrifying locked room mystery."

I rolled my eyes. "Well, that's what I'm here for." I grabbed the sergeant. Cloridan had only secured his arms with rope, but it was only going to be a short trip.

Captain Guertin jerked in surprise when I stepped out of the shadow but went right back to lecturing me.

"Ma'am, we can't protect you when you go off like that—"

"Hold that thought," I said. "I got us a prisoner that needs taking care of."

"Captain, you've got to listen to me!" the man babbled. Unfortunately, my Improved Blind spell had been cancelled by the shadow trip. "This woman, she's got you fooled!"

Captain Guertin scowled. "Take this fool away!" he snapped. Then he turned his glare back to me.

"Don't look at me like that," I said. "I'm helping!"

STORMING THE TOWER

The tower was an easier fight than the gatehouse. I think it was because word had spread among the soldiers that the Countess had abandoned them. She may have escaped capture, but she must not have had a way of communicating with her people once she was hidden in her new dungeon.

In addition to that, the soldiers in the gatehouse had seen our song and dance with the sleeper agents. Or, as they saw it, innocent civilians. What they saw wasn't as bad as if we'd cut them down while they fled, but they had managed to draw a variety of conclusions, most of which didn't paint us in a favorable light.

At least those impressions could be corrected. I hated to think how it would have gone if we'd tried to explain over the bodies of their fellow townsfolk.

It turned out that the watch sergeant had been hiding, just as it had appeared. He'd been fed all sorts of lies about me, mostly by a lieutenant of hers called Archambault. He'd been told that my social skills were so extreme to defy reason, allowing me to just mind-control whoever went up against me.

That sounded familiar.

Knowing that, as the one in charge of the outpost, he'd be targeted with whatever fell powers I supposedly had, he'd hidden in the storeroom in the hope of being overlooked. The other defenders had known this, but they'd been ordered to keep silent.

The looks on the faces of some of the captured prisoners had not been complimentary. I wondered if he'd have trouble holding the same position when things settled down. Maybe it would turn out that he'd had his memories changed and he could blame everything on that.

Of course, I did use Intimidate to crack him like an egg to spill the details on the Countess's remaining forces. The difference between that and mind control was . . . a bit thin, I'll grant you, but it *was* there.

Going in, we knew who we were up against. Their big hitters were Arnaud de Vautré, a level six Knight, Merrik Clayborne, a level five Earth Mage, and Stéphane Archambault, who didn't seem like much, but *did* constitute a valid excuse for me to be there.

"Honestly, once I've popped a few of his illusions, I doubt he'll even stick around," I said. "I've run into him a few times, and he flew off every time he looked like losing."

Captain Guertin stared stonily at me. "Fine," he finally said. "In the back line. No Shadow Stepping this time."

Koenig grunted in agreement. "We have our own people to take care of leadership this time."

This time, we weren't quite as worried about enemy casualties. The troops *here* were mostly the Countess's men, brought in with her to replace the soldiers that Hector had run off with.

The person in charge was Sir Arnaud de Vautré, a man with a brutish reputation. As far as we could tell, he was the only one in the tower with Leadership, so he was a priority. Chances were, though, that he would be leading from the front.

The tower had been crafted by pre-Empire stonemasons and Earth Mages. I wasn't sure if they just had higher skills or if they knew some tricks the modern craftsmen didn't, but the walls and gates were resistant to hostile Earth Magic. The walls were, anyway. This wasn't the first time the tower had been taken by force, so the gates were of a more modern construction.

Because of that, they'd been reinforced by the Earth Mage inside. The wood and iron had been covered over by granite, leaving no trace of the entrance. Our boys didn't seem too concerned, though—they had brought a ram.

In the movies I'd seen, rams were always massive tree trunks. Crudely hewn on site and carried by two dozen men. Things worked a little differently here. The raw material was part of the story, the strength of men's arms played a role, but the craftsmanship of the ram was a factor that could not be overlooked.

Here, the ram was smaller, about three meters long. It was made of stone, a long, thick cylinder of granite that must have weighed a literal ton. It was lifted by steel bars that pierced right through the shaft, and it was tipped with a steel wedge.

It was carried by six men, but any of them could have lifted it on their own. Together, they jogged with it, getting it into position. Normally, they would have had to worry about archer fire, but with the walls held by our people, we had plenty of vantage points to suppress anyone who tried to shoot at them.

The ram hit with a thunderous crash that I felt in my bones. The stone covering shattered, leaving the doors unprotected against the next swing. They held up better, creaking and groaning under the assault but still standing after the second swing. A third saw them burst asunder, and my men charged in.

Koenig was at the front. He held his main axe close, his hand just behind the head while his other hand held a smaller axe, more useful in close quarters. He was hoping to encounter Sir Arnaud.

We moved forward, too. Close enough to see the action and move up if we were needed but far enough back to not be caught up in the fighting. This was a very natural spot for Felicia to be in, and Kyle was never happier than when he was protecting her, but Cloridan was looking a little antsy at missing out on the fighting.

"Me?" he protested when I mentioned it. "You're the one itching to go hammer their backlines."

I denied it, but my heart wasn't really in it. I did get satisfaction from slipping past defenses and attacking . . . monsters from the safety of invisibility. It gave me a sense of superiority. I guess I got that from human opponents as well, as much as my civilized sensibilities told me it was wrong.

Ahead of us, spells were flying, swords were swinging, bones were shattering, and flesh was failing. Everyone ahead of us, our side and theirs, did not subscribe to the notion that violence against others was wrong.

Was this my life, now? Wasn't I supposed to civilize this place, to teach people that there was more to conflict resolution than a bloody knife? Or should I go with the flow and find gold, glory, and excitement in the heady press of combat?

I had no home that wasn't here. I had memories, but I'd never *lived* anywhere but here. The gods were just mortals now—they couldn't try to guide me or manipulate me or whatever it was I was fighting against. I was free . . . to do what?

My introspection was cut off when one of the fallen bodies ahead of us shimmered under my Dispel Image spell.

"Behind you!" I yelled, as the "corpse" came to life. I cast Improved Blind on him, just to be on the safe side. One of the adventurers whirled around and cut him down for real this time.

"Weak sauce, Archambault," I muttered. "Should have done more than one."

Or . . . was that right? It was a chaotic mess out there, but our people would have been suspicious of a large group of unexplained corpses. Whatever. I kept casting Dispel Image. I didn't limit myself to corpses, though I was careful not to cast it *indiscriminately.*

Mostly, I cast it on our guys. Any time I saw them behave in a way that seemed odd. Look, it was a mess out there. It was easy enough for someone to get turned around or confused. I didn't want to judge, but I didn't want to take the risk either, so anyone who looked a little bit funny got a Dispel Image in the face.

Not that they noticed, since none of the ones that I'd targeted so far had been disguised assassins waiting to strike. But one of them would be.

I also targeted the occasional wall, on the ground that it looked too smooth, or I thought there should be a door there. I *had* been in this place a couple of times. I hit the jackpot on my fifth cast.

There *was* a door there, and behind the door was a bunch of troops, looking to get behind us. They did not achieve this ambition. The leader of the bunch that charged out was a broad-shouldered man with a weathered face, wearing a wolf's-head cloak.

"De Vautré! We found de Vautré!" one of our soldiers yelled. I winced as he was quickly cut down, and acted as fast as I could to give them support.

[Improved Blind].

Impressively, he was only slightly slowed down by this. I saw this a lot with the high-end fighters. Even blinded, they were still better than me. He must have clocked me before I cast the spell, because he headed my way at speed. One of the adventurers tried to stop him, but Arnaud body-checked him out of the way, barreling right through.

"I've got this," Cloridan stated, stepping forward. I let him.

The pair clashed in front of me, sword and dagger versus paired long knives. Cloridan must have had the edge, what with the other guy being blind and all, but I couldn't see that he was winning.

Then Arnaud made a strangled grunt and fell to the floor. I poked my head around Cloridan to see Koenig. His axe was buried in de Vautré's back.

> **Your party has killed Arnaud de Vautré – your experience share is 120 XP.**

"Not an honorable kill, but we're not fighting for points," Koenig said, almost philosophically. He pulled his axe out and turned back to the fighting. "Who's next?" he yelled.

You could feel the fight go out of the enemy as they lost de Vautré's Leadership. They started surrendering in droves.

> **Your forces have defeated Arnaud de Vautré in a Large Scale Combat. You have earned 1,045 XP.**
> **You have defeated Marianne Rankin in an Intrigue. You have earned 180 XP.**
> **You have taken control of a Territory: City of Talnier. Claim? [Y]/[N]**

[Y], I thought.

[Territory Status].

[Territory Name]: Talnier [Territory Type]: Free City Population: 3,789 [Territory Points]: 4 [Roles] [Customization]	Liege: Kingdom of Latorra Vassals: Seren County (Unreliable) Threats: Marianne Rankin

It gave me a certain grim satisfaction to bring up the blue box, even if it wasn't useful right now. Threats were down to just one, which was downright reassuring. I guess none of the gods were actively gunning for me, which was great.

Unless they were subtle enough about it to not trigger on the screen. They knew a lot more about it than I did. The new vassal was a surprise. Seren County was ruled from Anchorbury, so the screen was telling me that Aubert was my vassal.

That wasn't how feudalism was *supposed* to work, but I suppose it wasn't telling me anything I didn't already know.

All around me, people were cheering, having gotten their own notifications of our victory. I had to chivvy a few people into holding off the celebration until the enemy troops were all accounted for. Captain Guertin was thankfully on the case, organizing prison details and so forth. There was talk of a party that night, but I shut that down. The Countess was still at large, not to mention Archambault.

It was hardly unexpected, but the Illusionist had slipped our net. As I recalled, he had Air Magic, so he had probably flown invisibly off the roof of the building. We'd been watching for it, but invisibility was hard to detect at the best of times, and I'd had better things to do than spam the roof with Dispel Image for the entire battle.

In the end, there was a *small* celebration, once all the prisoners were tucked away. Everyone needed to be up bright and early to winkle the Countess out of her den.

And so it was, the next morning, that I stood outside the Ogre Temple with as strong a fighting force as we could muster.

"Okay, hear me out," I said to Koenig. "Have we considered just Breaking the dungeon?"

OGRE TEMPLE

Koenig looked at me as if I'd gone mad.

"Are you crazy?" he asked. "Break the dungeon?"

"Let's take this conversation private," I said. "It concerns Guild secrets."

Koenig narrowed his eyes, but he followed me far enough away from the others that Privacy would work. Nadine followed.

I cast the spell and paused for a moment to gather my thoughts.

"You know the Countess has taken over this dungeon."

"Aye," Koenig said. "As you have, for Oakway's."

"That name is hardly relevant anymore," I complained. "But because I *did*, I know what a mage can do with a dungeon they control. Do you?"

The two of them looked at each other awkwardly. I clapped my hands. "Focus, people! The cat is out of the bag!"

"We know," Koenig grumbled. "We're just not used to talking about it."

"So you know, but aren't ready to admit, that the dungeon can cast *her* spells with *its* mana," I said. "And it has a *lot* of mana."

"Aye," Koenig admitted reluctantly.

"So lots and lots of mind-control spells, then," I said. "What was your countermeasure?"

"We've got the priestesses," Koenig said defensively. "And the amulets you gave us. Dungeon spells don't have a great spell total, so the amulets can probably handle them."

"You haven't tested it, though, have you?" I asked. "And the Countess is in there somewhere, perfectly capable of casting her *own* spells . . . which we can't counter!"

Koenig shrugged. "Dungeons are never easy," he said. "We've got a big crew; one of us will get through."

I shuddered. "Or," I countered, "we could Break the dungeon, and force it to use all its mana on monsters."

"Which we'd have to fight, all at once," Koenig said.

"We can fortify this clearing with Earth Mages," I pointed out. "Like they do in the capital. And they don't all come out at once, they come in waves."

"Even so . . ." Koenig objected.

"And when we're done," I kept talking, pressing my point, "we go in and face a Countess *without* extra mana, without extra monsters, and without any traps she made when she saw us come in."

"Hmm," Koenig rumbled.

"I have an objection," Nadine said. "What if she responds by Breaking the Forbidden Laboratory dungeon?"

"How?" I asked. "She's stuck in *this* dungeon, isn't she?"

"She might have bound that dungeon as well."

"Even if she did, she'd have to be in it to give orders, and . . . can a Dungeon Master order a dungeon to Break?" I asked. I didn't think so, but I'd never asked.

Nadine started to answer but then stopped, struck. "I— don't know," she said. "It seems strange that an ordinary person can do something the Dungeon Master cannot, but I've never heard of a case."

Koenig grunted. "She can always step out and catch herself a beast, like we would," he said.

"I can't see her doing that," I confessed. "And if we've got someone watching the entrance, she can't. We should have someone watching the entrance."

"We do," Koenig grunted. "Though they might need more specific instructions. Returning to the subject at hand, if Lady Rankin can Break the Laboratory, she can do it whether we're in the Temple or outside of it."

He frowned, thinking the scenario through. "The rest of your points stand. We'll Break the dungeon."

He turned and started yelling orders at the adventurers.

It wasn't long before we were ready. The Earth Mages had built a wall a fair way back from the entrance. We had the forces to man it, and the farther back it was, the longer our ranged attacks had to whittle them down.

There was a lot of nervousness in the air as we waited for the hunter to come back. Some of the adventurers here were beast-kin, more used to the idea of Breaking a dungeon. They were used to laying trails for the maddened beasts, sending them where they wanted them to go. Sometimes that was a human settlement, at other times it was for something as mundane as feeding a herd of useful monsters that ran wild outside.

For the Latorrans, Breaking a dungeon was pretty much a war crime. So many of their settlements were built near dungeons that letting the beasts out was essentially a mass civilian attack. Surprisingly, it wasn't actually illegal under the King's Law. Nadine had told me that there *were* legitimate, if rare, reasons to Break a dungeon. Between those reasons and the unfortunate fact that someone who would risk such an event wouldn't care about the law, had led to jurisdiction being handed over to the local lords or affected communities.

That was me, so we were all right there. That might have had something to do with Koenig's lack of resistance to the idea.

Surrounded by the wall was the entrance to the dungeon. This was a simple three-sided stone building. There were columns along the outside of the walls, either for additional support or for decoration. The invisible line where the fourth wall would be marked where the dungeon started. Inside was just a staircase leading down into the dungeon proper.

The hunter approached with a struggling spider jaguar in his grip. He threw it in without ceremony. The monster froze for a second and then dashed down the stairs. The hunter ran back and climbed up the ladder that was lowered for him.

It took a minute. Then, the first ogreling scrambled out of the dungeon's maw on all fours, its spindly limbs jerking with unnatural speed. Its beady eyes gleamed with feverish anger, and its nostrils flared as it sniffed the air for prey.

Behind it, more poured forth, clawed hands scraping against stone, their ragged breath hissing between jagged teeth. They moved with a manic energy, their sinewy frames twitching, their heads snapping in different directions as if barely containing the urge to lunge. Then they surged forward, a tide of bloodthirsty malice, driven by nothing but the raw instinct to kill.

The archers saved their arrows and the mages saved their mana. Ogrelings went down easy.

[Identification]: Ogreling – Threat: 6 – Properties: None

Most of the fighters here could kill them in a single blow, and slowed down by the wall, they weren't a threat. Heads went flying as fast as they could climb up.

The next wave was only incrementally more dangerous.

[Identification]: Orc Slave – Threat: 8 – Properties: Berserk

These guys warranted a few arrows, if only because triggering their Berserk meant they killed a few of their own before they got to the wall. These guys hated their ogreling masters almost as much as they hated humans. Having the remaining ogrelings between them and their targets must have given them a brief moment of happiness.

[Identification]: Ogreling Villager – Threat: 6 – Properties: Skilled

A sudden jump in difficulty. These were the guys who had enslaved the orcs, after all. They may have had a lower threat value, but Skilled was a multiplier on all their attack and defense totals. These guys were a serious threat to a level three adventurer—even a level four, in enough numbers. Our force, though, was split between levels five and six.

[Identification]: Ogreling Warrior – Threat: 8 – Properties: Skilled

These guys, I was sad to admit, were a good match for me. That was more an indictment of my combat capability than anything else. They were still small and weak enough for our fighters to cut them down with one blow. Skilled didn't give monsters more hit points.

I didn't see the Ogreling Chieftain. He had a leadership effect, so the mages blasted him as soon as he appeared. The next wave came hard on the heels of this one. Ogorcs had longer legs and moved faster than the smaller ogrelings.

[Identification]: Ogorcs – Threat: 10 – Properties: Berserk

Seven feet tall, with grey skin and uglier faces than either an orc or an ogre, these monsters were purported to be a cross between the two species. They were tough and strong, but that was it. It now took our fighters two or three blows to take them down. The Orgorc Champion was more of a challenge, enough to attract some ranged attacks as he rushed forward, but he fell before he reached the wall.

[Identification]: Ogre Thrall – Threat: 12 – Properties: None

More slaves, at least within the context of the story that the dungeon was trying to tell. These were full-sized ogres, just missing the crude weapons that they preferred. These monsters took at least three blows before they fell, and they were tall enough that they could reach up to the top of the wall and pull themselves up.

That didn't mean any of them made it. They didn't seem to grasp that doing that left them open to attacks on their hands and faces. None of them lived long enough to learn the lesson. The next wave was close behind them.

> **[Identification]: Ogre Warrior – Threat: 14 – Properties: Skilled**

At least the numbers were reducing, because ogre warriors were where it started to get dangerous for us. With skill totals comparable to a level five human warrior and more than 1,300 hit points, they were a serious threat to a lot of people here.

A barrage of arrows and spells hit them as soon as they stepped out. That thinned their numbers some, but they charged forward undaunted. They crashed into the wall with a thundering roar, cutting down the few thralls left in front of them.

Warriors had enough reach with their weapons to attack the defenders directly, but the angle was bad for them. The height of the walls had been carefully chosen to encourage that behavior and *discourage* the alternative of trying to smash the wall down. A few tried it anyway, but the mages managed to keep up with repairs.

We felt the next wave coming before it arrived. The stone underneath our feet trembled, and both the ogres and the defenders redoubled their efforts. On some level, it was amusing to see the realization flit across the faces of the brutish ogres that they were going to be treated the way they had treated the thralls. But it was tempered by the knowledge that *we* would soon be facing the brunt of it.

The first Ogrehulk had to climb the staircase on its belly. It was too big to walk out. Someone must have had the bright idea of blocking the exit with its body, because arrows and spells started flying at it before it even left the dungeon. It roared with pain and thrashed enough that I thought it would bring the building down on top of it.

> **[Identification]: Ogrehulk – Threat: 20 – Properties: None**

It lay there for a few seconds, giving the archers the opportunity for another shot, and for a second, I thought it might work. Then, the hulk *flew* forward, injured but still alive, roaring with pain. The monsters behind had pushed it out of their way.

The first one didn't make it to the wall. It got up and roared with anger and pain, but it only got a few steps more before it fell. The next Ogrehulk almost made it out of the entrance before it started attracting fire.

This one made it to the wall. Standing over sixteen feet tall, it could easily reach the defenders. It tried to sweep a section clear, but the crenellations, put there for exactly this purpose, got in the way. They didn't escape unscathed, but the Earth Mages could put them back.

The level fives had to step back now and concentrate on the remaining ogre warriors. We tried to manage three level sixes on each hulk, but as more of them squeezed through the stairway, that became untenable.

Koenig was trading blows one-on-one against a hulk, and it was awesome to watch. Standing on a ten-foot wall, he was about the same height as the monster. If the Ogrehulk had been smart, it would have hung back for a reach advantage, but it came in close, just as eager to use its teeth as it was its weapons.

I started helping out, casting Improved Blind on the heads of the hulks as they came out. Cloridan and Kyle didn't have to worry about mana and had been on the wall since the beginning. Now that there were injuries, Felicia and the other healers came into play, keeping our fighters fresh and unbloodied.

Koenig's opponent finally fell with a shuddering crash. Four of the hulks were still fighting when the final wave started coming up the stairs.

They emerged from the dungeon with slow, deliberate steps, their hulking forms wrapped in layers of furs and bone charms that rattled with every movement. Their tusked mouths twisted in guttural chants, voices thick with the weight of devotion to some ogre god. Each carried a weapon that was more a relic than a tool—a massive iron cudgel, a jagged obsidian blade, or a staff crowned with a skull. Their faces were smeared with war paint, crude symbols of their faith scrawled across grey flesh.

The monsters from the final floor. The ogre priests.

[Identification]: Ogre Priest – Threat: 15 – Properties: Skilled, Caster

RELIGIOUS DISPUTE

Oh yeah, the ogre priests could do magic. They could throw fire-balls, heal, and remove "curses." Curses that included, unfortu-nately, my Improved Blind. Even as they came out of the gate, they started throwing cures at the remaining Ogrehulks. Some were heals, which were bad enough, but one broke a hulk's blindness.

Right. That's just about enough of that.

The problem was, with four of them, I couldn't just cast Improved Blind four times. The spell stopped sound, and they needed to chant, so it stopped that one from casting. But the three others would cure him. In the dungeon, they came in pairs, so it wasn't *as* bad.

I'd come up with a solution. I'd cleared it with Koenig beforehand, and he'd spread word of what I was doing around. He needed to because, without context, what I was doing would seem crazy and more than a little counterproductive.

I cast Greater Invisibility, and the first ogre priest disappeared.

Not to me, of course, nor to himself. He didn't notice that anything had happened and threw out his hands to cast a spell. I'm sure he was surprised when that didn't work.

The other priests looked surprised, I think. It was hard to tell on those faces, but they goggled at the space where their companion had been for long enough that I got to cast again.

[Greater Invisibility].

Even if they had figured out what was going on, I didn't think they'd be able to do anything about it. Invisibility wasn't a curse, and they couldn't target someone they couldn't see. I hoped.

With their second companion gone, the remaining two seemed to remember they were in a fight. They cast some more cure spells on the ogres fighting in front.

[Greater Invisibility].

The first ogre priest seemed to realize his spells weren't working and decided to switch to hand-to-hand. He started charging forward.

That was . . . the main flaw in my plan, but there was only one left now. I cancelled the first invisibility and cast Improved Blind on the one remaining. The defenders were startled by the sudden appearance of the ogre, but they would have been more startled by an invisible attacker.

The two ogres that were still invisible seemed confused by the sudden reappearance of their friend. That bought me time to blind him. Seeing the sudden reversal of fortune for their pal, they wasted a round casting cures on him. That was another one blinded, and I cancelled his invisibility.

The final unblinded one ran at the wall. His mouth was open; he was probably screaming. Once again, I cancelled the invisibility spell and blinded him when I got the chance.

That was all four spellcasters . . . not neutralized; they were still quite capable of wreaking havoc in melee. Their combat effectiveness had been greatly reduced, though.

Two of the priests were engaged at the wall, and the other two were stumbling around blindly. They'd find their way there eventually, but a few of the level five archers were keeping them busy, trying to lead them around in circles.

All in all, not a bad job. I think I'll hold on to the rest of my mana.

I watched as Cloridan savaged the arms of an ogre warrior, as Kyle took the blow of an Ogrehulk on his shield, and as Felicia did what she did best. The crew here knew what they were doing. It took time to whittle down the monsters, but they demolished them in the end, slowly but surely.

In the end, no one even died.

> **Your party has cleared a Dungeon Break! Your experience share is 3,750 XP.**
>
> **Your party has cleared a Dungeon Break (8 levels)! Special award: 8,000 XP.**

It seemed this Dungeon Break didn't rate a full-on event like the other ones did. The System must have known that we had it in hand. The special bonus confused me, but then I remembered that some dungeons gave a bonus for clearing a level. I made a note to ask Rhis if we did, and if so, why.

"Right!" I called out. "Fresh volunteers only for the raid!"

Groans were heard all around, and someone called out, "Right now?"

"Right now!" I gestured at the hole in the ground. "That dungeon is regenerating mana even as we speak. We need a small team to get in there and . . . ah, neutralize the Countess."

"We're not taking everyone?" Koenig asked.

"This many people would be chaos going after one person," I answered. "And in all the mess, it would be a lot easier to sneak up and pick off an unwary straggler. Plus, we don't have protection amulets for everybody."

I gingerly jumped down to the ground inside the wall. I landed on a dead Ogrehulk, which made for surprisingly stable footing. Cloridan, Kyle, and Felicia jumped down after me.

"I dunno if you guys are *fresh* . . ." I hedged.

"Shut up, we're coming," Cloridan said. "If anything, *you* shouldn't be going."

Captain Guertin wasn't here, so he couldn't agree with that. He was back defending the town. This was adventurer business.

"If you want something done *right*, do it yourself," I said grimly. "At least I can scout with an emissary that she can't control. Felicia, you've got the highest Soul out of any of us, so I'm counting on you to resist her."

I looked up at the wall. "Therris and Aelira, you're a part of this, so get down here."

The two priestesses reluctantly jumped down. Despite their robes and the rough footing, they landed gracefully.

"Not me?" Tonet asked from the top of the wall. "Not that I'm not grateful."

I grimaced. "I need you to cleanse anyone who comes out of the dungeon," I said. "And while we're at it, we need to put some kind of barrier across the entrance. If she beats me, she might have me turn her invisible."

"Understood," Tonet said. "Hopefully, it won't come to that."

"I'm coming," Koenig said. "I may have fallen victim to her before, but there's not many that can say they haven't. You too, Nadine, we need another mage."

"That's my line!" Janie said. "You can all rely on Fire Magic's special counter against Mind Magic."

"And what would that be?" I asked. I was fairly certain she was joking, but she *had* made it through the occupation untouched.

"If you're on fire, you can't do Mind Magic," Janie said, completely seriously.

I groaned. "I would complain, but I would quite like to see the Countess on fire," I admitted. "You're in."

No one else volunteered, and the party was starting to get unwieldy, so without further ado, we entered. As soon as we passed the threshold, I sent my emissary out.

The stairway went down a long way in the dark, a clear violation of Occupational Health and Safety rules. I was a little surprised that it hadn't been made slippery. Maybe the dungeon was thinking ahead to the times when it would Break. Imagining the Ogrehulks slipping down the stairs like a greased pig seemed both possible and funny.

"So, Lady Rankin will be able to tell what floor we're on," I said. "If we were all on different floors, she might have trouble telling who was where, but we're going to stick together so that won't be an issue for her."

"She can't just . . . see us?" Koenig asked.

"No, the dungeon can, and she can *ask*, but . . . Rhis, at least, has a lot of trouble telling humans apart. He's right about gender about eighty percent of the time."

"We've started shielding you," Therris announced. "In conjunction with the amulets, it might be enough."

"Let's hope so," I said, trying not to sound grim. My emissary had reached the bottom and was headed across the first level.

The Ogre Temple was a series of open-air levels, broken up by a maze of walls and buildings. You could find your way through the maze, killing ogrelings the whole way, or you could avoid them by climbing up and walking on the walls.

Doing that let them *see* you, though. They'd throw things at you, which was annoying, but they'd also follow you. You would acquire a crowd of angry ogrelings, and at some point, your paths would intersect.

For some, this was simply a more efficient way to kill lots of ogrelings. For others, it was a deadly trap. Right now, for us, it was simply an easy obstacle course. My emissary jumped lightly to the top of one of the six-foot walls and kept running. I was keeping an eye out for the Countess, but I didn't expect to find her here. No, she'd be at the bottom level, waiting for us.

The rest of us weren't far behind. I marveled at my ability to handle two sensoriums at once, my real self managing the uneven footing of the walls just as easily as my shadow had.

"Oh, I might not have mentioned," I said as we walked over the empty passageways. "The Countess might not be able to see through my illusions, but she has some sort of mind sense which tells her if a mind is there. So she can tell if she's looking at a Phantasm."

"Unfortunate," Nadine commented. "Can she recognize the mind that she sees?"

"That didn't come up, so I don't know if she can do it with a glance," I admitted. "But she can always read a mind if she's uncertain."

"Then she can see invisible people?" Cloridan said with dismay. "*Target* invisible people?"

"Probably," I said. "And I don't know if it's linked to her sight or if she just senses minds within a certain radius."

"That'll make it hard to sneak up on her," Cloridan grumbled.

Janie laughed. "Fire Magic's looking better and better! Did you know you can't be mind-controlled if you're on fire?"

"Yeah, nah," I said, rolling my eyes. "I don't think anyone's going to take you up on that offer."

We pressed on. The Temple had a fairly simple floor layout. Each floor descended in giant steps, about thirty meters across and two deep. If you were following the passageways, there were tunnels that took you down a step; otherwise, you just had to jump.

When you got to the bottom of a floor, you took a right to find yourself at the top of another, differently laid out maze. The main difference was that the inhabitants changed. The pattern continued, descending like a giant spiral staircase.

As we descended, the houses became relatively better built. They got bigger as well, to accommodate their larger residents. Two-story buildings became common, sticking up out of the maze and forcing us to go around, through, or over them. The decisions would have been more fraught if a horde of ogres had been chasing us.

But they weren't, so we picked our way past the dwelling of the ogre warriors, through the fighting pits where the hulks had fought, until we came to the end.

The final floor was mostly empty, I guessed so that we could appreciate the architecture of the massive edifice at the end of it. This was the Ogre Temple.

The three entrances were set in a structure fifteen meters in height. The archways were ten meters from ground to top. One of the archways was a dead end and a trap. The dungeon switched them around from time to time. The other two entrances normally held two ogre priests and an Ogrehulk. They hadn't managed to respawn yet.

I sent my emissary through the middle entrance, and it made it through unscathed. It walked into a huge chamber dominated by a statue ten meters tall. This was the supposed Ogre God. Twice the size of the biggest ogre, four arms, and a ferocious, snarling expression.

There was a betting pool running at the Guild for when the statue would come to life or get replaced by a live version. Today was not the day.

"Middle door is clear," I announced. "And . . . the Countess is there."

LITTLE CHAT

The Countess watched me approach with distaste written clearly on her face. She'd set herself up with a comfortable chair and a small side table for some tea. There were some other chairs, for guests, arranged to emphasize her importance. They were all facing her, but none of them were directly opposite. They were also smaller and less comfortable. I resolved to ignore them if we ever got to the stage of sitting down.

"Ugh, another of those hollow images of yours," the Countess sneered. "Show a little courage, why don't you?"

"I'm getting here," I said mildly. "Don't think for a second I'll be approaching this close in my real body, though. We can kill you from way over there."

I waved vaguely at the entrance.

"Not even trying to engage in a Social Contest? I thought that was your specialty."

I shrugged. "I like to think *winning* is my specialty, and engaging in conversation with a Mind Mage doesn't strike me as a winning move. I work with other people to cover the areas that I'm lacking in. Like killing."

I glanced ostentatiously over my shoulder at the entrance. We were still a little while away, but it never hurt to make your opponent feel nervous.

The Countess laughed, but even without my skills, I could tell it was fake. "As if you could kill me, here in the heart of my domain," she said.

"Got plenty of mana, then?" I asked idly. "Gonna summon a bunch of ogres? Or are you saving it for spells?"

Her face twitched. If I hadn't been operating through an emissary, I'm sure I would have gleaned a novel's worth of information from that twitch, but as it was, I was just pretty sure I'd hit the mark.

"I don't need spells," she said scornfully. "There's nothing you can do to defeat me. I just need for you to realize that."

"I hadn't noticed that becoming a Dungeon Master made you immune to fireballs," I said dryly. "Is that a thing?"

"There really is no getting through to you," she sighed. "Oh, well, I suppose I'll come back later and try again once you've had a chance to think things through. Sitting through a person's education is so *tedious.*"

She wiggled her fingers at me in a half wave. "Bye now," she said and disappeared in a flash of yellow light.

"What the hell?" the real me yelled. I was so startled that I tripped on the steps leading up to the Temple.

"What happened?" Felicia asked.

"She just . . . disappeared!" I said.

I'd searched dungeon floors before, but not for people. It had always been for treasure or body parts, gruesome as that sounds. The Ogre Temple was a pretty easy search, consisting as it did of four large, empty rooms. No secret doors had ever been found, but we looked for them. I got cleansed to make sure I hadn't been manipulated into remembering wrong. Nothing worked. Or rather, everything worked as it should, but no Countess was revealed.

Eventually, we ended up in the fourth and final room. The core room.

"You're sure it wasn't an illusion?" Nadine asked.

"I'm *not* sure," I repeated. "She didn't disappear like a cancelled spell would, but I could have made it look like that. Some of the tea was drunk, but if she wanted to beat me at my own game, she could have faked that easily enough."

"And we don't think that being the Dungeon Master allows you to teleport around the dungeon." Koenig stared at the dungeon core as if he were interrogating it.

"It never has for me. I never asked Rhis about it, though."

I looked at the core myself. In all this time, I'd never done an Identification of a core. I guess it was because I'd never had any question of what I was looking at. There was some useful information there, though.

> [Identification]: Dungeon Core – Level: 6 – Controller: Maan –
> Master: Marianne Rankin

"So . . . we should destroy it?" I suggested.

"Are you mad?" Koenig snapped. "Destroy one of Talnier's dungeons? They're the only reason this town even exists!"

"What's the alternative?" I asked. "Let Lady Rankin control one of Talnier's dungeons? Wherever she's gone, we've got to assume she can come back any time she likes. Then she mind-controls all the adventurers, and this whole thing starts up again."

"Is that why she didn't put up a fight?" Nadine asked. "And where do *you* think she's gone?"

"That would be one interpretation of what she said when she left," I agreed. "As to where . . . my guess is that one of the perks of owning two dungeons is the ability to teleport between them."

"So right now, she's back in her county," Koenig growled.

"Earldom," I corrected. "I . . . think? But that's not important right now."

"If she can flick across the kingdom like that, it might explain how she hoped to get away with all this," Nadine said. She pursed her lips thoughtfully. "If scattered complaints about her are coming from here and she's safe at home . . ."

"It can't be all of it, but memory alteration covers a lot of sins." I looked at the pair of Guild officials. "So, any alternatives to smashing it?"

"Could you . . . wrest control of it from her?" Nadine asked.

I looked at her through narrowed eyes. "I thought I was done with this Chosen One nonsense. Couldn't *you* wrest control of it from her?"

"Our oaths prevent us from doing such a thing."

"Those oaths are broken," I pointed out. "Not in the sense that you violated them, but the geas is broken. You can do anything that you like."

"We're not Reynard," Koenig said firmly. "Just because there is no magical compulsion, we're not going to forsake our Guild."

"You're just going to stand by and watch me violate the precepts you hold dear." I raised my eyebrows and looked at them skeptically. "That's what you're saying?"

"Under the circumstances," Koenig said awkwardly, "it seems like the lesser of available evils."

I looked at my party.

"Right behind you, fearless leader!" Cloridan said.

"Oh, I could never," Felicia averred. "I'm not good at confrontations."

Kyle nodded and drew her close. "My job is to look after her," he said. "I can't do that in a dungeon."

I sighed and turned to the priestesses.

"Wait, you're not even going to ask me?" Janie demanded.

"No one wants for you to have infinite fireballs," I told her.

"Hold on, no one said that was part of the package!" Janie exclaimed. "*Infinite* fireballs, or just a whole lot?"

"Never you mind," I said firmly and turned back to the priestesses.

"Ah, the Guild wouldn't be happy with a Dungeon Master of foreign nationality," Nadine put in.

"Jointly managed, remember?" I said with a grin.

"Even so," Therris said, bowing slightly. "We seek to return to the Tree as soon as this situation is resolved. We don't want a permanent posting."

"Traitors, every one of you," I muttered. "But even if we accept, *for the sake of argument*, that I'm the one to do it, it's still a bad idea. The Countess as much as told me that she had to kill me *before* she could take over Rhis."

"When I hear that," Koenig rumbled, "it just makes me think that she couldn't beat you in a fair contest."

"That—" I stopped. "I thought it meant that you *couldn't* contest a binding like that."

"If *that's* true, then there's no problem," Nadine pointed out. "You touch the core, nothing happens."

"Huh." I thought about it. "The other possibility is that it's a coin flip with unknown stakes. I could get sucked into the core if I lose."

"I think your bond with Rhis might protect you from that happening?" Felicia suggested timidly. "Maybe?"

I glared at her, but when I thought about it, she might be right. "Maybe," I agreed. "But still! It's a big risk!"

"But the alternative is letting the Countess win *or* destroying Talnier's economy," Nadine said. "She might well have bonded the Forbidden Laboratory as well."

"Ugh, so if this goes *well*, I'll have to do it all again?" I complained. But, thinking about it, I didn't see any alternatives. "Fine. But I want you two to have cleanses at the ready! If anything starts looking funny, I want you to clear out any malign mental influences!"

"That's what we're here for," Therris agreed.

"Great. Now, nobody panic. If it takes me more than five minutes, I'll stop. If I *can't* stop, then someone should cleanse me. If that doesn't work, move my hands to put it back on the pedestal without touching it.

"What are you talking about?" Nadine asked.

"You'll see," I said. Then I had my emissary pick up the core and hold it out to me.

> **Dungeon core has been removed from external mana construct. Five minutes before external construct unravels.**

I was pretty sure that everyone would get to see that one. From the startled and worried looks on their faces, I was right. I had another notification to deal with, though.

> **Network detected . . .**
> **Multiple networks detected . . .**
> **This node is claimed by Marianne Rankin (2-node network).**
> **Do you wish to claim this node for Kandis Hammond (1-node network)? [Y]/[N]**

Well, that might be some good news hidden in there.

Not wanting to waste time, I selected *[Y]* with a thought. Instantly, I was thrown into the maelstrom.

I'd been so foolish. How could I imagine that any attribute of mine could have affected this contest? The times when I'd touched a core that was still connected to its dungeon—the external mana construct—I'd felt the power of the intellect behind it. It wasn't "vast and cool and unsympathetic." It was cold and hateful, filled with the desire to bring about the end of everything.

I'd avoided its power before by unplugging the core. That was how I'd bound Rhis, and it was why I'd unplugged this core. But this wasn't a fight between the two of us. The core—Maan, if Identification was to be believed—was still connected to the Countess. Maan might have lost their external mana construct, but the Countess still had her snake dungeon. She brought it into the fight.

All that power, firmly leashed under her control. She must have used the same trick I did, because I could feel her power, and it was nothing compared to her dungeon.

I would have been in trouble if I hadn't had a dungeon of my own.

The will and the darkness and the hate of Rhis flung itself into the clash with the snake dungeon. Maan was nothing more than the bone they fought over, and the Countess and I were mere afterthoughts.

It was troubling, even as it worked to my advantage. I liked to think that I'd moderated Rhis, at least a bit. Now I saw that all I'd done was put a leash on the beast. He followed my orders; that was all. The Rhis that I knew, the one that I'd talked to before planting my dungeon, was only the relatable face of the monster.

It was a coin flip after all, her dungeon against mine. To my surprise, Rhis was winning.

It wasn't clear to me what gave him the edge. At first glance, you might think that he was the underdog. His dungeon was less than a year old, and I was willing to bet that the Countess was not short of mana to feed her source of power.

But Rhis wasn't just the Tower of Learning, only a year old. He'd been Oakway's dungeon for a long, long time. Starved of mana, slowly working his way to a fourth floor. He *might* be older than the snake dungeon. Big powerful dungeons were desired, fought over, and sometimes destroyed. It made sense that a small unwanted dungeon might survive longer.

If that *was* the reason, then I should be grateful that the gods had sent me to Oakway first. Rhis saw the other dungeon off with a contemptuous burst of disdain. He presented Maan to me like a cat bringing in a mouse.

The Countess was gone. Fled, probably, in the confusion.

I opened my eyes—I hadn't realized I'd closed them.

Dungeon core has been removed from external mana construct. Two minutes before external construct unravels.

Three minutes had passed? It had seemed . . . I don't know how it had seemed. My emissary was still there, so I had it put the core back where it belonged.

Node claimed.
Reconnecting to the external mana construct.
Connecting to Kandis Hammond (2-node).

A humanoid figure about four feet tall stood next to me. They had a pointed nose with long whiskers and rounded ears. Their face was furry, and they had rounded animal ears sticking up near the top of their head.

They looked absurdly cute, and I had a feeling that only I could see them.

"Hello, Master!" they said, and I tentatively assigned them as female based on the voice. "Who would you like to kill today?"

CLEANING UP

They found my money, for which I was particularly grateful. The Countess had stashed the gold and mana crystals that the Bank of Talnier had been holding in reserve in her personal quarters.

That wasn't all the money that had been deposited, of course. Most of it had been loaned out to various businesses. But the Countess hadn't gone after the books. Whether that was from a lack of understanding of how banks worked or if she just had a disdain for any information that wasn't kept in people's heads, it didn't matter. I could reestablish the bank just as it had been.

Maybe even better. The dungeon network offered interesting possibilities for growth in the future. If I kept expanding the network, I could offer a branch in every dungeon. Something to think about.

Right now, we were too busy cleaning up to think about future expansion. Arrests needed to be made, victims needed to be restored, and institutions needed to be brought back in line with the laws. Trials needed to be held, which meant judges needed to be *found*. At least we already had one judge to start with.

Most of the trials were fairly perfunctory. Mind control was a perfectly good excuse, much better than "only following orders." We had the priestesses to confirm that the victims had been under the influence as well. It was possible that a person who had been mind-controlled to do one illegal thing had gotten away with *another* illegal thing. . . . We were letting that go.

The town as a whole seemed to want to forget the whole affair as soon as possible. Cleansing didn't remove the memories of what you'd done, just your reasons for doing it. A lot of victims were looking back at their actions with remorse and embarrassment. The fact that the perpetrators of the deeds had been victims themselves helped avoid a lot of recrimination and blame.

The trials were still important, though. Even if they ended without a sentence being delivered, they still provided us with an official way of cataloging every crime that the Countess had committed. After all, if the verdict was not guilty for the reason of mind control, that put the onus on the *mind controller*.

I didn't expect the packet of legal documents that we would be sending off to the King to accomplish much. The Countess was a noble, and I—we—were not. Still, it was something else she had to deal with, and it would give the King leverage to use against her. If he was interested in doing that.

"I've sent the report to the Guild," Koenig told me. This time, he was in *my* office. It was only appropriate as he was reporting town business to an official and not chewing me out for my questionable activities as an adventurer.

"Will *it* accomplish anything?" I asked, still a little bitter about the lack of action my missive was going to provoke.

"Perhaps," Koenig said with a shrug. "I'm not privy to the reports that the Serpent's Cavern is sending headquarters, but that dungeon is under Guild administration. If they haven't told him about the Countess having free access to the dungeon—"

"Let alone binding it," I added.

"Yes," Koenig agreed uncomfortably. "If that has been missing from the reports, then Grand Master Voight will know that the Guild there has been compromised."

"Which is all moot if *he's* been compromised," I pointed out. "Lady Rankin has access to the King; she may well have had a chance to influence him."

"There are precautions taken at that level," Koenig objected. "Lady Rankin has been careful so far about getting caught. She wouldn't risk her magic being seen."

"Nothing about her actions here seems *careful*," I said with a grimace. "Except the running away part. It's possible that she feels invulnerable out here in the provinces, or . . ."

"Or she's stopped being so careful," Koenig agreed. "That could be because she feels invulnerable now, or that she's become desperate."

"Neither bodes particularly well for me," I muttered.

"We shall see what the future holds." Koenig got to his feet. "Oh, I should mention that there will be a temporary Guild master here soon. Nadine and I have to go back and renew our oaths."

"Both of you are going back?" I asked. This was hardly a crisis, but Koenig had been a useful ally, and I didn't want him replaced by a random official.

"I'll go once the replacement arrives. Nadine will stay here to keep them up to speed. She'll go once my oath is done and I return."

"Won't that take all of a minute?" I asked. He laughed.

"There will be reports to give, meetings to be held, and I might well go for a dungeon run while I'm there," he said. "I could be a while."

"Oh, so it's like a vacation. You're going on vacation while I have to stay here and keep cleaning up."

"Ha! Vacations are for nobles, and neither of us are one of those." Koenig turned to leave.

"Is that why you agreed to me binding the Ogre Temple?" I asked. "It's still a Guild-managed dungeon."

Koenig stopped and paused with his back to me. Then he slowly turned around.

"There might be some discussion about that," he admitted. "The King allowed you to bind your first dungeon, but no one is going to be happy about you having *two*."

"You practically pushed me into it, so I don't want to hear complaints about it now."

"Oh, I'll be getting an earful about that, don't you worry. What do you think all those meetings are for?" He shrugged. "But in the end, it will be easier working with you than against, so I think they'll see reason in the end."

"Is there even a way of giving up a binding?" I asked.

"You'd know better than me," he said. "If someone tries to bind it, you could let them?"

"Would the Guild allow that?"

"Oh no. They'd rather have one dungeon holder, however exceptional, than two. But I'll let you know what they say."

"I'll look forward to it," I said to his departing back.

Huette popped in as soon as he was gone.

"What's next?" I asked.

"We just received word that . . ." She broke off and looked at her notes again. "The goddess Duit will be arriving next week. The delay is so a suitable welcoming party can be assembled. They put in an application for a parade."

I glanced over it. "It seems fine. There's no mention of Isidre coming?"

"I heard she was out of the country? With the other Champion?"

I sighed. Old habits died harder than gods, it seemed. I wondered if Isidre and Kaito had heard the news yet.

"Get this to Guertin for approval," I told Huette. "Is there anything else?"

"No, that's all for today," she said.

"Fantastic," I replied. "I'll be at the bank for the rest of the day."

The way it felt to walk along the street had changed again. I'd been a complete nonentity, someone with a few friends and then a popular politician. Each role had received a different treatment from random passersby as I walked through the market or, in this case, the business district.

Okay, "business district" might be too grand a term for Talnier. But my bank was here, and that made it a business district.

Anyway, before I left on my trip, I'd been popular. People approached me, thanking me for something I'd done or asking me for favors. Sometimes there were gifts, just in the hopes of staying on my good side.

Now, people were more wary. The looks I got weren't unfriendly. People still smiled when they saw me. But they stayed back, hesitant to approach. It must have been the fallout from my sudden notoriety. I'd been denounced, then restored to power. People had been told that everything was okay again, but it would take some time to get them feeling it again.

I walked in the front door of my almost reopened bank. We were still short on staff. Those of my employees who hadn't been trapped in the dungeon had gone into hiding, and we still hadn't found all of them. Some of them may have left town. I hoped that was the explanation.

We were taking deposits, because I'd be damned as a banker if I stopped taking people's money, but we weren't yet able to offer loans. All the remaining staff from that side of the desk were chasing up our existing debtors and reminding them that, yes, we still existed, and yes, they still had to pay.

"How's it going?" I asked Delmar.

He looked up from his books and pushed his glasses up on his nose as he looked at me.

"Surprisingly well, Director," he said.

Finally, a title I can be happy about!

"We've had very few problem clients. Most of them were easy to find and accepted our reiteration of their obligations."

Delmar was finally learning to speak like a financial officer. I was so proud.

"Some of them . . ." He paused, looking puzzled. "Some of them expressed happiness or gratitude that we were back in business. I don't understand that at all."

"We don't just take their money, Delmar," I explained. "We provide services. Some of them will have had deposits with us as well as loans, and some of them have friends or family members in need of a loan."

"I see . . . so even though it costs them money, it is opening opportunities again."

"Exactly. Well, if everything's good, I'm going to check out the vault. Is anyone in there?"

"There shouldn't be," he said with a bit of uncertainty, looking around the front room. I knew that he had the habit of getting lost in his bookkeeping.

"All right, I'll be back soon if anyone comes looking for me."

"Yes, Director."

Stepping over the threshold was like coming home again. Rhis had moved the portal back to the vault level and had repaired all the damage that had been done by the Countess's raid. Golden walnut paneling on the walls, a white marble floor, and tasteful lighting gave just the right impression. Stability. Elegance. Wealth.

"Greetings, Master!" Rhis said, popping up out of nowhere. "Is everything to your satisfaction?"

"It looks great, Rhis. You've done well."

Rhis looked pleased at the praise. "Um, Master?"

"Yes?"

He looked down and twisted his furry toe back and forth against the smooth marble floor. "I was wondering, since you had Maan go back to killing people, I thought I could kill a few people as well?"

He looked at me with soulful eyes. I sighed.

"No, Rhis, no killing people in the bank."

"Except robbers!" he said quickly.

"Robbers are a special case," I agreed. "Maan has gone back to what she's doing because that's what the Guild wants. And she hasn't killed *anyone*, it's just been level sixers going through to test that nothing has changed."

"I'm sure she will eventually, and then she'll never shut up about it."

Yes, dungeons could communicate through the link. I don't think that meant they were talking *through* me, I certainly didn't feel anything of the sort. I felt it was more like all dungeons were linked, and these two were authorized to talk to each other. I'd yet to find out if there was a way to turn it off.

"If that happens, you'll just have to be the bigger dungeon and be happy for her."

"Bigger? I'm not bigger, I'm—oh! Are you going to authorize another level?"

"Maybe," I said. "We've got a lot of planning to do. I want to reopen the school in here and maybe have some beginner monster floors for the lower levels. *And* we need to work on vault security. I need to go through your settings and your catalog and see if there's a way to move goods through dungeons, not just me."

I took a deep breath. "We've got a lot to do, Rhis."

"Yes, Master! I'm ready to get to it!"

"Let's start with your experience points . . ."

ABOUT THE AUTHOR

Christopher Hall, also known as Maxlex, is the author of the Phantasm series. Hall started writing his first novel while sailing the Tyrrhenian Sea one summer, the salty night air flavoring and enriching his worldbuilding. Since then, he has continued to hone his craft while holding down diverse jobs in metalworking, marketing, perfume sales, and briefly, modeling. In addition to writing, Hall's interests include illuminated lettering and artisanal brewing. He endeavors to convey a sense of l'esprit in all his creative pursuits.

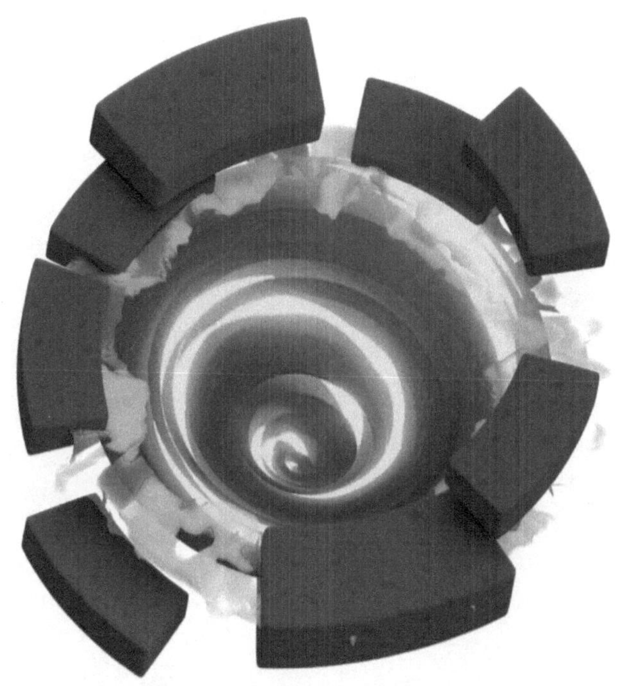

RESPAWN YOUR CURIOSITY

follow us on our socials

 podiumentertainment.com

 @podiumentertainment

 /podiumentertainment

 @podium_ent

 @podiumentertainment